S0-BQA-091

To Love a Stranger

Marjorie Shoebridge

POPULAR LIBRARY

An Imprint of Warner Books, Inc.

A Warner Communications Company

POPULAR LIBRARY EDITION

Copyright © 1990 by Marjorie Shoebridge
All rights reserved.

Popular Library® and the fanciful P design are registered trademarks
of Warner Books, Inc.

Cover illustration by Bob Sabin

Popular Library books are published by
Warner Books, Inc.
666 Fifth Avenue
New York, N.Y. 10103

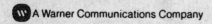 A Warner Communications Company

Printed in the United States of America

First Printing: January, 1990

10 9 8 7 6 5 4 3 2 1

"HOLD ME," SHE PLEADED. "DON'T LEAVE ME YET."

Clare's arms rose to encircle the neck of the man who had gathered her into his arms when she screamed. She clung to him, her cheek against the curve of his neck, then as her terror left her she stirred, not wanting to leave the comfort of his body but knowing she must.

"I'm sorry," she whispered, raising her eyes. "You must think me mad."

"No, not mad. Just a girl who has been harried intolerably."

Clare stared into his face. Of course, he still thought her a whore, she realized. If she told him the truth, would he leave her? He probably wouldn't believe her innocence anyway.

Behind her back his fingers moved. Clare caught her breath as her shift came free and was tossed aside. She saw his gaze wander over her naked breasts and resisted the urge to draw away. His eyes rose to hers and he smiled, his lips firm, not slack with lust like Lord Rayne's had been.

"Do you want your shift back?" his voice was teasing but implied the choice was hers to make.

For a moment she lay still, looking into the bearded face. "No!" Her voice spoke clearly.

His mouth came down on hers . . .

MARIA LUISA YEE

To Love a Stranger

◆ *Chapter One* ◆

Clare Harcourt took her father's arm as they left the wind-swept churchyard and walked the short distance back to the house. Rain, leafless trees, and the swirl of the January wind made the occasion more depressing. Half of the parson's words had been swept away, his cassock had flapped wetly, and the pitiful group of mourners had held on to hats and tucked their chins deep into their collars.

Mrs. Harcourt had been laid to rest, no doubt thanking God for her release from her insensitive, ill-humored husband. Clare, her face half hidden by the black veil, slid a sideways glance at her father. Oh yes, his eyes had watered at the graveside, but she knew it was the effects of the cold wind, not grief. Neither had she cried, although she had loved her mother. Perhaps that would come later. At the moment, her mind was too hot with contempt for George Harcourt, the man who had accepted condolences with the air of one robbed of a treasured companion.

Clare released her father's arm as soon as they had reached the lych-gate and did not take it again. Her mother, that poor, fragile creature, soon to be a mere name on a headstone, had scarcely reached her fortieth year when death had taken her unresisting hand. And who had put her in the graveyard? Ask

yourself, George Harcourt. Clare clenched her teeth to keep
from speaking. Eight miscarriages—the arrogant impatience
of a man who wanted sons and had only sired one living
daughter—had ruined his wife's health. If that was marriage,
Clare wanted no part of it.

At seventeen years old, she was confident that her father
would never succeed in marrying her off, even to rid himself
of the daughter he despised and hardly noticed. Who in his
right mind would take the penniless daughter of a man bur-
dened by debts of his own making and an old, uncared-for
house that was falling apart? Since the servants had departed
to seek positions that paid in cash rather than in promises,
Clare was all he had in the way of housekeeper and laundress.
In four years she would reach her majority—not long for a
patient girl who had lived for seventeen years in a state of
near-poverty. The day she woke to her twenty-first birthday,
freedom would be hers.

Now that the niceties of the occasion had been observed,
George Harcourt preceded his daughter into the house. As
expected, he made directly for the brandy bottle, lowered
himself into a shabby armchair by the fire, and looked
thoughtfully at Clare as she removed her hat and veil.

"What do you think of that Lawson widow? A finer-bodied
woman I never saw." He drained his glass, missing the sudden stillness of Clare's hands.

She drew in a steadying breath, anger flaring that he should
look at another woman while his own wife's coffin was being
lowered into the ground.

"Mrs. Lawson?" she asked evenly. "I scarcely know the
woman and was not aware that she held Mother in sufficient
esteem to attend her funeral. They were not friends."

"No, they weren't. She always thought your mother a bit
delicate in her ways."

"Delicate? In what context? Mother was not strong—"

"Not delicate in that way," Mr. Harcourt said impatiently.
"A bit high in her manner to the townsfolk."

"That's nonsense!" Clare returned hotly. "Mother was
kindness itself, though heaven knows," she went on bitterly,

"she could hardly play Lady Bountiful with what you allotted her."

George Harcourt's color deepened and he glared. "I need no pert remarks from you, my girl. I have too many expenses to throw money away on those who should work harder to make their own living. You're not a child—" He paused, his eyes sharpening as he took in the becomingly flushed face, dark curls, and clear grey eyes. "No, by God, you're not a child." The last words were muttered in an undertone, and for some reason Clare's heart beat faster.

She forced herself to speak calmly. "You were speaking of Mrs. Lawson. What has she to do with anything?"

Mr. Harcourt's face assumed its normal color. Clare stared at him with distaste but hid her feelings as best she could. Her father was now on his second glass of brandy—good cognac, she noticed, from the label on the bottle. Had he allowed his wife and daughter as much as he spent on brandy, they would not have needed to fashion and remake every garment they wore. Mother's trousseau had long been exhausted, the fine silks and lace collars made over so many times that they were mere fragile relics of a happier age. Happier, that is, for her mother, who had been able to recall balls and parties, and her presentation at court as the only daughter of a rich baronet.

Clare looked at her father, trying to see in him a handsome young man, the romantic hero who had charmed her mother into marriage after a whirlwind courtship. Poor Mother, so young and innocent of the world and its ways. Had she foreseen that twenty years later her impetuous lover would turn into a faithless, brandy-loving gambler, she would have fled from his arms.

Mr. Harcourt emptied his glass and fixed his eyes on Clare. His lips twisted into a knowing smile.

"A decent, obliging woman is Dora Lawson."

Clare was well aware of his meaning, having heard the gossip concerning Mrs. Lawson. "Indeed? Quite the paragon," Clare said lightly, arching her brows.

George Harcourt's eyes narrowed. "Don't use that haughty

manner with me, girl. You've too much of your mother in
you.'' He paused. ''Though maybe it's not a bad thing.''

Clare felt again that jerk of the heart. It wasn't like her
father to pass even a hint of a compliment. Had it been a
compliment, or was something devious stirring in his brain?
She could not, for the life of her, imagine what it was, but
instinct warned her to curb her tongue. After seventeen years
under his roof, she had learned a caution and cunning of her
own. She softened her tone and smiled.

''Forgive my interruption, Father. Do go on about Mrs.
Lawson. A handsome woman, I agree.''

Mr. Harcourt relaxed in his chair. ''Buried two husbands,
she tells me, and each time was the better off for their going.''

Clare nodded. ''Which accounts for her style of living, no
doubt. I've admired that pair of matched bays drawing her
carriage through the town and the carriage itself—all that red
velvet and gold paint is most dashing.''

''She's a dashing woman, and many's the time we've
shared—'' He broke off, and stared moodily into his glass.

He stayed silent for so long that Clare began to move toward
the door. He seemed so sunk in thought, she decided to leave
him. If he was brooding upon anything, it was certainly not
his wife's passing. Her fingers were reaching for the knob
when she heard his murmur.

''It's too soon, dammit. Six months, at the least—'' He
lapsed into silence, as if unaware that his daughter was still
in the room.

Clare slid quietly away and went upstairs. So that was it.
Her father was already lusting after another woman—this
handsome, bold-eyed Mrs. Lawson, who was a widow twice
over and wealthy. And now George Harcourt was a widower,
free to pursue Mrs. Lawson, if he was not already doing so,
as Clare suspected.

What had they shared together? A bottle? A bed? Either
or both was perfectly possible, but now it seemed that her
father hoped to legalize their relationship. Clare entered her
bedroom and began to remove the shabby but expertly re-
paired black dress. She slipped into a brown woolen gown,
just as old but equally refurbished with care. Sewing had

become an art as well as a necessity for the Harcourt women, and both had shown flair in redesigning elaborate tea gowns and silk-frilled bonnets.

Clare brushed her hair before the looking glass that had lost half its silvering through damp and age, and thought of Mrs. Lawson. A stylish widow of independent means might accept the attentions of many men, pick and choose her companions while retaining the right to welcome or rebuff. Marriage ended independence; a woman was given—lock, stock, and barrel—into the ownership of a husband. She became his property, and whatever she owned became his by law.

A decent, obliging woman, her father had called Mrs. Lawson, but remembering those shrewd dark eyes at the graveside, Clare suspected that the lady might not be so obliging as to give herself and her fortune into the grasping hands of George Harcourt. Why should she, indeed? Her father's character and way of life was no secret in the county. He would have no more difficulty in running through her fortune than Clare's mother's.

She stared at her own reflection, glad that she had inherited her mother's slender figure and good facial bones. Her brows were well-arched, her hair fine and dark, and her skin clear if pale in an oval face. What if Mrs. Lawson did take Father?

That tiny flutter of the heart came again. Would Father expect her to remain as unpaid housekeeper, or had that look suggested she was old enough to be bonded somewhere as a servant? With a new wife, why should he be faced each day with a younger replica of the wife he had despised? As a minor, she had no redress against anything her father planned for her future. How many years could one be bonded? Two, five, ten—surely not after reaching one's majority. In any case, she knew nothing of the law regarding bond servants.

She calmed herself by remembering her father's last words. She had six months, and that would make her almost eighteen. It was usual to grieve for a full year before embarking on matrimony again. Six months might seem indecent haste to the conventional, but the lure of Mrs. Lawson's wealth would outweigh all thoughts of keeping up appearances in Father's eyes.

What appearances? she asked herself wryly. They really had none to keep up. Let Father get his hands on Mrs. Lawson's money and the house would come alive again with his gambling cronies, men like himself—hard-drinking, high-staking parasites, who swooped and were gone like locusts, leaving George Harcourt the poorer for their company. Did he never win? Perhaps he did, but to the inveterate gambler, it was always the next card that would double his winnings and bring the gold pieces his way. His way, but not hers, and in the meantime, she must contrive a meal of sorts.

Taking an old woolen shawl from the drawer, Clare descended the narrow stairway to the cold, cavernous kitchen. She rarely used the main staircase, finding it more convenient to go the way the servants had, when there had been servants. The route lessened her chances, too, of meeting her father or encountering his odd friends. Since her mother's health had begun to fail, a year or so ago, the two women had kept to the upper rooms, creating their own sitting room—a smallish one, but it caught the sun. The larger rooms downstairs were far too damp and drafty for an invalid, besides being almost impossible to heat to any degree of comfort, so this room and Father's study, where he spent most of his time, were the only ones to have decent fires.

In the kitchen, Clare tied an apron about her waist and bent to coax the ashes of the iron stove into life. Logs were still plentiful, brought weekly from the estate, and the cost of their felling was paid by Mr. Harcourt without complaint, as was the bill to the butcher and grocer. However threadbare his wife and daughter, Mr. Harcourt was a man who valued his own creature comforts.

As Clare set a pan of vegetable stew on the now glowing fire, she pondered on her future. Mother, her only companion of seventeen years, was gone. Since Mother had been teacher in everything from French to fine embroidery, Clare had never been to school or mixed with other children. She had seen children playing in the fields and streets, of course, when she and Mother had driven into the town, and had often longed to join them, but at the sight of the Harcourt carriage, they had mysteriously disappeared. Not until many years later did she realize that George Harcourt's unpopularity as a landlord made people avoid them. It was years since they'd had a carriage, and now all those children would be grown. Some of them could even be married, with children of their own. Married? She gave an involuntary shiver, as if the very word was evil. Marriage was a trap she would avoid.

She relaxed and stirred the stew, smiling wryly to herself. There was no likelihood of some handsome gallant riding up to her door and demanding her hand. As a cook or seamstress, possibly, but as a wife, never!

Mr. Harcourt's voice boomed along the corridor leading to the servant's hall.

"Are you there, girl?"

"Yes, Father," Clare called back, damping down her annoyance at being addressed as *girl*, just as if she were truly some nameless kitchen skivvy.

"Bring my dinner to the study as soon as it's ready. I'm going out."

"Yes, Father."

Going out, was he? To begin his courting of Mrs. Lawson, now that he was a free man? She banged the soup ladle viciously on the side of the iron pot. A man of sensitivity would have stayed indoors on the day his wife was buried, but when had George Harcourt been sensitive? He cared nothing for the people in this small town of Bradford-on-Avon, or for the whole county of Wiltshire, for that matter. They went their way and he went his. She prepared a tray to take to his study. A few more years and she, too, would go her way.

As winter crept drearily away in winds and heavy rains, the promise of spring was in the air. Daffodil and hyacinth shoots appeared in the neglected borders of the driveway and the trees revealed young leaves. Snowdrops held up their heads shyly to greet the softer weather. After months of gaunt trees and barren hedges, the miracle of renewal was beginning again.

The house had been very quiet of late. Mr. Harcourt's frequent absences were a great comfort. She had no doubt that he was dancing attendance upon Mrs. Lawson and fretting over the slow passage of time. Another three months and he would offer for the lady, Clare had no doubt. But would the widow take him? True, her father was tall, with scarcely a trace of grey in his hair. His figure had not altered for as long as she had noticed him, but the face had coarsened, signs of dissipation clear.

As spring passed into summer, Clare's spirits rose. She was almost eighteen now, and the memory of her mother was fading. Out of their combined wardrobes, she had stitched and fashioned a small selection of reasonable wear for herself. A touch of lace here, a ribbon or frill there, and she had a half dozen respectable, if sober, gowns. A tweed cloak and, regrettably, an old-fashioned poke bonnet were all she could contrive for outerwear. But only occasionally did she walk through the streets of Bradford-on-Avon; and as it was hardly a center of fashion, like Bath, some eight miles away, her poke bonnet brought no stares. Tradespeople were polite, although she bought little, and she assumed that their deference was due to Mr. Harcourt's being landlord of some of their properties. It would have surprised her to know that her father had long since ceased to own much more than a few acres of wooded land and received rents from only a handful of cottages. Their courtesy, had she but known it, was extended in sympathy for the lonely, pale-faced girl who was so like the young and pretty bride her mother had been before time and George Harcourt had reduced her to a wan and fragile shadow.

Six months to the day on which her mother died, Clare was in the kitchen, chopping vegetables for the evening meal. It was a hot day and the back door was wide open. An old mobcap left by some long-gone servant covered Clare's hair and a long apron covered the rest of her. It had been a struggle to light the stove and she knew her face was damp and smoke-grimed. As she lifted the pot onto the stove, a shadow fell across the kitchen floor. She turned, startled, expecting the old woodcutter, but not the vision that confronted her.

Her eyes widened in astonishment at the man silhouetted

in the doorway. Of medium height, he was slim, with golden hair and curly side-whiskers. His jacket, unbuttoned to show a brocaded waistcoat, was of finest material and cut by some expert tailor. Buff-colored trousers met knee-high Hessian boots.

The stranger was the first to speak. "May I trouble you for a glass of water?"

His voice was pleasant, educated, and his smile friendly. Clare nodded dumbly, wiping her hands on her apron before going to the sink.

"I startled you. I'm sorry," the man said. "I did go to the front door, but could make no one hear."

"The bell is broken," Clare mumbled.

He smiled. "That accounts for it, but there is usually someone in the kitchen, so I took a chance and came this way."

"My—Mr. Harcourt's not in," Clare said, adopting a Wiltshire accent. This stranger obviously took her for a kitchen maid, so she must act the part. "Nobody's in," she finished.

"Ah, well," said the stranger. "It was mere chance. One of my horses cast a shoe so I sent the groom to find a blacksmith. As I am a trifle acquainted with Mr. Harcourt, I thought to pass the short time of waiting with him. However, since you have quenched my thirst, I will bid you good day and hope to meet my groom on his way back from town." He nodded and moved from the doorway into the sun.

Clare nodded briefly and turned back to the stove. Should she have called him sir and bobbed a curtsy like a true kitchen maid? No, that would be carrying pretense too far and she was not prepared to bend her knee to any stranger. He had been quite handsome, she thought—well-dressed and a gentleman. He had spoken to her in friendlier tones than one might have expected a gentleman to use to address a kitchen maid. She dismissed him from her mind and concentrated on peeling potatoes.

That night at dinner, as Clare and Mr. Harcourt sat at opposite ends of the dining table, she studied her father covertly. His linen was spotless, and surely, that was a new silk cravat? It was obvious that he had taken pains with his appearance. Was this the night he intended to offer for Mrs. Lawson? Offer what, for heaven's sake? He had no title, no stately home—just a crumbling old house and himself. Would that be enough for Mrs. Lawson, who was said to have crested carriages spend the night in her driveway? From her father's air of confidence, it was plain that he thought so.

She woke in the night as she heard the hoofbeats of her father's horse. Listening intently, as if every sound he made would give her some hint of Mrs. Lawson's answer, she heard the front door slam, then the clink of glass from his study, and finally, heavy footsteps coming upstairs. They were slow, not stumbling, yet seemed to move with weighty purpose, as if their owner was deep in thought. They paused outside Clare's door, and a rim of candlelight showed underneath. Clare sat up in bed, her body stiff, nerves taut. Why didn't he move on to his own room? The candle was steady. Was he listening, as she was? For what? Why should he care whether she was asleep or not? He had never cared before if his noisy parties had disturbed his wife and daughter.

There was sufficient moonlight from the uncurtained window for her to see the brass knob of the door turn slightly. She pulled the sheets up to her chin and watched the door open.

Mr. Harcourt, holding the candle aloft, looked at her. He swayed slightly and the flame flickered but he was not very drunk, she guessed. The only expression was in his eyes, which were slightly unfocused but somehow speculative.

"You're awake," he said, as if he had not expected that.

"Yes, I'm awake." Clare stared hard at the swaying figure, trying to read meaning into his intrusion of her bedroom. "Why don't you go to bed, Father. You're dripping candle grease onto your sleeve."

He frowned in irritation—whether at her or the candle, she couldn't judge. "She might take me, at that," he muttered.

Clare stirred uneasily. If he wanted to talk of Mrs. Lawson, why could it not wait until tomorrow? Had he proposed to the woman? His attitude showed neither the elation of the successful suitor nor the dejection of a rejected one. He was

staring at Clare so strangely that it might have been the first
time he had ever really looked at her. What was going on
behind that fixed stare? Whatever it was, it would not be to
her advantage, she surmised.

He moved and Clare's fingers tightened on the sheet. He
turned, spattering candle grease, and stumbled out of the
room. In the sudden gloom, Clare heard her door close and
she was alone. The moonlight shone softly on the panels of
the closed door.

◆ *Chapter Two* ◆

Clare stared mutely at the paneled door through which her
father had gone, chuckling softly to himself. The drink must,
at last, have affected his mind. What had he to chuckle about?

She lay down and drew up the covers. Tomorrow he would
be his old, ill-humored self, the night visit to her room washed
clean from memory. It was so ridiculous a conversation that
it must be dismissed as the ramblings of a drunken man. She
slept on that thought.

Over the next few days, it seemed that her assessment had
been right. No word was said that argued against it, and life
went on normally. The only discussion that held any signif-
icance occurred during a visit to her father's study. He had
asked her to take in his lunch on a tray, and as the door was
slightly ajar, she had entered, pushing wide the door with her
shoulder.

Mr. Harcourt, seated at his desk, had looked up quickly,
his brows drawn together in a frown. As Clare placed the
tray on the desk, she saw her father slide an official-looking
document under a newspaper.

"Thank you," he said, most surprisingly, and Clare, un-used to the simplest of courtesies from him, looked into his face.

"Do you have to dress like a servant?" he asked, a tinge of irritation in his tone. "That mobcap is really too much."

Clare laid her hands flat on the desk and leaned forward. "I dress like a servant, mobcap and all," she said slowly and distinctly, "because that is exactly what I am. However you may dislike my attire, you cannot like it less than I do. Should you not wish to have your meals cooked and your shirts washed, then you have only to say so and take into your employ a cook and a valet." Her eyes met his, chal-lengingly, over the desktop. "Until that unlikely day arrives, I shall continue to protect my hair and clothes as I see fit."

She stood back, awaiting his outburst. She would be eigh-teen next week and was no longer afraid of him. She was a woman, not a child to be browbeaten anymore, and it was time he realized that his own profligacy had brought her down to the status of maid of all work.

Mr. Harcourt leaned back in his chair, folded his arms, and looked at her. The furious outburst did not come. His expression was unreadable—neither angry nor friendly. If anything, it held a curious mixture of surprise and satisfac-tion.

Clare began to turn away when he halted her.

"Though your looks are your mother's, you've spirit she never had. There must be something of me in you, after all."

"God help me, then." The words came bitterly to her lips and she continued toward the door. It was an incautious remark, perhaps, but she was in no mood to care how he took it. She hated the thought of inheriting any part of his sensuous, reckless nature. Her hand froze on the doorknob as he spoke.

"It's your birthday next week. Don't think I've forgotten it."

Clare's head came around slowly. "Since you've over-looked the previous seventeen, why should you remember the eighteenth?"

His hand went under the newspaper and he drew out the parchment Clare had noticed. "Next Wednesday, isn't it?"

"Since you appear to be reading my birth certificate, there's no reason to query its statement of fact."

"Very true, and at eighteen, a father should contemplate his daughter's future. After all, your mother married me at that age. You're no heiress, of course," he said, not meeting her steady gaze. "But you've a neat figure and reasonable looks. There's no doubt of your pedigree, either, for the Harcourts are of good stock."

Clare's grey eyes narrowed a little. "You talk like an auctioneer at a bloodstock market, extolling the virtues of a young filly." She paused as his startled gaze touched her. "Would you have me trot around the ring to show off my paces?"

George Harcourt's fingers curled into fists, the knuckles white. "What rubbish you talk, girl. Too much imagination, that's the trouble with you. Just like your mother—all sensibility and no sense. You'll allow it's a father's duty to secure the future of his daughter, I hope?"

"Yes, Father. What did you have in mind? I am curious to know, since it concerns me closely."

"I haven't made any decisions yet. It's too early to say."

Clare's frown held perplexity. "I doubt there are many options available, save in domestic service."

George Harcourt looked offended. "My daughter, a domestic servant? Never!"

Clare smiled thinly. "You'll admit in your turn, Father, that I am well qualified in that respect." She bobbed a mocking curtsy. "Will there be anything else, sir?"

She swept from the study, leaving him glaring darkly after her. Back in the kitchen, Clare held on to the back of a chair until her heart stopped its fluttering. What was he up to? She remembered his mumbled words in her bedroom. *She might take me, at that.* Mrs. Lawson? She might take him—if what? Get rid of that daughter, first? What idea might she have put into her father's head? If only Mrs. Lawson knew it, Clare was eager to be gone, without any prompting from a possible stepmother. But surely that was a ridiculous supposition. A simple condition like that would not be enough to lure the rich widow into marriage. Her father's position would remain the same, with or without his daughter in the house. All she could do was wait and see, watch her father carefully, hoping to catch some hint of what was in his mind, if indeed there was anything, other than her own imaginings.

The following Sunday she attended morning service in the parish church, as usual, taking flowers to her mother's grave beforehand. She strolled through the churchyard and stood for a time before her mother's grave. A stone had been erected, the minimum of words engraved upon it. The stone was not of good quality; it was far less imposing than that of the baker's wife. Her lips curled involuntarily in a grimace of disgust as she thought how her father must have begrudged the cost of even this poor stone.

The sun was hot on her head and she pulled carelessly at the ribbons of her poke bonnet. It was too enveloping to be comfortable, and she eyed the summer straws of strolling girls with envy. *Well, better no bonnet than this old-fashioned one*, she thought, and she shook her hair free, uncaring of curious glances. There seemed to be more idle strollers than was usual in so small a town. A few family parties and a number of well-dressed men moved aimlessly, glancing now and then at a name on a gravestone. Since it was high summer, she supposed the strangers came from fashionable Bath and were seeking diversion in the nearby countryside.

Bradford-on-Avon was certainly worth a visit. As the center of the west of England woolen trade, the town had grown into a spread of narrow-streeted houses with crazy tiled roofs, while here and there stood solid medieval buildings. The massive Tithe Barn, the "chapel" on the bridge, and the Norman Church of St. Mary's were local attractions.

Clare tossed back her hair and wandered toward the lych-gate, swinging the old bonnet by its ribbons. In the shade of a yew tree, she glimpsed a man peering intently at the carvings on a gravestone. The sun caught his fair hair as he raised his head to glance as she passed. Something of familiarity stirred in Clare as the man's gaze turned back to his study of the stone. There had been nothing of recognition in his look, and Clare frowned. Yes, of course, it was the man who had asked for a glass of water at the kitchen door. Clare moved on quickly without looking back, her cheeks a little heated. In the kitchen she had been wearing a mobcap and apron, her face shiny with perspiration from the stove. Thank goodness he had not recognized her, although, had he done so, he did not look the kind of man who would acknowledge a kitchen maid. Why should he? Rich people paid servants to serve and remain unobtrusive in the background. No etiquette book suggested they be acknowledged outside of their duties. His manner at the kitchen door had been pleasant enough, for he was asking a favor.

She walked along the river before turning home. Home? Well, it had to be for the next three years, unless Mrs. Lawson went out of her mind and married her father. She smiled grimly to herself, remembering those bold, shrewd eyes at the graveside. No, Mrs. Lawson had not the appearance of a foolhardy woman. If she took George Harcourt, there would be something in it for her. She was well past her prime, so perhaps she thought it time to settle again into matrimony before marriage proposals ran out. Clare smiled again to herself. In his eager pursuit of the lady, could her father be unaware that she lacked the submissive nature of his late wife? Did he imagine it such a simple matter to acquire Mrs. Lawson's money?

It was not until Wednesday morning, however, that George Harcourt sought out his daughter to inform her, in a far too casual tone, she thought suspiciously, that he intended to throw a little party that evening. Clare looked into her father's overbright eyes. Brandy, so early in the morning—or had the widow given him hope of a happy outcome? She decided to ask no questions save material ones.

"For how many, Father?"

"Just a handful, my dear." He was smiling.

Clare blinked at the endearment. "Food?" she asked warily. "We've little enough in the house, and certainly not the kind for a party."

"Don't bother your head about food, my dear. They'll all have dined at the Swan. Just set out glasses and cards in the dining room. No need to light a fire; the evening will be warm enough."

"The dining room has not been cleaned for ages."

"Well, just give it a quick dusting. They'll not notice once I've brought out the cards."

"Oh, I see—a small gaming party. I'll leave the room ready before your guests arrive. You won't be disturbed then."

George Harcourt seemed to hesitate for a moment. "I—er—hope you'll wait to greet our guests, my dear. It will be a mixed company."

"Mixed? You mean ladies, too?"

"Mrs. Lawson and one or two of her friends who enjoy a game at the tables will be coming. They are most respectable females, my dear, I do assure you. I would not insult you by asking you to take the wraps of low-class females. A gentleman does not entertain the lower orders in his own home."

"Very well, Father." She made her voice noncommittal. After all, Mrs. Lawson might become her stepmother, so she must greet the ladies politely and attend to their needs before retiring to her own room. If it was merely a small card party, her presence would not be required.

"Put on your best dress, my dear," said her father jovially and patted her cheek—something he had never done before. "Not the apron and mobcap, eh?"

He gave a chuckle and walked out of the kitchen, leaving Clare to ponder his strange behavior. What had put him into such a good humor that he spoke to her as if she were a well-loved daughter? Surely his exuberance had something to do with the rich widow coming tonight. Had she taken him? Did she now want to see over the house and become mildly acquainted with his daughter?

As Clare dusted the drab dining room, she thought how

typical it was of her father to expect something to be accomplished without giving fair warning. The room needed to be aired and warmed, the dull surfaces of the solid furniture polished. If his visitors eyed it with disdain, that was his fault, not hers. She paused in her dusting, realizing that his behavior toward her had not been at all typical.

Put on your best dress, he had said. She had never had a best dress in her life! Every garment she had worn had been contrived and remade from her mother's trousseau. The black dress with its scrap of fragile lace that she had worn for the funeral was the best she had, so that must suffice for greeting the ladies. Remembering Mrs. Lawson's stylish gowns, she smiled. If the other ladies were of similar style, they need expect no competition from Clare Harcourt.

At nine o'clock that evening, when she heard her father's peremptory voice on the stairs, Clare smoothed down her wide black skirt, secured the ribbon holding back her hair, and hurried from her bedroom. A mingling of male and female voices reached her as she turned down the last steps of the front staircase. She paused, her hand on the newel post, and surveyed the company. More than one carriage had arrived bearing guests for there were three ladies, including Mrs. Lawson, and at least a half-dozen men.

There was a lull in the greetings as all eyes turned to her. Clare raised her chin and fixed a smile on her face. They should not find her wanting in the social graces. Her blood was as good as any of these richer people—perhaps better, in some cases. She approached deliberately with a touch of hauteur in her aspect.

She looked first at Mrs. Lawson, the only person she recognized.

"Good evening, Mrs. Lawson. How pleasant to have you call. Father has spoken of you quite often." She touched the outstretched hand briefly, then raised her brows in question to her father.

He gave her the names of the other two ladies and said, in fond tones, "See to the ladies first, my dear, then bring them to the dining room, where I will make the rest of the company known to you."

He had swept the gentlemen away into the dining room before Clare had time to see them clearly, and she was left with the three ladies. As she had supposed, they were expensively gowned, their coiffures elaborate. Perfume hung heavily in the air.

"Please follow me, ladies," Clare said pleasantly and led them into the drawing room. The air was musty, the chair covers faded—in fact, the whole room had a dismal, neglected air—but Clare's raised chin and steady gaze defied the ladies to pass adverse comment.

"What a pleasant room," said Mrs. Lawson with patent insincerity, and the other two women nodded in agreement.

Since Mrs. Lawson had made the first move, however insincere, Clare allowed herself to shrug dismissively, as if the room held little importance.

"In my mother's day it was kept up most admirably— quite a pleasant room, as you say, Mrs. Lawson—but it is so little used now, and with the servant problem as it is—" She spread her hands, intimating the difficulty of hiring good, reliable servants.

"I understand perfectly, Miss Harcourt," said Mrs. Lawson, giving Clare a shrewd but approving look. "With only two people to share a large house, it is quite commonsense to close off the larger rooms. Don't you agree, Louise, Emily?"

The ladies had laid their wraps on the couch and were now peering into a large, gilt framed looking glass over the empty fire grate, smoothing their hair and examining their faces. Without turning, they agreed that it was so and commended Miss Harcourt on her decision.

Clare kept her expression smooth, but she was perfectly aware that the two ladies had exchanged glances through the looking glass. Those white, beringed hands, Clare supposed, had never lifted a stew pot onto a stove in their lives, nor had those well-dressed heads been stuck into mobcaps. She caught Mrs. Lawson's eyes, unaware that amusement showed in her own. There was a hint of sympathy in Mrs. Lawson's gaze, and Clare smiled. Of course, the widow knew the situation exactly, whereas the other two—Louise and Emily, was it—were strangers to the district. At least, Clare thought so, for she had never seen either before and had already forgotten their surnames.

"If you're ready, ladies, I will show you to the dining room."

They followed her and she held the door open for them, then crossed the hall and opened the door to the dining room. As they passed into the already noisy room, Clare decided to slip away before her father could make good his promise to introduce her to the male guests. There seemed no point in remaining, for she would not be acquainted with any of them.

To her surprise, Mrs. Lawson put a hand under her elbow. "I can see that you mean to abandon us, Miss Harcourt. Please do not, for we are outnumbered by your father's friends and it would be a kindness if you stayed for a while. One or two of these gentlemen are strangers to me, too."

Mrs. Lawson's dark eyes were inviting her to strengthen the female ranks. Clare hesitated, a little unsure what to do. If she refused, it might be considered a discourteous gesture, but on the other hand, she shrank from joining this party of people who were here for cardplaying.

Her father turned and Mrs. Lawson's hand still rested under Clare's elbow. The moment to slip away was gone.

"Why, there you are, ladies," said Mr. Harcourt with loud good humor. "And you, too, my dear Clare. Come now, don't be shy. These gentlemen are wishful of making your acquaintance. Bring the child forward, Mrs. Lawson, my dear."

The widow cast a rueful glance at Clare. "Too late to flee, my dear. You must do as your father asks."

Her fingers tightened on Clare's arm and she was propelled forward. All eyes seemed to rest on her with an intentness she found embarrassing. Why should any of them be eager to meet her, as her father implied? He had never presented her to any of his friends before. She glanced at Mrs. Lawson, who had now released her arm. That lady's face was blandly impassive. Had she held Clare by the door until her father had caught sight of her for some reason of her own? No, it was imagination, yet these three ladies now talking and laughing with the gentlemen seemed in no need of an extra female. They appeared well-versed enough to hold their own without her company.

Mr. Harcourt laid an arm about Clare's shoulders, holding her firmly.

"Gentlemen," he said, beaming around. "And ladies, too, I hasten to add. I think it only fitting that we drink a toast to my daughter before getting down to the business of the evening. Today, she has achieved her eighteenth birthday and, as you see, she is now a young lady in all respects, as pretty and elegant a creature as anyone could hope for. Charge your glasses, my friends, and wish her well on this auspicious day."

Auspicious? thought Clare. It had been a day like any other as far as she was concerned, except that her father had organized this card party. She stared at the circle of well-dressed men, who had all risen and were regarding her with interest. Their ages varied—somewhere between thirty and fifty years, she guessed—but they were politely raising their glasses. They were all strangers to her, save one. There was no recognition in his eyes, but she realized that he was the man who had glanced at her in the churchyard and who had stopped at the kitchen for a glass of water.

She smiled vaguely, allowing her gaze to pass over them without stopping at that particular gentleman. Mr. Harcourt identified each one but Clare's mind retained none of the names. Why should she make the effort to learn them, when she had no intention of staying longer than was polite. Her father might gamble away his home and land for all she cared. He must be a fool to indulge this crazy addiction. She glanced around, staring a little more closely at the men's faces, and found a similarity of look. They were gamblers' faces—hard-eyed—and in play, no doubt impassive. Even their present smiles seemed perfunctory—a mere politeness to their host and his daughter. The hard eyes were glinting as if impatient to begin the true business of the evening.

Mr. Harcourt's arm moved from Clare's shoulder. He

smiled down at her and she saw his own eyes take on that hard glint.

"There, my dear, the company has drunk your health. Since you care nothing for cardplay and have always kept early hours to bed, I shall excuse you from spending a boring evening. Good night, my dear. Run along and get your beauty sleep."

Clare turned, hearing the murmured good-nights from the company. At the door, she glanced back at her father. He was not looking after her; his gaze was fixed on Mrs. Lawson. As if some secret message had been passed between them, Mrs. Lawson gave an arch smile and the tiniest of nods.

◆ *Chapter Three* ◆

Clare was too thankful to leave the company to ponder on that exchange of glances. Perhaps Mrs. Lawson, too, was eager to start the cardplaying and approved of Clare's dismissal after so short a time. Inside her own bedroom, Clare relaxed. She was far enough from the dining room to hear nothing if the play became noisy. She recalled the row of bottles on the sideboard. There were so many, she wondered how her father could have afforded them. He had displayed an impressive array, she supposed, to convince his visitors that he was a man with the means to gamble. Pray heaven that he had some luck tonight, for the contents of the larder were meager as it was.

She undressed slowly and moved to the washstand. The brass knob of her door winked in the candlelight, reminding her of her father's unannounced entry into her bedroom a few nights ago. She turned the heavy key under the knob, wondering why she did so, but deciding that unannounced entries might not be confined to her father. It was silly, of course, but she wanted no one blundering into her room, mistaking it for the bathroom on the same corridor. She pulled her nightdress over her head, snuffed out the candle, and climbed into bed.

She thought of the two ladies she had just met; they were well-dressed, perfumed, and jeweled. She wondered if they were widows, left comfortably off like Mrs. Lawson. Clare's mother would have considered them not quite the thing with their rouged lips and cheeks, the overabundance of rings, and the too-heavy scents. Mother had always told her that when dressing for a party or ball, one should look at one's reflection and remove a piece of jewelry. Clare had never questioned the advice, assuming that her mother was pointing out the line between elegance and vulgarity. *Poor Mother*, Clare thought sleepily. Her dowry jewels had gone long ago, and what chance had her daughter of removing one piece of jewelry when she had none to put on in the first place?

She woke to the sound of scratching on her door. For a moment she lay still, thinking it imagination, but it came again. Someone was in the corridor and trying to attract her attention as quietly as possible. But why? She sat up, her mind fully alert now. The sound came again. She slipped her legs out of bed and fumbled for the matches. With the candle alight, she stared at the door. The knob turned and she remembered her turning of the key. Thankfully, she was safe enough, but who was it?

Padding barefoot to the door, candlestick in hand, she put her ear to the panel. The scratching turned into a soft, insistent tapping.

"Miss Harcourt, wake up."

The voice was male, soft with urgency.

"Who is it?" Clare hissed.

"Philip Rayne, Miss Harcourt. I must speak to you."

Clare frowned. "I don't know you. Please go away."

"I want to help you and you do know me by sight. I came to your kitchen door and also saw you in the churchyard. I knew you for Miss Harcourt on both occasions."

"Well, what of it, and why should I need help?" *He must be drunk*, she decided, although his voice was not slurred.

"Miss Harcourt, I implore you to listen. Won't you open the door?"

"No—not to a stranger. I prefer it to stand between us."

"A wise precaution in this house tonight, but it will avail you nothing tomorrow. That will be much too late."

Clare stared at the door in perplexity. "I don't understand a word you are saying."

"Naturally not, but since you will not allow me to explain face-to-face, I must whisper and hope to God no one is listening."

"Are you drunk, Mister Rayne?"

"I am not, and neither am I Mister Rayne, but Lord Rayne, although my title is by the way. It is not important, but your safety is—at least, to me—for I disapprove most strongly of what your father is doing."

"Gambling, I suppose you mean, but did you not come here yourself for that very purpose?"

"Yes, I admit that, but I can afford it. Your father cannot, and things have gone badly for him. He is in the devil of a temper and is staking everything he owns. You may know little of gamblers, Miss Harcourt, but believe me, when a stake has been declared, it is a matter of honor on both sides that the result holds good."

"What are you trying to tell me, Lord Rayne? That my father has put up this house and all he possesses as a stake?"

"Exactly. And he has lost. The winner is quite without mercy. He will extract every last thing your father staked."

"Why do you tell me all this, Lord Rayne? It will not grieve me to leave this house."

"Then I suggest you dress and do so immediately, before its new owner takes possession. At the moment he is very drunk, and with luck should stay so for several hours. Your best chance is now, and I offer you my protection."

Clare felt confused. "In the middle of the night? Surely this man will allow us time to find other accommodation?"

"My dear Miss Harcourt, you have not understood me

aright. The winner has offered to withdraw his claim to the
house and property under certain conditions.''

"What conditions?"

"That he takes you instead."

Clare's heart jerked and her mind dizzied for a moment.

"Me? That's ridiculous. He couldn't . . ." Her voice
trailed away as she remembered her father's surprising jo-
viality, his request for her to meet the guests wearing her
best dress, that hard-eyed Mrs. Lawson taking her arm, preventing her from slipping away, and the unusual toast drunk
to celebrate her eighteenth birthday. Why would he make
such a show of her unless it was for his guests to assess her
qualities should his luck run so badly that only she remained
of value?

"He couldn't," she said aloud.

"He did," came the firm reply.

"But I have no value," she said desperately. "I am quite
without money. Who would be fool enough to make such an
offer?"

"A man of lecherous mind, Miss Harcourt, who would
not hesitate to rob you of virtue. What is to prevent him when
the offer was accepted by your own father? A gentleman is
bound to honor his gambling debts or he ceases to be welcome
in any company of gentlemen."

"Honor? You talk of honor, my lord, when it is my honor
that is at stake." Clare felt surging anger sweep through
her body. "Damn my father's honor! He lost that in my
eyes by the way he treated my mother for so many years. I
care nothing for him, nor has he ever cared for me." She
paused, thinking. "Does Mrs. Lawson have knowledge of
this?"

"Yes, Miss Harcourt. I rather suspect she put him up to
it as the price of marriage."

"But how will she profit by it if my father retains only the
house?"

She heard the hesitation in Lord Rayne's voice, then he
spoke gently. "It pains me to tell you, Miss Harcourt, but
there was a monetary transaction involved. When—er—your

possession is accomplished, your father will be richer by the sum of five thousand guineas.''

Clare leaned against the door, shaking. ''Oh, my God! He has sold me in order to marry that woman. May he be struck dead for his vileness!''

''Miss Harcourt, I beg of you to dress quickly and come with me to avoid this fate. I am a man of honor and will not be a party to this iniquity. Trust me, please. I will help you, but hurry—before the men recover their senses. They will all come upstairs soon to witness the possession. Believe me, I know their kind. We must get away quickly.''

His urgency communicated itself to Clare. ''Yes, yes, I shall hurry.'' She flew about the room, dressing quickly, stuffing a straw bag with spare clothes, adding a few toiletries, and finally pulling out her cloak and old poke bonnet. Only then did she turn the key in the door.

Lord Rayne was peering down the corridor, his attitude one of listening intently. A faint rumble of voices came to Clare. She stared hard at the handsome profile of the man. He turned quickly toward her.

''Ah, good. You are dressed. We must waste no more time. I have alerted my coachman. All is ready.''

Clare hesitated, her mind suddenly full of doubt. Leave the house in the middle of the night because of some tale this stranger had told her? It was madness. He could be lying, for some obscure reason.

Then a picture flashed vividly through her mind of another man holding a candle aloft—a man also standing by her open bedroom door, rousing her from sleep. She recalled the speculative gaze and the muttered words. ''She might take me at that,'' he had said. She knew her father had come from Mrs. Lawson's house that night. Was it possible they had planned this thing together, with the widow promoting the idea of a card party and possibly supplying the refreshments, in order to lure old gambling cronies to the house? They must surely be aware of George Harcourt's financial straits, yet they had come.

She shivered, remembering the circle of hard-eyed, rather

dissolute faces staring as her father had introduced her. A true gambler would need to view the stake before agreeing to play for it. No, no, it was quite mad, a fantasy of the night, yet this man was telling her it was so.

"I can't believe this is true, Lord Rayne," Clare said in a wavering voice. "Is this some unkind game you are playing? You ask me to trust you, but how do I know that you speak the truth? If this is a bet—"

She paused as he raised his hand for silence. "Listen," he said.

The noise downstairs had risen, as if a door had been opened. She heard a man's voice, slurred and thick, the words barely distinguishable.

"Come on, George. Don't fall asleep, man, before you've given me direction. How's a fellow to find the right room? I'm in the devil of a sweat already."

More slurred voices floated up the staircase. "A fine fancy piece, that widow Lawson of yours, George. Dammit if I don't cut you out and marry her myself. Not that I'm the marrying kind, mind you. Never needed to, yet."

There was a burst of laughter and the coarse kind of remark offered a man on the threshold of marriage.

Lord Rayne looked at Clare and she stared back miserably.

"Do you not gather from that," he said gently, "that your father now has the means to marry that rather vulgar woman, Mrs. Lawson. Forgive me for describing her so but, as a lady yourself, I feel sure you have remarked upon it." He regarded her pale face for a moment. "There is little time, Miss Harcourt. As a gentleman, I am loath to leave you unprotected, yet the decision must be yours. Will you stay to be despoiled by one of those downstairs, or accept my offer of protection?"

"What kind of protection do you propose, Lord Rayne? You say you are a man of integrity. What am I to judge from that?"

"I offer you my name, for my intentions are honorable, Miss Harcourt. Your future will be safe in my hands."

Clare made up her mind. "The choice is simple, Lord Rayne. I go with you."

Lord Rayne smiled. "A wise decision, Miss Harcourt, and

one that relieves my mind. Lock your door from the outside.
We will toss the key into the bushes. They will need time to
force the door, and that will enable us to be on our way to
London.''

"London?" Clare asked wonderingly.

"It would be better to go to my London house rather than
to the one I own in Bath. That city is rather too near this
place, should your father come asking questions. You will
be safer in London.''

"What will he do when he finds me gone?"

Lord Rayne looked at her steadily. "Do you care?"

Surprisingly, Clare felt an inclination to giggle. "Not in
the least," she managed, feeling light-headed with the lifting
of tension.

"Where are the back stairs?" his lordship asked.

"I'll show you." Clare donned her cloak and bonnet,
scooped up the straw bag, and led the way.

There was little need for excessive caution—the servants'
quarters had been empty for years—but they went silently
down the stairs and out the back door. She gripped Lord
Rayne's arm tightly as they crossed the courtyard to the stables, hardly able to believe that escape could be this simple.
A light glowed dimly, and Clare saw two men come to attention as Lord Rayne entered the stables.

"Harness up quickly," he ordered and helped Clare into
the closed carriage. She lay back on the leather seat as he
tucked a rug about her legs. Her eyes closed and she let her
mind relax.

A few minutes later Lord Rayne joined her, and then the
carriage began to move slowly down the driveway, the wheels
making little noise. Once outside the main gates the horses
were urged into a gallop. Soon, thought Clare, today or tomorrow, they would reach London and she would become
Lady Rayne. Sleep overcame her and she rested her head on
the shoulder of the man who had rescued her and made her
such a generous offer.

◆ *Chapter Four* ◆

When Clare awoke, it was full daylight and the carriage was pulling into an inn yard. She felt most refreshed from her sleep and also enormously hungry.

"Where are we?" she asked, her voice alert and tense.

"This is the Bear Inn at Devizes," Lord Rayne returned in calm tones. "I thought we'd break our journey here and have an early luncheon. We'd best stay overnight, too. The horses need a rest, as I hadn't planned on driving to London, only to Bath." He smiled down at her. "I'm sure you wouldn't be averse to a good night's rest. Heaven knows, you had little last night."

"You're very thoughtful, my lord."

Lord Rayne caught a note of doubt in her voice and thought it prudent to reassure her. "I have sent in my groom to speak for their two best bedrooms," he said, and noted a relaxing of the rigid little figure.

"How far have we come from the house?"

"Fifteen miles or so. Don't worry, my dear. If your father is in any condition to go searching, he'll make for Bath or possibly Bristol, where a girl could lose herself easily. He'd never dream of your setting out for London. As far as he knows, your traveling will be on foot."

"Could he guess that you had helped me?"

"Not at all. He has no reason to think that I was in any way responsible for your disappearance. Come now, we'll go and see what they have to offer for luncheon."

They took their meal in a small private parlor and Clare ate with great enjoyment. There had been nothing so lavish at Harcourt House.

Lord Rayne watched her consideringly over the rim of his wineglass. She had good bones—perhaps a little too prominent, but better food would take care of that. Her hands and arms were slender. He guessed that beneath that dowdy gown her body would be slim and supple. He drank deeply, pushing away the intoxicating vision of the sweetness that was his to taste when they reached London. Like good wine, she would keep. His task now was to gain her trust and keep his desires under control. No good rushing things. They were not out of the woods yet, and she could still escape him if alarmed. With a prick of irritation, for he was not a man to deny himself unless greater pleasure resulted, he regarded the poke bonnet with distaste.

"Where on earth did you find that hat, my dear? It is positively prehistoric! Oblige me by discarding it at the first opportunity."

Clare giggled. "It is rather enormous, isn't it? It came from Mama's wardrobe, as did the cloak. I imagine they were quite fashionable when she was young. I'm afraid I don't own very much myself."

Lord Rayne reached out and laid his hand on hers. He leaned forward, and Clare stared into the face so close to her own. In the cruel light of day she noted the slight pouches under his eyes and the lines that ran from his nostrils to the corners of his mouth. He was somewhat older than she had judged at their first meeting, and it struck her that the fair hair and side-whiskers were a little too golden to be true.

She smiled. Even men were entitled to quirks of vanity over their looks. Why should he not dye his hair if he wished? At least he disdained the use of cosmetics she had heard were popular with some of the dandy set. She turned over her hand and returned his clasp.

"You know that you have my gratitude, Lord Rayne, and I will try to repay your kindness in every way I can. I am not used to moving in higher circles. Be patient with me and I will try to be a credit to you."

"I have every confidence, my dear, and now you must go and rest. In the meantime, I will ride into Devizes and buy you some more suitable clothes. Perhaps if I purchase an evening gown, you will honor me by wearing it tonight?"

"Oh, indeed I will. You are most kind." Clare's eyes sparkled and a rare, enchanting smile lit up her face. A real evening gown! Could there be anything more exciting?

Much to her surprise, she slept soundly all afternoon and woke to a gentle tapping on the door.

"Come in," she called, pulling up the covers to hide her old shift.

A smiling maid entered with a tray of tea. "I will bring up your hot water directly, my lady, together with the boxes my lord has ordered me to deliver."

"Thank you," said Clare, enjoying to the full the unusual situation of being waited on and addressed so grandly.

Later, after the maid had brought the hot water, Clare bounced out of bed and tore the wrappings off the collection of boxes. She stared in wonder as an amber-colored dress of fine silk slid through her fingers. Tiny beads of deeper color were stitched about the neckline and the high waist. Another box contained a delicate shift of filmy gauze and a pair of stockings far finer than any she had ever seen. Soft evening slippers and a gold-colored ribbon to thread through her hair completed the purchases.

Clare sank back on her heels, marveling at Lord Rayne's generosity. He had no need to buy her clothes until they were married, but remembering his distaste of her bonnet, she smiled. Well, she need not wear that again, but her old dress and cloak must suffice until they reached London.

After washing, she slipped the new shift over her head. It glided down her body so lightly, it hardly seemed to be there at all. The gown was almost as weightless, and she glanced at her reflection in the dressing table glass and gave a gasp of dismay. With the neckline cut so low and the waist shaped so tightly, her breasts were barely covered at all. Lord Rayne had misjudged her size, she decided, but what should she do? He would expect her to appear for dinner wearing his gown, as she had promised. She remembered her shawl. It was old, but had been of good quality once. She brushed her hair until the silken strands glowed like polished jet, then threaded the ribbon through the vibrant curls.

With the shawl about her shoulders she glided down the stairs in the feather-light kid slippers. Lord Rayne would be amused at his mistake over the dress, but understand that she wore it out of gratitude.

He was in the dining parlor as she entered, elegant in a waisted jacket of superfine cloth, his buff-colored pantaloons clinging tightly to his legs before disappearing into Hessian boots. He turned as she greeted him, and for a moment, his scrutiny was so intent that she was embarrassed.

"Take off your shawl, my dear, that I may fully see how my choice of gown becomes you."

She slid the shawl down her arms reluctantly and gave a shy laugh.

"I believe your choice was a little in error, my lord. As you see, the gown was designed for a person even smaller than I."

"Not at all. It fits you perfectly."

Her hands fluttered over her breasts. "But it is so revealing! I cannot imagine the ladies in London being quite so—so exposed."

"By society standards, my dear, the neckline is quite modest. Even ladies of the nobility have been known to damp their dresses to make them cling to their figures more closely. You are merely unused to such finery, my poor child, but that is nothing out of the way, I assure you. You look divinely virginal, and I shall be the envy of all when I present you to my friends."

"But it hardly seems respectable," she protested.

"Is that what you want to be—respectable?" He had moved closer and his fingers played with a curl at the nape of her neck. "Perhaps you would have been happier to mate with a tradesman. Does a life of drudgery and constant child-bearing appeal to your sense of respectability? Tell me now before I involve myself further in protecting your honor."

Clare stiffened and her grey eyes glowed indignantly. "I was reared a lady, my lord, in spite of my father's way of life. I have the accomplishments of gentility, not those of a tradesman's wife."

"And what you lack, I will teach you gladly." He bent and kissed her lips. "I hope to find you a willing and eager pupil."

His lips were warm and moist, and the hand he placed on her shoulder seemed to burn through her skin. She looked

into his face. There was a sheen of perspiration on his brow
and the pale eyes held a glitter she had not seen before.
Unaccountably, her father's face flashed through her mind;
and as Lord Rayne's fingers touched the beadwork on the
neck of her gown, she flinched.

Lord Rayne sensed her withdrawal and cursed himself for
a fool. She was so desirable he had almost cast caution to
the winds. It was too soon. She would fight him and he would
lose all the advantage he had gained. And with the wine he
had already drunk weighing heavily on him, she could well
be fleeter of foot and elude him completely. Better to control
his lust until they were in his London house, surrounded by
his servants and with no one to aid her.

He stepped back. "Forgive me, my dear. You looked so
enchanting that I was overwhelmed by my desire for you. To
admire so deeply can be painful, but I will restrain my feelings
until you come to me willingly, as I pray you will. My first
duty is to carry you away from all danger, for we are not yet
safe. We need to set off at first light."

Being reminded of her danger made Clare realize that she
had no choice but to accept Lord Rayne's help. Only he could
protect and carry her swiftly to London. He had said he
admired her, and unused as she was to tenderness, she must
try to return his feelings. For her sake he was acting unlaw-
fully by spiriting her away from her father's domination.

Had her mother flinched each time her father touched her?
Was this strange feeling of revulsion the total of all a wife
could expect? Was it only the harlots who found pleasure in
being fondled?

As Lord Rayne swayed to the door after dinner, Clare
smiled at him brightly, determined to show her gratitude. He
had drunk a great deal, but that was the way of gentlemen,
she supposed.

"Sleep well, my dear," he said, his voice slurring, his
hand squeezing her shoulder.

"Thank you for everything, my lord," she replied, forcing
herself to lean forward and kiss his cheek.

He turned his face and met her lips greedily, his slack

mouth covering hers. Before she knew it, his fingers were inside her bodice, cupping one small breast. Her inclination was to pull away but she held herself still, though her body went cold. His fingers moved to caress the nipple as his mouth slid to her neck.

"Clare, my dove," he murmured, and brandy fumes filled her nostrils.

"My—my lord," she gasped. "You will tear my gown."

"Call me Philip, sweetheart, and to hell with the gown. I will buy you a hundred."

She felt the threads crack and panic ran through her. "You must not, my lord. Philip—you promised to wait! This is not the time—I will not allow it."

He raised his head and she was shocked by the fierce glare in his eyes.

"You will not allow—!" His words were tinged with outrage. Then, suddenly, the heat died from his eyes and sanity took its place. He withdrew his hand and Clare pulled the silken bodice up over her naked breast, her cheeks crimson.

Lord Rayne pushed back his damp hair. "You are right, my dear. This is not the time or the place. You did well to remind me. I was intoxicated by your nearness into a moment of madness. I have never desired anyone so much, but I must be patient. Forgive me for alarming you."

"Of course. Good night, my lord." She gave him a trembling smile and slid quickly from the room, her heart thumping uncomfortably.

Once in her room she locked the door and sank onto the bed to examine her feelings. One thing was very clear. If marriage meant submitting to the pawings and squeezings of Lord Rayne, she could not do it. If she was revolted by his mere touch on her breast, what then of the unspeakable indignities he must hope to inflict on her in the marriage bed? Yet she dare not repulse him irrevocably at this point, in case he returned her to her father in anger.

She bit her fingers in indecision. It was a choice between her father's drunken friend or Lord Rayne. But, was it? If she could hold off his lordship's amorous advances until they reached London, might there be an opportunity to evade his watchful eye and lose herself in such a big city?

The maid called her early the next morning. Clare donned her own clothes, parceling up the new ones carefully and putting them into her straw bag. When the time came, she would not be too proud to take them with her. They were a gift, after all.

As she was returning to her room after breakfast, an idea struck her.

"Oh, Philip," she said sweetly. "The maid has been so good to me that I would like to give her a generous tip. Would you approve?"

"Of course, my dear." Lord Rayne beamed his relief at her friendly tone. Thank God he had not ruined his chances last night. He must not drink so much again; it always brought out the sensualist in him. He produced a leather purse and handed it to her. "Tip what you will, my love, and return the rest to me in the coach." He could afford to appear magnanimous if it achieved his ends.

Back in the bedroom Clare emptied the purse onto the bed and her eyes widened. Ten golden guineas! She put two into one pocket of her cloak, dropped the purse into the other, then sought the maid and handed her one gold piece. The girl was overwhelmed. Few people gave her a whole guinea and she was profuse in her thanks.

Clare put on her ugly bonnet and, with her bag over her arm, wandered into the inn yard. Lord Rayne was settling with the landlord, and from the glimpse she had of him through the bar window, he was also indulging in a parting glass of brandy. She strolled toward the Rayne carriage, looking about her. Two men were lounging near the stable door, watching the ostlers lead out the horses.

"Better get his lordship's cattle out now," called one to an ostler. "His temper's none so good this time of day and he wants to be in London tonight."

"What's his hurry?" queried his companion. "The fancy piece is with him, isn't she?"

The first groom laughed. "He had to book two rooms last

night. He's in a hurry to make it one, and that's got him in a devil of a state.''

''Must be a different kind of female he's got in tow this time, then. Teasing him along, is she? Getting him so hot he'll set her up in better style than the others?''

Clare listened with growing horror, unable to move. She was half hidden by the carriage and had not known which men were Lord Rayne's.

''What happened to the last one? Pretty blond thing, I recall.''

''Threw her out. Got tired of her, I expect. His lordship always did run through his women fast.''

''Wonder what his lady wife thinks of his fancy women.''

''Glad he goes elsewhere, I should think, poor soul. Come on, Bob, here's the first horse. Back him into the shafts while I hold his head.''

The blood suddenly ran cold through Clare's veins. So, Lord Rayne was already married! His intentions were merely to install her in some house as his mistress—just another bedmate until he tired of her, too, and she was thrown out on the street!

What a fool she had been to believe he had fallen in love with an eighteen-year-old, country-bred child. How simple-minded she was to suppose she could enter society as Lady Rayne! There was no point in going to London now. She recalled his remark about a girl being able to lose herself in Bristol. Why not? It was as good a place as any.

She moved slowly toward the stable. The Rayne grooms were backing in the first horse between the carriage shafts. An ostler was bringing a second out of the stable.

''Is that Lord Rayne's horse?'' she asked.

''Yes, ma'am.''

''Thank you.'' She took the bridle from him, threw back her skirts, and scrambled onto the bare back of the horse. She wheeled it around and tucked in her knees, set the straw bag on her arm, then dug in her heels. The horse leapt forward, and before the startled gazes of the two grooms, she thundered out of the inn yard.

◆ *Chapter Five* ◆

As the cottages thinned she reached a crossroad and slowed her headlong gallop to read the signpost. She was on the London road, heading in the wrong direction for Bristol! But she dare not return the same way, for that would mean passing the inn. A cross-country route would be best, circling the villages and towns to put herself back on the Bristol road. She turned into a lane and set the horse to a steady canter.

The sun rose higher in the sky and the air warmed. She felt clean and carefree. Whatever happened, she was her own woman, and never again would she allow a man to arrange her life and dictate her actions.

She pictured Lord Rayne's face when he was told of her flight and laughed aloud. But then she sobered, remembering the purse still in her pocket. She had stolen nine guineas and a horse belonging to him. Would he be furious enough to seek her arrest on a charge of robbery? Was Bristol big enough to hide a thief and a runaway?

The sun had passed its zenith when she found a tiny, tumbledown inn, tucked away in the fold of a valley. She was hungry and must rest the horse. Instead of riding into the inn yard, she halted and slid from the back of the horse, then smoothed down her creased skirts and tucked her curls under the enveloping bonnet. It would be more seemly to lead the horse in.

An ostler stood by the stable door, his hands thrust in his pockets. He watched her approach, eyeing her insolently, without removing himself from his lounging position.

"And what might you be wanting?" he asked.

Clare answered meekly. "Will you please feed and water this horse?"

He ran an experienced eye over the Thoroughbred. "Yours, is it?" He seemed surprised.

Conscious of her plain attire and not wishing to rouse

suspicion, she said, "My lady has gone for a picnic and wants the horse rested for an hour. I am to eat here myself and return to her later."

He nodded. "I thought it too highbred to belong to a girl like you. Go you then to the public parlor while I give him a rubdown."

"Thank you."

Clare had never been in a bar parlor before but she went in bravely, keeping her head low, trying to remain unobtrusive. Surprisingly, the room was quite full, but she noted with a sinking heart that, apart from the barmaid, she was the only female.

She managed to whisper her order for a meat pie and a glass of cider before being noticed by any of the customers. To her chagrin, this was brought about by the barmaid herself. The girl, a large, blowsy-looking female, placed her hands on her hips and regarded Clare searchingly.

"Let's see the color of your money first," she demanded, her hard gaze taking in the faded cotton dress and dust-stained cloak.

Clare's grey eyes flashed with anger and her chin came up haughtily.

"I can pay!" she snapped, and slammed down a guinea on the table.

The barmaid's eyes widened. "You got nothing less than that?"

"No, I haven't. Does it matter? Now be good enough to fill my order."

She couldn't quite restrain the imperious note that crept into her voice.

The barmaid eyed her with new respect. "Nobody ever paid with one of those before. Where did you filch it? You ain't dressed like gentry."

"How dare you suggest such a thing!" Clare flared. "It was a gift, if you must know. And I expect the right change without being cheated."

"All right, miss, but I wish I knew a gent who was as free with his gold. He must have been right satisfied with you."

She turned away, leaving Clare with burning cheeks at the

implication. Only then did she realize there was an odd silence in the room. She glanced up to find herself the object of all eyes. Some were amused; some were watching her in speculation.

A man in a seaman's jersey and woolen cap sauntered over. "Mind if I join you?" he asked with a knowing leer.

"I mind very much," Clare replied fiercely. "Go away."

"Come on now, girl, be friendly. You must have been more accommodating to earn yourself a guinea. I'm just a sailing man but I've a pocketful of back pay. You'll not get a guinea that often, but I'm a generous fellow. What do you say?"

"I have nothing to say to you," she hissed. "Now, leave me alone and get back to your drinking."

"Little spitfire, aren't you?" he said admiringly, his hand grasping her wrist. "I like a bit of fire in a whore."

Clare's indignation spilled over and she lashed out with her free hand.

"I'm not a whore!" she screamed.

"No?" he caught the flailing arm and jerked her close, grinning

"Tom!" A voice cut through the dimness of the tavern like a knife. "Leave the wench be. She wants none of you."

Clare glimpsed the tall figure of a man leaning against the bar. He was half-turned away but she noted the curly black beard, the woolen cap covering shaggy hair, and a lean, brown cheekbone. His voice had a commanding ring.

"But, Cap'n—" the man protested.

"Do as I say. If the girl's earned a guinea she'll be too worn out to bother with the likes of you."

There was a guffaw of laughter and the man, Tom, shrugged and rose.

"Some other time, spitfire. I'll look out for you when I'm this way again."

He rejoined his friends at the bar and Clare, eyes dimmed by helpless anger and humiliation, saw the barmaid put down her order and slap coins onto the table. She slid the change into her pocket, drank deeply of the cider, and walked out with the pie in her hand. She didn't look back.

Under a tree in the nearest field, she ate the pie slowly, willing her heart to slow its wild beating. She shivered in spite of the sun. Could she find work in Bristol? Or would eventual destitution force her into accepting the role intended by Lord Rayne and presumed by the seaman?

She must have dozed for a time because the sun was much lower when she came to herself. It would be dark in a few hours. Could she reach Bristol before night? She brushed down her cloak and went cautiously to the inn yard. In the stable she found the ostler yawning. He had done a good job on the horse. She paid him and led the horse outside before mounting. A signpost pointed the way to Bristol and she set off once more after checking her straw bag and the money she had left.

Her spirits rose. Some household in a big shipping city like Bristol must need a maid or a sewing girl. She was prepared to work hard. Her lips curved wryly. When, indeed, had she ever lived like a lady?

It began to grow dark and she glanced at the sky. Black clouds were building up and the sun had disappeared. The breeze turned cool and a few spots of rain fell. She looked about her. There was only countryside for as far as she could see. Bristol should not be far away, but she could do nothing by arriving in the middle of a storm after darkness had fallen. A distant rumble and a flash of lightning made the prospect of a storm immediate. Then there was a crash and the clouds let loose the torrent.

Across a field she saw the lights of a farmhouse and turned the horse toward it. The rain was blinding now and the wind hurled its force across the open field, billowing her cloak behind her. The horse stumbled and neighed in terror as lightning tore the clouds apart. Clare reined in, slipped from the horse's back, and talked soothingly to the nervous animal as she fought her way along. The rain was soaking her through and the sodden earth threatened to suck off her shoes.

Looming up in the gloom, a barn caught her eye, and she decided to take advantage of its shelter. She could not be expected to ask permission with the storm at its height. The door was almost blown out of her hand, but she hung on and urged the horse inside. It went readily, and as she hauled the door shut behind her, she looked around.

It was a tidy barn, with farm tools stacked neatly. The sweet smell of hay, rising from bales down its length, was pleasant. There was a water butt, and from this Clare filled a tin bucket for the horse and pulled down some hay before tethering the animal. She could settle the cost with the farmer. She discarded her bonnet and cloak and spread the cloak on the hay. She gave the horse a perfunctory wipe with a handful of straw, then turned her attention to her own condition.

Although the barn was dry, it was cold, and her soaked skirt had become uncomfortably clammy. She sat on the hay and peeled off her shoes and stockings, then removed her dress and damp undergarment. Her shift was reasonably dry, and clad only in this, she crossed to the water butt and rinsed her muddied hands, then dried them on the hay.

It was still raining fiercely and the light was dim, coming only through a few split planks in the wood of the door. The wind still howled, crashing against the wood as if demanding entry. She was suddenly very tired, and the piles of hay were inviting. There was no reason for the farmer to visit the barn tonight. Surely tomorrow would be soon enough for her to call at the farmhouse to pay for the accommodation and perhaps buy breakfast.

She stepped onto the hay, reaching up to draw sufficient down to make a pillow. Without warning the barn door swung open, crashing against the wall, and a cold wind swept through. Clare froze as she heard a man's voice, then a horse plunged through the doorway.

"Come on, my beauty, get in. You're as timid as a tabby at a dogfight. Shame on you, Bella. Get over now while I shut the door."

The wind was cut off as a shoulder slammed against the door. Clare stared at the dark figure with the seaman's cap pulled low. For a frozen, terrified moment, she thought the man who had taken her for a harlot had followed. Her gasp of horror brought the man's head around with a jerk. He searched the barn, then his stare found her. She saw a curly beard and broad shoulders and her tension lessened slightly. It was the man who had stopped the other one's pestering, but even so, her situation was hardly improved.

For his part, the man saw a slightly built, waiflike creature; a cloud of black curls framing a pale, oval face. Clad only in a scanty shift, her long, slender legs were bare to the thigh. Her pose was as rigid as a marble statue, and her whitened knuckles gripped clumps of hay. He saw the terror in her wide gaze and smiled reassuringly.

"Take no heed of me, child. If it wasn't for this skittish mare, I wouldn't have taken shelter." He glanced over at Lord Rayne's horse, then noted Clare's clothes spread over the hay. "I see you had the same idea. Are you alone?"

Clare nodded, then wondered if she should have admitted that fact. He seemed unconcerned as he set about rubbing down the mare, and even turned his back to her. Clare took the opportunity to burrow into the hay and pull her cloak over her. She watched him warily as he tossed off his dark jacket and woolen cap. He wore a grey flannel shirt tucked into tight dark breeches and his body looked slim and hard. Without the cap, his hair was dark and untrimmed, a trifle curly, like the short beard.

He finished his task and led the horse to the water butt. Glancing over his shoulder he grinned at her, white teeth glinting in the brown face that crinkled in amusement.

"I'm not the devil come to steal your soul, child, so relax your guard. I think you'd best close your eyes now."

"Why?" asked Clare, suspiciously.

He laughed. "Because I intend to remove my breeches."

"Oh!" Clare felt her face flood with color. Even in the dim light he seemed to notice, and a soft chuckle escaped him.

She closed her eyes and heard the creak of leather as his boots came off. After a few moments the hay rustled and he said cheerfully, "You can open your eyes now."

She did, and discovered that he was bedded down not two feet away. Under her outraged stare he threw back his head and laughed.

"What a suspicious creature you are. Does your mother teach you that all men seek your virtue and not a one can be trusted?"

Clare turned her head away. "My mother is dead and she had no need to teach me that lesson."

"So you learned it the hard way. When I came in just now I had the impression you feared it was another. Are you running from someone?"

She nodded and he lay back, his arms under his head. "So am I."

"You?" She stared at him.

He glanced sideways, a small grin on his face. "There's a young lady who thinks it time I settled down. When I begin to feel hemmed in, I run."

"Do you always go back to her?"

"It's in my best interest, at present."

"You sound quite unprincipled. I'm sorry for her if she —if she loves you."

He raised himself on one elbow. "Why the doubtful tone? You speak as if such a thing doesn't exist."

"Does it?" she asked bitterly.

He leaned forward suddenly and took her chin in his hand. "I thought I recognized you. You were at the tavern earlier today—the girl who spurned poor Tom because she'd already earned herself a gold piece."

"I didn't spurn him for that reason," she returned furiously. "And I will not be called a whore."

"Then, why go to such an out-of-the-way place? It's well known for its whores and fly-by-nights."

"You might know that, but I didn't! I was lost. All I wanted was something to eat and feed my horse."

"And where did you get the gold piece?"

"I did not earn it in the way you mean. It was—it was a gift."

"You mean you stole it."

"I did not!" She saw his eyebrow rise quizzically and finished lamely, "I just borrowed it. And you have no right to ask me questions."

He laughed softly. "I won't ask you any more except, are you hungry?"

"Starving. I've had nothing to eat since that pie."

He sat up, pulled his saddlebag close, and drew out a bottle and a cloth-wrapped packet. Beef sandwiches, cheese, and apples were displayed, and Clare accepted a share gratefully.

He uncorked the bottle and drank from it. With his head back, Clare noted the strong column of his neck below the hard chin. His shoulders were well-muscled and his bare chest, with the fine mat of hair, tapered to a firm waist. He offered her the bottle.

"What is it?"

"Brandy—good, strong brandy. It will keep you warm until your clothes are dry." Clare took a long drink, as he had done, and the breath left her body as she gasped for air. The spirit surged like fire throughout her whole being.

"I told you it was strong," he said with a grin as she coughed and wiped her eyes.

After the first shock, the brandy spread a warm glow through her and she lay back in the hay with her arms behind her head.

"Where are you headed?" the man asked casually.

"I don't know. Possibly Bristol may suit me. If not—" She shrugged.

"I'm often in Bristol myself. Maybe we'll meet again."

"Maybe. Maybe not."

"Perhaps in the course of business."

"I don't know your business."

He smiled and touched her cheek. "Then in yours, I expect." His fingers brushed her tangled hair and she flinched at their gentle touch. He withdrew his hand and regarded her intently. "I think you have not yet met with tenderness in your dealings with men."

"The only people who were kind to me were tradesmen."

"What of your father? Or was your mother an unfortunate, too?"

A languorous feeling was creeping over Clare. *No wonder*

men drink, she thought lazily. *It really makes one feel glowing and clear-minded.*

She gazed at the man who lay on his elbow, smiling down at her. He smelled somehow of meadows and orchards, leather and sweet hay. It was altogether a pleasant aroma, so unlike the sickly body smell of Lord Rayne.

"My father hated me because I was a girl. He would have sold me, but Philip came and I thought— But he was worse—"

A shudder racked her, bringing those past moments of despair horrifyingly alive. The heightening of her senses, induced by the brandy, sent her brain reeling into a clarity of vision too great to bear. Her overtaxed mind tried to thrust away the pictures, but they spun about her in a confused blur.

Her body was icy cold. She could see the men's faces looking at her, then fingers thrusting into her dress. They were laughing, all of them—her father, Lord Rayne, Mrs. Lawson, and the others, all together. They were staring, cynically amused by her innocence. Hands were reaching and she could not move.

A scream tore itself from her throat, and she fought the arms that were trying to hold her down. How could they do this? Then her face was pressed against flesh—hard, warm, living flesh—and the voice was not laughing anymore but murmuring softly. It was a comforting sound. Her body was no longer stiff and cold but warming to the heat of another.

The visions receded, and as her body lost its tautness, the arms relaxed.

"Hold me," she pleaded. "Don't leave me yet," and her arms rose to encircle the neck of the man who had gathered her into his arms when she screamed.

For a few moments Clare clung to him, her cheek against the curve of his neck. Then, as her terror left her, she stirred, not wanting to leave the comfort of his body, but knowing she must.

"I'm sorry," she whispered, raising her eyes. "You must think me mad."

"No, not mad. Just a girl who has been harried intolerably. How old are you?"

"Eighteen."

"Good God! What impatient fools those men were! Your body is too exquisite to be treated roughly. There must be satisfaction on both sides, and I'll wager you've never come near to enjoying any."

Clare stared into his face. Of course, he still thought her a whore, she realized. If she told him the truth, would he leave her? She didn't want to be alone in case the terrible pictures came back. He probably wouldn't believe her innocent anyway.

She smiled shakily, smoothing the fine hairs on his chest. "Exquisite? Me? I think the light deceives you, or your words are kindly meant."

Behind her back his fingers moved. Clare caught her breath as her shift came free and was tossed aside. She saw his gaze wander over her naked breasts and resisted the urge to draw away. His eyes rose to hers and he smiled, his lips firm— not slack with lust as Lord Rayne's had been.

"To me you look perfect," he said and dropped a kiss on her brow. "Do you want your shift back?" His voice was teasing but implied the choice was hers to make.

For a moment she lay still, looking into the bearded face. "No!" Her voice spoke clearly and she shook her head.

His mouth came down to hers and he kissed her gently at first, then with more passion. After the first shock, Clare's lips softened and parted slightly and she returned the kisses. His lips touched her cheeks, her eyelids, then slid to her throat, lingering in the curve of her neck.

She felt his fingers on her breast and gasped at the sensation of pleasure that ran through her. His lips moved lower and his mouth was on her breast, his tongue touching the nipple that had hardened. She gave a soft moan as his hand slid over her stomach, fingers lightly probing her tender flesh.

Her body was on fire. The reckless blood of her father rose, drowning the passive nature of her mother. Her fingers closed around the back of the man's head, drawing him close as his mouth wandered over her breasts. He rose to her lips again and she locked him fiercely in her arms. His body pressed against hers, one leg easing her own apart. She moved

them herself without realizing it, and the hardness of his
thighs forced them wide. She felt the swell of his manhood,
the slow, deliberate entry into her, and her body arched to
the flame of desire.

Her gasp as he thrust rose to a muffled scream and the pain
stabbed. Then their loins were joined as one and a rhythm
took them both. Clare's hips rose and fell with the motion
and their bodies fused together in a fiery heat. It seemed an
eternity of the fiercest and sweetest pleasure Clare had ever
known.

They lay locked together as the fire died into a glow. Clare
was content to curl in the shelter of his arms until her heart
slowed its pounding. She was filled with a sense of well-
being. A stranger in a barn had brought her to womanhood,
she mused, and he was still nameless! Her lips wandered up
his throat. His beard tickled her nose, and she found herself
looking into eyes that regarded her frowningly. What had she
done wrong?

"You were a virgin!" he said at last, his tone accusing.

She smiled. "Yes, I was, but not anymore."

"You said you were a whore!"

"No. You said I was a whore."

"Oh, God, what have I done?" he groaned. "Why did
you let me?"

She put a finger on his lips. "Don't blame yourself. I was
afraid that if I told you the truth, you would leave me when
the rain stopped. I couldn't bear to be alone tonight. There
are too many ghosts."

"But, who are you? Your father will call me to account
—and with reason."

She shook her head and the black curls hid her face. "I
am alone in the world and must stay that way. It is better if
we part in the morning as strangers. I hope to earn an honest
living somewhere, but if I must become what you supposed,
then I shall know that such acts can be beautiful, not simply
cruel and lustful. Give me this night to dream on, and if it
please you, remember a girl you once met during a storm."

He reached for her and held her tightly against him. "Tomorrow we will talk—" he began, then was silenced as

Clare's lips brushed his, teasing him with tiny kisses across his cheek and neck. He was surprised at the passion she showed, unaware that affection had never figured in her life.

He drew her on top of him, cupping her slim buttocks and holding her firmly to his hips. The fresh young body pressed to his sent a flame of desire leaping through his entire being. Clare twined herself about him, moving sensuously, and they rolled over in the hay until she was beneath him again and he was entering the soft, secret places of her body.

The crowing of a cock woke him. He lay still for a moment, staring at the rafters of the barn. He was flat on his back and the sun streamed through the cracks in the door. Where the devil was he? Memory came flooding back and his blood raced as he thought of the exquisite creature with whom he had spent a night like no other he had ever known. His arm went out to touch her. His fingers met only hay. Where was she?

He sat up and stared about him. The barn was empty. His horse stood alone. Had he dreamed that ecstasy of passion in some fevered sleep? No, it had been real. Another memory pierced him, like the prick of a knife. He had taken the virginity of an eighteen-year-old!

He sprang to his feet and dislodged a small object that rolled along the earth floor. He stared, then bent to pick it up. In his hand lay a golden guinea! He grinned, and closed his fingers on it. The saucy wench had reversed their roles. She had paid him a guinea for his services! And dared lay it on his stomach as he slept! He gave a low chuckle. But then, hadn't she practically seduced him?

His smile died. Find her he must, for she was no whore, but an innocent, unworldly child. And who knew what might result from this stormy night of passion?

◆ *Chapter Six* ◆

It was like seeing everything for the first time—the glory of a new world, a rebirth of being. Her eyes followed the flight of birds and rested, as the birds did, on hedge and tree, while her heart sang with them. After the rain, the countryside was fresh and green, the sky a heavenly blue, sun shafts lancing down to turn the odd pool of rainwater into molten gold. Clare breathed deeply and joyously of the spring air and hummed softly to herself as the horse trotted along. Though her body ached a little, it was not enough to dispel the euphoric haze that enveloped her. As the distance from the barn increased, so the bliss became part of a once-in-a-lifetime dream—a moment sweet with the surrender of her being to another.

While her body remembered, her mind tingled with the shock of realizing she was capable of such passion. Was she a whore at heart? The man had not forced himself on her; quite the contrary, she had invited his lovemaking! Her cheeks began to burn as she recalled her wanton behavior. Had he not discovered her virginity, he would have taken her for an eager, lustful harlot.

In spite of the warm sun, she felt suddenly chilled, but she took comfort from the fact that there had been no exchange of names or information. They were still strangers and might possibly pass each other in the street without recognition. The barn had been gloomy and even the later moonlight had shadowed their faces, and all women's bodies, she supposed, were much the same to men. But now that she realized the measure of her Harcourt blood, she must never allow herself to think of that night again, or of the one man who had the power to rouse her senses. Lord Rayne had not succeeded, and she doubted if any other man could, but she would not put it to the test. Her attitude from now on must be as retiring and meek as her mother's had been. How else would she find employment as a sewing maid?

So engrossed in her thoughts was she that her hands had lain slack on the reins. The horse had dropped into a walk and taken its own direction. Clare raised her head and peered from under the brim of the bonnet to find herself staring across a wide channel of water. Small ships, sails furled, were drifting on the tide, making for a small harbor below the hill on which the horse now stood, motionless. Clustered round the harbor were warehouses and streets of buildings, and on the hillside were a number of farms. Sheep and cattle were in the fields beside the lane where she sat the horse and the fields were hedged between clumps of trees.

The Bristol Channel! It must be, and yet the town was small—too small to be Bristol. That city must be farther up the estuary. She became aware of hunger and decided to descend to the town and seek direction while she purchased some food.

As she urged the horse back to the main thoroughfare a voice, desperate with appeal, floated toward her.

"Miss! Please, miss, help me."

She stared about her, seeing no one.

"Look up, miss. I'm in the tree. Please help me." The voice was young and nervous.

Clare scanned the branches of the tree nearest to her. A flutter of pink caught her eye and she glimpsed a small figure clutching tightly to the trunk. She guided the horse closer and looked up.

"You're not so very high. Can't you put your feet on that lower branch and hold the one beside you?"

"It's my dress, miss. It's caught fast on a sharp twig. If I move it will tear, and it's my best dress!"

Clare laughed and slid from the horse. "All right, I'll come and release it, but what on earth are you doing, climbing trees in your best dress?"

The child gave a nervous giggle. "I was going to tea at the farm when I met the boy with the billy goats. He doesn't like girls and always drives the goats at us so that they dirty our dresses. I had to climb the tree to keep out of the way."

"So now your dress is clean but in danger of being ripped. Well, hold on, I'm coming."

She swung herself into the lower branches, finding firm footholds, and edged slowly upwards. Almost level with the child, she was able to stretch out a hand and ease the pink cotton from the twig that had pierced the hem. The face that regarded her gratefully was of a girl about eight years old, brown-haired, and with enormous grey-green eyes.

"Oh, thank you, miss, I can manage now."

"Come down slowly and I will steady you at the bottom." Clare swung down and held out her arms as the child descended carefully. "Apart from that little tear in the hem, I think you look quite respectable enough to go on to your tea party with the ladies and gentlemen at the farm."

The child gave her a sweeping glance from eyes that twinkled, showing more green than grey. "It's not a grown-up party, miss, only Kate and Milly."

"And what is your name?"

"Sara."

"Do you know how far we are from Bristol, Sara?"

"No, miss, but they'll tell you at the farm. Is that where you're going? Bristol?"

"I hope to do so when I have found somewhere to buy food for myself and my horse."

Sara slid her hand into Clare's. "You can do that at the farm, too. Kate says we're having ham for tea and scones with lots of cream."

Clare looked down into the pretty face of the child and laughed aloud. "What a delicious thought. I believe you said that on purpose, you little temptress! How can I resist when you talk of lots of cream. Shall we ride there?"

Sara nodded eagerly and Clare lifted her onto the horse's back before swinging up behind her.

"Do you always ride without a saddle?" Sara asked.

"Not always, but I was in a terrible hurry and didn't bother."

Sara twisted her head around and gave Clare a glowing look. "Were you running away from your wicked stepmother?"

Clare couldn't restrain the smile that tugged at the corners of her mouth. The child had a vivid imagination.

"Not really," she replied, but as she noted a dimming of that glowing look she continued, "I am running away, it is true, but from a life I could not endure anymore."

Sara brightened. "And are they chasing you, these bad people?"

"I hope not." She smiled down at the child. "What do you know of bad people, young Sara?"

"Nothing, miss, but in stories there is always a wicked stepmother."

"And there is always a fairy godmother who puts everything right."

Sara giggled and gave Clare a twinkling look over her shoulder. "You must be my fairy godmother, then, because you rescued me and I shan't be late for tea. What shall I call you when we get to the farm?"

"My name is Clare and I am eighteen. How old are you?"

"Nearly eight. Can I call you Clare?"

"Please do. *Miss* makes me feel like a schoolma'am."

They reached the farm and Clare helped Sara down. She tied the horse's reins to a fence, then removed her bonnet and ran her fingers through her curls in an effort to tidy them.

Sara took her hand. "Come on, Clare, I can smell the ham."

"So can I, and it's making me faint with hunger."

Two small girls erupted from the doorway of the farmhouse. "Sara! We thought you were never coming." They halted abruptly, eyeing the stranger uncertainly.

"This is my friend, Clare," Sara said proudly.

Over their heads, Clare saw a pleasant-faced woman staring at her.

"Please forgive my intrusion," she said. "Sara told me you might give me directions to Bristol. And if it would not be too much trouble, I would like to buy a little food from you. My name is Clare."

At the sound of her soft, cultured voice, the farmer's wife came forward swiftly. "Indeed, I can do both, miss." She called to a boy in the yard. "Take the lady's horse to the stable, Jack, and look after it." To Clare she said, "Follow me, Miss Clare, please. I've set the tea in the kitchen but it'll be no bother to serve you in the parlor. I'm sure you'd rather have a meal in comfort than on the road.''

"Thank you, ma'am. I would, indeed, but please allow me into the kitchen too—that is, if Kate and Milly don't take exception to my presence.''

She smiled at the two little girls, who blushed rosily. "Sara, you have neglected to tell me which is which of these pretty friends of yours.''

Sara performed the introductions gravely and Clare learned that her hostess was Mrs. Clark.

Any unease the Clark family felt at entertaining a lady in their kitchen was quickly dispelled by Clare's attitude toward them. After slipping off her cloak, she took the chair proffered and was soon eating as hungrily as the girls and laughing with them as Sara recounted her meeting with the billy goats. Her acceptance was complete when she complimented Mrs. Clark on her delicious scones and vowed she had never tasted better.

After tea, the three girls ran out to play. As Clare and Mrs. Clark lingered over large cups of tea, Clare asked about the town below the cliffs.

"'Tis Clevedon, Miss Clare, and a fine little town, too. I'm not so fond of Bristol, myself—too many streets and strange people. A lot of good families live here that have made money from shipping in Bristol. Will you be joining your kin there?''

"No, Mrs. Clark, I have no one now. My mother died recently and I go to Bristol to take up a post as—as a dressmaker.'' Her pride upgraded the position as she saw Mrs. Clark's brows rise. "My father—my late father,'' she said firmly, "was not exactly clever with money.''

Mrs. Clark made a sound of understanding. "'Tis often the way with gentlemen. The money just slips through their fingers if they've no good estate manager to guide them. And so a well-brought-up young lady, like yourself, must seek a genteel occupation through no fault of her own.''

"And why not, Mrs. Clark? I'm young and strong and it's quite an adventure, really. I'd rather do something I enjoy, like sewing, than live in idleness and spend my time being bored to death with tea parties and gossip.''

"Bravely spoken, my dear, but you are so young and pretty, I hate to think of you being at the mercy of those idle young men who pursue young females without kin to protect them. And mark my words, Miss Clare, you'll find the young bucks not slow in escorting their womenfolk to the dressmaker's when they've once glimpsed that pretty face of yours.''

Clare felt her heart give a little jolt. "But I shall only be a dressmaker's assistant, far beneath anyone's notice.''

"Not for what the young men have in mind, my dear,'' Mrs. Clark pronounced ominously. "Why, even a sewing maid in a grand house has to watch herself if there are any young gentlemen living there. Servant girls are considered fair game, and who would believe their word against that of the son and heir? And you being such a slip of a girl, how could you hope to fend anyone off who was determined to seduce you?''

Clare laughed uneasily. "You make it sound as if I was headed for a life of debauchery, but I have no alternative. I must make a living somehow. I thought Bristol would be the best place.''

"If I were you, miss, I'd write to that dressmaker and tell her you've changed your mind.''

"What good will that do? I still need to earn money.''

Mrs. Clark leaned her elbows on the table. "I've a suggestion to make. You'll please yourself, of course, but I'll put it to you straight. Until a month ago, the town had a dressmaker—couturiere, she called herself—and though she was a bit uppish, she sewed well enough to please the ladies. She made my girls' dresses, though it was plain to see she preferred the carriage trade. As I rented her the cottage cheap, she had no option but to take the orders I gave her.''

"Why did she leave?'' asked Clare.

"Ambition, miss. She was as honey-tongued as you like to the ladies, but I knew she was out to catch one of the rich merchants. She was not the sort of girl who'd be content to stay a dressmaker all her life.''

Clare smiled. ''And did she succeed in capturing her merchant?''

''She did that, and good luck to her, for she'll need it! A widower he was, and as tight-fisted as they come, though plump enough in the pocket. I've known him a long time and suspect he only needed a housekeeper and mother to look after his four children. The silly girl jumped at the chance to be a rich man's wife, though she'll be hard put to pry much out of him.'' Her eyes dwelt on Clare's face kindly. ''What I had in mind, miss, was that you take her place. The cottage is small, but dry and snug, and I'll not be charging you rent until you're established. When the word gets around that we've a new dressmaker—or couturiere, if you prefer—the ladies will be as pleased as punch at not having to travel to Bristol.''

''You're making me an extremely generous offer, Mrs. Clark,'' Clare said with a tremulous smile. ''But we've only just met, and you know nothing about me.''

''I've got eyes in my head, miss. I can see you're a lady fallen on hard times, but not the sort to sit wringing your hands and moaning about it. The girls have taken a fancy to you already, and you ate in the kitchen like one of us, without any uppity airs. I'd worry myself sick to think of you on your own in Bristol, though you've the spirit to try your fortune there. And don't be thinking I'm offering out of charity, for I'm not. I'm all behind with the mending and sewing since the last girl left, so I'll keep you busy until you get some customers from town.''

Clare felt as if a weight had been lifted from her shoulders. Without realizing it, she had dreaded the thought of wandering around Bristol seeking employment, her money gradually dwindling until she was destitute. Tears pricked her eyes and she rose swiftly to give Mrs. Clark an impetuous hug.

''Dear Mrs. Clark! I accept with pleasure and thank you most sincerely for your kindness. Fate must have put Sara in my way, for I would never have met you if she had not climbed that tree.''

Mrs. Clark turned rosy with pleasure at the hug. ''There,

then, it's settled. Sep's been keeping the cottage aired and tidy. I'll get him to take you there. He's an old seaman who does odd jobs around the farm.''

As they moved to the doorway, the girls came racing toward them. They received the news with cries of pleasure, and Sara beamed as proudly as if she had arranged the whole thing from the start.

"May I take Clare to the cottage, too, Mrs. Clark?"

"Of course, dear, if our new couturiere wishes it."

"Oh, Mrs. Clark," laughed Clare. "I believe I will stay just a dressmaker. Couturiere sounds far too grand for a beginner."

Mrs. Clark smiled approval. "I'll send the girls over with some food later, and you may tell them if there's anything you lack."

"Thank you, ma'am. I will keep an accounting so that we start off on a business basis."

The old man leading her horse from the stable had a rolling gait that left Clare in no doubt that this was Sep, the old seaman. He was short and thickset, with grey, grizzled hair sprouting from under a faded peaked cap, but his eyes were amazingly blue in his brown, wrinkled face. He touched his cap and grinned, showing tobacco-stained teeth.

"'Day, ma'am. I'm to be showing you the cottage, these young ruffians be telling me. Woke me up, they did, just as I was aiming to blow old Boney off his poop with me four-pounder muzzle loader. Had him right in me sights, too."
He sighed heavily and beetled his brows at the girls, who fell into giggles and regarded him with adoring eyes.

"Oh, I'm sorry, Mister Sep," Clare said, smiling.

"Not your fault, miss, but I'll get him next time, if these pesky landlubbers will leave a man in peace without coming at him like yelling heathens. 'Minds me of the time I was captured by Arab slavers. Just such a racket it was." His scowling countenance only threw the girls into fresh giggles, but Clare could see that old Sep was as fond of them as they were of him.

"Will you be mounting the horse, miss?"

"No. I think we'll walk to the cottage, and you can tell

me of your dreadful experience at the hands of the Arab slavers.''

Old Sep grinned as he stumped along. "What's the use of a lifetime at sea if you can't tell a few tall tales now and then?''

"Indeed, I agree entirely. You must have had many adventures—apart from the Arab slavers. Storms and shipwrecks, at the very least.''

"Plenty of those, miss, and lost many a good companion I did. See, there's the cottage just by the cliff. 'Tis a trifle windswept at times, but there's a rare view over the channel. It's as right and tight as an admiral's quarters, you'll find.''

Clare looked at the small, whitewashed cottage with interest. She was intrigued by the tiny mullioned windows and the solid wooden front door. It appeared to be all on one level and within view of the farm, which was a comfort.

As Sep had said, there was a breathtaking view of the channel from the main room. Opposite the window was a large open fireplace with a beamed overmantel. The walls were of whitewashed stone, inset with wooden uprights rising to the beamed ceiling. This, it appeared, was the central room, with doors leading from it to a flagged kitchen, a small bedroom, and a tinier room containing a commode and large tin bath.

"Do you like it, Clare?" asked Sara.

Clare swung Sara up and around in happiness. "It's perfect, Sara. Just imagine us sitting by that fire in the winter making toast for tea! And the girls and Sep and everyone! It's better than lodgings in Bristol. I think you must be my fairy godmother! If I ever see the boy with the goats I must thank him for sending you up that tree! Without him we should never have met and I wouldn't have a home and a position, all in one day. Promise to be my first customer, Sara. Bring this dress to me and I'll mend that little tear, just as soon as I've bought some needles and thread.''

"No need, miss," said Sep. "There's a drawerful here— scissors, too. The last young lady must have thought she'd not be needing any such thing. Married rich, I heard, so she'll be having someone else to do her making.''

"Then I must get myself some books on fashion and place an advertisement in the town newspaper. I hope there are lots of rich ladies there who will read it."

That night, Clare sat at the window seat in her small bedroom, staring out across the water. It was hard to believe that only a week ago she had gone to bed at Harcourt House, an innocent seventeen-year-old. Now she was eighteen and no longer innocent, but a young woman determined to carve out her own future by herself. Today, by good fortune, she had acquired friendship, freedom from fear, and the chance to remake a shattered life.

♦ *Chapter Seven* ♦

The next few days passed in a whirl of activity for Clare. With her fast-dwindling guineas she purchased two dress lengths of plain twill, one of olive green, the other of deep blue, together with a length of cotton for a nightdress. A bundle of cheap remnants caught her eye in the modest draper's shop she visited and she purchased these to make petticoats and pantalettes. A pair of lightweight house shoes were added and a thick hair net. After placing her advertisement in the newspaper, she rode home satisfied, a fashion paper tucked into her cloak pocket.

She had decided to drop the first syllable of her surname, so her advertisement stated that "Miss Court is available for fine sewing and dressmaking." With her flair for needlework, it did not take her long to cut and sew two plain, long-sleeved, high-necked dresses. She stared at her reflection in the long cheval glass she had asked Sep to move into the main room. The dresses were plainly styled, but quite elegant in an austere way, she decided. Her customers must view her as a woman

of quiet taste, as befitted her position. To this end she brushed
her curls mercilessly until they lay smooth before enmeshing
them in the heavy net at the nape of her neck. Hairpins held
them rigidly in place.

She nodded with satisfaction. No one would recognize the
tangle-haired, shabby creature who had traveled the countryside. No one, not even the man who had— Her thoughts
stopped abruptly and her color rose. She must not think of
that night. It was too shameful! But just thinking about it
brought a new terror to her mind—one she had not considered
before.

It wasn't until the end of a long week of occupying her
mind feverishly with making her purchases into petticoats
and nightdress that relief came flooding in on her. She woke
one morning to find irrefutable evidence that she was not
pregnant. Her prayer of thanks came from the heart. It would
have been an unwanted complication in her new life, and
how would Mrs. Clark have viewed her protégée?

So thankful was she that she rode singing to the farm after
breakfast and insisted on gathering up every single item that
needed a stitch. In spite of Mrs. Clark's protests, Clare promised to have everything done by the following day.

"It's the least I can do for all your kindness, Mrs. Clark.
Who knows but what I shall get a fine lady wanting a trousseau
any day now? I won't have as much time then. Have you
seen Sara this week?"

"She's been here but I bade the girls to leave you for a
couple of days to get yourself sorted out. They all wanted to
be off to the cottage but Sep said you were sewing away like
you were off to foreign parts on the next tide."

Clare laughed. "Well, I was. I've made two severe gowns
to impress my customers with my sobriety and respectability.
How do you like this green one?"

"You made it, miss? Why, it's so stylish I'd have guessed
you had it made by a fine establishment in Bath or London."
She eyed Clare critically. "And you've got your hair all
severe, too. You look all of nineteen or twenty. Not a bit
like that little gypsy who came to tea the other day. Why,
the girls will be quite in awe of you!"

"I hope not. This will be my professional face, but as soon as my customers have gone, that gypsy will reappear. Do tell the girls and Sara that I am now at home to them."

She rode off, leaving Mrs. Clark with a few private misgivings. In spite of Clare's optimism, Mrs. Clark had noted the tilt of the chin and the indefinable aura of gentle birth about the girl. She guessed there was a fierce pride beneath her outward attitude and wondered how Clare would react to the ladies who considered dressmakers as little better than servants, especially the newly rich clients, who might be patronizing in the extreme, exacting and critical in their demands. But that very aura of class might enhance the girl's reputation and give a check to those who were a little uneasy in their own newly won status.

Mrs. Clark had done her best to circulate word of a new resident dressmaker. Her own doubts had been put to rest when Clare returned the clothes she had taken to mend. The stitching was as fine as one could ask, and even previous alterations had been neatened. Sara's dress, too, had been so cleverly mended that one would not have known there had ever been a tear in it.

Clare's first professional order was a milestone in her life and one she determined to execute to the best of her ability. A coming-out dress was requested by the middle-class mother of a hopeful young girl. They sat one on each side of the fireplace, four square to Clare, and riffled through her fashion book while Clare studied the girl intently. Isobel, a younger version of her mother, Mrs. Foster, was a tallish, well-made girl with mouse-colored hair and a slump to her shoulders.

It is not a promising start, mused Clare. She had to turn a duckling into a swan, with the girl's mother torn between white satin and feathers and pink taffeta with a wreath of rosebuds in her hair. The Empire line was still fashionable, but to put Isobel into that style would have the girl looking like a well-stuffed bolster. As Clare's grey eyes rose, they met the blue ones of Isobel. There was a defeated look in them, as if acknowledging her faults but appealing to Clare to minimize them to the best of her ability.

Mrs. Foster had decided: white satin with pink satin ribbons under the bustline, an Empire sheath gown with a train, perhaps three or four yards in length.

"Are you to have dancing at Miss Foster's debut into society?" asked Clare.

"Yes, indeed. We expect a great number of young people—all very well connected, of course."

"Then I would urge you to dispense with the train, ma'am. It is apt to be a terrible nuisance to handle and even more so when let down, as gentlemen are so inclined to catch their heels in it. As to white satin—" She paused, as if in thought. "It does mark so easily when one's partner forgets his gloves—invariable with the young, I find. Satin and taffeta seem so very ordinary, don't you think? And, indeed, one tires rather of the Empire line, this slavish copying of French fashion."

Mrs. Foster stared hard at Clare, her color high. Never before had her wishes been set aside so emphatically. "Then, what do you suggest—from your vast experience of fashion, Miss Court? You have made gowns for nobility, I suppose?"

"No, no, Mrs. Foster. I speak of my own experiences with gowns that were designed for me when I hosted my late father's gatherings. I always felt that the English gown, the *robe a l'Anglais*, as the French call it, was far more flattering than any design of the Empress Josephine. Mr. Gainsborough painted many beautiful ladies in that style of gown. Miss Foster would quite outshine any other, if the dress was made in forget-me-not blue to match her eyes, and of the softest silk, too. There is nothing as graceful as the sweep and fall of real silk." She smiled into Mrs. Foster's stunned face. "You do wish your daughter to be the belle of her own ball, do you not?"

"Well, yes, of course I do." Mrs. Foster suddenly doubted her own superiority as Clare's grey eyes quizzed her from under arched brows.

"Elbow-length sleeves finishing in soft ruffles," Clare went on. "And the softest fichu, both in a slightly deeper shade. You have a string of pearls for her to wear, I suppose?" She raised her brows expectantly. "It is, of course, usual."

"Her—her papa has promised her a string, yes."

"Splendid. Then her maid must thread an oyster satin ribbon through the curls the coiffeuse will make for her to highlight the pearls. A simple style would be best, so as not to detract from the overall effect." She smiled serenely at Isobel, whose face had come alive with hope. "Your daughter will be the envy of all her friends who cling to the Empire line, like a row of pouter pigeons. Perhaps you will allow Miss Foster to meet me at the silk warehouse tomorrow and we shall choose the color most carefully between us." Her tone excluded Mrs. Foster, and to her surprise, the lady found herself agreeing to let Isobel make her own choice.

As Clare escorted them to their carriage in her most regal manner, Isobel's gaze rested warmly on her, but her mother's look was a trifle bemused, as if she had been outflanked in some mysterious way.

Clare closed her front door and laughed softly to herself. An air of hauteur and a pretended knowledge of society life had taken her a long way. Now she must sketch out the gown she remembered from the Gainsborough painting that had once graced the walls of Harcourt House. It was the kind of challenge that appealed to her. Let others make run-of-the-mill gowns. She was suddenly determined to be known as the dressmaker who was different—the one who adapted, even created, styles to suit every figure. Isobel Foster must be the foundation stone of her reputation.

She watched the Fosters' departure from the window. As soon as their carriage had passed the farmhouse, three small figures raced up the incline toward the cottage. Clare smiled and turned to the kitchen to arrange a tea tray. She was on the doorstep to greet them.

Their bubbling high spirits died as they surveyed her uncertainly. Gone was the tangle-haired girl in the crumpled blue dress—the girl who had giggled with them over Sara's encounter with the goat boy. In her place stood a slim, graceful creature, hair severely restrained by the net, and clad in a long-skirted gown of elegant cut.

But her smile was the same, and when she drew off the hair net and the black curls fell to her shoulders, she was the Clare they knew.

"How glad I am to be rid of this ridiculous thing," she said, laughing. "Come in, do, and help me celebrate my first commission. Tea and buns are ready, ladies, if you would be good enough to step this way."

"Oh, miss, you gave us a fright then," breathed Kate. "For a minute, we thought your lady was still here, though we saw the carriage leave. You looked so different."

"I'm glad, for how would I get any orders if I looked like a disreputable gypsy girl? If anybody asks, tell them you think I must be twenty years old, at least. Now, give me a minute to put on my old blue dress. I cannot afford to stain my dressmaker gown. Will you do the honors, Sara, and serve our guests?"

Sara nodded, beaming, and the next hour passed hilariously as Clare gave them an imitation of Mrs. Foster's attempts to impose her will on a sewing girl who seemed annoyingly unaware that she was being so honored.

Clare's meeting with Miss Foster the next day was highly successful. Away from her mother, Isobel proved to be a friendly and appreciative girl with a taste of her own.

"I am so glad, Miss Court," she said, "that you talked Mama out of the Empire sheath for my coming out. I do so agree about looking pigeonlike unless one is positively lacking a bosom. "And as you can see," she spread her arms in resignation, "I am far from lacking. I am the despair of dressmakers, and Mama has tried several. However fashionable the style she chooses, I still make it look like an old sack, and I am too tall." Her shoulders slumped disconsolately. "I fear you are wasting your time."

"My dear Miss Foster. Nature may have endowed you too amply for your taste, but you make matters worse by slumping your shoulders. Certainly you are tall, but is that a fault? Hold yourself proudly, like a queen, for many have been taller than you. Do you realize that your waist measurement is a mere twenty inches? And who is to know that when it is concealed by these so-called fashionable styles?" She took Isobel's arm and whirled her into the silk warehouse. "What we shall emphasize are your good points, so bear with me on this. Attend to your posture and leave the rest to me."

Isobel laughed, suddenly hopeful. "I declare, you are not at all like any of the previous dressmakers. They do exactly as Mama tells them and never contradict her."

"Perhaps I shall prove unsuccessful by being too outspoken, but I cannot agree to something I am convinced is wrong for a client."

They spent the morning examining silks until they found the exact match for Isobel's eyes, together with the amount needed of a darker shade. After the parcels had been taken to the carriage by the Fosters' coachman, Isobel suggested tentatively that they refresh themselves at a nearby tea shop.

"How very kind of you, Miss Foster," said Clare. "Are you sure your Mama will not object to your entertaining your dressmaker?" she added on a teasing note.

"You are a lady, Miss Court—not like the others. Mama was secretly impressed, I know, though she never said a word."

"I'm flattered," said Clare, laughing.

"One can always tell," Isobel said solemnly as they entered the tearoom.

Clare was aware of the girl's curiosity but had no intention of satisfying it, and Isobel had the good manners to refrain from questioning her.

When they parted, it was agreed that Isobel should visit the cottage the following week for her first fitting.

Clare worked carefully from the sketch she had made of the Gainsborough painting. The ruffled fichu would minimize Isobel's bustline, but the darted waist would show to advantage the slender span between breast and hip. As the day of Isobel's debut grew nearer, Clare was thankful that she had, as yet, no other clients. It occurred to her that the Clevedon ladies might possibly be waiting to judge her efforts with Isobel first. She paused in her stitching of the sleeve ruffles for a moment and smiled to herself. Even Isobel had been startled at her reflection in the cheval glass and they had sworn each other to secrecy. Mrs. Foster did not accompany her daughter to the fitting, being far too busy organizing her household for the ball, so the dress remained a secret between the two of them.

Isobel had begged Clare to be present in her dressing room
on the night of the ball to supervise the last-minute arrangement of hair and ribbon, and Clare had agreed. She wore her
green twill dress, covered by the old cloak, and rode Lord
Rayne's horse to the house. Mrs. Clark had found her an old
saddle, and Clare was determined to add the cost to the debt
she already owed.

The house was ablaze with light and she could hear the
musicians tuning their instruments. As the front door opened
to the pull on the bell, the perfume of flowers flowed over
her. Confronted by a splendid individual in scarlet coat and
knee breeches, a powdered wig atop his young face, she
smiled.

"Please inform Miss Isobel that Miss Court is here. Oh,
and have the goodness to send a groom to stable my horse
for a short time."

She found herself eyed in some surprise. "Miss Court?
You're the sewing woman?"

"I am the dressmaker, yes."

"Then you've come to the wrong door. Tradesmen around
the back."

He was about to close the door, but reckoned without
Clare's sudden surge of temper. She placed a hand flat on
the panel and pushed. Her surprise move sent him back a
pace and she was in the hall before he had recovered. She
raised her chin dangerously and skewered him with a steel-
grey glance.

"How dare you! I am neither tradesman nor servant! Inform Miss Isobel at once that I am here." She flung her cloak
at him and stalked over to a chair, seated herself firmly on
it, and regarded him with outraged hauteur.

His mouth opened and closed, then his eyes quailed under
her intimidating stare.

"Yes, miss. Right away, miss." He laid her cloak almost
reverently on a chest and took himself off hurriedly to the
nether regions of the house.

A few minutes later, a maid appeared. "Miss Court?" Her
eyes stared about the hall and then returned to the slight figure
on the chair. "You are Miss Court, ma'am?"

"I am, indeed. Are you to direct me to Miss Isobel's room?"

"Yes, miss, but Carter, he says—" She caught back her words.

Clare smiled. "Something uncomplimentary, I have no doubt."

The maid gave a stifled giggle. "He was so put out I thought you'd be a fierce old dragon. Oh, excuse me, miss, but he looked so shaken that I didn't know what to expect. Come this way, miss, if you please."

Clare found Isobel seated at her dressing table, clad in a shift, stockings, and blue satin shoes. Her maid was teasing her hair into stiff, corkscrew ringlets that stood out from her head as if starched. She turned an unhappy face toward Clare.

"It's no use, Miss Court. That hairdresser has made me look like a shocked mouse. What am I to do with this mass of ringlets? Mama thinks them sweet, but I hate them!"

Clare regarded her consideringly, her head to one side. "They will not compliment the gown, that is true. Would you miss them if they were gone?"

Isobel stared at her. "Gone? You mean—?"

Clare allowed her gaze to rest significantly on a pair of scissors on the dressing table. She smiled. "Under all that tortured hair, I believe you have a little natural curl. Am I right?"

"Yes, but—"

There was a short silence. "Can you—?" asked Isobel.

"Certainly," returned Clare firmly, not in the least certain. She glanced at the maid. Isobel followed her gaze.

"You may go now, Susan."

Once alone, Clare moved behind Isobel, so both their faces reflected in the glass. She picked up the scissors. "Ready?"

Isobel took a deep breath. "Ready!"

There followed ten minutes of deep silence and heavy concentration on Clare's part. As the ringlets fell to the carpet, the weightless hair curled about her fingers. She snipped carefully, giving Isobel a cap of close curls with a tiny froth of fringe over her eyebrows.

They both stared into the glass with astonishment. What had emerged was a slimmer-faced girl, whose blue eyes looked enormous in their frame of baby-fine curls. Clare gave her hair a final brush to add gloss, and the job was done.

"That's—that's wonderful!" breathed Isobel. "I never would have believed I could look so—"

"So captivating?" teased Clare, who was thanking heaven for her steady hand.

A tap on the door startled them. "Madame is asking if you are ready, miss," came a voice.

"I'll be down directly."

Clare helped Isobel into the full-skirted blue silk dress, smoothed down the tight waistline, and fluffed out the ruffles. The oyster satin ribbon was threaded through the curls and the pearls fastened into place. Isobel stared at herself in the long looking glass of the wardrobe.

"I don't look like myself at all!" she whispered.

"You look magnificent, and if you're not besieged by every eligible young man here tonight, why—I'll eat all those ringlets I cut off!"

Isobel giggled and picked up her fan as they left the bedroom. At the half landing she paused uncertainly. Below in the hall could be glimpsed Mrs. Foster, taking up position as the doorbell rang.

"Will—will you walk with me as far as Mama?" Isobel asked hesitatingly.

Clare shook her head. "Apart from enraging your Mama, it would not be the thing. Hold up your chin and make a splendid, sweeping descent. With guests to greet, your Mama will not have time to study you in detail."

"Thank you for everything, Miss Court." She took a deep breath, straightened her shoulders, and sailed down the stairs like a stately galleon, the wind of her passing billowing out the full skirt in a whisper of silk, like sea over shingle.

After the party moved down the hall, Clare picked up her cloak from the chest and let herself quietly out the front door. She collected Lord Rayne's horse from the stable and rode home slowly, letting the soft, warm air drain the tension from her. She had completed her first commission, and taken upon herself more than dressmaking. She laughed softly. How would Mrs. Foster react to her daughter's new hairstyle? Was it the end or the beginning of her career as dressmaker extraordinary? Well, she would know soon enough if the cream of Clevedon's merchant society was present at Isobel's coming-out ball.

The next morning she gave the cottage a thorough spring cleaning, partly to fill the hours, but more so to keep all thoughts of the Foster ball at bay. She washed the chintz curtains, gave the old furniture a vigorous polishing, and rearranged the room. She dragged the long, cushioned sofa to one side of the fireplace and placed her chair and sewing table on the other side. In between the two lay the round, pegged rug someone had made from multicolored scraps of cloth. Opposite the fireplace was a sideboard with cupboards and drawers, in which she kept her sewing, and on this she had placed a small bowl of snowdrops from the garden. Apart from the cheval glass, there was no other furniture in the room, but she liked it that way. Its very smallness gave her the sense of security she lacked in the rambling old Harcourt house. No one could come upon her unaware in this cottage.

An alcove curtained off in the bedroom held her few clothes, and there was just a chest of drawers in addition to the bed. Beside the bed was another rag rug.

By midday she could find nothing more to occupy her time. She wandered into the kitchen and set the iron kettle on the wide, black-leaded cooking range while making herself a meal. Mrs. Clark had sent up one of the girls each day with fresh milk and provisions, and Clare was intensely grateful, as she had none of her guineas left. They had discussed how much Clare should charge Mrs. Foster for Isobel's dress and, to Clare's horror, Mrs. Clark had promptly doubled the figure she had chosen, declaring that the Fosters could well afford it, and ladies of her stamp thought more highly of things that cost dear.

There was a kind of logic in it, thought Clare, for if things were cheaply obtained they were considered of little value, and how could one build a reputation as a superior dressmaker if one charged a paltry sum? But the figure Mrs. Clark suggested was so high that Mrs. Foster must surely shy off, she was convinced.

As teatime approached, Clare changed into her blue twill gown and pinned up her hair. She was making out the bill she would present to Mrs. Foster when she heard carriage wheels. Through the window she caught sight of the Foster ladies descending from the carriage.

Isobel was wearing an attractive straw-and-lace bonnet, and as she turned to the cottage, Clare glimpsed a smile on her face. With a return of some confidence she opened the door and ushered the ladies inside before seating herself demurely on her sewing chair.

"May I offer you tea, Mrs. Foster?" she asked calmly.

"No, thank you, Miss Court. We already have a tea engagement and must not be late on our first visit." Mrs. Foster's smug tone indicated that the invitation pleased her excessively and was possibly, Clare surmised, a small step up the social ladder. "We called to tell you of the great success of Isobel's ball. She looked quite ravishing, and your Gainsborough gown was commented on by everyone! So many of those boring Empire styles were worn, it was quite laughable, but dear Isobel was the star of the evening. One could hardly see her for beaux!"

"It was so exciting, Miss Court," interposed Isobel, her blue eyes brilliant. "I never thought to have so many young gentlemen begging to be allowed to call. And I was complimented, too, on my hairstyle!" She glanced at her mother, whose lips had pursed slightly.

Clare turned her gaze fully on Mrs. Foster. "I trust you did not disapprove of my action, ma'am," she said with a hint of ice in her voice. "I could not allow my creation to be ruined by that ridiculous hairstyle. Such ringlets are only worn by ladies of indeterminate age or theatrical inclination. Miss Foster is vastly more attractive in a softer style. Don't you agree?"

As she spoke, she handed over the bill, without removing her gaze from Mrs. Foster. It seemed to come as something of a relief for Mrs. Foster to break that intense gaze and lower her eyes to the neatly written paper. "Oh, indeed. So pretty and—and unusual." She fumbled in her reticule.

"I would be very surprised," continued Clare glibly, "if

Miss Foster did not soon find herself a leader of fashion for the young set of Clevedon.'' She could almost see Mrs. Foster mentally examining that new thought as she counted out a pile of golden guineas without a word of complaint.

Clare, with calm deliberation, kept her gaze firmly averted from the coins, but her spirits rose sharply.

"Then we shall continue to—'' Mrs. Foster almost said *patronize*, but changed her mind as she met Clare's eyes. "To do business together,'' she finished in a rush.

Clare gave a regal inclination of the head and rose, forcing the ladies to rise with her. Mrs. Foster found herself on the doorstep, feeling somehow dismissed. It was an unusual experience for one who was used to treating those people she employed in a rather overbearing manner. The small, upright figure watching them drive off seemed far too haughty to deserve her custom, but she had the common sense to realize that to be dressed by Miss Court might well become all the rage in Clevedon, and dear Isobel had been the first to discover her.

Her supposition was prophetic. Enchanted by Isobel's appearance in the "Gainsborough dress,'' as it came to be known, the ladies of Clevedon flocked to Clare's cottage. She retained an air of hauteur, refused to be rushed, and put forward her own suggestions in so confident a manner that her reputation as a very superior dressmaker grew.

April and May passed swiftly and daffodils took the place of snowdrops and crocus in her vases, but in spite of her industry, Clare still found time to visit the farmhouse and join the family in the kitchen for tea. Mrs. Clark was proud of her.

"You'll soon be moving into town and taking on staff, I can see,'' she teased one day.

"Never! Unless you give me notice, of course. I prefer to be alone, truly. I love the cottage and the view over the water. It's so peaceful and comforting, I don't want anything to spoil it. I need only you, the girls, and Sara for company. And Sep, of course. You've all been so very kind. I've never been so content.''

However fiercely Clare wished it, her words were not quite

true. During the day she was too busy to think of anything other than her work, but sometimes in the night, she woke with a strange longing in her. Staring up at the beamed ceiling in her bedroom, her eyes saw rafters and her body grew hot with remembered passion she had sought so eagerly. She buried her face in the pillow on these occasions, willing the wild blood of the Harcourts to leave her in peace, but there was no escape from the pounding senses.

Unable to sleep, she would wander naked into the main room and stand before the cheval glass, trying to see herself as the stranger had done. Her hair, tousled from sleep, framed her face like a cloud, and her slender body seemed ethereal in the moonlight. The cool air caused her breasts to tighten and she ran her hands sensuously down her body, trying to recapture the feel of his hands.

She wondered who he was and where he was. The beard and the seaman's cap were all she remembered, apart from the skill with which he had transported her into an unknown world. She shrugged. Did it matter who he was? To him she had been just another girl, eager to learn a whore's trade. He was probably many barns and many girls away and had no thought of the tormenting devils he had aroused in her.

♦ *Chapter Eight* ♦

It was inevitable in a small town like Clevedon, with a population of only hundreds, that the new dressmaker should figure in drawing room conversations. Not even the most traveled of them had heard of Miss Court before, and yet she sewed with such skill and designed with such originality— no two gowns were ever identical—that speculation on her origins was keen. She was Quality without a doubt, said those who had visited Bath and London, but any attempt to draw her out on her past life was met by a smooth change of subject or, if the questions became too personal, by a distinctly dangerous air of hauteur. Those soft grey eyes could hold a steely glint that made one uncomfortably aware of having committed a social gaffe.

Fond mamas found it galling to have their own suggestions dismissed by their offspring in favor of Miss Court's, but they grudgingly agreed that anyone who could make Isobel Foster a sensation at her coming out was not to be ignored.

What they didn't know was that Clare, with money in her pocket, could now afford to have the latest fashion papers sent to her from London. From every illustration she sketched her own designs, subtracting the outrageous and adding her own ideas, until she had a portfolio of original sketches, keeping in mind her young customers' shapes and sizes. She was able to increase her own wardrobe, too, adding a number of lightweight gowns, but still adhering to her austere mode of dress.

June came in with the promise of a long hot spell. The air was soft and scented, the sky a brilliant sapphire. The climbing roses peeping through her window, as if inviting her to join them, caused Clare to lay aside the gown she was sewing. She had never yet seen the small harbor where Sep spent most of his free time.

"'Tis a rare sight," he had said. "To see those schooners and brigs beating up the channel with all sails rigged. Most be merchantmen heading for Bristol, but now and then they need to be unloading something at Clevedon and they take in sail as neat as you like and come into harbor as gentle as a lamb nuzzling the ewe."

The object of her thoughts came into view from the direction of the farm. She rose to greet him at the front door and relieve him of the parcel he carried.

"Missus has been baking. Thought you'd like a nice fresh loaf and a batch of scones, miss."

"Thank you, Sep. Are you off to the harbor? It's a lovely day."

"It is that, miss. I hear the *Dolphin* was sighted off Lundy a while ago, and this tide'll bring her in pretty sharpish today. I want to be there.''

"The *Dolphin*?"

"One of the Patterson line, miss. Bristol shippers."

"May I come with you, Sep? It's so beautiful out there, it seems a shame to stay indoors all afternoon."

Sep's face developed a wide grin. "O' course, miss. 'Tis a long time since I took a dainty little maid along of me. You'll be right welcome."

Clare settled a prim straw bonnet over her netted hair and picked up her shawl. Miss Court would not be at home to callers this afternoon, she decided, closing her door firmly behind her.

They followed the footpath skirting the fields and reached the lane sloping down to Clevedon's small harbor. They passed the cottages with their geranium-filled window boxes and the stone walls that were host to a variety of purple and white flowered trailing plants. Clare lifted her face to the sun. The last two months had kept her so busily occupied that her complexion, she feared, had become a little pallid. She would have liked to remove her bonnet and loosen her hair and let the sea breeze riot through her curls, but if she were met by any of her customers, the carefully built image of the grave and so-proper Miss Court would take a sad jolt. As they reached the cobbled walk that ran along the jetty, Sep's eyes surveyed the incoming vessels. He nodded with satisfaction and pulled out a short-stemmed pipe, which he proceeded to fill with tobacco. He leaned his elbows on the harbor wall, first ascertaining that Clare was upwind of the blue cloud that enveloped his head.

"'Tis the *Dolphin*, like I said, miss. We'll have a good view of her from here."

Clare gazed from the harbor wall with only mild interest as the small merchant ship edged slowly up to the dock. All sails were furled, masts stark against the sky, and at precisely the right moment the ropes were tossed and made fast and she settled herself snugly between two other vessels like a sleepy kitten between its sire and dam.

Beside Clare, leaning forward intently, Sep gave a grunt

of appreciation. "Neat," he said. "Very neat," and rubbed his chin with a callused hand. The sound was that of an ax head drawn across a wire fence, and Clare flinched.

"A good captain, you'd say?" she asked quickly.

The old man rolled an eye in her direction and his lips held a cynical twist. "Nay, miss, not on this ship. That young fellow'd go broadside out of a twelve-yard channel if the handling was left to him. And in flat calm, too." He chuckled at his own words.

"Then, who brought her in?" queried Clare.

"The same as always—the first mate, Mister Mark."

Clare turned her gaze to the ship. They were unloading her already. Harbor porters swarmed over the decks, heaving crates and barrels to the gangway, assisted by the ship's men.

"Cornish clay and lime, I'd reckon," Sep commented.

"Clay?"

"'Tis best for the making of pottery, they say, so the Staffordshire merchants'll be bidding for it come sundown. They'll barge it to the Midlands, for it's cheaper that way than by packhorse, and a sight quicker."

"Did you ship in a merchantman yourself?" Clare asked with a smile. "You seem familiar with the cargoes they transport."

He showed her tobacco-stained teeth. "I was a seaman, aye, miss, but in the king's navy. Pressed, I was, and me no more'n fourteen at the time."

"Oh, how dreadful!"

"Mortal hard, miss, but I was on the parish anyway, and it taught me a trade. When I'd done my time, I shipped with Mister Mark many a day until I got too old. But the likes of him don't go forgetting old shipmates. He sees me right and tight."

"Which one is he? The one just coming this way off the gangplank?"

The old man peered down at the elegant figure passing below—a slender man of average height, dressed in fine broadcloth with a touch of lace at collar and wrist. He swung a tricorne hat, generously endowed with gold braid, carelessly between white fingers.

The old man spat with deadly accuracy and a jet of tobacco
juice hit the cobbles a foot behind the heels of the well-dressed
young man. Clare gaped, but Sep chuckled with delight.

"That be the captain, m'dear. The first to leave the ship
and the last to come aboard. I hear tell he loathes the sea and
loses his stomach regularly in stormy waters."

"Then, why on earth does he captain a ship?"

Her companion tapped the side of his nose. "He's the
owner's nephew, miss, and has to earn his keep. Old Patterson's such a skinflint he'll have no hangers-on who won't
pull their weight. No other course for him if he wants to keep
the old man sweet."

A commotion on deck claimed their attention. Howls of
strangled anguish were issuing from the mouth of a seaman
being held aloft by the neck of his thick jersey and shaken
like a rat. The tall, powerfully built man administering the
punishment was at the same time laying about the unfortunate
seaman with a rope's end.

Clare's eyes widened but a glance at her escort showed
that he did not share her revulsion. He was grinning, and
another look at the scene showed her that the rest of the crew,
and even the dock porters, had stopped work to watch this
engaging spectacle with appreciation.

Just as suddenly as it had started, it was over. The strong
grip on the jersey was removed and the man fell, moaning,
in a heap on the deck. He was jerked roughly to his feet, and
as words were exchanged, he fumbled under his jersey and
produced a package that had been held in place by his broad
leather belt. His tormentor took it, shaking his head like an
exasperated father, then cuffed the man about the ears and
pointed to a barrel.

The seaman shrugged and grinned, making for the barrel,
seemingly uninjured by his rough handling. Clare's companion chuckled and shook his head in grudging admiration.

"That Joe Binns! Every time they dock he tries to make
off with something, but every time he gets caught by Mister
Mark. You'd think he'd learn—you really would—but it's
as if he can't help it."

"So that's your Mister Mark, is it?" Clare remarked with

a touch of scorn in her voice. "A man of violence who cows his crew by physical strength. Why could he not just question the man without resorting to force?"

"It's what they understand best, miss. A soft man with fancy ways earns no respect from as rough a bunch of seamen as you're likely to meet. The old man don't pay the best rates, which is why he gets the scum, as Mister Mark's always telling him. Without Mister Mark on board, the young fellow that's captain wouldn't last long. Over the side he'd go and the ship's crew would turn privateer."

Clare looked at him uncertainly, but he wasn't looking at her. His face had split into a huge grin and his gnarled fist was raised in salute. Clare glanced down. The big man was on the cobbles below. A package was in his hand. He tossed it upwards and the old seaman caught it.

"Thanks, Mister Mark. I knew you wouldn't forget my 'baccy."

The first mate grinned, showing strong white teeth in his brown face. "I didn't forget but I had to shake it out of Joe there, the light-fingered ruffian."

"Well, I never! So that's what he was hiding!"

The big man's gaze moved from Sep to Clare. She suddenly became conscious of her own intent stare and the boldness of his and drew herself up, moving back from the wall, a pink flush staining her cheeks. But somehow she couldn't quite break away from the startlingly blue look directed keenly at her. The peaked cap shadowed his face but she noted the strongly boned lines, the firm, clean-shaven chin, and the humorous set of his lips.

He was just a rough, heavy-handed seaman, her mind said, and she should turn on her heel and walk away—dismiss him as beneath her notice. And yet her body refused her brain's command and she had the sense of being drawn down deep into the unimagined depths of a whirlpool that surged and frothed beneath a bland blue surface.

She gasped like a drowning woman and struggled to reality, resisting the magnetic quality of those eyes, which were far bluer than any sea she had ever looked upon.

A lick of heat seared her body as her mind steadied. It was

resentment primarily, but resentment tinged with anger that
a common seaman should have such a strange effect on the
well-ordered emotions of Miss Clare Court. She was quite
old and experienced enough not to be subject to whimsies of
the mind occasioned by a bold look. Her chin rose and she
was able to look calmly into the eyes that now held a hint of
amusement.

"You've a pretty lass there, Sep. Why is it you landlubbers
keep all the tasty dishes to yourselves while we sea dogs
make do with the scraps you've tired of?"

The old man almost choked with hoarse laughter. "Nay,
Mister Mark, you're allus first at table, I'll be bound."

"Then present me to your companion, you old rascal,
before I come up there and shake it out of you."

"Maybe she's not wanting to make your acquaintance,
Mister Mark," Sep said in a more sober tone. "Miss, here,
is a proper young lady."

"Then I'd best perform my own introductions to the lady.
Mark Conrad, ma'am, lately captain but now first mate on
the *Dolphin*, a three-master of the Patterson Line out of Bristol." He bowed and looked up inquiringly.

There was a pause as Clare fought a duel with herself.
Two pairs of eyes regarded her, waiting. She concentrated
on the old man. With his leathery skin, fringe of grey hair
around his bald skull, his long, rough cloth coat, waist secured
by a length of rope, he looked like some medieval friar. His
eyes were blue, sunk into wrinkled folds, but they had a kind
and simple look. He was obviously devoted to the first mate
and his expression was a little anxious—hopeful, she imagined, that his friend's insistence would be accepted as politely
meant.

Still, she hesitated. A simple introduction? A warning
tremor in her body contradicted that theory. Her instincts told
her that here was a man she should beware of—a ruthless
man who took what he wanted and be damned to the con-
sequences. How could she know this in so short a time, she
wondered in amazement? And yet she did. For hadn't he the
look of a man who takes life at a gallop? It was a steady
look, it was true, but behind that blue gaze there was some-

thing only a woman could recognize. The hard jaw and slightly hooded eyes reminded her of those long-gone adventurers and buccaneers who had stared down cynically from the walls of Harcourt House. They had taken what they wanted from life, shaking it by the scruff of its neck and leaving it, for the most part, by violence or glorious exit.

The man now awaiting her reply had that same reckless look, yet its strength was controlled and he was no idler. He worked on the ships and was kind to an old man. She acknowledged the difference but was not prepared to accept any man at face value. But what harm was there in a simple introduction? It was nothing more than a courtesy, after all.

Staring coolly down at him, she said, "I am Miss Court, and that is the extent of the information I choose to impart."

"I am honored, ma'am," said Mr. Conrad with a slightly mocking bow. "I thought for quite five minutes that I would not be allowed the pleasure of knowing your name. The rest I can find out for myself."

"Please don't go to the trouble," said Clare coldly. "It would be of no earthly use to you. I doubt we have anything in common."

"We shan't know that until we are better acquainted, shall we?" The question seemed mild enough, but Clare had a moment of panic, and her mother's nature made itself felt.

"I have no wish to further our acquaintance, sir, and trust you will have the goodness to respect that wish."

Beside her, the old man chuckled. "Regular little fire ship, ain't she, Mister Mark. Called you a man of violence. What do you say to that?"

Mark Conrad's smile was thin. "Only when the occasion merits it am I a man of violence, Miss Court. And certainly not toward the gentle sex." He shrugged as if he had lost interest in the conversation. "I have never found it necessary, I assure you. Good day, ma'am."

He gave a brief bow and strolled away down the quayside, leaving Clare with strangely mixed feelings. Far from putting the man in his place, and leaving him in no doubt of her distaste, she felt that he had come off best in the encounter. She and not he had been subjected to rejection. For no more reason than that, she found herself simmering with anger and determined that if ever she could do him harm, she would gladly.

"A proud one is Mister Mark," murmured the old man beside her.

"And overconfident of his own worth," snapped Clare. "Why he should imagine I wish to know him at all is beyond me. I regret even telling him my name."

"Mister Mark has a way with him, miss, and he's hard to resist when he sets his mind to it. But don't you be worrying he'll take advantage of knowing your name, for he's not one to be lost for female company. The lassies around here get in a rare state when the *Dolphin*'s sighted."

Clare knew that she should exhibit complete indifference to the dubious activities of a man newly arrived in port, but curiosity got the better of her.

"Why did he allude to himself as first mate but lately captain of the *Dolphin*? Did he lose that position through ill treatment of his crew?"

"Bless you, miss, no. 'Twas as I told you, old Patterson sent his nephew aboard and nothing would do but the young fellow must insist on being called captain. It makes no scrap of difference to the crew, for they still take their orders from Mister Mark."

Clare smiled without humor. "Maybe the crew didn't care, but I suspect it was a blow to your Mister Mark's pride. To be called first mate instead of captain has not the same ring about it. Rather less impressive, wouldn't you say?"

"'Tis no matter what a man's called, miss, as long as he does the job right." There was a hint of reproach in the old man's voice, as if he resented any criticism of his idol, and Clare was suddenly ashamed of her waspishness.

"I'm sorry, Sep. That was unkind of me. Our opinions on your friend differ, but you are in a better position to judge him, for I doubt if our paths will ever cross again. I rarely walk this way."

With a smile she turned away and followed the path up the incline, away from the Bristol Channel, whose tide had brought the *Dolphin* into the small harbor of Clevedon.

At the top of the incline, she paused. Across the field, high on the cliff, she could see her cottage and, to one side, the farm. A glance in both directions assured her that she was alone and she tweaked her bonnet ribbons, removing the plain straw that shaded her face. The sea breeze lifted the black tendrils of hair from her forehead and cooled her flushed cheeks. She left the hair net in place although at this point, within sight of the field she must cross, it was unlikely that her Clevedon ladies would materialize. Glancing back at the harbor, she saw Sep still leaning on the stone wall. Poor Sep. Had she been a little too hard on his friend? That look had held not only boldness but a strange intensity for a moment. Her withdrawal had been instinctive, a retreat into the cold practicality of her new identity. Nothing must threaten the life she had built.

Standing motionless at the top of the incline, she wondered why she associated him with a threat. He was a sailor, not an officer of the law. Only her father and Lord Rayne had reason to seek her out. Had she imagined the intentness of his gaze, knowing her own fear of discovery? But in light of Sep's remarks about the man's popularity with the local girls, it was probably, she thought with a wry smile, nothing more than the routine scrutiny of a new face. After her frosty response he had lost interest rapidly.

The sound of hooves brought her head around sharply and she clutched her bonnet and shawl to her breast in an agony of indecision. But then she relaxed. It was not a carriage but a solitary horseman. She stood still, waiting for him to pass before crossing the lane to the field. He came slowly and the sunlight was on him. The fair hair under the tricorne glinted and the pale blue eyes stared moodily down to the harbor. She recognized him as the captain of the *Dolphin*.

Suddenly aware of a figure in the roadway, the eyes moved to rest on her. The sun was behind her, outlining the slender figure and shining through the straying curls. She raised a hand to brush back a tendril of dark hair and the movement revealed the rise of her breasts beneath the plain cotton gown she wore. Captain William Oliver's gaze rose to her face and he found himself being regarded, somewhat clinically, by a pair of wide, dove-grey eyes.

He reined in his horse and stared down at her. She did not smile or bob a curtsy, as he was used to receiving from the cottagers hereabouts. She merely looked at him with sublime disinterest.

"Good afternoon," he said, putting a hint of hauteur in his voice.

"Good afternoon," the girl replied in a voice equally cool.

"What are you doing?" Captain Oliver asked, intrigued but slightly annoyed at her lack of respect.

"At this precise moment, I am waiting for you to pass by so that I may cross the lane," she said in a tone of infinite boredom.

"You are not, as I thought, from one of the harbor cottages?"

"No."

"Do you live in Clevedon?"

"No."

He stared down, feeling an unaccustomed sense of bafflement. Most girls he engaged in conversation would by this time be fluttering their eyelashes and giving him provocative glances, whether of his own circle or not. He gave her his most charming smile.

"You are not very forthcoming, are you?"

"No," she repeated, not returning or seeming to be affected by his smile.

"Then I shall remove myself instantly from your vicinity." This remark, uttered gaily at balls, usually brought a pout from his female companions, but this girl merely inclined her head and replied gravely, "Thank you. I am obliged."

"Devil take you," he muttered and caught a flash of amusement in her eyes.

"Very likely," she said calmly. "Good day to you."

She turned away and crossed the lane as he clattered off. From the shelter of the hedge beside the footpath, Clare gazed after him, a smile trembling on her lips. How foolish men were and how easily affronted when women did not respond in the way expected of them. She supposed he was much in demand in Clevedon society, just as that first mate was in local circles. He rode well, she noticed, and was no doubt rich if he was the shipowner's nephew. Why was it that every new female face presented a challenge? Was there a man anywhere, outside of a monastery, who didn't look upon a girl as a target for his gallantry?

She remembered the vow she had made to herself. No man shall ever take what I do not freely give. She was not stupid enough to suppose the two men she had met today had the slightest desire to know her better, but coldness was the strongest shield she possessed. There must never be gossip featuring Miss Court, or her career was ruined.

As she crossed the field she was reminded of the gown she had laid aside to take this walk. It was a simple morning dress she had promised to complete for Miss Foster, who was leaving for Bath the next day. Since her success at the ball, Isobel had worn her height proudly, and although she would never be fragile-looking, Clare had adapted the Empire line of dress for her by a slight lowering of the too-high waistline and a clever arrangement of filmy ruffles and flowery bows to minimize the top-heavy look.

By the time she reached her cottage, the sky had taken on a slightly leaden look and the breeze had turned into a chill wind. From her window she looked down over the wide channel. The waves seemed higher. The ships rose and fell as they headed up the estuary. She completed the dress, wrapped it carefully, and put it on the sideboard to await collection by the Foster coachman in the morning.

It was growing darker and the sky held a strange, greenish pallor. An ominous quiet seemed to hold nature in its grip. The roses at her window had stopped bobbing—they seemed to be holding themselves in breathless waiting—and she could hear no sound of cattle or sheep, as she had been used to. Did this peculiar quiet herald some vicious storm? She shivered and crossed to light the oil lamp. The grate held logs, prepared by Sep. Although it was only June, she felt the need to be warm and protected, so she set a light to them.

While the flames took hold, she changed into her old blue dress and loosened her hair, then secured all the windows

before curling up on the cushioned sofa with a cup of tea to
hand. This old cottage had weathered many a storm, she
surmised, and had triumphed over whatever the elements
flung furiously in its direction.

◆ *Chapter Nine* ◆

The elements were bothering Captain William Oliver a little,
too. Before he had reached the town of Clevedon he had
narrowly escaped losing his elegant tricorne twice. He had
it tucked under his arm as he finally turned into the courtyard
of the large town house of his employer. Why must Uncle
Thomas insist on immediate delivery of the bills of lading,
whatever the weather? What had promised to be a fair, balmy
evening had turned into a threat of bad weather. Thank heaven
they'd made port. He loathed the sea, even when mild, but
a storm was hell without a harbor in sight. And to mix with
the scum on the *Dolphin* was added torture. Even that damned
first mate, Conrad, was a superior swine, treating him with
exaggerated courtesy but overseeing all he did with the air
of one instructing an idiot child. But the old man wouldn't
listen to a word against him. Not because he had any great
affection for Conrad himself, but on account of cousin Eve,
the old man's daughter, who was engaged to him. What she
saw in the man, heaven knew, but he grudgingly admitted
they made a striking couple, he so dark and Eve so fair.

A further annoyance to Captain Oliver was the fact that
the Conrads were an older family in the history of the county
and could not be dismissed as upstarts. The man's ancestors
had served the Crown but had profited little by it, while the
Pattersons had seen the advantage of trade and made a fortune.
Discounting personal dislike of the man, it gave him a certain

satisfaction to know that Conrad, with his gentry forebears, was in the employ of Patterson the merchant.

He dismounted and flung the reins without a word to the waiting groom, then looked up at the ugly old house. Every window was ablaze with light. Uncle Thomas had hinted to him of a partnership, first insisting that William learn the business from the practical side before moving into the boardroom. Only that hint had persuaded him to accept the offer, but he had insisted on his position being ranked as captain. And for a Patterson, only the flagship of the fleet of merchantmen was suitable. As the flagship happened to be the *Dolphin*, and its captain Mark Conrad, it gave William intense pleasure to outrank Conrad, and address him pointedly as *Mister*.

Strangely enough, it hadn't seemed to dent the man's pride or have any marked effect on the crew. Whatever orders he issued, he had a sneaking suspicion that they were verified with Conrad by the crew members behind his back. But as the ship ran smoothly, he was able to overlook it and bask in Uncle Thomas's approval of his efforts. Surely it wouldn't be much longer before his exertions were rewarded? In that event, he would happily consign Conrad and the motley crew of the *Dolphin* to the devil.

He was reminded suddenly of the girl on the bridle path. She had not been outraged at his carelessly tossed blasphemy. Instead, she had shot him a look of amusement. It had lit her face like a candle behind glass. She was a plain, dowdy creature, he had thought, hair in a net save a few escaping wisps, too simply dressed for his taste, and not much of a handful for any man. And yet, when she had spoken in her soft voice and reacted to his remark with a flashing glance, she had become beautiful. Her previous lack of expression had made him think her a thick-headed, stupid village child. Obviously, he was wrong. She was young, yes, but that swift glimpse of rounded breasts declared her unmistakably a woman.

He shrugged away the memory and squared his shoulders, ready to face his uncle, and possibly the waspish tongue of his cousin, Eve. At least he would enjoy a good dinner after

a month at sea, and be allowed to revert to the role of the
gentleman he was.

Uncle Thomas was in his study and William was announced
in a gratifyingly unctuous tone by the butler.

"Captain Oliver to see you, sir," he breathed importantly.

The impression was spoiled a little by the raising of Mr.
Patterson's heavy brows and a complete lack of expression.

"Ah, there you are, boy. Expected you an hour ago.
Stopped by the way, did you?"

Captain Oliver bridled indignantly but held his temper.
"No, sir. I came straight here as soon as we docked. I considered it my first duty."

"First duty? I assume you secured your vessel and set the
unloading in motion first?"

"Well, naturally, sir," stated William, who had, in point
of fact, left that menial task to his second in command. "I
am aware of a captain's responsibility."

Uncle Thomas's slate-grey eyes examined him keenly. "I
would hope so. That is why you are aboard the *Dolphin*. Sit
down and let me see the bills."

There followed a trying half hour for William as he attempted to keep up with Thomas Patterson's swift assessment
of the profits to be accrued from this cargo. The questions
shot at him with the rapidity of cannon fire concerning quality,
quantity, commission to agents, reliability of supplies, and
current market values made his head spin. He almost complained that he wasn't some damned clerk in a countinghouse
but held back the words, for that was exactly how Uncle
Thomas's father had started the business. The Pattersons of
that day had owned but one ship, and they sailed it, shipped
goods from one place to another, marketed them, and performed the whole operation themselves. As proof of this
tireless industry, the Patterson Line now extended to six ships,
most of little more than two hundred tons but capable of
carrying great quantities of cargo. Each flew the house colors
at the masthead and together they had made Thomas Patterson
a rich man.

At last the inquisition was over and William rose, straight-
ening his damp neck cloth. Not even a brandy had been

offered him, he thought resentfully, eyeing the decanter at his uncle's elbow. It was almost a relief to see Eve entering the study, though he was not exceptionally fond of his cousin.

She gave him a brief smile. "Glad to be on dry land again, William?" she murmured sweetly, knowing his dislike of the sea. "Do tell me what the cargo was, so that I may arrange the seating at dinner in order to be upwind of you."

He glowered at her but Uncle Thomas laughed. "Now, Eve," he said fondly. "It's not a fishing fleet we run, so stop teasing poor William."

As they followed Mr. Patterson into the dining room, William muttered under his breath, "I wonder if you'd be so particular if it was Conrad beside you. Would being down-wind of him distress your sensibilities?"

She glanced at him coldly. "Mr. Conrad would never present himself reeking of any kind of cargo. He is most particular—a true gentleman."

William laughed softly. "I doubt you've seen the real side of him. He flogged a crew member today with exceptional viciousness. Can you handle him in a temper, dear cousin?"

"I have no reason to think not."

"A man of violent passions, I'd say," William continued, watching her from the corner of his eye, "especially if he doesn't get his own way." He shrugged. "With a man—or a woman. I doubt it would make a difference."

"But at least he's a man," she tossed over her shoulder scornfully.

"Oh, yes. You'll find he's that all right when you're married." He smiled at her, but his glance held meaning.

"If you're trying to tell me he frequents low places when you put into different ports," she hissed furiously, "I won't believe you! And even if I did," she went on, changing tack, "it is quite understandable, especially when a man is engaged to a lady of good reputation."

"You're quite right, Eve. It is best to pretend these things are of no importance, especially before marriage! After that, you'll find out for yourself." He gave her a gleaming smile and slid into his seat.

Eve tossed her head and concentrated on charming her

father. She had decided on a new wardrobe of clothes and intended to coax him into accepting the bills. As the richest and most attractive girl in Clevedon, she had expected to outshine every other at Isobel Foster's recent ball. It had come as a shock to see Isobel looking absolutely ravishing in a most unusual gown and sporting a very attractive new hairstyle. What was even more galling was that some of her own admirers had forsaken her to solicit dances from Isobel. Who would have thought that mousy, lumpy Isobel could be so transformed?

It hadn't taken Eve long to discover the author of this transformation. Clevedon society had talked of nothing else the following day but that adorable "Gainsborough" dress. She visualized herself in that style. With her blond curls and blue eyes, she thought a crimson silk might be striking. She was already "out," so she had no need to hold to white or pale colors. Crimson—or perhaps a deep violet—with a lower neckline to show off her magnificent breasts. Isobel Foster would be quite put in the shade when Eve Patterson appeared in her own stunning version of the gown.

"Are you expecting that young man of yours tonight, Eve?"

Her father's voice cut in on her train of thought.

"Yes, Father. He sent a message excusing himself from dinner, but he said he would come later when the cargo was in the warehouse."

"A thorough fellow," Patterson grunted. "A captain's duty is to make sure his freight is under lock and key."

"But William is the captain, Father," said Eve with a sly glance at her cousin. "Shouldn't he have done that?"

"Uncle Thomas asked for the papers right away," interposed William swiftly. "I considered that my primary duty."

"What if the cargo was stolen, Father?" asked Eve innocently. "Who would take the blame for that?"

"The first mate, naturally," William snapped. "I entrusted him to see everything stowed safely. If I had doubts in that direction, I would not have left."

"How lucky for you that Father finds him completely trustworthy," murmured Eve. "Isn't that so, Father?"

"Yes, my dear, but I still wonder if I did the right thing in giving William the flagship captaincy. It could well sour a good man to be demoted, as it were; although, of course, we are not the Royal Navy, where such a thing would be considered a stain on one's character. But Mark took it very well. Better than you did, my dear."

Eve pouted prettily. "I do think you might have considered my feelings before putting William on the *Dolphin*. Captain Conrad, my fiancé, has a ring superior to that of first mate. Indeed, it quite mortified me, almost as if I were engaged to a common seaman!"

"So you are, cousin," said William unpleasantly. "Whichever rank you prefer him to hold, he is still the same man."

"That will do, William!" Mr. Patterson spoke sternly. "When Eve and Mark are married, there will be changes to compensate them both."

William looked sharply at his uncle. Good God! Surely the old man was not contemplating offering the fellow shares in the company or, heaven forbid, a seat on the board? Why the devil had he not considered that possibility himself? A glance at Eve's smug face convinced him that if she had anything to do with it, and she was clever enough to twist the old man around her finger, a son-in-law of Uncle Thomas's could not possibly remain first mate on a merchantman. Eve would insist on a shore job and a position of importance—perhaps one even higher than his own might be. He, a true Patterson, might be passed over by Uncle Thomas in favor of a fellow only connected by marriage!

He was still deep in horrific contemplation when that fellow, himself, was announced.

"Captain—er, Mister Conrad," the butler announced, flinching as William's glare scorched him.

"Ah, come in, my boy," said Mr. Patterson genially. "You'll take coffee and a brandy? Pity you couldn't get here for dinner. Eve has been positively moping, haven't you, my dear? A month is a long time for young things to be parted."

Mark Conrad, impeccably attired in evening clothes, strolled forward and bowed over Eve's hand. His smooth,

tanned face under the thick black hair held a slight smile as
he nodded to the two men. His manner was assured, and he
wore his clothes with that innate grace denoting centuries of
gentlemen. However much William disliked him, he could
never quite quell the stab of envy as he took in the somehow
casual yet unconscious elegance of the man.

"Thank you, sir," said Mark Conrad, taking a seat beside
Eve. "A brandy would be welcome. The glass is falling
rapidly and I wouldn't be surprised if we were in for a gale.
But the *Dolphin*'s snug enough. I hope the rest of the fleet
makes safe anchorage. It'll be a rough night if they're off
this coast."

As if to corroborate this statement, a crack of thunder rolled
overhead.

Eve gave a squeak of dismay and clutched Mark's arm.
"How I hate storms! You will stay until it's all over, won't
you? I shall not be so frightened if you are beside me." She
gave him an appealing look and he smiled, thinking how fair
and pretty she was, rather like a butterfly in agitation.

"Of course I'll stay—unless I'm needed."

"Needed? What for?"

"Old Sep told me at the harbor that a fifty-tonner was due
in port this evening but hadn't arrived. A fishing boat reported
her with a broken spar this side of Lundy. If she's out there,
it'll be the devil of a job for her to make land if she's running
crippled before the storm. The coast guard is on the watch
and I expect the village is, too. Sounds like the *Venturer*."

"But, why should you go?"

"They'll need every hand they can get if she's in trouble.
We might get a boat out if she looks to be breaking up, but
the wind could just as well drive her onto the rocks."

"There'll be enough people there without you, dear
Mark."

"Very likely, but if I were in trouble at sea I'd like to
think someone was trying to effect a rescue. For all her
beauty, the sea can be hard and unyielding, just like a moody
woman," he finished, smiling.

Another roll of thunder shook the house and rain began to

hammer the windowpanes. A door slammed sharply and Mark frowned, draining his brandy. He rose.

"I think I'd best get back to the *Dolphin*, sir."

"But, Mark!" protested Eve. "You're not dressed for taking boats out."

"I can change on the *Dolphin*."

"Oh, Mark, I was so looking forward to our first evening together after your month at sea. It really is too bad of you to leave me now. I absolutely forbid you to go!" she said in a tone of annoyance, gazing up at him reproachfully.

Mark stood very still for a moment and the face looking down at her seemed carved from those sea-swept rocks, the eyes glinting like hard pebbles.

"I beg your pardon," he said softly.

She felt the cold prickle of danger and shrank from the edge of the abyss. Her eyes widened and she was able to force them to fill with tears. "I didn't mean that, Mark. I spoke without thinking in my fear for your safety. Must you go? I shall be in torment, imagining all kinds of things happening."

"Don't worry," he said shortly. "I've a fondness for my own skin, too. I shan't play the hero."

Eve stared over at William, seeking an outlet for her frustration. "Are you going too, William? It is your duty as ship's captain, you know."

"My duty is to the flagship," he returned defensively. "There is no point in risking the lives of the only two officers on the *Dolphin*."

"Then you should go instead—"

"Have done, Eve," said Mark coldly. "It's no concern of William's. I happen to know the crew of that vessel. I shall offer what help I can." He bowed and made for the door. "Excuse me, sir. Good night, Eve."

In the hall, the butler gave him a warm smile. "Godspeed, sir. I had your horse brought around. I knew you'd not sit idle while there's folks in trouble."

"How did you know?" asked Mark as he shrugged on his boat cloak.

"I heard you talk, sir, so I sent the boot boy up to the attic. There's a clear view down to the harbor from there. The boy reckons he saw a rocket go up, some miles out to sea."

"Did he, now?" said Mark, frowning. "The poor devils are in trouble, then. This gale's enough to bring down the mainmast on a small rigged ship, and without canvas on a night as dark as hell, they don't stand much chance. The steersman will need a beacon. I'll be off to see what's afoot."

He left the house, staggering against the force of the wind. His horse was stamping nervously, prevented from making for the stable again by a groom clinging grimly to the reins.

"Good luck, sir," he managed to gasp as Mark succeeded in mounting.

"Thanks. It's those poor souls out there who'll need it."

He swung away and urged the horse into a fast trot through the streets of Clevedon. His hat was stuffed into the pocket of his cloak and the wind tore and teased his well-brushed hair into a tangle of wild spikes, but his mind was not on sartorial things.

He clattered down to the harbor, scanned the darkness, then turned the horse toward a tavern. The sound of hooves brought out a reluctant ostler and Mark dismounted, thrusting the reins at him.

"Stable her, lad."

"Yes, Captain," replied the man, recognizing Mark.

"Mister Mark!" a voice called, and old Sep appeared out of the gloom.

"What's happening, Sep?"

"They're trying to get a fire going on the headland and we've set lamps around the harbor. The coast guard's on watch but there's not a blind thing to see. We saw a rocket go up, though she's most likely been swept from that spot long since."

"Come on to the *Dolphin*. I need to change, and we've got a telescope there."

Dressed in his sailing garb and with his peaked cap jammed firmly over his hair, Mark went to the bridge to survey the horizon through the telescope. Sep followed him.

"Any chance of launching a boat, Sep? Nobody knows this channel like you."

Sep scratched his bristly chin and pondered. "Against the wind and tide? She'd be thrown back on the beach, or else capsize. It'd be madness to try."

"We might try and get a line aboard if she hits rock."

"Aye. That's all we can do, but she'll break up fast in this weather."

It was over an hour before the ship was sighted, tossing on the high waves. It seemed to Mark that she had lost all masts, and her dragging canvas was impeding the efforts of the steersman. There was nothing they could do until the gale swept her inshore.

A second rocket went up, but the whole of the harbor village population was already alerted and the beach was dotted with tensely watching groups—women in shawls and wind-tossed cloaks, men in reefers and woolen caps. No one was speaking. It was like a rapt audience viewing the final act of an intensely absorbing stage drama. But would it end in tragedy?

Mark and Sep joined the group around a rowboat. It was manned by the younger men—sailors from other small ships who knew that their lives were at risk the moment they pulled off from shore, but whose faces would wear no sign of hesitation when the moment arrived.

The ship loomed abruptly out of the darkness. Although the rain and wind still pounded on the watchers, there seemed a lightening of the sky. The thunder was fainter and the storm less vicious.

The beacon on the cliffs bloomed and burst into a fierce, wind-racked blossom of fire, illuminating the headland and casting sparks high into the sky. The rocks showed green and yellow, but the little ship seemed to be heading inexorably for them.

"Steering gone," muttered Sep. "They'll just be seeing what they hit."

As if directed, the crowd began to move slowly toward the rocks. Mark and Sep moved with them.

♦ *Chapter Ten* ♦

The moon came fitfully through the racing clouds, illuminating the plight of the *Venturer* before swallowing it up again in darkness. There was nothing anyone could do but watch in helpless pity. The ship was tossed high by the breakers, only to fall headlong into each trough.

"If she goes broadside on, she'll capsize for sure," Sep muttered.

There was a splintering crack that merged into a roll of thunder.

"Mainmast over the port side," Mark exclaimed. "It'll slow her like a sea anchor. Come on, Sep. We'll chance a boat from under the lee of the cliff. Between the two, it may be calm enough to get a line out."

"There's Murphy's herring box. He anchors it in the cove yonder, but he'll not be keen to have it turned into tinder."

Mark was already running. "He'll not be allowed the choice, Sep," he tossed back over his shoulder.

Sep, puffing behind, caught the edge of recklessness in Mark's voice and sighed inwardly. If ever a fellow took chances with the sea, it was Mark Conrad. Never a one to ignore the thrown gauntlet, he took everything as a personal challenge, the sea most of all. But the idea was feasible, he admitted—the *Venturer* taking the brunt of the storm as protection for a smaller boat. It would be rough enough, but with the cliffs at their back, not impossible.

By the time Sep had scrambled over the shingle and low rock, Mark had reached the inlet where Tim Murphy tied up his fishing boat. Two pairs of oars were already being fitted into the rowlocks by four young fishermen, their eyes alight with the same reckless eagerness as that in Mark's eyes. A fifth man tumbled into the stern and grasped the tiller. Sep watched, aware that Mark would refuse his own help, and rightly so, for he was an old man. If it came to swimming for their lives, Sep admitted to himself that he would be the first to knock on Davy Jones's locker.

A dozen or more hands reached for the thick hempen rope Mark tossed out. The other end was knotted about his own waist, and he crouched in the prow of the boat.

"Cast off," he shouted, and willing hands let go of Tim Murphy's boat.

Sep glanced at the crowd and grinned. None of the Murphy brothers was there to raise any objection. Knowing Cap'n Mark, it wouldn't have made a blind bit of difference if they'd all been screaming their heads off.

Sep turned his gaze to the *Venturer* and his grin died. The poor old girl was laboring like a sick cow from side to side, not yet broadside on the waves, but perilously close. If that mainmast tore itself away and stopped the drag, she'd be up like a cork and the next heavy roller would toss her every which way.

It was usual to set axes to the mainmast to avert the tilt of the vessel. Maybe they'd tried and failed. Sep, himself, had seen many a seaman go overboard, trapped in rigging or sail when the mast broke free. He tried to make out Mark's boat, heading toward the *Venturer*. Like the moon, it was there one second and gone the next, appearing and disappearing, fighting the tide. For long moments it seemed to hold station, but Sep knew that four stalwart arms were pushing her along, inch by painful inch.

In spite of the cold night, he began to sweat. If the mainmast went before they reached her, she'd go up like a bird and come down like a cannonball, smack on Tim Murphy's boat! She was heeling to port as if lining up her target.

A voice beside him seemed to speak his thoughts aloud. "Lord have mercy. If Cap'n Mark don't get split apart when the masthead goes, she'll have them lads in a nutcracker between her and the rocks."

Sep didn't look around. His attention was riveted on the narrowing gap between the *Venturer* and the fishing boat.

"Heave, my hearties. Put your backs into it, do."

As if to help, the moon was thrusting its way between the clouds and the thunderstorm was less intense, but still the wind whipped the sea. The little boat, dwarfed by the high-sided *Venturer*, moved closer. Sep saw Mark, half crouching in the prow, raise an arm, sweeping it backwards to throw the weighted line. It struck the rail and fell back. Mark staggered, half plunging over the boat's side to retrieve the line.

The *Venturer* yawed wearily to port, cutting off all sight of the fishing boat. Sep swore in a muffled voice.

"You lazy, butterfingered landlubbers. A touch of the rope's end to your tails is a sight too good for a bone-idle lot of scrounging sea dogs. Can you see them, mate?"

If there was a reply, Sep didn't hear it in the screech of tortured wood. The *Venturer* drew herself up, relieved of the drag of mast, and drove forward. Just as violently she came to a shuddering, keel-grinding halt as underwater rocks caught and held her.

"She's aground on the reef," a man shouted. "And going down by the stern. Maybe she'll hold 'til low tide, God willing."

"Where's Murphy's boat?" growled Sep. "Can anybody see her?"

"There she is," a woman shouted, pointing, then fell quiet.

The crowd stared in silence as Tim Murphy's boat came in on the racing tide, keel uppermost.

"Lord save us, there's someone left," a voice screamed, and three heads bobbed, clinging grimly to the thwarts.

The crowd surged forward, dragging the three men from the sea. They lay gasping and retching, but one man managed to point seaward. Two more men, arms flailing, were thrown onto the beach like driftwood.

Sep scanned their faces. Six men had gone out, five had returned, and none of them was Mark Conrad. Had the sea at last picked up the gauntlet and won the contest?

"Where's Cap'n Mark?" he demanded.

Heads were shaken. One of the first arrivals managed to speak.

"He threw the line again, then the mainmast hit us and we capsized." Sep turned away as the man went on. "'Twas every man for himself then, Sep. You know the sea well enough yourself."

Sep turned back. "Aye, lad, I know. I wasn't holding you to blame. Do you think he got a line aboard?"

The man shrugged. "Don't know—" he began, when a cry went up from the group of men hauling on the rope.

"She's rising, men. Haul away."

There was a rush to help as the thick rope came free of the sea in a long, glittering line of cascading droplets.

"She's up, she's holding," they shouted as the line tautened. "Back, lads, back."

The handlers strained back, digging their boots into the shingle. The line rose, well clear of the sea, and every eye was on the swaying bulk of the *Venturer*, towering like a moated castle.

Sep's heart leapt. Captain Mark had got the line aboard her, that was certain, but had he hung on to it or been swept aside by the tangle of mast and rigging? He looked along the line to the rail of the *Venturer* and saw something detach itself—a breeches buoy. Of course! It was the only way. If the merchantman carried a dinghy, the sea would have smashed it to matchwood, even if it could have been launched.

The short canvas breeches buoy, into which a man could slide his lower body, was coming fast down the line. Sep blinked as he saw a pair of waving legs, a great bunching of skirts, and heard the thin wail that accompanied the swinging buoy. The master's wife! He would have her off first, without a doubt, if only to get rid of a wailing female.

Arms reached out and the woman was lifted out of the canvas breeches, soaked to the skin, her hair in disorder. She was pushed toward a group of women and the breeches buoy was hauled back to the *Venturer*. A dozen men, from cabin boy to first mate, took the journey. It was touch and go for her master, the last man to leave, as the *Venturer* broke her back on the rocks and began to founder.

Sep helped haul the master to his feet. "Where's Cap'n Conrad?" he asked hoarsely. "He's not still aboard, is he?"

The master looked blank. "Mark Conrad? Never saw him, mate."

"But he brought you the line, along with those lads here."

The master stared into Sep's ravaged face. "I'm sorry, Sep. We grabbed the line, yes, but I don't know who threw it. 'Twas bravely done and I give thanks to the fellows who risked out that boat and their lives to save us. If Mark Conrad's out there, God rest his soul."

They both turned seaward as the *Venturer*'s stern gave a last salute to the heavens and slid, sighing, into the sea. The line went limp and sank, too.

Among the women on the beach, Clare knelt with Mrs. Clark. They were soaked and windblown, but intent on the injured woman. Clare's head scarf had served to bind a possible break in the arm of the cabin boy. Fishermen's wives had sacrificed their own scarves and shawls to bind cuts and bruised bodies. All the crew members had sustained damage from falls as they had fought to keep the *Venturer* afloat.

The nearest cottages were being used to shelter the casualties, but the dwellings were small. Mrs. Clark offered the farmhouse to accommodate the overflow. She glanced up as her husband, wiping rope-scored hands, approached.

"This boy needs a doctor, Harry. We must carry him there, for sure. His arm may be broken."

"Aye, lass, we'll take the young'un. Looks scarce more than a twelve-year-old. Our girls'll fuss over him tomorrow, you see if they don't. Here's a couple more young fellows who could do with a cup of your strong tea, as well."

The crowd began to disperse, helping staggering men into cottages. Mr. Clark raised the half-conscious form of the boy into his arms. Mrs. Clark and the two seamen began to follow him up the path to the farmhouse. Clare glanced back to the wreck. Half of the *Venturer* still perched on the rocks. She noted a solitary figure staring out to sea. It was Sep, she was convinced. Making her way down to his side, she touched his arm.

"Come back to the farmhouse, Sep. You're wet through, and Mrs. Clark will be putting on the kettle."

He didn't answer and Clare looked at him worriedly. "Sep? What is it? All the men got ashore, and the master's wife, too."

"All except one, miss, and he was the one to risk his life for them all."

Clare felt a sudden chill. There was only one man who commanded such respect and affection from Sep.

"Your—your friend, the first mate on the *Dolphin*, Sep?"

He turned on her fiercely. "He'll always be captain of the *Dolphin* in my eyes, and he was the one to get the line aboard. Where is he now? Tell me that!"

"Oh, Sep, I'm so sorry. I didn't know. I thought everyone was rescued."

Sep's shoulders slumped. "Well, you weren't to know it, miss. Cap'n Mark's out there somewhere, dead or alive."

"Not dead, Sep, he can't be."

Clare remembered the tanned, arrogant face, the brilliant blue eyes probing into hers, the look that stirred something deeply hidden within her. That strong, vibrant life could not be snuffed out like some bedside candle, a lifeless corpse turning in a dance of death beneath the sea. Clare shivered at the thought. Why could he not? Other men died. Why should the thought of it bring her a sense of personal loss? The man was a stranger, a heavy-handed seaman who brought tobacco for Sep. He had cause to like the man. She had none; in fact, quite the reverse. Her instincts, at their introduction, had signaled danger to that side of her nature inherited from George Harcourt.

Clare touched Sep's arm again. "It's no good brooding here, Sep. You'll catch your death of cold. Let's walk back together."

"You go on, miss. I'll bide a while longer. The tide's bringing in wreckage. See, there's a mass of canvas and a bundle of flotsam."

"And who might you be calling a bundle of flotsam, you old sea dog?"

Sep gave a choking cry and plunged forward. "Cap'n, Cap'n! Where by the head of Neptune are you?"

"Trussed up in the old devil's beard, by the feel of it, and held tight as a chandler's purse string. You'd best have your gutting knife aboard, Septimus Thomas, for I'm damned if

I can fight my way out of this rigging much longer.'' The voice was suddenly weary.

Clare plunged after Sep, gasping as the cold sea swirled about her thighs. Between them, they pulled and tugged the mass of canvas beachward. At first she could not see the man enmeshed in the folds, but as Sep hacked the wet ropes he began to emerge, white-faced, eyes red-rimmed.

"I thought you were under hatches, Cap'n," Sep muttered as he sawed at the ropes. "Davy Jones can shut his locker this day. There'll be none to join him."

"None?" came the tired voice.

"None, Cap'n. They got your line aboard. All came off and your own crew got spewed back by the tide. Mind you, Tim Murphy's boat ain't what it was." He gave a throaty chuckle. "But he can argue that one out with the *Venturer*'s owner."

The man Sep and Clare pulled clear of the tangled rigging was barely able to stand. Seawater ran out of his hair and over his bruised face. They each put a shoulder under his armpit, and the limp hand Clare clutched to hold him steady was as cold as ice.

"Lean on us, Cap'n," Sep said. "We'll get you up the hill between us."

"We?" Mark Conrad squinted down at the small figure below his right shoulder. "Who's this, then? 'Tis small and soft enough to be female. You've brought Neptune's daughter, Septimus Thomas, to deny her old man the victory." The words came breathily, between gasps.

"Save your breath, Cap'n, do. You're as like to soused pork as I've ever seen, but a fire and a hot toddy'll do you the world of good. Where'll we take him, miss? That looks like the doctor's carriage at the farmhouse. He'll be tending the lad with the broken arm."

"Doctor?" muttered Conrad. "I'll see no sawbones, Sep. I've been keelhauled enough this night without getting prodded by an old quack."

Clare's eyes met Sep's below the lolling head. "I've a good fire going," she said, "though I've not the makings for hot toddy. I'll leave that to you, Sep."

"That's right good of you, miss." He glanced at the farm-house. "'Tis not but a step farther to your place, and the Clarks have a houseful already."

Sep beamed at her offer of hospitality to his friend, but Clare regretted her impulsive words immediately. She could not explain her reluctance, even to herself, yet her instincts warned her against this man. But how could a shivering, half-drowned man be any threat? It was only common decency to help the victims of disaster, and he had acted bravely in taking out a line to the battered *Venturer*.

They reached the door of her cottage. It opened onto the living room, where the fire threw out inviting warmth. Before the hearth, she and Sep released their support and Mark Conrad sank to his knees. He began to shudder violently, his face draining of all color.

Sep looked down anxiously. "Will he be all right, miss?"

Clare nodded. "He needs a hot drink inside him, Sep. You said something about a hot toddy. I'll put the kettle on."

"Aye, that's the way of it, miss. Hot inside and out. I'll be back in a minute with the rum."

Clare went into her small toilet chamber and returned with a large towel and a blanket.

"Mr. Conrad."

He looked up dazedly, his blue eyes blinking.

"It's best if you strip off your clothes and towel yourself dry. I've brought you a blanket."

She left him by the fire and went back to get a towel for herself.

In the kitchen, by the warmth of the range, she stripped quickly, toweled her body, and drew on a long, woolen dressing gown. She set the kettle to boil, then rubbed her hair vigorously. Freed of its scarf and hair net, it fell to her shoulders in wild disarray. A hairbrush was needed, but she would have to pass through the living room to reach her bedchamber. If Mr. Conrad had taken her advice, it would be too embarrassing to come upon him. She waited for Sep.

He arrived as the kettle began to steam. His voice sounded clearly through the closed door of the kitchen.

"That's the ticket, Cap'n. You'll be a sight warmer without those wet clothes. Now, wrap yourself up right and tight in the blanket and rest your weary bones. Miss won't mind if you lie on the couch now you're dry. 'Tis sitting down all wet that gives females the huff. Now, lie you there, Cap'n, and you shall have your hot toddy in a trice.''

Clare opened the kitchen door and peered out cautiously. Sep, with a bottle tucked into his pocket, grinned at her.

"He's decent now, miss, so if you've a mug or three, I'll brew up a powerful toddy. There's nothing like it for putting fire into the blood.'' He moved into the kitchen. "He's mortal pale, but looks better every minute.''

Clare set two enamel mugs on the square, scrubbed table. "Not for me, Sep. I've no head for spirits. I'll brew some tea." She smiled. "I'm glad you had the sense to change your own clothes. That wind was like a knife."

"I've lived through worse, miss, but I was a young fellow then." He gave her a wry look. "I'll not deny my old bones will be glad of a warm bed tonight."

Steam rose from the two mugs of dark brown liquid, and Sep carried them carefully into the living room. Clare took a small earthenware teapot from the shelf and brewed her tea.

As she sipped, she listened to the voices, reluctant to join the two men in the living room. After a while, the voices stopped and Sep came back into the kitchen, carrying the two mugs and an armful of wet clothes.

"That did the trick, miss. He's sleeping like a baby now. He'll be as right as ninepence tomorrow." He hung the wet clothes on the rack over the stove and turned a beaming face toward her. "I'll be off to my bed now, miss."

Clare set down her mug of tea carefully. "Septimus Thomas, has the seawater addled your brain? Are you suggesting that your friend should sleep the night in my cottage?" She rose and stared into his bemused face. "This is not a seaman's mission, and I am not some nameless tavern wife in foreign parts. What will people think when they hear where Mr. Conrad spent the night?"

Sep scratched his bristly chin. "I never thought of that, miss."

"Well, think of it now, Septimus Thomas. I should never have suggested my cottage. It was foolish of me, I realize that now, and you say he is fast asleep." She looked in anguish at the steaming clothes. "He must dress again and go. You do understand, Septimus? My reputation would be ruined."

"Aye, miss, you're right. I'd naught in my head but Cap'n Mark. Let's see now." His brow corrugated in thought. "I've a jacket and trousers, but the one'd be too small, and the other too big."

"Where does he live? Can't you get some of his own clothes?"

His brow cleared. "That's a bonnie idea. It's not far, but would his dragon housekeeper answer the door?"

"For heaven's sake, Septimus, why shouldn't she?"

"In the middle of the night? Females can be powerful nervous."

"You must try, Sep. Surely she knows you?"

"Well, yes, but she's not overfond of old sailors. Likely she'll think I'm drunk and call the law."

"Since she housekeeps for a sailor, what makes her so particular?" Clare said in irritation. "You can take my horse."

"Can't ride them danged things. They ain't shipshape."

"Oh, Sep." Clare sank down onto the kitchen chair and put her elbows on the table, cupping her chin into her hands. "What are we to do?"

"They've all gone to bed at the farm," Sep commented unhelpfully. "The lamps are out." He yawned as if the word *bed* had made him aware of his own weariness. He blinked rapidly to dispel tears. "Tell you what, miss. I always wake before dawn. That's habit from when the bosun used to roust us out. Cap'n Mark's clothes should have dried by then. I'll come over and take him away before the birds start piping to stations. How's that? There'll not be a soul about."

Clare hesitated. "Are you sure you'll wake? What if you oversleep?"

"Never been known to, miss. We'll sneak out before cock-crow."

"All right, Sep." Clare sighed. "It's the best we can do, but if you let me down, I'll have you—what is it you say? —flogged around the fleet."

Sep grinned. "I won't let you down, miss."

Clare accompanied him to the front door and let him out quietly. Now she must pass the couch on which the sleeping man lay, to reach her bedroom. A log fell into the hearth with a soft thud. Clare held her breath, but the man did not stir. The log was smoldering; she would have to lift it back into the grate. Moving silently, she approached the hearth and reached for the fire tongs. Without a sound, she replaced the log and laid down the tongs. The room was very quiet; only the gusting of the dying wind broke the stillness.

Clare glanced at the man, half buried in the blanket. The firelight played over the thick, dark hair, tousled from Sep's vigorous rubbing. The lower part of his face was shadowed by a blanket fold, giving the appearance of a beard. She was on the point of rising when his eyes opened.

Clare froze. The gaze was hazy, uncertain. There was a tiny furrow between the dark brows. Clare stayed utterly still, praying the eyelids would droop again.

"I know you," came the slurred voice, thick with sleep. "You're the one who—"

The eyes clouded over. Rum-induced sleep and the effort to concentrate warmed his face for a moment; then, the eyelids came down and sleep won the contest.

Clare rose, body and mind numbed with shock. Without knowing how she got there, she was in her bedroom, her back hard against the door. A lighted candle stood on her dressing table. She looked toward the mirror and saw herself as the man had seen her—not as the soberly dressed, slightly haughty creature beside Septimus at the harbor, but as that tumble-haired, wanton girl in the barn. Oh, yes, he knew her all right! And she, who had been fooled by the neat, clean-shaven appearance of first mate Mark, lately Captain Conrad of the *Dolphin*, knew him, too!

She turned the key in the door of her bedroom, exchanged her robe for a nightgown, and climbed into bed. Dear God, what appalling mischance this was, that the only man able to ruin her hard-won respectability was lying not six feet away on the other side of the wall. Why hadn't she carried on to the farmhouse and left Sep to brood alone by the seashore? And, in heaven's name, why had she suggested her own cottage as the place to bring a half-drowned man? It was all very well being wise after the event, but no one could retrace her steps and act differently.

Her mind went back to that isolated tavern, where the insolent barmaid had drawn her to the notice of the occupants. The bearded and peak-capped man at the bar who had called off the importuning seaman had, like herself, taken shelter in the barn on that stormy night.

Clare buried her face in her pillow, trying to shut off what had happened next. Her blood ran hot with shame, but the memory would not be dismissed. She had behaved in exactly the way of a common whore, almost as if she had been born to it. The tears ran hotly down her cheeks as she pictured the ladies of Clevedon cutting her dead, canceling their orders for gowns, and forbidding their daughters to soil their tongues with the name of Miss Court. Pride goeth before a fall, they said. Your sins will find you out. And she had been proud of her growing reputation, her facade of gentility. Now the facade would crumble, revealing a girl of low morals. Another memory stabbed. He knew, too, that she had stolen those gold pieces.

Why the devil hadn't that man asleep on her couch really drowned? She would have been safe then. *Dear God, forgive my wicked thoughts*, she prayed, appalled by her own vehemence. She fell asleep at last, but her dreams were haunted by the thought of facing Mark Conrad again.

◆ *Chapter Eleven* ◆

When Clare woke, the sun was streaming through the window. The wind had died, and the sky showed such a face of innocent blue that it was hard to imagine it had shown any other. Those black, thunderous clouds, the wind-seared beach, the laboring *Venturer* of last night might never have been.

Clare sat up, her heart leaping as memory clawed her mind. Dawn, Sep had said, and now it was full morning! If that man was still on the couch, she would be ruined! She listened, trying to control her breathing. The silence was eerie. She slid out of bed and pulled on her dressing gown. There or not, she was ruined anyway, she reflected miserably. Now that he had found her, it was surely too good a story to keep to himself.

Opening the bedroom door a crack, she peered into the living room. The couch was empty, but her gaze swept the room warily. No sign of him. The kitchen, perhaps? She went on bare feet over the polished boards. The kitchen door stood open. The clothes Sep had hung on the rack over the stove were gone. The mugs were back in place on the dresser and the iron kettle was hissing a tune over the low-burning, but surely remade, fire.

Clare looked about her, then returned to the living room. The rug was smooth, the cushions of the couch plumped up, and everything was in perfect order. A neatly folded blanket and towel, laid inconspicuously on a stool outside the bedroom door, were the only differences in the tidy room. Clare clasped her hands together.

"Oh, Sep," she breathed. "You kept your word. Thank you, dear Sep."

She carried the blanket and towel into the bedroom. The church clock was striking. Eight strokes, she counted as she washed and dressed. Standing before the mirror in her most severe gown, she brushed her hair, gathered the curls into a bunch, and secured them tightly into a chignon with an abundance of hairpins. Her cheeks were rather pale, her eyes shadowed, as she wondered about Mark Conrad. Would he remember that moment of recognition? He had been dazed and half asleep. With luck he might, if he remembered, put it down to a fantasy of imagination. Her spirits rose a little. She regarded her reflection, assuming a solemn expression. Spectacles and a grey wig would certainly dispel any flicker of resemblance. She almost smiled at the thought of Miss Court appearing to have aged twenty years overnight. Since she had neither wig nor spectacles, she must wear her own face and hope for the best. A shocked denial of ever having spent a night in a barn must be her only defense if the man told his story.

After tea and toast in the kitchen, Clare settled to her day's work. She had promised summer muslins to the daughter of a Clevedon businessman. They were to be collected this afternoon and needed only to be finished off. Just before noon a tap on her front door made her lay the sewing aside. Whoever was calling for the dresses must wait outside. She had made it quite plain that anyone who required her services must abide by her rules. She was not a sewing maid, to be harried and rushed.

As she reached the door, she schooled her expression into one of disapproval, her brows high in question. It was not a maid or coachman who faced her through the open doorway, but the tall figure of a man. His back was toward the sun and she could barely discern his face. Her brows rose higher.

"Yes?" she asked coolly, before recognition hit her.

"Conrad, Miss Court. Mark Conrad."

Clare stared at him blankly, her mind frozen by this sudden confrontation.

"You may not remember me, Miss Court, but I have good reason to remember you."

"Indeed?" Clare felt an icy touch down her spine. Her disapproving expression remained as if glued into place.

"I suppose one half-drowned wretch looks pretty much like another," went on the pleasant voice. "But Sep tells me you sheltered me last night, since the cottages and farmhouse were overflowing with the survivors of the *Venturer*."

Clare could see his face clearer now as her eyes became accustomed to the sunlight. There was nothing on his face but a smile of gratitude, nothing in his eyes that hinted of inner knowledge.

"Oh, I understand now, Mr. Conrad. Since I was one of the last to leave the shore and Sep appeared to need support, I was happy to help. I hope you are recovered from your ordeal."

"Quite recovered, thank you, Miss Court. I owe you a debt of gratitude which I shall not forget."

"You owe me nothing, Mr. Conrad. There were many helpers last night who all deserve thanks for what they did."

"Quite so, Miss Court, but a man considers his own survival a personal thing and gives thanks accordingly. To be given a second chance at life has an importance all of its own. Don't you agree?" He smiled.

Clare stared into the smiling blue eyes. Was there some oblique message in those words? A second chance at life? Wasn't that exactly what she wanted herself? She allowed her expression to relax slightly but still did not smile.

"I agree wholeheartedly, Mr. Conrad. I am convinced that the crew of the stricken ship will share your sentiment." She watched his eyes for a change of expression—one that said he was not including the seamen in his views—but his smile was the same.

He bowed. "I will take up no more of your time, Miss Court, except to say that old Sep had me whisked out of your cottage well before dawn and not a soul about to see."

"I am vastly relieved to hear that, Mr. Conrad."

"Septimus Thomas has a great respect for you, Miss Court, and threatened to have me flogged on a crosspiece if I didn't shake a leg." He chuckled softly. "He tells me you are a dressmaker."

"That is so."

"I understand his nagging now. He was fearful for your reputation."

Clare drew in a calming breath. "Reputations are fragile

things, Mr. Conrad, and once gone, cannot be recovered." She stared at him solemnly. "I hope your gratitude extends to discretion, Mr. Conrad."

He bowed again. "My word on it, Miss Court. Good day to you."

Clare did not wait to watch him stride away but closed the door quickly and leaned against it, feeling helplessly weak. Had it really been a simple conversation or had question and answer lurked under the spoken word? Did he know or guess? Was he assuring her that she had nothing to fear from him? If he truly remembered nothing of last night, then it was a simple conversation. If he knew, and out of gratitude said nothing, would that make her safe? And when gratitude wore off, what then? An expectation of renewing their relationship? A subtle form of blackmail? Accept my attentions or have your reputation ruined? She knew so little about him, she could not begin to guess. Sep thought the world of him, but they were fellow seamen, so it was natural. She could not, dare not, confide in anyone, and it might never happen. She had to go on as before, yet always with that nagging doubt at the back of her mind.

Clare's next caller arrived midafternoon and really was the coachman she had expected. Her nerves had jumped as the knocker sounded, but she told herself irritably that Mr. Conrad would hardly call again so soon. Why should he call at all, since he had thanked her sufficiently for taking him in, and even he would not risk a daylight approach if he intended a pursuit. The muslin dresses were ready, packed in tissue paper. Clare handed the coachman a sealed envelope containing her bill, together with the dresses. He saluted her most respectfully and drove away. As Clare was about to close the door, she saw Sep approaching in his usual rolling gait. She waited, smiling.

"Come in, Sep. I was about to put on the kettle."

"Thank you, miss. I'll step aboard for a tot with you." He knocked out his pipe on the heel of his boot and stuffed it into his pocket.

"A tot of tea is all you'll get from me, Septimus Thomas,"

she threw over her shoulder as he followed her into the kitchen.

He grinned. "'Tis a powerful smell, that hot toddy. I opened your window a mite this morning in case you were expecting early visitors. Some fine ladies have noses like bloodhounds."

Clare gave him a fond smile as she put on the kettle. "I am obliged to you, Sep. You kept your word, rekindled the stove, and left the cottage in prime condition. Did your friend reach home before his housekeeper was astir?"

Sep nodded. "Aye, and none the worse for being half drowned."

Clare turned her back to reach down the tea caddy. She kept her voice very matter-of-fact.

"He called earlier to thank me for housing him overnight. He looked quite recovered."

"Aye, he'd do that, miss. Always gives thanks where it's due. A real gentleman is Cap'n Mark."

Clare brewed the tea and set the pot on the table without comment. Perhaps to an old seaman any superior in rank was a gentleman—especially one who showed friendship by gifts of tobacco. She poured out the tea.

"How is the lad with the broken arm?"

"Chirpy as a newborn chick," Sep said cheerily. "Especially after young Kate and Milly turned into mother hens. Old sawbones set his arm on compass course and the young'uns wouldn't hear of him being carted off to the workhouse hospital. He's an orphan lad, you see, and got shipped off as a cabin boy when he was twelve."

"So now the *Venturer* is gone, and he's got a broken arm. Poor lad."

Sep chuckled. "I doubt it, miss. Fallen on his feet as it were, since he can't stand the sea, anyway. Likes dry land, he does, so Farmer Clark'll find him a job, if those two young'uns have any say in the matter. Quite taken with young Albert, they are."

"And the rest of the survivors?" asked Clare, smiling.

"All sorted out and gone their ways."

Clare looked down into her tea and spoke carefully. "Did Mrs. Clark mention me? Wonder where I'd got to last night, I mean."

Sep's shrewd old eyes twinkled. "Aye, but I told her I'd sent you packing off home after we'd beached Cap'n Mark, on account of you being soaked to the skin." His face assumed a pious expression. "Took Cap'n Mark home, I did, all by myself, and saw him safe there before I gave thought to my own condition."

Clare bit her lip in a grin. "So, you're a hero now, as well as an old rogue, but I thank the two of you."

Sep grinned and tapped his nose. "So that's between you and me, miss."

Clare hesitated. "And—and your friend."

"I told you, miss. He's a gentleman and never breaks his word."

Clare nodded, hoping Sep's faith in Captain Conrad was justified.

When Sep rose to go, Clare decided to walk with him as far as the farmhouse. Sep had announced his intention of visiting the scene of the *Venturer*'s shipwreck.

"Tide's backing out," he declared. "I'll maybe pick up a bit of driftwood for my fire."

Clare settled her summer bonnet in place and eyed his innocent face. "A round piece of driftwood with the bung still in place, you mean?"

Sep scratched his chin. "You've a sharp, suspicious mind, miss, and no mistake." His expression became one of injured innocence, then collapsed into a wry grin.

Clare laughed. "On your way, Septimus Thomas. I won't tell the revenuers if you get a lucky find, so don't you tell me if you do."

They walked the short distance between cottage and farm in companionable silence as Sep began to stuff his pipe. Clare watched in affection as the short, sturdy man went on down the hill. Then she turned to the ever-open door of the farmhouse.

"May I come in, Mrs. Clark?" she called.

"Come right in, miss. You've no need to ask and, in any
case, you'll be dragged in by the girls to view our stranded
fish."

Kate and Milly were before Clare in an instant, each grasping a hand.

"Come and see Albert, miss. He's broken his arm but he's
ever so brave and we're taking turns feeding him."

Clare allowed herself to be propelled into a small room off
the main living room. On a truckle bed lay a fair-haired shrimp
of a boy. A bandaged arm, held by a sling, lay across his
chest.

"This is Albert Smith, miss," Kate said proudly.

"Say good afternoon to miss, Albert," prompted Milly.
"We're going to fetch your milk now."

"Good afternoon, miss." The boy smiled sheepishly.

Clare returned the greeting, observing the thin, under-
nourished body. "Just an arm, is it, Albert?"

"Yes, miss. I can use my right arm, but these danged—"
He caught himself up sharply. "These young ladies are per-
ishing keen—I mean ever so . . ." He sought for a word.

"Obliging?" offered Clare.

"Yes, miss—to stuff me gizzard like I was a Christmas
goose." He smiled suddenly, and it was so enchanting a smile
that Clare smiled back. "Not that I've ever seen a Christmas
goose," he went on. "But I've heard tell of them."

There was no rancor in his voice, and he looked over at
Kate and Milly with something like brotherly affection in his
eyes.

"Well, you just thank your stars, young Albert Smith, that
you got yourself beached in this place. There's no family as
kind as this one, so take your punishment like a man and let
the girls fuss over you. You can put down your manly foot
when you're up and about. All right?"

"Yes, miss. It's just that I'm not used to it. Nobody ever
fussed over me before."

Clare saw Kate approaching, carrying a brimming glass of
milk. She looked down on Albert and raised her brows.

The boy glanced at the milk. "Why, thank you, Miss Kate.

Gabbing—I mean, talking, does make a body's throat dry,'' he said meekly, and took the glass from Kate's hand as she lifted it to his lips. '''Twould be a shame to get this good nightshirt sopping wet, and 'tis only the food I need helping with, honest.'' He shot Clare a bright look before burying his nose in the glass.

"He's getting better, isn't he, miss?'' Kate said, beaming and watching with rapt attention as Albert drained the glass.

Clare agreed. "I daresay if you cut up his food, he could handle it with a spoon very well by himself.''

Kate sighed. "Yes, miss, but I haven't had so much fun since we fed those baby goslings when the goose fell into the well.''

"Not—not the Christmas goose?'' Clare asked in a choking voice.

"It was, miss, the very one. We had to feed up another.'' She frowned, looking from Clare to Albert. "Why are you laughing? It wasn't funny.''

"N-not for the goose, no,'' Clare managed. "Just be warned, young Albert. Keep away from wells.'' She turned hurriedly and went in search of Mrs. Clark.

After talking at length about the events of last night, Mrs. Clark glanced at the kitchen clock.

"Young Sara will be over presently.''

"I haven't seen her for several days,'' Clare said. "Can I wait to say hello before she's dragged off to meet Albert?''

"Of course, my dear. She'd be sorry to miss you. The lass has taken a great fancy to you, which is quite unusual.''

"Is it?'' Clare asked, surprised. "She's a friendly child.''

"She's used to us and the girls, but on the whole, she doesn't make friends easily. Rather more reserved than shy, I'd say. A lonely girl, really.''

"Is she an only child?''

"Yes.''

"Perhaps I see myself in her,'' Clare said. "I was an only child, too. Maybe we meet on that inward plane of loneliness that is a sort of communication.''

Mrs. Clark nodded sagely. "Mrs. Winter is a well-meaning

body, but I doubt she understands Sara. The child is a bit fey, and Mrs. Winter is a very house-proud woman, a most matter-of-fact person, while Sara's a bit of a dreamer.''

"What about her father?"

"Mostly away at sea, but there's real feeling between them. Sara adores her father.'' Mrs. Clark looked at the clock again. "The child is taking piano lessons from the vicar's wife. Her father arranged it to give her another interest, and the vicar's wife says she has a natural talent for music.''

"That's wonderful,'' Clare said. "Dreamers aren't like other people. Their need is to express themselves creatively, as artists or poets or musicians.''

"Or sewing fine gowns?'' suggested Mrs. Clark with a smile.

Clare laughed. "Well, I suppose you might call me a dreamer, too, but my talent must earn me a living. I am in your debt for putting me in the way of that.''

"If you call that a debt, I've been well repaid, since you insist on renting the cottage and charging only half price for the girl's dresses.''

"Well, they're only half size,'' protested Clare. "And I can charge the ladies of Clevedon quite high, as you yourself suggested, don't forget.''

"And well worth it, too,'' commented Mrs. Clark, rising. "There's Sara now. Will you stay for tea, miss?''

"No, thank you, Mrs. Clark. Septimus Thomas called on me earlier and we took tea together. He said he was going down to the beach.''

"He won't be alone,'' Mrs. Clark said dryly. "There's always beachcombers after a wreck, but the coast guard will be keeping an eye on them to stop any thieving. Hello, Sara, dear. Miss Clare was waiting to say hello before she went home.''

Sara smiled, her eyes bright and her cheeks flushed. "Hello, Mrs. Clark. Thank you for waiting, Clare. I did so want to see you and show you my music.''

Clare eyed the fine leather music case. "I should love to see your music, Sara, but I fear you must deal with Albert first.''

Sara's eyes widened. "Who's Albert?"

Kate and Milly, hearing Sara's voice, surged into the room. "Sara, Sara, come and meet Albert. We've told him all about you."

"But who—" Sara began, but her voice was drowned in a double entreaty.

"Come on, do. He got washed ashore last night, just like a mermaid, and—"

"He wasn't washed ashore," Milly interrupted. "He came on the breeches buoy, and a mermaid is a girl, silly."

"Well, a merboy, then." Kate giggled. "But we're looking after him 'til he's better. So, come on, Sara."

Sara set down her music case. "I'll come in a moment," she said with quaint dignity. "I must first exchange a few polite words with Miss Clare, who has been kind enough to wait for me to come."

Kate and Milly looked a little abashed, and Mrs. Clark hid her smile as she shooed them back the way they had come.

"Sara will be with you directly. Don't be so impatient."

Clare went out of the farmhouse with Sara at her side. "You'd better bring your music to my cottage, Sara. Come to tea tomorrow. I haven't got an Albert to distract us."

Sara smiled up at Clare. "Will you come to tea with me tomorrow, instead? That's what I've been planning to ask you. Do say you will come."

"I'd love to, Sara, if you've asked permission."

"Oh, yes. There'll be cakes and scones and Papa always says I may invite anyone I like." She smiled up shyly. "And I like you, Clare." Her smile faltered a little. "You do like me, don't you?"

Clare felt her heart melt with sympathy for this lonely child. What kind of parents did she have? Didn't they understand that some children were changelings—strange, dreaming children in a matter-of-fact world? She knew well the feeling of being different, even when her poor, hard-pressed mother had lived, flitting like a poor, pale ghost through the house, shrinking at every footstep.

"I like you very much, Sara, and will be delighted to take tea with you. At what hour would you like me to call?"

"Four o'clock?"

"Splendid. Where do you live, by the way?"

"I'll come for you. It's not far. It's easier to walk."

"Then I'll tell my coachman that I will not be needing his services tomorrow. He may take the whole day off," she finished grandly.

Sara giggled. "And if the weather turns inclement, I will send you home in our coach."

"A kind thought," Clare said, smiling, then caught sight of Kate and Milly, hovering in the doorway of the farmhouse. "Your escort is waiting to introduce you to their shipwrecked mariner. Meanwhile, Miss Clare Court accepts with pleasure the kind invitation of Miss Sara Winter."

The grey-green eyes swept up in a look of surprise. "I'm not Sara Winter. Didn't you know my name? It's Sara Conrad."

◆ *Chapter Twelve* ◆

As Sara joined Kate and Milly at the door of the farmhouse, Clare stood for a moment in stunned disbelief. Sara Conrad? There was only one Conrad who lived hereabouts, and that was Sep's adored Captain Mark. Sara was his daughter, then, and Mrs. Winter the housekeeper Sep talked of—the one he had been loath to disturb and had avoided meeting by smuggling Cap'n Mark into his own house before dawn.

Clare walked slowly back to her cottage. Was Captain Conrad a widower? He must be, since he employed a housekeeper and Sara had not spoken of a mother. Clare had mistakenly assumed her mother to be the Mrs. Winter referred to by Mrs. Clark. And now she had committed herself to taking tea with Sara. If that man saw her again, and not briefly this time, but in full possession of his faculties, surely he would recognize her as that wanton girl in the barn.

No, she dare not meet him again. She must send a message to Sara, pleading a rush of urgent business, an indisposition—anything to ensure her anonymity. She bit her lip in annoyance. Sara was calling for her. She didn't know where the child lived. Sep knew, of course, but Sara might still call with offers of help for whichever excuse she used. She recalled the child's glowing look as she professed herself delighted to accept the invitation. No, she could not hurt the child by backing out, and anyway, she comforted herself, tea and cakes seemed unlikely for a seaman. With luck, he might not even put in an appearance.

Even so, as the hour approached the next afternoon, she donned a very plain dress of grey twill, with only a small frill of white lace about the high neck. Her hair was brushed back and knotted behind her head so that every strand lay flat under her straw hat. Low-heeled black sandals and a black fringed shawl completed the attire of a very sober citizen, as different from that hoydenish creature in the barn as she could manage. Would the memory of that night never leave her? A man might take and discard many girls, scarcely remembering their faces afterward. She hoped Mark Conrad was one of them. After all, he must have had a wife, and he had spoken that night of escaping some pressing female. Despite her own inexperience, Clare had sensed that he was well-versed in the art of lovemaking. Just another girl, an easy conquest she had been, so why fear he would remember?

She was able to greet Sara almost cheerfully. The child wore a pretty, rose-printed and frilled dress, her light-brown hair held back by a pink ribbon.

"How pretty you look, Sara," Clare exclaimed gaily.

Sara eyed Clare's somber attire and Clare knew what was in her mind.

"One day, Sara, I shall make for myself a dress with roses in the pattern, or maybe a muslin dress of lilac with lots of frills and flounces, but not this year. I am too busy making the young ladies of Clevedon their summer finery to have time for my own."

Sara said politely, "You look very nice, Clare."

Clare laughed. "A very nice moth, Sara dear, but one day I shall turn into a butterfly—just you wait and see."

They were walking up the hill and Sara took Clare's hand. "I don't think moths turn into butterflies, do they?"

"No, they're different, but I'd rather be a moth than a caterpillar. Just think of all those legs!"

"I'd rather not, if you don't mind," Sara said with a giggle. "Look, we're nearly there. Papa has a telescope in his bedroom and you can see miles out to sea through it. He says he can see Cardiff on a fine day. Would you like to look through it?"

"Good heavens, no, Sara! I would not dare go into your papa's bedroom. It would be most improper." She paused. Since Sara had brought her father's name into the conversation, she could ask the question that had been nagging at her mind.

"Will your papa be joining us for tea?"

Sara shook her head. "No, Papa is working on his boat."

"The *Dolphin*?"

"No, that belongs to Mr. Patterson's line. Papa has a boat of his own. It's not really big enough to call a ship, but Papa and Mr. Thomas are fitting it out with new sails and canvas. Mr. Thomas says she'll be as fine as fivepence when she's had a lick of paint."

Clare laughed. "That sounds like Mr. Thomas."

Sara gave her a bright look. "Mr. Thomas says he's going to paint her new name next week and then she'll be ready to sail to China and back. Guess what Papa is going to call her?"

"Since all ships are ladies, she can't be called Septimus, right?"

Sara giggled and did a hop and a skip in her excitement. "Of course not, but do guess."

"Well—it has to be the name of a lady, or a bird or a fish or a flower, or something very heroic. Let me think," she teased. "If I was your papa, what would I call my lovely little boat? Could it be after my lovely little daughter whose name just happens to be Sara?"

"Yes, yes! Isn't it wonderful? Papa says we'll have a christening party when she's finished." She whirled about, her skirts flying. "Sara, Sara, as fine as fivepence. You'll come, won't you?"

"To China?" asked Clare, laughing at the breathless girl.

"No, no, the party. Papa will like that."

"How on earth can you say that when your Papa doesn't even know me?"

"He will, he will. Papa knows everybody and he'll like you when he meets you."

Clare's mind edged warily around that thought. She said casually, "Well, not today. You did say he wouldn't be at your tea party?"

Sara nodded. "He won't be home until late. Look, there's our house now."

Clare glanced toward the few cottages, with their tiny front gardens. "Which one is yours?"

"None of those. They belong to Mr. Patterson's shipmasters. Our cottage is at the far end. There, that one with the wisteria over the front door."

Clare looked where Sara pointed and her eyes widened. "You surely don't call that a cottage! Why, it's three times as big as all those others put together!"

"It's really called Conrad Place, but Papa says his great-grandfather must have been a very pompous man to call it after himself when he built it."

"His great-grandfather built it? It must be very old, then."

Sara shrugged. "Hundreds of years, I think, but most people call it Conrad's, and Papa doesn't mind because he's not a bit pompous."

As they approached the wide stone porchway, inset by a brass-studded door, Clare had to revise her opinion of the man she had taken to be a rough-handed seaman. The age of the house and the fact that generations of the same family had lived in it did not, in itself, constitute gentry, but a prosperous line of Conrads. Perhaps like the Pattersons, of whom she had heard, they had been skilled tradesmen. She glanced about her at the stone troughs of flowers and the mullioned windows, beyond which were snowy-white curtains. Unlike the usual whitewashed cottages, this house was built of mellowed stone, a dusky pink in tone, perhaps the particular kind of stone quarried from the west of England.

The stonework was in good condition, evidently cared for by generations of Conrads and quite unlike the crumbling ruin of Harcourt House, she reflected wryly. Gentry might look down on trade in the social scale, but families in trade had the means to keep their properties in good order. The door opened and a plainly dressed, greying woman looked out.

"There you are, Miss Sara." She stood back, allowing them entry, and Clare felt the woman's eyes assessing her.

"Clare, this is Mrs. Winter, Papa's housekeeper. Mrs. Winter, this is Miss Court, my friend."

Clare smiled and inclined her head, approving Sara's presentation of Mrs. Winter to herself. A less well-taught child might have done it the other way about, allowing the housekeeper the privilege of hostess. Clare did not extend a hand.

"Good afternoon, miss," the housekeeper said and bent a knee slightly.

"Good afternoon, Mrs. Winter," Clare said pleasantly and removed her straw hat and shawl.

Mrs. Winter accepted them without a word and Clare smoothed back her hair in the gilt-framed wall mirror. First impressions always counted, she knew, and Mrs. Winter should not think that she was some sewing maid befriended by young Miss Sara. Naturally, Mrs. Winter would keep an eye on Sara's new acquaintances, and with Mr. Conrad away at sea, probably report on them all to her master, so Clare felt her touch of hauteur quite justified.

"Will you serve tea now, Mrs. Winter, please?" asked Sara. "I will take Miss Court into the drawing room."

"Yes, Miss Sara, right away."

Clare looked about the drawing room, impressed by its tasteful arrangement. She hadn't known quite what to expect in a seaman's home. The house was inherited, of course, but each generation had its own ideas of furnishing. The polished floor was almost covered by an Oriental rug of flower design, its colors picked to match perfectly with the deep-pink velvet curtains and the velvet button-back chairs with cabriole legs. Before the couch stood a low, rosewood coffee table and on this, Mrs. Winter placed a tea tray of heavy silver.

"I feel greatly honored, Miss Conrad," Clare said. "A Georgian tea service, if I'm not mistaken. How delightful."

Sara clapped her hands in delight. "Papa said I might use it for important occasions. It belonged to his papa, you know. Do you like the carpet? Papa brought it back from one of his voyages. Can you guess where from?"

Clare studied the carpet, trying to recall all the ones that had come and gone from Harcourt House. She thought of the ship, the *Dolphin*, and the tanned faces of the crew. Somewhere hot, but not, she thought, as far away as China.

"India, perhaps?" she hazarded. "I believe they make such flower designs in Kashmir. Turkish and Persian carpets are more inclined to be mainly red." She glanced up to meet Mrs. Winter's eyes. The woman was regarding her with respect. Good heavens, had she actually guessed right?

Sara confirmed her guess and as her eyes moved about the room, Clare protested, laughing.

"If we're having guessing games, my dear, the tea will become cold before we've finished, for I see Dresden and Sevres and heaven knows what else."

Sara giggled and brought her gaze back to the teapot, remembering her duties as hostess. As she poured the tea, she commented, "Papa has traveled a great deal, and he always brings something back with him, doesn't he, Mrs. Winter?"

"Indeed, Miss Sara. The master has good taste," she went on, turning to Clare. "Take this room, now. When the old master was alive, it was all dark brown with furniture to match. Mr. Mark changed all that."

"You mean that he designed this room?" Clare asked, surprised.

"Oh, yes, every bit of it. He said—" Mrs. Winter hesitated, biting her lip, but Sara took up the story with evident enjoyment.

"He said it was like living in the hold of a ship and he wanted none of it. Isn't that right, Mrs. Winter?"

"Well, yes, Miss Sara, but I wouldn't want Miss Court to think I was in the habit of gossiping about the master. I'll go and fetch the cakes now."

She left the room and Clare sipped her tea from the delicate china cup. The room certainly spoke of excellent taste. Sara and Mrs. Winter attributed it all to Mr. Conrad. Neither had mentioned a Mrs. Conrad, yet there had to have been, for here was Sara, the daughter of Mark Conrad. Clare decided against asking any questions. Since Sara had never spoken of a mama, it could well have been a long-ago tragedy with the child never knowing her mother.

In a corner of the room, set under a window, Clare saw a grand piano. It reminded her of Sara's wish to show her music scores. "You must play the piano for me, Sara. How long have you been taking lessons?"

"Only a few weeks, and I'm not very good yet, but Papa says that everyone should have another world to live in— one they can go into when they're depressed or unhappy." Sara looked up at Clare. "Do you think like Papa?"

Clare thought of her new, happy life and the one she had lived before. She nodded, answering seriously, "Yes, I think I do. We must always be able to escape from life. If we can't do it physically, we must retreat into our minds and make our other world more beautiful and enchanting. Music can create that other world for you, Sara, if you love it enough."

Sara was listening with rapt attention. "Have you found your other world, Clare?"

"Yes, I think I have." Clare stared unseeingly at the pink, button-back chair opposite. "At least, I hope I have."

Sara looked at Clare's somber expression for a moment and politeness held back any question. Instead, she returned to the subject of her father.

"Papa has another world, too. He says it's a dream, really, but one day he will make it come true."

Clare came out of her abstraction and smiled. "A dream? Does he want a fleet of ships like Mr. Patterson?"

"He wants a steamship—one that can travel without needing the wind in its sails; in fact, one that doesn't even have sails."

"Well, that certainly is a big dream. I have never heard of a steamship."

"Papa will make one," Sara said with firm conviction. "He always gets what he wants."

Clare felt a pulse twitch in her throat and she glanced at the clock on the mantelpiece. She was reassured to see the hands point at half-past five. She must be gone before Mr. Conrad came. That last remark of Sara's had made her father sound like a ruthless man. The less she saw of him, the less risk she would run of his thoughts being stirred by the sight of her.

They had finished tea and Mrs. Winter had removed the tea tray. Sara brought out her music case and spread the scores on the coffee table. Apart from the exercises, there were simple versions of Brahms, Chopin, and Strauss melodies. Clare remembered the early days when she herself had played these pieces, but not on such a fine-looking instrument as the piano by the window. Even the old, out-of-tune upright piano had been taken in payment for one of her father's bills.

Sara led her to the piano and looked up shyly. "I'm not very good yet at getting both hands to work together."

Clare laughed. "I think everyone who ever learned the pianoforte has said that." She sat beside Sara on the wide piano stool. "Let me turn the pages. What shall it be first?"

Sara gained confidence under Clare's smiling approval and sailed through the pieces with surprising aptitude, despite her few lessons. A natural talent, the vicar's wife had said, and Clare believed her right as she watched Sara's light touch on the keyboard.

They were indulging in a noisy duet, with Clare taking the lower notes, when a slam of the outer door startled them. Clare froze at the sound of a male voice. Her gaze sought the clock—ten minutes to seven.

"It's Papa," Sara exclaimed.

"But Sara, you said he would be late home." Clare heard her voice come out like a squeak.

Sara looked at the clock, then back to Clare in some surprise. "But it is late—almost seven—and Papa is usually here at six o'clock when he's in port."

"Oh, Sara," breathed Clare. Of course, to a child of eight years, seven o'clock might appear late. Why hadn't she thought of that? She rose quickly to her feet. "I must go. Thank you very much for inviting me." She glanced out the window. "How dark it is getting, and quite windy, too. I must hurry before I get caught in a rainstorm." She knew she was babbling, but she must get out of this house before Mark Conrad came looking for his daughter. He would very likely go upstairs to change first, and she could slip away before he came down.

"Won't you stay and meet Papa?" Sara asked.

"No, I can't, I'm sorry. I've just remembered that I promised to have a dress ready for early collection tomorrow, and—"

She broke off as the door opened abruptly. On the threshold stood a tall, dark-haired man, scowling brows lowered over blue eyes. His stare seemed to pin her to the spot and she felt like a clubbed animal. Dear God, her mind said, he knows me after all, and considers a fallen woman no fit company for his child!

Then, suddenly, the scowl was gone and the piercing blue eyes were regarding her with mild interest.

"Papa, this is my friend, Clare." Sara had run to her father and taken his hand.

Mark Conrad looked down on his daughter and there was no doubting the affection in his softened gaze. He glanced back at Clare and bowed. "So you are Clare, the young lady my daughter never ceases to talk about." His smile was polite, but there was a glint of something in his eyes. "We have met before, have we not?"

Clare felt a dryness in her throat. "I—I don't recall it, Mr. Conrad." Her voice came out low and flat, but she held his gaze without blinking.

"Ah, yes, I have it now," he said, smiling. "I remember our first meeting."

Clare felt a strong impulse to hurl herself forward, brush both Sara and her father aside, and run like the wind back to the refuge of her cottage. But her limbs were rigid, her stare fixed. Only her mind spun away, and that wasn't enough to take her from this house. Surely he was not going to speak of the barn? Her wits steadied and a grain of common sense returned. What a stupid thought. Of course he would not mention the barn with his young daughter at his elbow. The night he had spent in her cottage? Not that either, she reasoned, for it was unknown to any but the three of them—herself, this man, and the old seaman.

"Septimus Thomas," Mr. Conrad said, as if putting a name to her last thought.

Clare jumped. "What?"

"Septimus Thomas introduced us, the day the *Dolphin* berthed." He rubbed his chin and gave Sara a look of wry amusement. "I am not surprised that your friend has forgotten that meeting, since I was dressed in rough seafaring clothes, but Septimus introduced us." His eyes seemed to hold sardonic humor. "Miss Court was most reluctant, if I remember correctly."

Clare felt her nerves relax. If only that *had* been their first meeting she would feel much easier. They shared the knowledge of the night in the cottage, of course, but it was to their mutual advantage to hold silent on that.

The rain pattered sharply on the windowpane as Mark Conrad said, "Would you care for a glass of sherry, Miss Court?"

"Oh, no, thank you, Mr. Conrad. I really must go. Thank you so much, Sara. I—I have enjoyed taking tea with you."

"It is kind of you to come," Sara replied in her quaint, grown-up way. "Papa, can Clare take the carriage home? It sounds quite windy out there."

"Sorry, my dear, Perkins has the axle off and must make a new part. But don't worry. I will escort Miss Court home."

"There is no need, Mr. Conrad," Clare protested. "It is only a short walk and the rain is very light."

They were in the hall and Clare picked up her shawl and straw hat. Mark Conrad looked at the flimsy garments.

"Don't you have a cloak?"

"Of course, but not with me. The weather was fine when we set out. It will only take me a few minutes. Please don't trouble yourself on my account."

In answer, Mark Conrad took down a long boat cloak from the hall stand and swung it about Clare's shoulders. He grinned. "This will guarantee you from any weather but I can promise nothing for that straw hat."

Clare felt herself flush with annoyance at having the cloak forced on her, but she answered as calmly as she could. "Then I must shelter it under the cloak. Thank you. I will ask Mr. Thomas to return it. Good evening to you both." She moved quickly to the front door.

Mark Conrad opened it, still smiling, and Clare was unprepared for the wind that flung back the boat cloak and tugged her off balance. Mark caught her arm in a steadying grip.

"We are placed higher than you, Miss Court, and the wind comes straight off the sea." He gave her a bland smile. "Therefore, you must resign yourself to being escorted if you wish to keep your feet. In any case, I need my boat cloak for an early start in the morning, so there'll be no need to put Septimus to the trouble of bringing it back."

"Very well, Mr. Conrad. Good night, Sara."

When the lights of Conrad Place fell away it was very dark; the clouds seemed to hang directly overhead. Clare was thankful for the strength of the wind, for any word spoken would be lost in its howl. The path past the cottages was unfamiliar in the early darkness, and she was glad of the guiding hand under her elbow. Even so, she was very conscious of the closeness of Mark Conrad. They had, one other dark and stormy night, been closer still. The mere thought of it made the heat rise in her body and she was glad of the darkness that hid her flushed face.

As the ground dropped away, the wind noise was muted by cliffs and became less fierce. Mark Conrad still held her elbow and her other arm, clutching the straw hat, was imprisoned in the boat cloak, making it impossible for her to keep her knotted hair in place. Then the rain began—great, blinding droplets that were flung horizontally into their faces by the gusting wind. Clare knew that she was leaving a trail of hairpins as her curls broke from their restraining knot. She tried to hurry, conscious of the rain's effect on her hair, turning that severely brushed hairstyle into a tangled froth of curls.

"Don't hurry so; you'll fall," Mark Conrad said. "Only your hair will be wet, and that's no problem, surely?"

Clare didn't answer as she saw her own cottage come into sight. Almost home, and at the door she could take off the cloak and thank Mr. Conrad for his escort, then retreat into the anonymity behind her closed front door. On the step, she paused and faced him, sliding out of the cloak.

"I am most obliged—" she began, but he had reached past her and opened the door.

"I must see you safely inside, Miss Court, or Sara will want to know why. Is there a lamp in the hallway? I will light it for you."

"There's really no need—" Clare began again, but saw she was too late. He had lifted the glass chimney of the lamp and was applying a match to the wick. The soft bloom of light etched the strong planes of his face in gold for a moment before he lifted his head. Clare retreated toward the window, dropping the hat onto a chair and trying to smooth down her hair.

"Thank you, Mr. Conrad. I shall be quite all right now, so—" Once more she fell silent as he crossed the room and set a light to the lamp on her sewing table.

He turned and smiled. "There we are, Miss Court. Safely home, two lamps alight, and not a stowaway or ruffian in sight."

He picked up the boat cloak from the chair where she had dropped it and draped it over his arm. He looked at her for a long, unsmiling moment.

"Miss Court, there is something I must ask you. It has been on my mind for quite a while now." His gaze moved around the room, then returned to her with an intensity she found startling.

Clare's heart began to beat faster and she stared into the handsome face with the brows drawn tightly together, as if in mental struggle. His expression was that of a man who, while fearing the answer, forces himself to ask the question.

He drew in a deep, harsh breath. "I must know. Miss Court—are you expecting a child?"

◆ *Chapter Thirteen* ◆

Clare's hands dropped to her sides and she stared at Mark Conrad in frozen silence. The curls, now loose from her restraining fingers, fell in disorder to her shoulders. They faced each other, motionless, her grey eyes unable to tear themselves away from the hard blueness of his intent gaze. Her mind was stunned by the shock of his question, the starkness of it. She should have known the truth would come out. The barn had been shadowed, but he had seen her face clearly in the tavern, despite the old-fashioned bonnet. It hadn't taken him long to link that face with the primly severe one of Miss Clare Court.

Her legs began to tremble and she felt sick with the hopelessness of her situation. Now she would have to move on. She sank onto the couch, staring now into the cold ashes of the hearth. A shiver ran through her. She was cold—as cold as on that night when Philip Rayne had told her she was forfeit for her father's debts.

Mark Conrad had not moved. He stood, feet slightly apart, his hands clasped behind his back. Clare knew that his eyes had never left her face.

She looked up at him. "No, Mr. Conrad. I am not expecting a child." Her voice was surprisingly calm and she managed to edge it with cool disdain. As she saw the flush start on his cheeks, she rose to her feet. "I will take up no more of your time, Mr. Conrad. Thank you for your escort, and good night."

For a moment he stared at her and she wondered if there was some uncertainty behind the relief in his gaze.

"Will you call on Sara again?" he asked, and there was a strange note in his voice.

"I am an extremely busy woman, Mr. Conrad. I have little time for socializing. There are many orders I must complete before closing my business."

His brows rose. "You're leaving?"

"Yes."

"But, aren't you happy here?"

Clare hesitated. Hadn't the man any sensitivity? "Yes, very happy, but I feel it is time to move on."

"Where will you go?"

"Probably to London." As she said the words, Clare visualized that large metropolis with its millions of people, every one a stranger, and the endless searching for a position in a respectable establishment. Her mind shrank from the thought, yet how could she remain here?

"Why?" Mark Conrad asked and Clare looked up, bemused by her imaginings. What a ridiculous question. Surely he knew why she could no longer remain here, so close to the man with whom she had shared a night of passion.

"Need you ask such a question, Mr. Conrad? I would have thought my reason obvious. I have, even in this short time, achieved a small reputation. I—I have no desire to lose it." She was annoyed that her voice wavered slightly.

"Sit down, Miss Court. Let me bring this fire to life, then we will talk."

"We have nothing—" began Clare, but he was on his knees in front of the hearth, putting a flame to the small sticks and blowing them to life.

He glanced at her white face once. "Go and make a strong brew of tea. You are cold and your hair is damp. Change to slippers, too." He bent to the fire again.

There was a note of command in his voice, and since his words coincided with her own wish for hot tea and warmth, she obeyed.

Her slippers and comb were in the kitchen and there was

no point now in doing more than comb her damp curls and set the kettle to boil. When she returned to the living room with a tray of tea, Mark Conrad was on his feet, brushing his hands together. The fire was burning well. He took the tray from her and laid it on the side table.

"Sit down by the fire, Miss Court. I'll pour the tea. Do you take sugar?"

It was such an ordinary, domestic kind of question that Clare relaxed a little and sat in her sewing chair, leaving the couch to him, if he wished to sit. He did, and after placing a mug beside her, he sat cradling his own on the couch.

Clare stared into the flames and sipped her tea, waiting for him to speak. Was this thoughtfulness a prelude for certain conditions if she wished to stay in this cottage? He must have guessed she really didn't want to go to London. Who, in her right mind, would exchange this cottage and a flourishing trade to become a sewing apprentice in some garment workshop? She was quite untrained, had only her flair and expertise with the needle, both learned of necessity, and could produce no references from any previous employer.

Mark Conrad's voice startled her, although he spoke softly.

"Shall we be quite honest with each other, Miss Court?"

Clare shrugged. "Why not, since you are in a position of strength?"

"I doubt that very much, Miss Court. I feel the advantage is yours."

Clare looked at him, frowning. "Let's not fence, Mr. Conrad. I admit to being that girl in the barn, and I suppose you knew it all along. One word from you and my reputation is gone. You will be believed because your family is an old, established one. I am a stranger who appeared from nowhere."

Mark Conrad leaned forward. "The point I am trying to make is that my own advantage lies in us both remaining silent about that night."

"Don't men usually boast of such things?"

"Some might, but I am not one of them. I have no wish to hurt anyone, and other people could be involved if that episode came to light."

"Other people?"

"Sara, for instance, and I care greatly for her. My employer, Mr. Patterson, is a very straitlaced fellow and might deny me his house, and I have need to keep on the right side of him for personal reasons." His lips curved suddenly into a smile. "My old friend, Septimus, too. I'd be lower than bilge water in his eyes, for he thinks a great deal of you. And there's Mrs. Clark and your customers—so many people to consider. What do you say?"

Clare, her mind whirling, stared at him. Was she really to be freed from the burden of uncertainty?

"Are you saying that my reputation is safe and you will never speak of that night to anyone?"

"I swear to it, Miss Court, if you will return the compliment."

"Oh, I will, I will." Clare felt light-headed with relief. "Since we both have reasons to keep silent, you have my word on it, too." She eyed him for a moment. "You really mean it, don't you?"

"I mean it." He moved toward the door and Clare moved with him, no longer afraid of the revealing lamplight. With his hand on the knob he paused. "You didn't answer my question concerning Sara."

"Don't worry, Mr. Conrad. You will not come upon me in your house again." She gave him a thin smile. How like a man to have double standards, even if he was party to the indiscretion.

Conrad's hand dropped from the doorknob, the boat cloak fell to the floor, and he took her shoulders in a firm grip. His face was taut with anger.

"You misunderstand me entirely, Miss Clare Court. Do not judge me by other men. I do not forbid your association with Sara; in fact, I welcome it. She is a very reserved child, but has talked of nothing these past weeks save her friend, Clare. Since I am away so often at sea, I would take it as a kindness if you continued to befriend her. Did you suppose I would despise you after taking your innocence? I just thank God that no harm resulted from that action."

His face was so close to hers, his hands still imprisoning

her shoulders, that Clare felt an overwhelming longing to be gathered into his arms. She held herself rigid, trying to control her senses. He was thanking God for his release from the responsibility of fathering a bastard child. Any man would do the same, especially if the recipient of his favor did not figure in his future plans. It was crystal clear that she did not, save as companion to a lonely child.

"I second your thanks, Mr. Conrad," she said dryly. "It would not have been a happy situation for me, either."

"Then you will stay here in this cottage?"

Clare nodded, looking down. "As long as our bargain holds, Mr. Conrad."

"It will hold." He paused. "My name is Mark and yours is Clare. Does it not seem a little foolish to be so formal with each other? Can we not be friends, as well as partners to a bargain? For Sara's sake, shall we say?"

Clare raised her head. "Perhaps. I don't know."

"Well, at least we can seal the bargain in traditional fashion."

Clare was prepared for a handshake but not the kiss that took her unaware and left her weak and breathless. It had been firm, friendly, and quite without passion, yet it had set her pulses racing. Then the door had closed behind him and Mark Conrad was gone into the night.

Clare knew then, beyond all doubt, that she could never love any other man as she loved Mark Conrad, the passionate stranger she had met in a barn.

Clare saw nothing of Mark Conrad for several weeks after their talk in the cottage. He had no reason to call on her, she argued. Indeed, it might have precipitated the kind of gossip neither of them desired. And yet he had talked of friendship—a sop to his conscience, obviously. She tried to dismiss the man and his kiss from her mind. Good heavens, she had much more worthwhile things to think about, such as her increasing clientele.

Isobel Foster's summer wardrobe had been much admired by the young ladies of Clevedon and Clare's services were much in demand. Mothers of nubile girls, persuaded to visit the dressmaker in the small, whitewashed cottage, arrived, prepared to indulge their offsprings' quirks and patronize this sewing person. They left with the feeling that they themselves had been patronized—not overtly, but in subtle ways. Miss Court, it appeared, was not to be dismissed lightly. She listened gravely to every suggestion as to color, style, and fabric, then put forth her own ideas linked with the coloring, figure, and features of the girl to be dressed. There was no humility and desire to please in that soft, cultured voice and steady grey gaze. Neither would she be pressured into unreasonable haste. Two fittings for each garment was her rule. Here Miss Court smiled gently and with only the slightest hint of reproof in her voice stated that inner seams and hems were quite as important in the finished garment as those the eye could see.

Over mugs of tea in the farmhouse kitchen, Clare told amusing stories about her clients to Mrs. Clark.

"I would as soon the girls came alone, for we should get on famously, but naturally, they must be chaperoned. Why do these fond mamas think it necessary to have their girls festooned like Christmas trees? Such a frothing of bows and frills draws attention away from the girl herself."

Mrs. Clark chuckled. "Some wear their wealth on their backs, my dear, like a sign to let the world know how rich they are."

Clare smiled. "I shouldn't be critical, since they pay well."

"And you make their girls look elegant and ladylike," commented Mrs. Clark. "That's worth paying for, in my opinion, if it's something not born to them."

As Mrs. Clark refilled her mug, Clare asked after the girls.

"They're fine, miss. Getting on well at school."

"Oh, and I forgot, what happened to the boy?"

"That young Albert Smith? Given up the sea, he says, and he all of twelve." She chuckled. "Took one look, he did, at the two plough horses, and decided to become a farmer instead. Mr. Clark has taken him on for his bed and board, just to see how he frames the while. For all he's a skinny lad, he's the wiry sort."

"I expect the girls are pleased."

"They are, indeed—as proud as peacocks. You'd think they'd fished the lad out of the water themselves and brought him back to life." She paused. "I met Mrs. Winter in the grocer's the other day. It seems you made quite an impression on her when you went to tea with Sara."

"A good one, I hope," Clare said, feeling her cheeks grow warm. She lowered her head and sipped her tea, trying to forget the events following the tea party. With her eyes downcast, Clare asked the question that had been teasing her mind. Her voice came casually. "What was Sara's mother like? Sara seems not to remember her."

"No. The poor mite was only a baby when Mr. Mark brought her here. I imagine she gets those greenish eyes and light hair from her mother, though there's no doubting she has the Conrad bones."

Clare looked up. "You imagine? Didn't you ever see Mrs. Conrad?"

Mrs. Clark shook her head. "Mr. Mark didn't live here until he came into Conrad Place when his father died. Here as a boy, of course, but took to the sea early." She pursed her lips. "Old Mr. Conrad rather let the place go; more's the pity."

"Really? It looked remarkably well cared for when I saw it."

"It was Mr. Mark who brought it around when he came to live there with Sara."

"On the pay of a first mate?" Clare could not resist saying. "Mr. Patterson must be a generous employer."

"He gets his money's worth. Mr. Mark is a fine seaman and he won't be a first mate for long, you mark my words."

As Clare's income and trade increased, she invested in a tailor's dummy on which to hang the gowns, enabling her to stand back and eye her creation critically. In the absence of a human form, it helped her see just how the gown hung. In addition, she bought an attractive walnut bureau to set under the window. On its drop front she could write her accounts, make out bills, and, more useful than ever, keep notes of her clients—their sizes, previous garments made, preferences, and personal comments of her own.

Mrs. Clark had said, laughingly, that Miss Court might soon outgrow the cottage—wish to take on staff and move to a larger establishment. But Clare had grown to love the long, low-beamed living room, the square kitchen with its large, black-leaded cooking range, the neat bedroom and convenient dressing room. It was her first real home, snug and secure from the world, and its views were magnificent. Unless given notice or the cottage was required to house a married daughter, she would remain a permanent fixture, she had replied, much to Mrs. Clark's delight.

Clare, sewing by her open window, smiled as she recalled the conversation. How lucky she had been that day to come upon Sara in that tree. It was as if her whole life had only started then and she could forget her father, Lord Rayne, and the fate that had only been averted by an overheard remark.

The rumble of carriage wheels drew her mind back to the present. Isobel Foster, her first and most favored customer, was due to call and collect two fine velvet gowns to prepare for late-summer events. Clare laid aside her sewing and moved to the door, casting a swift look into the gilt-framed looking glass. It was another new purchase, but worth the money, for it gave her time to pin back any curl that strayed from her chignon before opening the door.

The knocker sounded and Clare opened the door, seeing Isobel Foster—not the radiant Isobel of their previous meetings, but a reversion to the girl she had first met, slumped shoulders and all.

"Do come in, Miss Foster," Clare said, stepping back and smiling.

What had happened to the girl who had walked straight and proud, supremely confident in her new style of dress? The clothes were the same; it was the girl herself who was lackluster.

As Isobel passed her, Clare saw the man hard on Isobel's heels. Of medium height, he was stocky with a pale, rather petulant face. He walked by Clare without looking at her, crossed the room, and flung himself down on the couch. Clare felt an upsurge of anger at his lack of manners and glanced at Isobel. The girl was fiddling with her bonnet strings, a look of utter dejection on her face.

Clare moved toward the couch and stared down stonily at the young man's upturned face. "Won't you be seated, Mr.—?" She raised her brows haughtily.

A red flush welled up into the pale face. He glared. "Mr. Palmer is my name, and I am already seated."

"I meant outside, Mr. Palmer," Clare said in her coldest tone. "You are in my private sitting room."

"Well, what about it?" There was an edge of bluster to his voice.

"I do not recall giving you permission to enter my house, let alone make yourself at home on my couch."

He tried to outstare her, but Clare was well-used to holding a client's gaze. She stood quite still until his dropped. He hauled himself to his feet, muttered something that sounded like "damned upstart dressmakers," and strode to the door. He turned and fixed Clare with a venomous look.

"Don't be long about it," he added to Isobel. "I've no mind to nursemaid you to your sewing wench." He went out, slamming the door.

Isobel turned her brimming eyes on Clare. "I'm so sorry. Mama said it would be quite seemly to further our acquaintance —in an open carriage, of course."

"Come into the kitchen, Miss Foster. We both need a strong cup of tea."

"But he will expect—" She darted an anxious look at the door.

Clare smiled and went into the kitchen to set the kettle on the stove. "That young man needs a lesson in manners, if you don't mind me saying so."

Isobel had followed her, and now she sank into a kitchen chair, her elbows on the table. She remained silent while Clare made the tea and sat down opposite her.

"What has happened to you, Miss Foster? You seem almost afraid of that man. Are you betrothed to him, by any chance?"

Isobel wiped her eyes and took a sip of tea. "Mama thinks him a good match."

"Is he rich?"

"Very." The girl was recovering. "Mines and factories."

"Does being rich excuse bad manners?"

Isobel gave her an uncomfortable look. "He's polite enough with Mama, but he thinks—" She faltered, and stared into her tea.

"I know. Servants and dressmakers are unworthy of his politeness." She began to laugh. "Don't be distressed, Miss Foster. I can take care of myself."

Isobel broke into a sudden giggle. "If he could have seen his own face when you ordered him out. He is quite unused to being ordered; it is usually the other way about."

"Then I hope you will refuse him if he proposes. A man may order his wife about in any way he chooses."

Isobel sighed. "I don't care for him at all, Miss Court, but Mama is so strong-minded."

"But, my dear girl, don't you see that you have the advantage?"

Isobel raised startled eyes. "In what way?"

"No one can force you to walk down the aisle with someone you dislike. Good heavens, this is not the Middle Ages!" Clare rose to her feet and took Isobel's hand. "Come with me, Miss Foster. I want you to see something."

She led Isobel to the cheval glass and stood her before it. "Now, tell me what you see."

Isobel gave her a bewildered look. "Only myself."

"Exactly. See those drooping shoulders, those miserable eyes? They remind me of the girl I first met. What happened to that elegant, straight-backed young lady who walked like a queen into her coming-out ball?"

Isobel smiled and pulled back her shoulders. "How I wish I had your self-confidence, Miss Court. It just isn't in me to flout Mama."

"Doesn't she want you to be happy? I cannot see you being so with that young man outside. Surely you met others at your ball?"

"Oh, yes, but none as rich as Mr. Palmer."

Clare sighed. "Well, it is not my place to pass comment on Clevedon society, being merely—as your friend said—a sewing wench, but it seems to lack an element of romance."

To her surprise, Isobel's cheeks became pink. She darted a quick look at Clare. "I did meet a most charming man— not at my party, but at a picnic. We have met a time or two, but I dare not tell Mama, for he admits quite cheerfully that he cannot compete in the fortune stakes."

"But you like him, nevertheless?"

Isobel nodded, her face transformed. "He is so kind and gentle. He makes me forget how serious life is, for he jokes about it all the time."

"He sounds an excellent young man. What does he do— for a living, I mean?"

"He farms, he says. Can you imagine Mama considering a farmer?" she finished bitterly.

"Hard to imagine," Clare agreed. "Shall we start the fitting now?"

"Oh, my goodness, yes. I had quite forgotten Mr. Palmer with telling you of Perry."

One of the dresses fit perfectly. The other required a small alteration. Clare promised to attend to it immediately and bring it over to the Foster house that evening.

"No such thing," Isobel said firmly. "I will send the coach for it after Papa gets home at six o'clock. Will that be all right? I shan't need the dress in a hurry."

"Thank you. That is a kind thought." Clare laid the completed dress in a box and packed it carefully into tissue paper.

As Isobel put on her bonnet, Clare opened the door. "I will carry this box to the carriage. I doubt your escort will lower himself to take it from me."

Isobel grimaced. "He would consider it that way, but Perry would not."

Clare paused in the doorway. "I should rather like to meet that estimable young man."

There was an eager glow in Isobel's eyes. "Would you

really? It would be lovely to talk to him here, without feeling that every eye in Clevedon was upon us. People do watch so.''

"Then I will invite you both to tea, on any day of your choosing. I will chaperon you as strictly as any maiden aunt.''

They walked out of the cottage to find Mr. Palmer lounging on the bench beyond the door. He rose slowly, a scowl on his face.

"A deuced long time I've been kicking my heels—'' he began, but Isobel, her mind obviously dwelling on the delights of Clare's invitation, broke in.

"Don't be such a bear, George, and take that box from Miss Court. If you drop it, I'll never speak to you again.''

Clare held out the box to him and he took it automatically, bemused for a second by Isobel's crisp words. He stared at the box, then looked at Clare, his scowl deepening.

Clare gave him a cool smile. "How kind. Thank you, Mr.—er—Farmer, was it?''

His scowl deepened further. "Palmer!'' he snarled. "Mr. Palmer,'' but Clare had turned away and Isobel was climbing into the carriage.

"Do hurry, George,'' Isobel called imperiously. "You were the one complaining about time, and now you stand there like a statue, as if we had all the time in the world.''

As Clare moved into her doorway, out of sight of Mr. Palmer, she shot Isobel a laughing look and nodded approvingly.

"Thank you so much, Miss Court,'' Isobel returned gaily. "The coachman will come for that dress about half-past six.''

As they swept away, Isobel waved, but George Palmer did not turn his head.

Clare went into the cottage, still smiling, and slid the dress onto her tailor's dummy. The problem was soon corrected and Clare folded the dress, wrapped it, and laid it on the hall table for collection later. Since there was nothing of great urgency to be completed, Clare decided to take a walk—not down to the farm or up to the Conrads', but over the field to

where she could see the bay. She liked the solitude and the
immensity of sea and sky. It was good to feel the breeze
refreshing her mind and body. On the headland she sat, her
chin on drawn-up knees. The swell of the ocean, surging up
the estuary to Bristol, was soothing, almost hypnotic in its
magnificence, and yet it had swept the *Venturer* to a violent
death. Did those men of the sea both love and hate the oceans
of the world?

She looked down into the sheltered cove of the bay. Did
Mark Conrad tie up his boat there? Not the Patterson line
ship, of course, but the one Sara had told her of—the one
named after her. Narrowing her eyes, she examined the few
craft drawn up in the cove. Men were moving about down
there—Mark Conrad and Septimus Thomas perhaps, getting
the boat shipshape.

Clare shook her head. Why did her every thought come
back to Mark Conrad? Her heart knew the answer and her
mind acknowledged it, too. Why dwell on it? Hadn't he
made it quite plain that for personal reasons he needed her
silence?

The breeze was cooling now and Clare rose with a shiver.
The sun was turning a dusky red and clouds were building
up on the horizon. How long had she been sitting here?
Joseph, the Foster coachman, might well be at the cottage
already. She had several fields to cross, and if this was not
the beginning of twilight, it must therefore be the buildup to
a summer storm. Whichever it was, she had to hasten back.
The sea looked flat calm but held a milky sheen on its surface.
Her last glance showed boats being hauled inshore, a precaution in either event.

Clare walked quickly, climbing stiles and shortcutting
through copses to avoid the longer way by road. She saw the
carriage drawn up at her front door. It must be half-past six
then, for Joseph was always a prompt man. She liked Joseph.
He was always pleasant and polite. He treated her with deference and was never annoyed at being kept waiting. If she
were engaged in some intricate decoration, he would grin
cheerfully and reassure her that his life as a coachman was

made up of waiting, and could he be making her a nice cup
of tea?

She had always answered his grin with a wave of the hand
toward the kitchen, declaring there was nothing she'd like
more and bidding him take a cup himself, which was exactly
why Joseph had offered in the first place.

There was no sign of Joseph's sturdy figure by the horses'
heads or on the box seat. The bench beyond the door held
no figure, either. She glanced about in the half gloom and
noticed that her front door stood wide. She knew she had not
left it so. It was unlike Joseph to enter unbidden. He had
always shown her the courtesy of waiting for an invitation.
Perhaps he had arrived early and taken the liberty of putting
the kettle on in anticipation of her arrival. In view of the
threat of rain, it was a kind thought, but still a liberty that
she must discourage in the kindest way possible. For the sake
of her reputation, she could not have any man—even
Joseph—making free with her kitchen.

At the door, she paused. The hall lamp showed no glow.
Had the day been lighter when he had arrived? She entered
the cottage and looked toward the kitchen door. It was closed.
*He may even now be lighting the lamp to see what he is
doing*, she thought.

"Joseph?" she called. "Are you in the kitchen?" She
moved to the kitchen door and pushed it open. The room was
dark and deserted.

A slight creaking sound brought her head around sharply.
The carriage was outside, things should be normal, but she
knew with a rush of panic that something was wrong. *Run,
run*, her mind screamed, *run while you can. Something or
somebody is here, lurking in the dark. Light the lamp, face
it—no, no, there isn't time. Run, run!* She swung about,
giving in to the instincts of a trapped animal. The front door?
The room was dark, but escape lay in the rectangle of grey-
ness.

She sprang forward, urged on into mindless terror by a
harsher creak and a quick succession of dull thuds. She was
almost at the door when an arm caught her about the throat,

choking off her scream. She was jerked back, arms pinioned,
and in a half daze, found herself dragged across the living
room.

The arm left her throat and she dragged in a deep breath.
The odor of sweat and wine was in her nostrils and she gasped,
recoiling instinctively. Fingers bit into her shoulders, then
pushed her backwards with a violent gesture. Clare felt herself
falling, but not to the floor. Her own couch caught her and
she lay still for a moment, gasping air into her lungs. Then
she tried to struggle upright. Her action was halted by the
flat of a hand striking her on the side of her face. The force
of the blow jerked her head sideways, but a backhanded slap
on her other cheek spun her head around in the opposite
direction.

She raised her hands and tried to protect herself, but both
wrists were gripped and the blows continued. Her mind was
dizzied by the strength of the attack and she tried to scream,
but the blows took her breath.

"Show me the door, would you!" a voice hissed. "Me,
who could buy the best whore in town. Come the haughty
with me, would you? A puffed-up sewing wench ordering
me about, pretending to forget my name. You'll not forget
it again. You'll have good reason to remember this, and not
be a ha'penny richer for it, do you hear?"

Clare barely heard for the singing in her head. She felt
faint and sick, but recognized the voice of her assailant, which
went on and on, spilling venom and gutter language in a mad
tirade. His hands stilled their slapping only to drag and pull
at the fabric of her dress, ripping and tearing it like some
maddened beast.

◆ *Chapter Fourteen* ◆

Clare longed for oblivion to wipe out the nightmare, but although she felt deathly sick with pain and shock, her mind refused to let her sink into blackness. As loudly as it had screamed run, run, before, it now screamed fight—fight this animal whose claws were dragging at her skin. Her mind sharpened, a surge of heat ran through her body, bringing unknown strength, and she began to fight back. Whore, she was not, and this coarse, foul-tongued creature would not use her as such.

His large head loomed over her, and she brought up both of her hands, fingers curved into claws, and raked savagely at his cheeks. Droplets of blood splashed her own face as he reared back, mouthing obscenities. Clare's heart leapt with mixed revulsion and pleasure. Her fingers bunched into fists, and with all her force, she drove them forward into his face. Her knuckles jarred on his cheekbone and he grunted with pain. A slight relaxing of his heavy weight allowed Clare to half drag herself away and take in a deep, gulping breath. Her mouth opened in a scream but two thick hands caught at her throat and squeezed. The scream was choked as the pressure increased. Clare writhed, flailed arms and legs, but the fingers pressed harder. An agonizing pain tore at her chest; her head seemed to swell and float away. Through bulging, wide-stretched eyes she saw lights—red and yellow—flash, explode, and re-form into one large, glowing ball. Her head fell back, and lolled on the cushion of the couch.

Somehow, the pain in her chest was not so bad. Her head had come back to her shoulders and, strangest of all, she could breathe. It was a great effort to lift her eyelids, for the glowing ball of light was still behind her lids. It was still there when her eyes were fully open. Her gaze rested upon it without immediate comprehension; then, it assumed the shape of a lantern. She did not possess such a lantern, yet it stood beside her own oil lamp on the hall table. Yes, the oil lamp was hers—or, at least, Mrs. Clark's. She stared hard at the lantern. If she closed her eyes it would go away. At the moment, she felt too ill to focus on anything.

She was very cold and her body insisted on trembling. She knew she must make a fire and put on the kettle for a hot drink, but somehow, her limbs refused her brain's command. There was something else, too—thudding and grunting noises outside. At least her ears were working. Men's voices were growling and swearing between each thud. Then there was a heavier thud than before, the sound of a slap, then a clattering of hooves. Had he taken the gown for Miss Foster? Who? Joseph, of course. No, no, it hadn't been Joseph, it had been—her mind jerked back into full consciousness, yet her body was rigidly unmoving.

He was back—that wild animal—and this time, he would carry out his threat. *Fool, fool*, she cried to herself. *Why did I not have the sense to lock the door before he came back.* There had been time. Now the dark shape bulked in the doorway and he was locking the door!

Move, damn you, move, she told her flaccid limbs, but their response was only sufficient to roll her off the couch. Her outstretched fingers touched metal. Yes, thank God. She clawed the object toward her. Her hand closed about the head of the poker. On her knees now she turned, gripping the weapon, sucking in her breath to scream and scream like the madwoman she was.

The figure stopped short of her and dropped to its knees. "No, no, Miss Court—not the poker, please. You've no need to scream, either. You are quite safe."

Clare blinked and stared. The voice had been gentle, soothing. It belonged to Mark Conrad.

The poker dropped with a clatter to the hearth. Clare gave a muffled whimper and covered her eyes with her hands. Tears trickled through her fingers and her breathing became ragged. Tearing sobs shook her body and she collapsed onto the rug, huddling herself into a small, vibrating bundle.

Mark Conrad regarded her in silence for a moment, unsure of his next move. She had dropped the poker, thankfully, but might still tear at him if he attempted to touch her. What would he have done if this distress had been Sara's? Take her in his arms, talk soothingly while he carried her to bed? This was no child, but a silly girl who must have asked for what she had received from that lout, George Palmer. Pity mixed with his irritation. Hadn't she been long enough in the world, a girl alone, to recognize the varying natures of men? Still, he was glad that he had happened to be passing at the time.

He rose to his feet. She could not be left in this state, that was obvious. He opened the door to her bedroom, drew the curtains, lit the bedside lamp, and turned down the bed covers. Then he went into the kitchen and set the kettle to boil. He hadn't seen her face clearly, but a towel and bowl of hot water might be needed.

When he returned to the living room she still lay on the rug, but now the tearing sobs had lessened. He went down on one knee beside her and spoke as if to Sara. "Come, my dear, let me help you to bed. Don't cry so, there's a good girl. The sun will come up again tomorrow, and you'll wonder what all the fuss was about."

He scooped her up into his arms, pondering ruefully on the inanity of his words. This was not a child who had taken a bad fall but a young woman attacked by a man with rape in mind. He was surprised at her lightness. Her body still shook but she made no resistance. He carried her into the bedroom and laid her down. Illuminated now in the glow of the bedside lamp, he bit back a gasp of shock as he looked down. Where her skin was not ashen, it was red-streaked and swollen. Her lips and cheeks were puffy. His gaze moved down to the torn bodice of the light fabric of her dress. The fingers ripping the dress almost to the waist had left red weals, as if the fingernails had been used in a deliberately vicious way. His lips tightened into a straight line as he removed her shoes and drew the sheet up to her neck. He walked out of the room.

A few moments later he returned, carrying a bowl of warm water, and set it beside the lamp. His gaze noted the door beyond the bed. Towels and cloths were in there, without a doubt.

Clare's eyes were open when he came out, a towel draped

over his arm and a facecloth in his hand. Her gaze was strangely incurious, he thought, uneasily. Well, it would be easier to do what he had to do if she was still in a state of shock.

Sitting on the bedside, he tucked the towel about her neck and proceeded to wipe her face gently. "You're lucky," he said conversationally. "The skin of your face is unbroken, and with a cold compress later, the swelling should go down. You were not so lucky below your neck, for your skin is scored and your dress ruined. But those scratches will not be seen when you wear another dress." His eyes narrowed on her neck as he slowly drew down the sheet. "You'd do well to wear a light scarf for a day or two. Your throat is bruised. Do you feel strong enough to sit up and remove your dress?"

Clare obeyed without comment and Mark bathed the scratches between her breasts. He frowned in concentration but was all too aware of the young breasts, pink tips showing through the light shift. Every few seconds they rose in a convulsive jerk as a tremor ran through her body. Drawing up the sheet, he quelled the memory of those breasts lying in the palms of his hands that mad night in the barn. This sweet body had been his for the taking and he had taken it. No, not quite taken, but accepted with an abandoned joy. Yet she had been no harlot, but an untouched girl. What had she become since that night? He frowned again and rose with the bowl.

"I will bring you cold cloths to lay on your face." His voice sounded curt in his ears as he looked at her. Her eyes had clouded over and he regretted his tone.

"Don't start to cry again," he said more gently, "or you'll undo all my good work. Here, take the towel. It will help you keep afloat."

Clare pressed the towel to her eyes, trying to stem her tears. Mark Conrad's curtness suggested that he might do the same for any lame dog or an injured seaman. It was a duty to be performed by the nearest at hand, impersonally and without emotion.

Clare laid her head back on the pillow. Thank God Mark Conrad had been nearest at hand. A child or stranger seeing a darkened cottage might have passed straight by. What had made him investigate? She had not had the breath to scream. He came into the room then, carrying two mugs of steaming liquid. He set one on the bedside table and stood with his own.

"Th—thank you," said Clare, blinking hard against her tears. "I am so very cold. This is most kind of you."

"Cold?" He looked about. "Do you have extra blankets somewhere? I can get them."

"In the top of the wardrobe, if you would be so kind."

He spread two blankets over her and picked up his mug again. "Don't keep thanking me for being kind. I am, in fact, rather angry with you."

"I'm sorry, but—but you have been kind and I appreciate it, nevertheless."

Mark sipped his tea and eyed the girl in the bed. "How long have you been acquainted with George Palmer? It's none of my business, but I confess to curiosity."

"I met him only today."

Mark's dark brows shot up. "Only today?" His lips seem to twist into a sardonic line. "And you entertain him in your sitting room before nightfall? At least, I assume you expected entertainment but got more than you bargained for."

Clare stared at him, appalled by the conclusion he had drawn. She licked her swollen lips and steadied her mind.

"You assume incorrectly, Mr. Conrad. He escorted Miss Isobel Foster here for a dress fitting earlier. I did not invite him to call this evening."

"Well, he did call and you obviously let him in."

Clare's head moved tiredly. "No, that was not the way of it. One dress needed a slight alteration. Miss Foster said she would send for it."

"And sent George Palmer?"

"No. She said Joseph, her coachman, would call. It was Joseph I expected."

"That doesn't explain why George Palmer was in your sitting room, wrestling with you on the couch. Had you changed your mind after offering him temptation?"

"Mr. Conrad, I thank you again for helping me, but that

does not give you the right to insult me." She turned her head away and tried to keep herself from shaking.

The bed sagged behind her. Mark Conrad's arms reached out and took her in an embrace. "I'm sorry. Forgive me, Clare. The fellow's such a crude oaf, I could not bear the thought of you and him—" His voice trailed away as he held her against his chest. "Tell me what happened, please."

Clare raised her eyes to the intent, dark face. Even under these circumstances she could feel her heartbeat quicken. Whatever he said or did, she loved him.

"I—I was out, taking a walk. I wasn't in the cottage at all. When it began to grow dark and look like rain, I hurried home. The carriage was outside. I thought Joseph must have gone to the kitchen—"

"The kitchen? Why would the coachman do that?"

"It's a sort of joke we have. He's a very nice person and most respectful. If I haven't quite finished the garment he has come to collect, he always offers to make me a nice cup of tea. It's because he wants one, too, and I see no harm in it."

Mark nodded. "I believe I know the coachman you mean—a good, sturdy fellow. So, you thought he was in the kitchen. But your cottage was in darkness. Why had he not lit the lamp?"

"I believed he had arrived before the skies went so dark and had not needed to. I was a little puzzled that he had gone in without invitation, for he is never presumptuous, but the kitchen was empty. I cannot understand why Joseph did not come at all to collect the dress."

Mark was silent for a moment, absently stroking her hair. "I begin to smell a bilge-water rat in this. Palmer took his place on some pretext and let himself into the cottage to lie in wait for your return." He looked down into Clare's grey eyes. "Had you made yourself agreeable to him when Isobel Foster came?"

Clare managed a tremulous laugh. "On the contrary. I reproved him for entering and seating himself without a glance at me. And since I have only the one room for fitting, I asked him to wait outside."

A deep laugh rumbled in Mark's throat. "So, it was revenge he sought."

"You sound amused," Clare said, shivering. "What if he comes back?"

"He won't." Mark's tone was so final that she stared at him.

"How do you know?"

"George Palmer will be in no state to show his face anywhere."

Clare looked more closely at Mark. One eyebrow appeared a little out of true and there was a reddish tinge on one cheekbone. Her eyes widened and she gasped. "Of course —you fought him. I was aware of vague noises outside. Oh, Mark!" Her fingers smoothed his face gently. "Oh, Mark," she said again, her voice a whisper. "You might have been badly hurt, and it would have all been my fault."

"Not a bit of it," Mark said cheerfully. "I'm a hard, rough seaman and Palmer's a well-fed landsman with muscles like porridge." He took her hand and touched the palm to his lips for a moment. "Hold to your first impression of me, my dear—a heavy-handed first mate. Isn't that how you saw me?"

"Yes, I suppose it was, but I know you differently now."

"Tell me." The blue eyes regarded her with amusement over the tea mug.

"You're from an old and respected family. You have very good taste in house furnishings, and your daughter adores you. So does Septimus Thomas."

Mark grinned. "So I can't be such a rascal with those things to commend me." His grin faded. "Even so, my dear, I intend to bring around the family fortunes by any means within my grasp. I have plans from which I will not deviate."

"I understand that." Clare held the cold cloths to her face. Her lips felt less swollen. With luck, she would look normal tomorrow. "I have my own plans, too—my very own, and not those dictated to me by others." Her eyes looked unseeingly into his for a moment and Mark caught the bitterness in her voice.

"So," he said carefully. "The night we met, you were avoiding those dictates by running away."

"Yes."

"Do you regret what happened?"

"Oh, no, not in the least." Her expression was one that Mark had never seen before. There was something of cynicism and satisfaction in it. "What I do not possess can no longer be taken from me."

Mark shook his head. "I do not pretend to understand you, but we will talk no more on delicate subjects. Are you well enough to be left?"

"Thank you, yes." Clare felt a cold dejection at the thought. She didn't want him to go, but of course he must. She forced a smile.

"Don't forget to bathe your own face before presenting yourself at the dinner table. Sara will be sure to ask how you won your bruises."

Mark smiled back. "A bruise on a seaman is no cause for comment. It's a hazard that goes with the occupation." He stared down into the grey eyes, so large and luminous. It was like looking into the heart of the sea on a moonlit night, seeing only the sheen of grey but knowing that depths of turbulence and mystery lay beneath, quiescent one moment then erupting into savagery the next. The girl was like the sea, he thought—one face prim with dignity, the obverse that wild, passionate creature in the barn. His heart gave a sudden lurch and he was swept into a tenderness he had never known for a woman. He loved Sara, but this girl brought out his protective instinct, a longing for that abandonment he had experienced just once on that stormy night.

He bent and took her face between both hands. "Clare, will you promise me something?"

"Of course. Anything."

"Lock your door when you are away from home and keep it locked every night. It was by chance I saw the carriage and wondered why your cottage was in darkness. You are a girl alone. Take no chances, my dear."

"You don't suppose George Palmer will—"

"No, no, I'm sure he won't. He'll be lying low with two

black eyes and a loss of dignity. Do you know, I doubt he even knew who hit him, but he'll walk warily in future. You will heed my warning, won't you?''

"I promise. I would not want to put you in this position again.''

"It's your position I am thinking of, not mine. I can take care of myself." He leaned down impulsively and kissed her full on the mouth.

He remembered with startling clarity the soft, yielding warmth of her lips and the feel of her body that night. Then his arms went about her and he pulled her close. Clare's hands slid around his neck and she was answering his kisses. Time seemed to roll away, as if nothing had happened between that night and this. It was a continuation of their wild lovemaking, joining past with present.

The blankets covering Clare's previously chilled body fell to the floor, together with Mark's shirt and breeches. She was no longer cold but hot with desire, completely lost in a world where only Mark's body had any reality. How could she deny that at this moment, George Harcourt's sensual nature was part of her—the part of her she had striven to suppress? And yet she gloried in the strength of Mark's loving, his care of her even in the height of their passion. There was strength but no brutality, a tenderness that was not lustful. His lips did not bruise nor his fingers bite into her soft flesh.

All the vague longings of her life since she had run from Philip Rayne were answered in the caresses of Mark Conrad. For her there could be no other, but for him, what? As they lay still clasped in each other's arms, Clare's mind came back to the real world—to those words he had spoken, those plans from which there was to be no deviation. She touched his face gently and smiled into the blue eyes so close to hers. They held a bemused look, as if wondering how he had come to be lying in her bed.

"Though your head lies on my pillow, dear Mark," Clare said softly, "it is in no sense a way to retrieve your family fortunes.''

The blue eyes lost their bemused look and clouded over. "I am a fool, Clare! But a very nice fool.''

He smiled ruefully. "I resolved not to have this happen again. Why did you let me?"

She laughed. "So, now I am to blame. Your defense must be that I tempted you, like Eve."

Mark's face suddenly came alert. "Eve? Dear God, what am I doing?"

Clare looked at him curiously. "Doesn't Adam usually excuse himself that way?"

"What?" He swung his legs over the side of the bed. "You don't understand, my dear. I wouldn't hurt you for the world, but why must you be so irresistible?"

Clare sat up and ran her fingers lightly down the strong, brown back. "There is nothing with which you need reproach yourself, Mark. I was a more than willing party to this deed, but I seek no profit from it. You have that much trust in me, don't you?"

Mark turned to look at her. "Yes, my dear." He reached for her hand and held her fingers to his lips. "I would trust you with my life."

"Then you have nothing to fear. I know you have plans and I wish you luck."

Mark's brows rose in question. "You know of my plans?"

"Some inkling only," Clare admitted. "But enough to know that if you set your mind to it, you will succeed. How else may you restore the family fortune?"

Mark was dressing slowly as she spoke and he looked up from buckling the belt of his breeches. Clare was kneeling naked on the bed, her hair a mass of tangled curls. Her cheeks were flushed, her eyes wide and luminous. Mark's gaze moved over her and he smiled in such a way that Clare's heart twisted with love.

"Your likeness should be carved in oak and set on the prow of a ship—my ship, and the flagship at that. I give you my word on that, my sweet Clare."

He turned and moved from the bedroom. Clare heard the front door close very quietly and Mark Conrad was gone from her cottage.

◆ *Chapter Fifteen* ◆

Clare woke to a fine, sunny day that accorded well with her mood. Before rising, she turned her head and smiled at the imprint of Mark Conrad's body on the sheet. Even the thought of him lifted her heart. She slid from the bed and padded into her small dressing room. Anxiously, she scanned her face in the glass, then sighed with relief. His quick action with the cold compresses had halted the swelling on her face. That, and his quicker action in pulling George Palmer away from her, gave her cause for gratitude.

A wry smile reflected back at her. Did a lady express her gratitude in total surrender of her body? She had no clear recollection of how it had happened, save that it had and she was not in the least bit sorry. She shrugged and poured water into the basin. Perhaps she was a wanton at heart and there was more of her father in her than she knew. All she did know was that Mark Conrad would never be repulsed, even if he came night after night.

As she dressed and brushed her hair, pinning it tightly into a knot, she realized that Mark Conrad would, for his own sake and the plans he had, steer a safe course in the future. And for her sake, too, for there would be two reputations at hazard if it became known that he and the dressmaker were lovers. Steam engines in ships, Sara had said. Well, to achieve that improbable dream, Mark Conrad, who had little money of his own, would have to persuade his employer or any likely sponsor to invest in the project for future gain, if such was possible.

As she passed through the living room into the kitchen, the memory of Isobel Foster's dress flashed through her mind. The sideboard was empty. She stood for a moment in thought. George Palmer must have tossed the parcel into the carriage before returning to lie in wait for her. She was glad he had taken it, and no doubt he was, too, she reflected cynically.

Had the dress remained on the sideboard, Miss Foster would surely have asked why it hadn't been collected. She decided she could dismiss George Palmer from her mind. It was unlikely he would come again, even as escort for Isobel Foster.

By teatime, Clare had completed several commissions and they lay, neatly wrapped and labeled, along the top of the sideboard. She was tempted to take a walk across the fields to look down into the harbor, and get a breath of air before putting the kettle on for tea. Remembering Mark's words, she locked the cottage door and slipped the key into the pocket of her skirt. As she skirted the lane, she saw the stocky, rolling figure of Septimus Thomas heading toward the harbor.

"Sep," she called. He looked back over his shoulder.

His leathery, bristled face broke into a grin. "Why, miss, would we be going in the same direction?"

She caught up with him. "Well, that depends where you're heading, doesn't it?"

"I've set my course for the harbor, miss, and I mean to lie to for a spell and watch the *Dolphin* weigh anchor."

"Where is she off to this time?" Clare hoped her voice sounded casual. Mark Conrad would be on board.

"Just up to the Clyde with a cargo for Glasgow." He lifted his face to the sky, then slanted a sideways look of unholy glee at Clare. "Wind's against her. She'll be tacking all down the estuary, and if he don't get his feet wet, then I'm a Dutchman."

Clare glanced at him, her lips twitching. "Septimus Thomas, you have the look of a dog who expects a haunch of venison to come his way. Do you expect the *Dolphin* to make heavy weather out of the harbor?"

Sep grinned. "Why, miss, you're picking up the lingo." He winked. "There's heavy weather and heavy weather, if you take my meaning, but it's all one to the captain."

"I'm not sure that I do take your meaning. I thought you considered Mr. Conrad a fine sailor, whatever the conditions."

"Bless you, miss, and so I do. If Cap'n Mark took her out, she'd go as smooth as silk and waltz through it like a ballerina. But he's not."

"Who is, then?" As she caught the sly twinkle in Sep's eye, she knew who was taking the *Dolphin* out. "That elegant Captain Oliver?"

Sep's lips pursed as if he would like to spit, but he collected himself in time and grinned instead.

"Aye, miss, that's the fellow. It'll be a rare show, I tell you."

"You have little faith in Captain Oliver, Sep. I believe you are set against him only because he outranks your friend."

"Maybe, miss, but the fellow's a landlubber at heart, and he's no taste for grog, would you believe?"

There was such outrage in his voice that Clare could not help laughing. "If by grog you mean rum, then I shall take his side, Septimus Thomas. If the taste is anything like the smell, I would as soon have a cup of tea."

"Only natural, miss, you being a lady and all, but a drop of Nelson's blood puts fire into a man's belly. See, miss, the *Dolphin*'s letting go. She'll be off on the next swell."

He hurried to the harbor wall and Clare joined him. She wondered why Mark Conrad was not on board for this trip, but nothing would have made her ask Sep. They stood, elbows on the wall, just as they had done the time before when Mark had forced an introduction. Her heart quickened at the memory of how far that introduction had progressed. An introduction, yes, but not their first meeting. She pushed the thought aside and concentrated on the *Dolphin*.

There was Captain William Oliver, scowling from the bridge—slender, fair-haired, clad in dark blue broadcloth. On the sleeves of his jacket he wore the gold braid rings of a captain. He was hatless, having decided, she supposed, that his gold-trimmed tricorne would be safer below. The handsome, slightly discontented face turned this way and that, watching the seamen's actions closely.

"Sep, you said Captain Oliver was a landsman at heart. Why does he choose to sail?"

"He's no choice in it, miss, if he wants to keep on the right side of Mr. Patterson, who owns the line. 'Tis his uncle, see, and that young middie's looking for a share in the business. Old Patterson only has a daughter. The old man served his time on a merchantman and'll have no one taking his place without knowing a thing or two about sailing."

"Oh, I see. The *Dolphin* is by way of being a carrot dangled before the eyes of Mr. Oliver."

"That's the size of it, miss. Would you look at that now. She's swinging too hard to port. The lads are fending her off the dockside with boat hooks."

"You're enjoying this, Sep," Clare accused. "I believe you'd like to see the *Dolphin* take out the dock wall."

"Oh, no, miss. I wouldn't want a lick of paint taken off her." He turned a look of innocence on Clare. "The lads would get the blame, for sure." His innocence changed to contemplation. "Though I'd not mind seeing a lick of paint come off the high admiral yonder."

Clare gazed down at the harassed face of William Oliver and felt a touch of sympathy. "Well, I'm sure the poor man is doing his best. Not everyone is born to the sea."

The man she was looking at raised his head to glance at the harbor wall, which was lined with grinning fishermen and old salts like Sep. For a second, his gaze seemed to meet Clare's and she gave him a sympathetic smile. He did not appear to recognize it as such and the color in his face deepened as he swung about.

The *Dolphin* moved out and was picked up by the tide. As Sep had said, there was not a following wind. A rather wayward one filled the *Dolphin*'s sails with erratic gusts. Small figures clung to the rigging as the *Dolphin* bounced along, veering first to port and then to starboard.

As the ship ploughed on, diminishing in size down the estuary, Sep turned an almost purple face toward Clare. His shoulders were shaking and he had difficulty in speaking. "There's a sight for sore eyes, miss," he gasped. "Sails like a haystack, don't she?" His chest rumbled and he erupted into laughter. "Lundy lighthouse better hop back a pace when she sights the *Dolphin* or she'll be getting a dozen fresh hands to man the lights—not invited, like."

"You're a terrible man, Septimus Thomas," Clare said severely. "I vow I will have nothing more to do with you. Good day, sir."

She walked away from the harbor wall and Sep fell into step beside her. Clare raised her chin and stared ahead, trying to keep the disapproving expression on her face. She knew she could not hold out very long, and was aware that Sep kept glancing at her sideways.

Sep's voice came, penitent as a child's. "'Tis only a bit of fun, miss. Old sea dogs like me are mortal sore we're not still afloat. Jealous, we are, really, which makes us skylark a bit." He gave a deep, gusty sigh. "Well, I'll be off, miss, to think on the past while I brews up a cup of strong."

Clare bit her lip and slanted him a look as he shambled beside her. His eyes were on her and she recognized the hopeful twinkle in them.

"Apart from being a terrible man, Septimus Thomas, you're a dreadful old humbug! Don't think for a moment that your soft words have touched my heart, for I can see right through you. You have designs on my teapot, if I'm not mistaken. Confess it, you rogue, and don't try to soft-soap me with that injured expression."

Sep grinned and Clare could hold onto her dignity no longer. She grinned, too. "All right. Set course for my cottage, bosun." She thrust a hand into her pocket and produced the door key.

Sep looked ahead at the sound of children's voices. "Seems we've got boarders, miss." His voice rose to a roar and Clare flinched. "Avast there, shipmates."

An excited babble floated toward them and three young girls pelted down the last slope from the cottage.

Kate, Milly, and Sara came to a laughing halt, flushed and breathless. Sara spoke first.

"I told you it couldn't be Captain Oliver. And not Papa, for he went to Glasgow last night."

Clare's heart jerked. Glasgow last night? How could he, since he had spent the night in her bed? She kept her voice calm.

"What couldn't be and what precisely are you talking about?"

"It was Albert," Kate said. "He told us."

"Told you what?" Clare asked with a feeling of dread. Had Mark been seen leaving the cottage?

Milly giggled. "Said he'd seen you walking out with a sailor." She and Kate clutched each other and fell into a fit of the giggles. "It was only Mr. Thomas, after all."

Septimus drew himself up to his full height of five and a half feet and glowered at the girls from under his bushy brows. "Only Mr. Thomas, is it? I'll have you know, you young rips, that Septimus Thomas has walked out with a Tongan princess and a mandarin's daughter in China, and they both begging to become my missis. And not to mention the time I got shipwrecked off the Araby coast and was taken in by a sultan's lady, who, being his fourth wife and needful of attention, would have followed me anywhere, save the Royal Navy didn't hold with females on the gun deck." He blew out his chest in a great sigh, which caused Milly and Kate further merriment.

Clare smiled at Sep. "Well, so I was indeed walking out with a sailor. Albert was right. Now I'm taking my sailor friend to drink tea in my cottage. You may all come, too, providing my friend will welcome you after your unkind words."

Kate and Milly hurled themselves at Sep. "We're not unkind; you know we're not." The girls grasped his hands and looked up appealingly. "We only said *only* because you couldn't marry Miss Court anyway. You've got six wives already."

"Just like Henry the Eighth," murmured Clare. "Come to think of it, I can see the likeness. He was fond of tall tales, too," she added dryly.

"What's a tall tale, miss?" asked Milly.

"One that ain't short, you young varmint," Sep growled. "Now, stop bothering my lady friend or I'll take a rope's end to you. Only Mr. Thomas, indeed! You'd think I was no more than a barnacle to be scraped off a hull."

Clare unlocked her front door and led the party inside. The sun slanted through the living room, brightening the chintz covers on the couch and chair. Clare opened the lattice window to allow the cooler breeze in and turned to her visitors.

Sep cocked an eyebrow. "Shall I be putting the kettle on, miss?"

"If you would be so good, Mr. Thomas. Meanwhile, be seated, ladies, while I fetch in the plum cake. I baked it myself, but sadly, it falls short when compared with Mrs. Clark's cakes."

"I'm sure it will be very good," Sara said politely. "May we not have tea in the kitchen?" She glanced about at the gowns of fine fabrics hanging on the rail beside the cheval glass, and the one on Clare's sewing table. "It would be too bad if any of these dresses were soiled."

Clare observed Kate and Milly sitting a little uneasily on the edge of the couch and realized, with affection, that Sara's words had meant something quite different. That large kitchen of the Clarks' was the focal point of the two girls' lives. The parlor was used only for entertaining the vicar or local doctor. Crumbs from the table or mud from Mr. Clark's boots would never be allowed to fall in the pristine parlor.

"Good idea, Sara. Then we may all put our elbows on the table and speak with our mouths full. Can you imagine what one of my fine ladies might say if they found a piece of plum cake adhering to a satin gown?"

Kate and Milly giggled but rose quickly and followed their hostess into the kitchen. Clare took down the plain white cups from the dresser, and compared them mentally with the fine bone china tea service from which she and Sara had drunk at the Conrad house. One day, when her fortunes increased enough, she would purchase a flowered tea set of better quality. She could not aspire to a Georgian silver tea service— no, that was putting expectation too high.

The kettle was singing and she took the brown earthenware teapot to it, after spooning in the tea leaves. Stools were put to use beside the two wooden chairs and ten elbows vied on the wooden tabletop as Clare and her guests consumed plum cake and tea.

It was Sep who brought up the subject of Mr. Conrad's visit to Glasgow. Clare was glad. She wouldn't have dared to mention it herself in case her face changed color.

"Papa will return on the *Dolphin*," Sara explained. "But

he had leave from Mr. Patterson to go and look at a boat called *Charlotte Dundas*. It is just a wreck, really, and has been lying for ages in a canal.''

"Has it something to do with steam, Sara? You told me your papa was interested in that subject.''

Sara wrinkled her brows in thought. "Yes, I think so. Something to do with paddles, as well. Papa said it was invented by Lord Dundas, who named it after his daughter.'' She smiled brightly. "Just as Papa calls his boat after me.''

"What does he expect to find, looking at some old wreck?'' put in Septimus.

"It wasn't wrecked, really,'' Sara said earnestly. "Papa said it worked well up and down the canal, but people said the swell it made would wash away the canal banks. I expect poor Lord Dundas was very upset, so he just left it there and went away.''

"What's Cap'n Mark want with it, then?'' asked Sep.

"I expect he wants to see all the parts that were worked by the steam.''

Sep grunted and took a gulp of tea. "Canvas is the thing. You ask Admiral Nelson.''

"I don't know Admiral Nelson,'' Sara said. "Do you, Mr. Thomas?''

"Well, now,'' began Sep, then caught Clare's sardonic smile. "Well, not personal like, but we've had a hand in a few battles together against them Frenchies.''

"Tell us a story, Mr. Thomas,'' asked Kate eagerly.

"Well, now.'' Sep scratched his chin. "I mind the time in ninety-eight when I was on the *Vanguard*. We found the Frenchies a-hiding in Aboukir Bay. That's nigh on Egypt, you know, and as thick with Arabs as fleas on a dog's back.''

"Was that where you met the sultan's lady?''

"'Course not,'' Sep said scornfully. "There's no time for females when you've got a battle to fight. Where was I? Ah, yes. Well, our Nel was but a rear admiral then; been made up the year before. Well, we thrashed them Frenchies and sent them scuttling and, do you know, afore the year was out, it was Baron Nelson of the Nile. Those lords of the Admiralty knew a good sailor when they saw one.''

"You've a good memory, Septimus," Clare said gently.

"'Tis what most of us are left with in the end, miss."

Clare nodded. How true that remark was, although to many, it might appear trite. How could she look cynically on Sep's inventive narratives when her own mind dreamed of things that could never happen? Without wife or child, Sep had only memories of the seafaring life. Why should he not embroider his adventures to amuse the children?

"From baron to viscount, from rear admiral to vice admiral, our Nel went," Sep was going on. "Against the Danes, then back to those danged Frenchies, and old Boney. And him with only one arm and an eye left."

"And then came Trafalgar," Clare said. "That must have been a sad day for you, Septimus."

"Aye, miss. Aboard the *Victory* or not, it was a sad day for the whole country as well as every man jack in the fleet."

"With men like you to remember him, he'll never be forgotten, my friend. Have some more tea and tell us how you escaped the sultan's wrath when he discovered his lady's fancy for you."

Septimus gave Clare a long look, then grinned. "Aye, miss, I will, but you'll never believe it."

Clare smiled back. "On my word, I will. I'm as much agog as the rest of your audience, so weigh anchor and proceed under full sail."

♦ *Chapter Sixteen* ♦

After the plum cake had been eaten and Sep's tall tale swallowed whole, the tea party broke up in the cheeriest of spirits, with Sep's assurance that he would escort Miss Sara to her door, as befitting a gentleman of the Royal Navy. From the cottage doorway, the three of them watched the farmhouse until Kate and Millie had reached the paddock.

Clare prepared for bed some time later. Her thoughts rested on Mark Conrad and the information Sara had given them concerning his whereabouts. It had not been really late when he had let himself out of the cottage. He could have caught the night coach to Glasgow. Later, he would return on the *Dolphin*. It was ridiculous to feel her heart quicken at the thought. There was no earthly reason for him to call at the cottage again. His passing last night had been mere chance, and hadn't they made a bargain? In spite of what had happened last night—and that must be put down to a feeling of pity and a desire to comfort—the bargain that preserved their reputations must be kept.

He wanted ships completely powered by steam, no canvas. Such a radical change in shipping needed similar enthusiasm from men who were exceedingly rich and could afford to research the project. Mark was not rich, but his employer was a wealthy man. Was Mr. Patterson content to run his fleet in the conventional way, or did he share Mark's vision? She didn't know. All she knew was her own lack of fortune—something she would gladly have given to Mark Conrad in return for his love. She climbed into bed and blew out her candle. In the dark, she might imagine him beside her.

In a small hotel room in Glasgow, Mark Conrad was preparing for bed, but his thoughts were not on Clare. They were on the *Charlotte Dundas* lying forlornly in a creek off the Forth and Clyde Canal. Her inspection had been worth the ruin of his trousers in the mud and canal water. She had been lying neglected for a dozen years, and he knew she had been looked over by many men before him, and all to their profit. He took the stack of notes and sketches he had made and lay back in bed to peruse them again.

Over the previous two weeks he had, by post, engaged old friends and colleagues in the shipping world to make certain investigations for him. He was vastly indebted to a college friend for his notes on maritime history, before and after the launching of the *Charlotte Dundas*. Since his employer had no interest in steam, and declined to allow him time to make his own investigations, Mark Conrad was glad of any information gathered by willing friends.

He read with interest the notes on Robert Fulton who, like himself, had made drawings of the *Charlotte Dundas* many years ago and had incorporated those findings into the building of his own steamship.

"An enterprising fellow, this American," Mark murmured to himself as he read on. "Sailed up and down the Hudson River with passengers as well as freight, and called his ship the *Clermont*."

The *Comet*, a steam-powered paddleboat that plied the Clyde had been introduced in 1817. Mark grinned at his friend's comment on the *Comet*. Passengers desirous of reaching port had to be prepared to take their turn on the flywheel of the paddles, should the engine become overheated and thus exhaust its energy.

Then there was the *Marjorie*, in 1814, which might be considered the first steamship in the country. She went down the east coast from Scotland to London, then carried passengers from the capital to Margate and back.

Mark laid aside the papers and stared at the ceiling, his hands behind his head. This revolutionary method of powering ships would bring a new age, dependent on neither wind nor tide. Ships without sails—that was the future, and he wanted desperately to be a part of it. But to fit out a ship with boilers and pistons, the dozens of different parts, required money. Could Patterson be persuaded to invest in just one ship? That prospect seemed doubtful, for Thomas Patterson's merchant fleet was doing very nicely under sail.

And what about William Oliver, nominal captain of the *Dolphin*? He would give much to be done with the waywardness of the wind, and steam a straight course, but Oliver was no friend of his, and would not risk his uncle's displeasure. All William Oliver wanted was a seat on the board of Thomas Patterson, Shipping Merchant.

The papers began to slide off the bed as Mark's mind drifted into sleep. He turned his head on the pillow and in memory

looked into a pair of grey eyes—soft, loving eyes that rested
on him without demand or coquetry. Clare's expressive eyes
showed kindness and intelligence, yet held back their secrets.
What did he know about her? Not a thing, save that she was
a runaway. From what? If she did not choose to tell, he would
never know. Nor did he wish to know, he told himself, for
involvement with Clare Court could only endanger his future.
And yet, as he drifted into sleep, his hand reached out as if
to draw that slender body close.

The *Dolphin* came sweetly into harbor, having made good
time with a following wind. Clare resisted the urge to go with
Sep and watch her tie up. She might have glimpsed Mark,
but the harbor was a public place, and only the politest of
words could be exchanged. And why should she put her heart
in turmoil, since nothing could come of it? That night should
never have happened, would not have happened, had it not
been for George Palmer. Her needle stabbed into the cloth
she was sewing and pricked her finger. A drop of blood fell
onto the cloth. Thank goodness it was only a tea towel she
was hemming for her own use; she would have preferred it
to have been the throat of George Palmer.

She went into the kitchen to rinse her fingers. Really, she
must be more careful. What if she had been sewing some
delicate lace or chiffon? The kettle was on the hob and she
determined to compose herself with a cup of tea before picking up some further sewing. After the noisy tea party, the
kitchen seemed too quiet and lonely. The girls would not
come again so soon and Sep was at the harbor. A walk over
the fields? No, definitely not. Mark Conrad might be walking
home and meet her with embarrassment. *I didn't mean this
to happen*, he had said, and that was an indication that no
serious commitment was intended.

As Clare returned to the sitting room, she heard a carriage
draw up outside. Was she expecting anyone? No parcel
awaited collection. Glancing into the glass in the hallway,
she smoothed back her hair and waited for the knock on the
door. One must not appear too eager and have the door standing open in welcome if it should be a client. It had to be, of

course, for she had no friends with carriages—indeed, few friends at all. She grimaced at her reflection.

She opened the door on the second knock, and was faced by a complete stranger—a thin-faced, sharp-eyed woman in her thirties, she guessed. She was dark-haired and wearing the soberest of gowns, and her olive-skinned face wore no smile.

Clare, feeling the sharp scrutiny, lifted her chin and stared back, also unsmiling. "Yes?" she queried, raising her brows.

"You are in, then," the woman said without preamble.

"You observe correctly," Clare returned coolly. "What is your business?"

Her cool tone seemed to disconcert the woman for a moment, and the dark eyes flickered. "My mistress will instruct you on that count, having ascertained by me that you are at her service."

"You have ascertained only that I am at home," Clare said softly. "Please carry that information to your mistress." She caught the hostile flicker in the woman's eyes again as she turned away and took a position near the cheval glass.

If this woman was maid to one of Clevedon's ladies, why the hostility, she wondered? Did a maid consider herself far above a dressmaker? Clare mustered all her dignity and waited for the entrance of the peculiar creature's employer.

The doorway darkened and a wave of perfume entered first, followed by a tall, very slender woman in a blue silk cloak. A young woman with fair hair, elaborately coiffured, looked at Clare from hard blue eyes. She was in her twenties, Clare hazarded, with the delicate, creamy complexion of those who avoid the sun.

A long-fingered white hand released the cloak loop at the neck and the garment fell, to be caught neatly by the maid. Clare could not help thinking it was a practiced gesture, meant to suggest an abundance of silk cloaks that could be tossed aside carelessly.

Clare half-smiled at the thought and at her visitor. "Good afternoon, ma'am," she said.

"Good afternoon," came the reply, and the blue eyes took in Clare from top to toe, resting at last on her face.

"You seem very young."

"For what, ma'am?" Clare asked calmly.

"To be this maker of dresses I have heard so much talk about. Is your name Court?"

"I am gratified if talk there has been and yes, I am Miss Court, the dressmaker. Perhaps you will be good enough to tell me your own name."

"I am Miss Patterson." She waited for a moment, but as Clare only inclined her head in acknowledgment, she went on. "My father is the owner of the Patterson line." She waited again, as if to allow Clare to recover from this startling revelation and compose her awestruck mind.

Clare's expression did not change. She nodded briefly and smiled. "Do I take it then, Miss Patterson, that you propose a commission for me?"

"Naturally. Why else would I be here? It has always been my habit to bestow my custom upon couturiers in Bath or London, and occasionally in Bristol. However, I am pressed for time at the moment and have decided to patronize, on this one occasion, a dressmaker nearer at hand," she said. Without looking over her shoulder, she added, "Bring in my material from the carriage, Marie."

"Yes, miss," the maid said and retreated quickly.

Miss Patterson looked idly about the room as she waited. Clare watched her gaze travel over the furniture, stop for a moment on the walnut bureau for which Clare had paid quite extravagantly, and come to rest on the half-finished gown on the dummy. She did not speak until Marie hurried in with the parcel.

"Spread it out on the cleanest surface you can find," Miss Patterson ordered.

Clare said coolly, "You will have no difficulty there, Miss Patterson, for all my surfaces are clean. It is a special point with dressmakers who work on fine fabrics."

"Quite so," Miss Patterson said absently, her eyes on the scarlet silk being unfolded. "Don't catch your nail in a thread, Marie. You know how expensive it was."

"No, miss." The maid stood back. "If a thread gets pulled,

it will be no fault of mine." She glanced meaningfully at Clare.

"Wait in the carriage," ordered Miss Patterson, and the woman withdrew. "Now, Miss Court." The blue eyes fixed on Clare. "I was a guest at Miss Foster's coming-out ball, and I want you to make me a replica of that fancifully named Gainsborough gown. How you managed to make that girl look attractive is quite beyond me, but she was quite the belle of her own ball."

"Surely, Miss Patterson, that is the hope of every young debutante. I imagine you expected no less at your own ball."

Miss Patterson paused and eyed Clare keenly. "Naturally, I was the belle of my own ball. That goes without saying, but I had not the difficulties to overcome."

"Difficulties?" Clare asked in apparent innocence.

The blue eyes hardened. "Come, Miss Court, you know what I mean. Miss Foster has hardly the Venus figure."

"Quite true. She's a little more Juno than Venus, but both were goddesses, were they not, and Juno the more magnificent in pride and carriage?"

The blue eyes narrowed. "I applaud your tact, Miss Court. It is an admirable quality for those in service."

Clare let the insult pass and looked at the scarlet silk. "I regret, Miss Patterson, that I cannot make you a replica of that dress. I designed it exclusively for Miss Foster, and no dressmaker—or couturier, for that matter—would duplicate a design without loss of confidence from the original customer." Clare noticed the tightened lips and went on. "If you would care to look through the pages of my pattern books—?" She gestured toward the sideboard.

"Oh, very well." Miss Patterson began to flick through the pages impatiently. "I would have made it worth your while, nevertheless." She slanted a glance at Clare, as if hoping for a change of heart at the mention of reward.

"I'm sorry," Clare repeated, and moved away a pace or two, letting her prospective client leaf through the pages.

So this was the daughter of Mark's employer—this blond, elegant creature who believed in the power of money to gain

her ends. Was that unfair? Did she only reveal that side of
her character when dealing with those she considered her
inferiors? To make a gown for the daughter of the richest
man in Clevedon and possibly Bristol might set the seal on
Clare's success, but she was not attracted to the woman, as
she had been to Isobel Foster. This interest in a local dressmaker, when she could afford the most expensive couturier,
seemed odd. It was an experiment, perhaps, in the light of
Isobel's success at her own ball. Miss Patterson had attended
that ball. Had she, herself, expected to be the belle of that
and every other ball in the neighborhood? To be overshadowed by Isobel must certainly have taken Miss Patterson
aback.

Clare looked at the yards and yards of scarlet silk draped
over the couch. Dressed in that brilliant color, her blond hair
coiffured to perfection, Miss Patterson could not be over-
looked or overshadowed by anyone. Every eye would be
attracted to that flash of color. Anything worn by others in
paler shades would look quite insipid beside it.

"This one," said Miss Patterson. "Unless, of course,
you have already made an exclusive model for someone
else."

"No, Miss Patterson. None in that book has been made
exclusively. I remove the patterns if I have done so and keep
them elsewhere." She looked at the picture Miss Patterson's
finger rested upon. She nodded.

"That will be an original to you, Miss Patterson, you may
be assured of it. Will you require any additional decoration?
Perhaps not, since it has six flounces."

Miss Patterson considered. "I shall wear my diamonds, of
course. Perhaps it should have silver thread edging every
flounce. Are you able to do that?"

"Certainly, but that will take time. When is your ball, may
I ask?"

"On Saturday."

"Of this week?"

At Miss Patterson's nod, Clare said, "Today is Wednesday. I cannot possibly agree to have the gown ready by
Saturday."

A look of vexation crossed Miss Patterson's face. "But that gives you almost three days. Surely, in that time—"

"Miss Patterson," Clare interrupted, "your usual couturier has, no doubt, a workroom full of sewing girls to pin and tack the sections together and also, without doubt, a team of more experienced women to edge each flounce in the manner you have suggested. I have no such help."

"How long does it take you, then, to make a gown?" The tone was slightly offensive, but Clare controlled herself.

"Two weeks, Miss Patterson, and I positively insist on two fittings."

"I told you, I think, that I am pressed for time. Is that the best you can do? It would be to your advantage to have me patronize your little establishment."

"But not to my advantage if I turned out a gown hastily made."

"So, you refuse."

"No, Miss Patterson. I will make you the gown if you still require it, but it must be on my terms. I would not feel easy in mind if I thought the slightest exertion might cause one of my dresses to part at the seams. If you cannot bring yourself to accept my terms, then I must regretfully refuse your kind commission."

Clare kept her gaze steady on Miss Patterson and saw a mixture of surprise and curiosity in the look returned to her. Had Miss Patterson never been thwarted before or had her demands rejected? Did she suppose that money and power were as irresistible to others as they seemed to be to her?

Clare smiled. "Shall I parcel up your silk, Miss Patterson?"

"No, no. I want you to make the gown." She shrugged. "After all, I have others I can wear on Saturday." She paused reflectively. "Yes, I think two weeks will suit me better. I shall wear the gown on that night." She smiled, much to Clare's surprise, and added almost gaily, "You will make me look absolutely enchanting and quite—quite irresistible, will you not?"

"I shall do my utmost," Clare murmured. "May I take your measurements?"

"Of course, of course." Miss Patterson's eyes seemed to glitter like polished blue stones. "Call Marie, if you please."

As Clare went to the door to beckon the maid, she was puzzled by the change that had come over Miss Patterson. She had become quite gay, unlike the domineering mistress trying to put a servant in her place. Had her own firmness had anything to do with it? Perhaps, but something to happen in two weeks' time seemed to be occupying her mind now —some special occasion at which she would appear in the gown for the first time.

Miss Patterson handed her reticule and lacy shawl to Marie as Clare took out her tape measure and set pencil and notebook on her sewing table. After taking very careful measurements, and ascertaining that Miss Patterson wanted a very low neckline and an extra flounce to give the appearance of a full-blown rose when she curtsied to the gentlemen, Clare was finished.

"Will you call a week today for your first fitting, please?"

"Yes, indeed," Miss Patterson said, twisting a ring absently on her finger. Her mind seemed still to be occupied, and Marie looked curiously at her mistress.

"Thank you, Miss Patterson," Clare said. "I think we have prepared the ground sufficiently today."

For a moment Miss Patterson did not move. Then she glanced down at the ring and righted it, so that the diamond-encircled ruby was visible. She spread out her fingers and stared at it. "A good match for the silk, is it not?"

"An excellent match," Clare replied.

"My father ships consignments of precious stones from time to time, but this particular fine stone was chosen by my fiancé."

"An admirable choice, Miss Patterson." Clare wondered why she was being favored with these reflections and why Miss Patterson seemed disposed to linger.

"Admirable in all things, including his choice of lady," Marie put in with a sycophantic smirk. "I daresay even a dressmaker may have heard of the fine gentleman."

Clare smiled faintly. "Fine gentlemen do not cross my path—only their ladies."

"But, living so close——"

"Oh, do be quiet, Marie," Miss Patterson said irritably.
"I expect Miss Court has heard of the house. Who hasn't?
It has stood there for hundreds of years. Come, we must be
going. Hand me my shawl."

Her maid looked sulky as she obeyed. It was obvious she
did not care to be reproved in front of a mere dressmaker.

"I only thought since Mr. Conrad lives so close——" She
cast a sideways look at Clare, who had been rolling up her
tape measure.

Clare felt the venom of the look but kept her eyes resolutely
on the tape measure. She must not allow that jerk of the heart
to set her fingers trembling. Mr. Conrad? Mark Conrad? He
was the only one of that name living close by. Mark Conrad,
the man who had been in her bed, was Miss Patterson's fiancé!

◆ *Chapter Seventeen* ◆

Clare tried to think clearly as she closed the door on Miss
Patterson. She glimpsed her reflection in the hall looking
glass. Was she a little pale? No matter. It was hardly a thing
Miss Patterson would have observed. Her mind had been
preoccupied by some special event at which she would appear
in the glory of scarlet silk and rubies.

Mark Conrad was engaged to be married. Failing Miss
Patterson's bed, and she was far too respectably middle class
to allow such familiarity before marriage, he had come to her
own bed. What did that make Clare Court? Was she to be
the companion of his body until he could claim Miss Patterson's by marriage? Clare stared at her reflection and drew
down the corners of her mouth in a wry smile. How could
she be angry with him when her own body had betrayed her?

He would have been gentleman enough to leave her had she protested, but she had denied neither him nor herself.

You are charged, she told her reflection, with complicity, inasmuch as you accepted the loving of a man who belonged to another. Her mind dwelled on Miss Patterson for a moment. She was a handsome, arrogant young lady with a very rich father. Did Mark love her or was he attracted by the wealth she could bring him to further his ambitious plans? Clare turned from the glass and went into the kitchen, her spirits at their lowest ebb. Why seek a reason? Miss Patterson wore the proof on her hand that Mark Conrad was betrothed. When Miss Patterson came for her first fitting, Clare must, she decided, be most circumspect and speak only of the dress. That maid, Marie, was a sly, sharp-eyed creature against whom she must be on her guard. The woman looked a born tale-teller, a pryer into other people's business—not from devotion to her mistress but a desire to ingratiate herself. Thank heavens that Clevedon was some miles away, so the woman would not be in any position to spy on her. Clare had an instinctive feeling of the woman's capabilities in that direction, although she had no logical reason to support it.

When Clare climbed into bed that night, she believed she was quite reconciled to the fact of Mark Conrad's marriage. Looked at logically, a gentleman in straitened circumstances must surely seek a wife who, although not so well born, possessed the virtue of wealth. Clare Court, lately Harcourt, was a lady in straitened circumstances. In these respects, she and Mark Conrad were two of a kind, but Clare lacked the ingredient so necessary to an ambitious man. The logic was plain. She must think only in those terms and ignore the pain in her heart when she visualized Miss Patterson in Mark's arms.

Daylight came after a restless night, and Clare rose early to rake out the ashes of her kitchen stove. There was a slight chill to the morning. A pot of hot tea would revive her spirits. With the stove glowing and a mug of tea in her hands, Clare contemplated her future. Sewing gowns for fine ladies was a good livelihood. Her store of money was increasing, and she had friends and a comfortable home. A dressmaker might find employment for years ahead until age or some other feebleness ended her career. There was much to be thankful for; and yet, on the day that Mark Conrad married, her heart would feel the withering of all happiness.

How morbid and sentimental can a girl become, she thought angrily, banging the enamel mug on the wooden table. Nobody died of a broken heart, save weak-minded females in novels. For a girl who had run from home, escaped the degrading role planned by Lord Rayne, and set up her own flourishing business, she had more spirit than one of those swooning, tearful maidens of fiction.

With her resolve revived, she cleaned the cottage and shook out the rugs. Milly called on her way to school with milk and fresh eggs. Clare greeted her cheerfully and remembered to ask how young Albert was getting along as a budding farmer.

"Pa says he's a marvel with the horses, miss. They've taken to him no end." She giggled. "Albert says he'll plough the straightest furrow in the whole of Somerset, come ploughing time."

Clare laughed. "That's a proud boast from a lad not long from the sea. I'll come and watch if you'll let me know when he's to be let loose with the plough."

It was toward teatime when Clare heard carriage wheels. She rose, laid aside her sewing, and tidied her hair in the hall looking glass. On opening the door, she beheld Isobel Foster.

"Good afternoon, Miss Foster. What a pleasant surprise. How are you?"

Even before her polite inquiry, Clare could see that Isobel Foster was in glowing good spirits. Gone were the anxious expression and drooping shoulders. Isobel looked radiant in a blue muslin made by Clare, and with a flower-trimmed bonnet of fine straw.

"You did say, Miss Court, that I could bring Perry to tea one day?"

"Yes, indeed. Your friends are very welcome." Clare paused. "Well, perhaps with one exception."

"Strange you should say that, Miss Court. The one to

whom you certainly refer has gone out of town. Called away on sudden business, his note said, but there was no address appended, so no one has any idea where he is. I suppose he said nothing to you?''

Clare's eyes widened in astonishment. ''I? What on earth do you mean by that?'' Her heart seemed to rise in her throat. Had George Palmer been seen leaving her cottage that night?

''Oh, forgive me, Miss Court. I meant no offense. It's just that Joseph told me Mr. Palmer had offered to collect that dress that wasn't quite right. Joseph was very surprised, as Mr. Palmer is not usually so obliging to servants. He could not argue, but thought he should mention it to me.''

''And did you receive the dress?''

''Oh, yes. It came the next day with his note, and I haven't seen him since.''

''Neither have I since he called for the dress, and Mr. Palmer did not confide his movements to me, I assure you.''

Isobel shrugged dismissively. ''I would as soon he never came back.'' Her face brightened. ''May I introduce you to Perry?''

Clare smiled. ''I shall be happy to make the acquaintance of your friend.''

Isobel turned and beckoned to a young man leaning against the door of the curricle.

Clare looked at him curiously. So this was the gentleman Isobel favored above all others. He was a farmer, she had said, and one who acknowledged his lack of fortune with good humor. Clare saw a tall man approaching, strongly built, but with a leisured grace of carriage that was quite uncultivated. He had the healthy look of an outdoor man and she could imagine him in tweed jacket and gaiters, yet his present attire was of good cut and worn with a natural elegance that put him at odds with his own description of himself.

He bowed before her and Clare extended a hand. ''Good day to you, sir. Miss Foster has not favored me with your surname so I am at something of a disadvantage. My own name is Court—Clare Court.''

''I am happy to make your acquaintance, Miss Court.''

He shot a tender, amused glance at the flushed Isobel. "Permit me to rectify that oversight. I am Peregrine Knightly."

"Then I bid you welcome, Mr. Knightly. Will you both step inside?"

As Clare released his hand and stepped back, smiling, she was aware that his grip had been firm on hers but not rough and calloused. There was a little mystery here. What kind of farmer was this?

As she brought in the tea tray, Mr. Knightly rose from the couch and took it from her. "Thank you, Mr. Knightly. On the side table, if you please."

He waited for Clare to sit down before resuming his own seat on the couch beside Isobel. Clare passed cups of tea and plates of scones. As they talked, Clare was aware that Mr. Knightly was studying her as closely as she was studying him, while neither appeared to stare overlong. Clare found herself liking this large young man with his amiable charm and casual references to men of importance in the world of commerce in Bristol and Clevedon. He seemed neither impressed nor disconcerted by their richness.

Isobel, on the couch beside him, looked almost fragile, if a large-boned, healthy girl could look fragile. He was easily a head taller than she and perhaps two heads taller than Clare.

"I believe you describe yourself as a farmer, Mr. Knightly," Clare said. "Do you farm in this county?"

"No, Miss Court, in Wiltshire, just a few miles over the county border. Do you know anything of farming?"

"I'm afraid not, although my landlord is just down the lane and he appears to have a thriving farm. I think you would call it a dairy farm, but he cultivates the land, too."

Mr. Knightly's face showed interest. "A dairy herd is something I am trying to build up myself. One of my reasons for coming to Somerset is to look at suitable cattle. I hoped for advice from a friend, but he is out of the country until month's end, and I have no excuse to linger, since there are two weeks to go. Yet, should he cut his journey short for any reason, I would lose all advantage by not being here." He lifted a brown, well-manicured hand. "It is little enough, yet I cannot forgo it and return to Wiltshire lest I lose all chance.''

Clare smiled into the hazel eyes, knowing that he was not referring solely to his absent friend. This man was vastly different from that dreadful George Palmer. Isobel was obviously head over heels in love with him, but what chance did the poor man stand? In such a moneyed society as Clevedon, he would be looked upon as an adventurer, even though he had freely admitted his lack of fortune. And was Isobel the kind of girl to elope? Her upbringing had been far too restricted.

"Shall we take a walk to Mr. Clark's farm?" suggested Clare as she cleared away the tea things. "The evening is warm and Mr. Knightly might care to hear another view of dairy herds before his friend returns."

Mr. Knightly looked at Isobel and raised a brow quizzically. "Would it bore you terribly if I took advantage of Miss Court's suggestion?"

"Not in the least. I should rather like to learn a little myself, and I much prefer to be out in the fresh air." She glanced quickly at Clare and blushed. "Oh, forgive me, that sounded most ungrateful. I love your nice airy cottage and have so enjoyed our tea, but a walk would be most refreshing."

"Since I suggested it," Clare said, smiling at Isobel's confusion, "there is no need to wear such a guilty face. I have to return Mrs. Clark's basket, anyway." She glanced at Mr. Knightly. "The farm supplies me with eggs and milk and most delicious cheese. There are two delightful little girls, Milly and Kate, who keep me in stock on their way to school."

They left the cottage and walked down the path to the farm. Mr. Knightly looked over the fields and commented on the crops, seemingly impressed. The farmhouse came into view. The upper windows glinted gold in the evening sunlight and the white-washed farmhouse had a look of prosperity. Milly and Kate were sitting on the step shelling peas. At the sight of Clare with her visitors, they smiled shyly, then Kate set her basket aside and retreated into the kitchen.

Mrs. Clark appeared and Clare introduced her visitors, then inquired for Mr. Clark.

"We have not come to disturb you, for I see the girls are occupied, as I daresay you are yourself, but Mr. Knightly is a farmer, too, and would be most obliged to have a word with Mr. Clark."

"He's yonder in the paddock, miss, but I'll send one of the girls to fetch him." She looked up at the large, smiling young man as if not quite believing that a man claiming to be a farmer could dress so elegantly.

"No, no, ma'am," Mr. Knightly protested. "I have not the slightest wish that Mr. Clark should wait on me. With your permission, I will proceed to the paddock and beg an interview." His gaze encompassed the farmhouse and the series of barns. "As neat and well run a property as I ever did see." His gaze came down to Mrs. Clark's face. "May I compliment you, ma'am, for as they say, behind every good man stands a good woman."

As Mrs. Clark stared in some bemusement, he laughed softly. "There you have it in a nutshell, ma'am. I've a great, drafty place that serves, but have not yet the gift of a woman's touch."

As Mrs. Clark seemed at a loss for a reply, Clare came to her assistance. "Mr. Knightly has plans for a dairy herd, and I could think of no one better to advise him than your husband, Mrs. Clark. The paddock, you say?"

"Yes, miss. You'll be more than welcome, I'm sure." She gazed in fascination as the large young man bowed and Isobel said, impulsively, "Thank you so much, Mrs. Clark. I am delighted to have met you."

As they turned away, Mrs. Clark whispered to Clare, "Well, I never. 'Tis not like the fine folks of Clevedon to bow and bob to a farmer's wife. If that young man hadn't looked so honest, I'd have said he was making game of me. But if they're friends of yours—" Her brow lifted.

"Miss Foster is my favorite customer among the rich ladies of Clevedon, and a very sweet girl. Mr. Knightly, I believe, has a fondness for her, but his case is hopeless since, as he admits quite openly, he cannot afford a wife."

"Ah, the poor man." Mrs. Clark's expression became sympathetic. "And they make a pretty couple, don't they?" She shook her head. "Those rich merchants in Clevedon think only of money and marrying it to money. But that lass is taken with him, isn't she?"

"She is, indeed, but depend upon it, her wishes will be overruled in the end."

"And two young people will be unhappy." Mrs. Clark sighed. "There's times when money is no blessing at all."

"Except to those who set great store by it and order their lives accordingly."

By the time Clare reached the paddock, Mr. Clark and Mr. Knightly were deep in a discussion of milk yields, the pros and cons of Jersey and Hereford cows, and the types of butter and cheese produced by various breeds.

Isobel smiled at Clare. "I haven't the faintest understanding of any of this, but Perry is so knowledgeable, and they're getting along famously, aren't they?"

"Farming is very hard work," Clare said. "And a farmer's wife seems always to be working, too. I know you like Mr. Knightly, but could you really see yourself in that role— milking cows, churning butter, and searching for eggs in the strange places hens choose to lay them? Why, I don't believe Mrs. Clark has ever had a ball gown, let alone gone to a ball," she added teasingly.

Isobel's smile was wistful. "I have to go to balls because Mama insists, but I cannot flirt or say witty things. I believe Mama really despairs of me, for I am not even a very good dancer."

"Has your Mama met Mr. Knightly?"

Isobel's lips twisted into a smile. "She has now, for we were both at a party given by the mayor, who introduced him to her as a stranger to Clevedon. Mama was quite gracious at the time, but it won't take her long to discover his unsuitability and forbid me to see him again. I wish Perry were not quite so honest!" she finished vehemently.

"An uncomfortable virtue in Clevedon society," Clare said dryly. "But it is to Mr. Knightly's credit that he makes no pretense of wealth. He is a gentleman in that respect."

Clare thought suddenly of Mark Conrad—another gentleman who lacked wealth. In both these men there was the ambition to succeed, but Mark Conrad had not been as honest as Mr. Knightly. It had taken Miss Patterson to reveal the betrothal between them. Would she, Clare Court, have given herself so completely to an engaged man, had she known? Could she keep him at arm's length in the future? Since he was to marry Miss Patterson, it was eminently desirable to run no risk of producing a fatherless child.

Since the two men had moved on into the realms of cattle fodder, Clare and Isobel strolled back to the farmhouse. Kate and Milly had finished their pea shelling, and emerged carrying straw-lined wicker baskets.

"Egg collecting?" asked Clare, and as they nodded, she smiled at Isobel. "Well, now is your chance to learn a little of the duties of a farmer's wife, or, in this case, her daughters."

She half-expected Isobel to cast a doubtful glance at her dainty slippers, but Isobel's face lit up with enthusiasm.

"Oh, may I, please?"

"I wasn't serious, Miss Foster. You are not dressed for such an occupation."

"But, I'd like to."

"Your shoes are too delicate and, good heavens, what would your mama say?"

"We've some pattens, miss, if the lady really wants to come."

"Of course—pattens. I never thought of that. They're thick-soled shoes to replace your own and raise you above the dirt," she explained to a puzzled Isobel. "They're invaluable in wet or muddy weather, too."

The pattens were brought and the visitors led to the hen run. Kate and Milly soon lost their shyness as Isobel produced her first egg from beneath a wheelbarrow. The search led from the hen run to the hedges and into the barns, where Isobel delved happily into bales of hay.

"What independent birds they are," she commented, her face flushed. Wisps of straw clung to her hair and the hem of her muslin.

Clare made a mental note to repair her condition at the cottage before allowing her back to Clevedon.

"Are the other animals as inconsiderate?" asked Isobel.

"Yes, miss," Kate said with a grin. "Pa reckons the ewes drop their lambs in the spring as far from the house as possible out of sheer cussedness. And if the snow stays late, we've got to go and dig the little things out. But Milly and I don't mind that, for we can take the lambs into the kitchen and give them a warming before their mothers come bleating to have them back."

"It's different with cows," put in Milly. "Pa makes sure to shut them in the field—those carrying calves, I mean."

The girls basked in Isobel's admiration and answered her artless questions with the pure common sense of youngsters whose lives revolved around farming matters.

"Oh, look," called Kate. "There's Albert, bringing in the cows. We'll be milking soon, miss. Pa says Albert's become a dab hand with the milking."

"I thought he wanted to be a ploughman," Clare said.

"He does, too, but Pa says he has to know every job on the farm before he lets him loose with the plough." The girls burst into laughter. "Pa says he's no mind to watch Albert play charioteer across his best acres and finish up with the furrows looking like dogs' hind legs. Albert is ever so impatient," Kate finished proudly, as if impatience was a special virtue.

Milly looked up at Isobel. "Shall I teach you to milk, miss?"

Clare had a sudden vision of Mrs. Foster's horrified face. For her, milk was something delivered in measures at the kitchen door. Cows were seen grazing calmly in fields on summer rides. The process of transfer was not alluded to in polite society, and young ladies were protected from such knowledge, which included the sight of a milk-laden cow.

"Another time, perhaps, Milly," Clare said hastily. "I really think it time we returned to the cottage. One is apt to misjudge the lateness of the hour in the summer."

Isobel sighed. "I have so enjoyed myself, but Miss Court is right, and I do have an engagement this evening."

"Sit down on the bench, miss, and I'll take off your pattens," Milly offered.

"And I'll pick those bits of straw from your hair, miss," Kate said with a giggle.

Isobel's eyes met Clare's and they laughed, too.

"What would Mama say?" murmured Isobel.

"Don't worry. I shall return you to pristine condition before I let you leave my cottage," Clare assured her. "Let us hope I shan't have to do the same for Mr. Knightly."

They watched the two men, still deep in talk, approach the farmhouse. Isobel's eyes softened.

"It is really too bad, but there is no way around it with Mama's blessing. And Papa's, too, although he is usually of Mama's opinion."

Clare eyed the two men closely, paying particular attention to Mr. Knightly. He was, thankfully, not at all in disarray, so she had only Isobel to make tidy. She smiled at the thought of putting Mr. Knightly tidy, as if she were some kind of nanny. But Mrs. Foster had sharp eyes. A grass stain or wisp of straw might provoke interrogation.

The two men shook hands in the greatest of good humor and the ladies took leave of Mrs. Clark and her daughters with good wishes on both sides.

Back at the cottage, Clare took Isobel into her bedroom to wash and brush her hair, and remove wisps of straw Kate had overlooked. A little dust had to be shaken from her muslin skirt, but her slippers were unmarked.

When they rejoined Mr. Knightly, it was agreed that no mention of the farm visit would be made. They had merely taken tea with Miss Court and driven the long way back to Clevedon.

"It is better that way for Miss Foster's sake," Clare said. "But I hope that you, Mr. Knightly, have profited by your talk with Mr. Clark."

"Immensely, and I am indebted to you for that introduction, Miss Court."

"I am sure you will be kindly welcomed should you choose to call there again."

"Oh, that would be wonderful," breathed Isobel. "I

should like it above all things. What fun we had searching for eggs. Do you know, Perry, I was invited to milk a cow!''

For a second, Mr. Knightly looked stunned. Then he grinned. ''Milk a cow, indeed! I'm glad you didn't try, for a cow can be fractious under strange hands and might have kicked you.'' His face softened at Isobel's crestfallen expression. ''But I daresay that you could come to grips with the cow if it was necessary, while in no way will it ever be.''

''No,'' said Isobel in a small voice. ''I don't suppose so, but it was a lovely visit anyway.''

Clare saw them off, silently commiserating with Mr. Knightly. If only he had money, everything would be simple. Isabel adored him, but Mr. Knightly would never speak for her, since he knew his own position too well.

As the evening darkened, Clare lit the lamp by her sewing table and opened her bureau flap. In alphabetical order, the pigeonholes contained small packets pertaining to her clients—names, ages at a guess, their particular preferences, and the patterns of gowns previously made. In her neat script she added her own comments, such as a tutor might append to the report of a pupil.

Tomorrow she must journey into Clevedon to replenish her stock of colored silks and purchase the silver thread that was to edge the flounces of Miss Patterson's gown. She draped the scarlet silk over her tailor's dummy and snipped off a tiny piece of the material. The thread she bought must match exactly. No critical eye should find the minutest flaw in the perfection of the gown. As a leader of fashion, Miss Patterson's recommendation would be invaluable.

Clare stood back and eyed the draped silk. With her blond hair, Miss Patterson would indeed look irresistible on that special occasion in two weeks' time. Even a girl with dark hair like her own might look good in such a color, with diamonds or pearls perhaps.

Her musings stopped as someone tapped on her front door. She caught her breath sharply and stared at the door as if to see through the solid wood. The tap had been soft, almost furtive, and her mind flew to George Palmer. No, he was out of town, according to Isobel, and would hardly expect her to open the door to him of her own accord. It was too late for the children, and Sep's knock was always of the boisterous kind.

She moved close to the door as the tap came again. "Who is there?"

"Clare, it is Mark Conrad. Please open the door."

"Why? What do you want, Mr. Conrad?"

"Mr. Conrad?" he repeated. "How formal we sound, Miss Court."

"What do you want?" Clare repeated.

"Will you keep me on the doorstep in full sight of every passing laborer? Think of your reputation."

There was such a mocking note in his voice that Clare felt her anger rise. She unlocked the door quickly and Mark slipped inside. Clare glared at him.

"How dare you force entry by blackmail? You put my reputation in jeopardy by calling at this late hour. I thought better of you, Mr. Conrad, but it seems I was mistaken to credit you with consideration for my position."

"My dear Clare—"

"I am not your dear Clare!" she flashed back at him. "Not now or ever. State your business and leave me to mine."

"No one saw me, I assure you." He looked into her flushed face quizzically. "Why so angry?"

"I am not angry. At least, I wasn't before you came, but I thought we had agreed on the best course for both of us."

"So we had, but I wanted to see you."

Clare looked into the handsome face and felt her cheeks grow hot and her pulse race. If he touched her, she would have no defense against him. She turned away abruptly and put distance between them. Was he regretting their bargain and thinking to carry on a secret relationship while openly engaged to Eve Patterson? However much she longed to have him in her bed, it would be disastrous to give in to such desire. She would be no better than a whore. It was a risk she was not prepared to take.

As the thoughts flashed through her mind and he made no move toward her, her mind steadied and she regarded him gravely. She was jumping to conclusions. Perhaps he really meant to keep their bargain. Why, then, was he here? She put the question.

Mark smiled. "You're very blunt tonight, Miss Court."

Even his smile had the power to make her heart jump. She made no answer.

"May I sit down?" he asked, and Clare made a gesture of assent toward the couch, not trusting herself to speak. She remained standing.

Mark Conrad sighed. "I cannot sit while you stand, and since your attitude prohibits a friendly conversation, I will state my business for calling upon you. I should have made my position clear to you at our last meeting. It was a cowardly act of neglect and I apologize. I rather hope we can remain friends, for Sara's sake."

"There is no need for apology, Mr. Conrad. Although you were less than honest, I understand perfectly. I have no fortune to offer and you are in dire need of one. I am aware of your engagement to Miss Patterson. She told me of it herself."

Mark looked startled. "Eve has been here?"

"Certainly. Miss Patterson has commissioned me to make a gown for her." Clare pointed to the tailor's dummy still draped in the scarlet silk. "There is her material." Her voice became bright and brittle. "Don't think that I will betray you as the unfaithful lover to your fiancée, Mr. Conrad. After all, we both have interests in keeping the lady sweet." She put her head to one side and said archly, "If you feel any obligation toward me, I hope you will use your undoubted powers of persuasion to have Miss Patterson commission me to make her trousseau. I will charge extravagantly, of course, but money is the greatest temptation to those who have little or none. Miss Patterson is the proverbial golden goose, wouldn't you say? Since we are both of a mind to lighten her purse, what better reason could we have for a conspiracy of silence? I am sure we are in full agreement on that, are we not, Mr. Conrad?"

◆ *Chapter Eighteen* ◆

Clare leaned back against the closed door after Mark Conrad had gone. Her eyes were closed and she had one hand pressed to her breast. He had looked at her thoughtfully for several seconds before walking out of the cottage without another word. That look had been quite unreadable. She hoped he would view her now as a mercenary woman and not some jealous creature who might ruin his plans. And yet her outburst had been prompted by jealousy of Eve Patterson—that rich, spoiled girl who had Mark Conrad for the taking. If he had said he loved Eve Patterson, Clare might have held back her sarcastic remarks, but he had listened in silence, then left. Was it from disgust, or a tacit agreement with her words regarding his fiancée?

She pushed herself away from the door and went into the kitchen. With trembling hands she set the kettle on to boil. Would he withdraw his offer of friendship and forbid Sara to see her? Dare he do that without giving reason and still hope for her silence? Of course, she would never betray him, but could he be sure of it? How foolish she had been to let her tongue run away with her. She carried the mug of hot tea into her bedroom and contemplated the future moodily before falling asleep.

Sara Conrad called the next morning, a large parcel under her arm. Clare's heart sank a little to be reminded so soon by the family likeness. Her heart was still sore but it was not the child's fault, so she greeted Sara with as much cheerfulness as she could muster.

"Hello, Clare. Papa said I was to bring this parcel to you before I went to school. We chose the material together and Papa asks if you would be kind enough to make me two plain dresses. Will you, please?"

"Of course I will, Sara. Do you want to look at my pattern book?"

"I liked the last one you made for me in pink. There is some blue stuff and yellow in here, and if you could make them just the same, I don't need to look in your pattern book, thank you."

"All right, Sara. Put the parcel on the sideboard, please. I will open it later. I must finish this list of things I have to buy in Clevedon."

Clare rode to Clevedon on the horse she had stolen from Lord Rayne. He was so far in the past that she gave neither him or her father a thought. That had been in another lifetime, and for all they knew or cared, she might have been on the streets of Bristol. She left the horse at her usual livery stable and proceeded, basket over arm, to the shop she patronized for sewing materials.

She needed scarlet and silver thread for Miss Patterson's gown, and blue and yellow for Sara. She consulted her list. Isobel Foster and her mother were coming in two days' time to collect the almost-finished gowns for their forthcoming journey to Bath. Even Mrs. Foster had succumbed, Clare thought, smiling inwardly, and had commissioned a black bombazine gown trimmed with jet. Ah, yes, she needed jet beads.

As she waited for them to be counted and secured in a cotton pouch, Clare glanced out the bow window of the merchant's. Directly opposite was a small shop where the ladies of Clevedon met their friends for morning coffee. Wasn't she now a lady of Clevedon? She glanced at the shopkeeper laboriously counting out the two hundred jet beads. Better not interrupt the poor man. She beckoned to a young assistant and whispered to him. "I shall take coffee and return for my goods. Please tell Mr. Witherspoon, but not at this exact moment," she warned. The boy grinned and nodded.

Emerging onto the pavement, Clare glanced up and down the street. The figure of a large young man caught her eye. Hands thrust into his pockets, he was staring moodily at the cobblestones as he came slowly in her direction. She waited until he was level, but he did not raise his gaze. He would have passed her had she not spoken.

"Why, Mr. Knightly. I shall take it amiss if you cut me dead."

The man started and glanced up. His hand went automatically to his tall hat and he removed it. "I beg your pardon, Miss Court. I did not see you."

"Are you so intent on counting cobblestones? It will take you an age, I assure you."

Mr. Knightly smiled weakly. "No, Miss Court. I have no interest in cobblestones. I was—" He shrugged. "Merely passing time and deciding whether to leave Clevedon immediately or wait until my friend returns." He shrugged again. "I believe I will opt for the first course."

Clare studied his face. Gone was the glowing happiness she had seen yesterday when they had visited the Clarks' farm. He looked quite cast down.

"I was about to take coffee, Mr. Knightly. Since you are, as you say, merely passing time, would you care to escort me across the road? I don't ask you to take coffee with me —it is not perhaps to your taste—but I would appreciate your company to the door. There are so many carts and carriages, it must be market day."

"Of course, Miss Court. It will be an honor to see you safely across, and if you could bear such miserable company as mine, I should be delighted to take coffee myself."

"By all means, Mr. Knightly. I should welcome your company, since this is my first visit to the coffee house."

They said no more until they were seated in a secluded corner of the shop and the coffee cups had been placed before them. Since Mr. Knightly seemed to be engaged in probing the depths of the dark liquid in his cup, Clare observed him almost openly. It was not her place to ask what ailed him, but there appeared nothing wrong physically. Since, on his own admission, he had no fortune to lose, his only problem was the winning of Isobel Foster, and his present attitude did not bode success in that direction.

Clare's commonplace comments were answered politely, if monosyllabically. She edged the conversation nearer to home, declaring that the day was as fine today as it had been yesterday. She preferred the freshness of the hills and fields about the farm to the noisy clattering of hooves on cobbles in town but was compelled by necessity to obtain her materials in Clevedon. As she mentioned the farm, Mr. Knightly's head came up and he looked directly at her.

"Ah, yes, the farm," he said, and relapsed again into gauging the coffee's depth.

"What about the farm?" Clare asked. "I was under the impression that you enjoyed your visit and found Mr. Clark a great help."

He looked up quickly. "I did, indeed, and Mr. Clark is a splendid fellow. Forgive me, Miss Court. I am an abominably low-mannered host today."

"Incorrect on two counts, Mr. Knightly," Clare said briskly. "Since I persuaded you into this coffee house, you are my guest, not my host. As to being low-mannered, that phrasing is ill-constructed. You may tell me that you are low-spirited, but never low-mannered. It is not in your birth or nature—nor, if I may say so, is surrender."

Mr. Knightly stared at her; then his face creased into a genuine look of amusement. "So, to leave Clevedon is, in your opinion, running away?"

"Without accomplishing one thing or the other, yes," Clare said carefully. "It's not my place to pass any judgment, but—" She paused, eyeing Mr. Knightly closely, waiting for a change of expression.

"Please go on," he said encouragingly. "I would value the opinion of an equal." As Clare raised her brows, he went on. "You may be a dressmaker, Miss Court, but you are a lady dressmaker, which is why the new rich of Clevedon vie for your attention."

Clare smiled. "I am grateful for their attention since it affords me an honest living, but that is by the by. You are asking my advice about Miss Foster, I presume, or am I being too presumptuous?"

"Not at all. And yes, the subject is Miss Foster. What am I to do when I have nothing to offer?"

Clare thought fleetingly of Mark Conrad. Poor as he was, she would gladly have thrown in her lot with him and disregarded their poverty. It would not be a new experience, since she had never been rich herself. But Isobel was used to riches—had been bred to life as the child of a rich merchant. Could the love of a man compensate for the lack of money and the pressures of her family?

Clare sighed. "There is little comfort I can give you, Mr. Knightly. It is hard on a gentleman to be poor, but Miss Foster would miss you dreadfully if you curtailed your visit. I am sure you are aware of her affection. If reduced to an unhappy state by your defection, she might be persuaded to marry George Palmer, and that would be a dreadful mistake."

Mr. Knightly's eyes narrowed. "I know the fellow's a dreadful bounder, but you speak as if you have personal knowledge of him."

Clare felt caught in the trap of her own vehemence and flushed. Her disgust must have shown in her voice. "He is contemptible," she said flatly. "I will say no more, save to pray Miss Foster will never become Mrs. Palmer. It would be a most withering experience."

Mr. Knightly breathed heavily, squaring his jaw. "Then, for as long as I am able, I will stay in Clevedon. It will do no good in the long run, and Mrs. Foster gave me quite a frosty reception when I returned Isobel last evening, but I will make myself impervious to all hints."

As they rose to leave the coffee house, where Mr. Knightly refused her attempts to pay the bill, Clare gave him a hopeful smile. "Something may turn up in the nick of time. Don't abandon hope."

He smiled down at her from his great height. "A useful philosophy, Miss Court, but it lacks practicality in application. Hope will not put a fortune into my pocket."

Clare shrugged. "Nor in mine, I fear, so we share equality in that respect."

Outside the haberdasher's shop they paused, eyeing the proprietor in surprise. He stood in his doorway, wringing his hands, an air of gloom over his pale countenance. The grey fringe of hair about his bald pate stood out as if tugged in anguish.

"Ah, Miss Court, ma'am. Sir." He bowed to them both. "A dreadful catastrophe, I fear, and by myself, personally, for I can blame no other. I offer my deepest apologies."

"A catastrophe?" Clare asked. "What on earth do you mean? Has your shop caught fire? I see no flames. A flood, perhaps? No, it cannot be on this fine day. What else?"

"A mutiny in your staff?" Mr. Knightly suggested, amused.

Mr. Witherspoon, the haberdasher, gave him a reproving look and turned back to Clare. "I have only one hundred and seventy-four jet beads, ma'am." He wrung his hands again and stared at her dolefully.

Mr. Knightly's stifled grunt, which he immediately buried into a pocket handkerchief, made Clare want to burst out laughing, but she controlled her expression with difficulty and spoke with only a tiny quiver in her voice.

"Oh, how vexing for you, Mr. Witherspoon. It is surely an oversight in ordering, an error anyone could make."

"You are most gracious, Miss Court, but it is quite inexcusable of me when you have given me so much custom." His face drooped. "It is only fair to tell you that my competitor can supply the difference. In fact," he added with a touch of bitterness, "he refused my plea for twenty-six beads and declares he must supply the whole two hundred, at a discount to you."

"And expect my trade there afterward, I suppose?" Clare asked.

Mr. Witherspoon's chin was almost on his chest. "The implication was there, ma'am. I would not blame you if you took up his offer."

"I shall do no such thing," Clare declared indignantly. "I am perfectly satisfied with the present arrangement if you will only order more beads quickly. I need them by Friday afternoon, at the latest. Is that possible?"

The haberdasher looked like a man reprieved from the scaffold. His head came up and a flush touched his cheeks. "Oh, indeed, ma'am, indeed. Most generous, I declare. I will go personally to collect new stock and bring them to you myself. I will close the shop to avoid further inconvenience for you and—"

Mr. Knightly emerged from his handkerchief. "Close the shop and deprive other customers?"

"But Miss Court must have them and the boy cannot safely be left—"

"Then I will collect them myself," Mr. Knightly said firmly.

Clare glanced at him in surprise, but Mr. Knightly continued, "I wish to consult with Farmer Clark, and Miss Court's establishment is no distance away. I am staying down the road at the White Boar. Your shop is on my route to the farm. It will be no trouble at all."

"Why, thank you, Mr. Knightly," Clare said. "If you are sure it will be no trouble to you."

The haberdasher was most voluble in his thanks and they left him on the pavement.

"It is very kind of you, Mr. Knightly," Clare said. "I hope you will not change your mind when you know the beads are to be sewn upon Mrs. Foster's gown."

She gave him an upward look of merriment, and he returned the look with a chuckle of laughter and shook his head.

"That melodramatic episode has quite lifted my spirits, together with our chat over the coffee cups." He gave her a lazy, amiable smile. "May I drive you home?"

"No need, Mr. Knightly. I have my horse at the livery stable, thank you."

"Until Friday, then." He touched his hat to her as they approached the stables and turned about.

The ostler brought out Clare's horse and she dropped her purchases into the pannier basket attached to the saddle. As she mounted, the ostler removed the straw he was chewing from his mouth and grinned up at her. He jerked his head toward a man standing idly by the entrance gate and spoke laconically. "Fellow there, miss, seems mighty interested in your horse."

Clare paused, looking down on the ostler who had always cared for her horse. She gazed briefly around the livery stable. "Since you trade in horses, as well as stable them, is that unusual?"

"'Tis when a fellow don't bother looking at any others," came the reply, and for some reason, Clare felt a chill of apprehension.

"Only mine?"

"Right, miss. Properly taken with this beauty, he was. Full of questions, too."

Clare glanced at him doubtfully but his grin reassured her.

"There's none so thick-headed as an ostler, miss, when he don't like the look of a cove. Not a gent, that one, and I don't take kind to being offered money for information."

"You mean, he tried to bribe you to find out about this horse?"

"Not only the horse, miss."

Clare's eyed widened and her heart gave a jerk. "What—what impertinence," she gasped.

They both turned to look at the man but he was no longer there. He must have slipped out as they were talking. She frowned, trying to recall what little she had seen of him. He had been stocky, with a hat pulled over his eyes. She had the impression of a gaitered figure, but she had had no time to study him.

"Sloped off, miss. Maybe not used to dealing with ladies. Some kind of foreigner, I reckon."

"Foreigner?" She looked back at the ostler.

The man shrugged. "Foreign parts, maybe, but not from over the water. Kind of sharp and twangy, down the nose kind of voice."

"A Londoner, perhaps?"

"Maybe so, miss. I've heard some visitors talk that way —folks come down from Bath in the summer."

Clare paid her fee and rode home slowly, thinking of the strange man. Why hadn't he approached her if he thought to offer for the horse? What information had he wanted, and why? Only one person knew the horse did not belong to her, and that was Lord Rayne. Her fingers jerked on the reins. Dear God, surely he was not searching for her? What was the loss of one horse to him? She remembered the scene in the inn when his lust had almost overcome him. Was it the loss of her and not the horse that mattered? How ridiculous to suppose that. There were dozens of girls he could have, even though he was married—girls willing to share his rich life for the sake of jewels and fancy living.

The only difference was that she had thwarted and eluded him. Well, he could have the horse back if he wanted it, but he couldn't have her. She felt comforted by the thought that Lord Rayne would hesitate, for the sake of his reputation, to bring charges against her for theft. Her father, however much he disliked her, might see profit in a countercharge of abduction of a minor. Her lips twisted into a scornful smile as she thought of George Harcourt. He would instantly become the loving parent if there was money to be had without effort. According to Lord Rayne, he had used her as a stake in his ambition to marry that dreadful Mrs. Lawson. That scheme had come to naught by the action of Philip Rayne, yet even he had expected reward.

Clare urged the horse onward. Confound all men with their arrogant deviousness. Mark Conrad was no exception, for he needed money and was prepared to marry Eve Patterson to get it. She tried to put him out of her mind but thoughts of his devastating smile, the gentleness of his hands on her body, kept intruding. It was madness to think of him. She tried to concentrate instead on the necessity of earning a living and the tedious sewing of black jet beads on Mrs. Foster's gown. How kind Mr. Knightly was in offering to deliver them. He was a nice, uncomplicated man, ideal for Isobel Foster, but who else would see it that way?

She was still thinking of that amiable giant when she reached the farmhouse. Sep was by the gate, puffing at his abominable pipe. He grinned up at her.

"Good day to you, Miss." He removed the pipe from his mouth and knocked out its contents on the heel of his boot. "You want me to stable that critter for you?"

"Not just yet, thank you. I'll go on to the cottage and empty my basket first."

"Right parching weather, ain't it, miss? You'll be glad to put on your kettle, I'll be bound. I'm as dry as a fish, myself." His blue eyes twinkled up at her and Clare laughed.

"A kipper, I shouldn't wonder, from smoking that obnoxious mixture. As to putting on the kettle," she paused in solemn contemplation, aware of Sep's hopeful look, "well, I did take coffee in Clevedon, not an hour since." She met his gaze. "Will you walk up and collect the horse in about ten minutes' time?"

"Aye, miss," came the resigned voice.

Clare urged the horse for a few paces and looked over her shoulder, giving him a teasing grin. "I daresay the kettle will be boiling nicely by then."

Sep's low chuckle followed her as she cantered the rest of the way. Outside the cottage she dismounted and tied the reins to a ring by the front door. She removed the basket and carried it into the sitting room, dropped her bonnet and shawl on the hall table, and went through to the kitchen. The fire in the stove was low, but a few sticks coaxed it into a blaze and she set the kettle on to boil.

Back in the sitting room, she was bending over the basket when a shadow seemed to pass momentarily across one of the latticed windows. Sep already? He was eager for his cup of tea. She moved to the front door and glanced out. A man stood by the horse, but he was not Sep. He seemed startled by her sudden appearance and backed away.

Shock made Clare's voice harsh. "What do you want?" she demanded.

"Nothing, miss. I—er wanted to take a closer look at the horse."

"Why?" Clare looked at the middle-aged man in gaiters and pulled-down cap. This was surely the man she had last seen in the livery stable.

He smiled ingratiatingly. "A fine horse, miss. A real goer, I'll bet."

Clare's tight expression did not relax. "I asked you what you wanted. Did you follow me from the livery stable?"

"Well, yes, miss. That oaf of an ostler wouldn't let me near the horse. A nice lady like you, now, wouldn't swear at a fellow for just admiring a horse, would she?"

Clare's fingers had reached the riding whip holster and she drew it out, feeling safer with the stock and thong between her fingers. She moved into full view of the man and swung the whip casually. She saw his gaze drop to the leather.

"All right, so you followed me from the livery stable. I did not see you, but we will let that pass. Why is this particular

horse of interest to you? It is not extraordinary in any way.
What is your object in coming here?"

"I told you, miss." The man eyed the horse whip nervously.

"You told me nothing," Clare snapped, losing patience.
"I can have you taken up as a horse thief unless you give
me better reason for following me."

"Oh, no, miss, I'm not a horse thief," the man said hastily.
"I've no orders for that." He stopped abruptly, as if the
thought of being hanged as a horse thief had overridden his
caution.

"Orders? Whose orders and to what purpose?" Clare kept
her voice level, but her pulses had quickened.

Was her instinct about Lord Rayne right? Was her past
catching up with her, after all? Almost without thinking she
gave the whip a savage crack and the man jumped. He eased
his damp neck band with a thick finger.

"Well?" Clare put all the arrogance she could into that
one syllable.

"I don't know, miss. Honest, I don't. My guv'nor said to
find a chestnut gelding with one white sock and a scar behind
its right foreleg." His eyes slid to the horse but he was not
in a position to examine the right foreleg. He made a slight
edging movement closer and Clare's voice came like ice.

"If you take one step nearer, I shall call for help and have
you arrested. Go away."

"But, miss—"

"Damn your eyes, man! Don't you understand English?
Go away now or I'll have you charged with assault as well
as theft." Out of the corner of her eye, Clare saw Sep stump-
ing up the incline and her relief was physical. "I have only
to scream and you'll be talking to the magistrate."

Her gaze moved past him and he swung about, following
its direction. Sep, though short, was stockily built, and a life
at sea had muscled his chest and arms. He looked quite
formidable as he rolled up the hill.

"All right, miss. I don't want no trouble. I'll go quiet, but
I'd still like to see—"

"Get out!" Clare snapped. "And don't come back."

The man obeyed with a shrug, and a minute later she saw him ride away on a horse he had apparently stationed on the side of the cottage. Clare had only a few moments to compose herself before Sep arrived. She hurried into her dressing room to bathe her hands and face in cold water from the basin.

Despite her show of hardness, her body felt weak with emotions. A man who was seeking a horse with a scar behind its right foreleg was looking for a specific animal—the horse she had taken from Lord Rayne's carriage. She, Clare Harcourt, was the horse thief, not this man who was employed by someone in the services of Lord Rayne.

She buried her face in the soft towel. Dear God, she was not only a horse thief. What about the purse of golden guineas? Was the penalty hanging or prison? Would Lord Rayne care which?

◆ *Chapter Nineteen* ◆

Septimus Thomas found his hostess a little distracted and seemingly not in the mood for another of his tall stories. After consuming two mugs of dark-brown tea he took his leave, pondering on the mysteries of females. He had never married, so his experience was of taproom wenches. But his experience had made him a shrewd observer of the human condition. The lass, he observed sagely, had the same pale look of shock to be found on the face of a raw young seaman who sees his first man swept overboard. It was not the devastating shock of seeing your mate blown to bits, but bad enough. There had been only ten minutes between their two meetings—not time for anything terrible to happen—and there'd only been that horseman moving up the lane. Maybe it was the heat and the exertion of her ride from Clevedon. Aye, that was it—overtired, she was.

"Come on, you four-legged critter," he growled at the horse he was leading. "You're a-shambling all over the place like a tarpaulin in a gale. Too many feet on you by half, which is all I've got, and a better job I'm making of it." He grinned at his own joke and the horse yawned, showing enormous teeth. Sep moved his fingers hastily down the lead reins.

He had just finished stabling the horse when he saw the tall, familiar figure of Mark Conrad striding up the hill. Mark was hatless, and the breeze tossed his dark hair over his tanned forehead. He wore his white shirt open at the neck, and dark breeches met knee-length boots of scuffed leather.

"Ahoy, there, Cap'n," called Sep, waving the currycomb.

Mark turned his head, his eyes narrowed against the sun. He grinned. "Ahoy, shipmate." His gaze passed to the open stable door and the horse and his grin widened. "Which shipyard laid down that keel? And you doing the pretty as if it was the *Victory* herself."

Sep scowled. "'Tis my generous nature. Always been my greatest fault but I can't change it at my age." He sighed heavily and glanced over his shoulder. "It's got enough teeth to take your arm off at the shoulder."

Mark laughed. "I'd watch both ends if I were you. They've a kick worse than a mule if you give them a fright."

"Me? Give him a fright?" Sep paused. "Maybe that was it. Pesky critters, I'd guess, when they've a mind to it. Enough to make anyone look a bit overcome, like."

"What the devil are you talking about?" Mark's dark brows drew together and he stared at the shorter man intently. "Isn't that Miss Court's horse?"

"Aye, it is. Fine as fivepence when she rode up the hill, but sort of gone away in her mind when I went up for a sup only ten minutes later."

Mark frowned into the stable. "The horse looks quiet enough. Did it play up when you brought it down?"

"A fair enough passage, 'cept it yawned in my face." Sep shrugged. "Maybe tired, just like Miss up there."

"I'll look in as I pass," Mark said and nodded his farewell to Sep.

As he walked up the incline, he remembered his last meeting with Clare—the formality of her reception and the dreadful archness of her manner. He had left the cottage abruptly for he deserved her words and had no defense against them. He should have told her about Eve. There was no escape from that engagement, nor did he want to escape, for only by that connection could he realize his ambition. Old Patterson must be persuaded to see that the future lay in steam, not sail. As part of the marriage contract, he must wring out of the old man the promise of at least one steam-powered vessel, and he, Mark Conrad, must be its captain.

After that and his marriage to Eve, he must prove himself by working twenty-four hours a day to show a profit by swifter passage between ports, more trade to fill the Patterson coffers further. And Eve was a beautiful girl. He would be envied that blond beauty on his arm and in his house. Of course, he loved her. She would fit perfectly into Conrad Place.

And Clare Court? Like himself, she had a future to create and there must be no diversions, yet he could not rid himself of the memory of that girl in the barn—the loving, giving child who had run from something so terrible that she had been flung into a nightmare. His loving had eased it for her and her passion had been a purely natural gratitude. Why the devil hadn't he left it there? George Palmer had been the reason for that second night of loving. He could not have left her hurt and vulnerable, as before. It was only Christian to comfort the child—as he would have done had it been Sara. His mouth twisted sardonically. What was he trying to do— justify his actions by comparison with a real child? Clare was not a child but a woman—a young woman, yes, but capable of astonishing passion.

Aye, and there's the rub, as that fellow, Shakespeare said. Clare Court had a passion to equal his own; and though the girl was in his blood and mistress of his senses, she could not be his. Ambition and Eve Patterson stood in the way— a formidable barrier to weakness. Better to endure Clare's anger and scorn than risk his future.

He paused in the open doorway of the cottage, wondering why he had told Sep he would call. She was probably just tired, as Sep had said, yet he could not walk past the door and ignore the nagging fear that something might be amiss.

He peered in, the sun still bright in his eyes. It would take a moment to accustom his sight to the dimmer interior. A rasping, indrawn breath met his ears but he was unprepared for the figure that threw itself forward.

Clare had been startled by the sudden blocking of light into the room. The figure outlined seemed enormously large; it cut off the sunlight. It was not the man who had come before—he was shorter. It was someone else—a confederate! Dear God, not Lord Rayne, himself! He must not come in. He would close and lock the door, trap her in the sitting room. Panic gripped her. She must fight free before the door closed. Animal instinct, the sense of the hunter closing in, took her flying across the room. Claw, beat, kick—anything to stop him from closing the trap.

"Get out! Get out!" she screamed, her voice edged with raw terror. "Take your damned horse and go!"

The man fell back under her onslaught and Clare's teeth clenched in a savage grimace as she pounded his chest and crooked her fingers to tear at his face. Out, out, her mind stormed, her vision clouded by blind fear. She felt her wrists gripped between strong fingers before her nails had time to reach the face. Squirming, kicking, she struggled to break free. None of her kicks landed—the man was too agile— but he was out of the cottage, and that was a victory in itself.

"I shall think twice before calling to ask after your health in the future," came the calm but perplexed voice of Mark Conrad. "One might leave in worse health than the inquiry warrants. Calm yourself, Clare. I don't want your horse, damned or otherwise."

Clare felt the fight and fury drain from her body. Her fingers went slack in his grasp and she blinked into the dark face looking down at her. Mark Conrad? Where had he come from? He was still holding her wrists, and with an attempt at humor, he spoke. "In the interests of life and limb—my own, naturally—may I release you, or will you renew your unprovoked attack?''

Clare shook her head dully and dropped her gaze from those probing blue eyes. Mark released her wrists and Clare turned, wanting only to retreat into the farthest corner of the cottage and hide from reality and Mark Conrad.

Mark followed her inside. "What is it, Clare? What is wrong?''

"Nothing," she muttered. "I'm sorry. Please leave me alone.''

"How can I, when I know there is something wrong?''

Clare sank bonelessly onto the couch and stared straight ahead, trying to stop her body from trembling.

"Please go. There is nothing you can do, and it is not your business.''

Mark stared at the pale oval of her face, the shadowed eyes and twisting fingers. He wanted to shout that everything concerning her was his business, but he knew he had no right to say it.

"Perhaps I can help," he said instead, and was shocked by the mirthless smile that twisted her lips. "For the love of God, Clare, what kind of scrape are you in? Every problem has a solution. Can't you share the problem and accept help?''

"Haven't you enough problems of your own? Why take mine on your back?''

"Because—'' Mark paused. Because he loved her? No, he could not say that—it would be cruel in this situation.

"Because I feel responsible, in a way.''

And so he did, he thought—responsible for the frightened girl in the barn. But she was no longer the girl in the barn but a successful, self-possessed woman, albeit a young one. Yet that self-possession had gone when she flew at him. Was it something from her past that she hoped had been buried? It had to be that, but he could not force her to tell.

Clare pushed herself up from the couch, her hands automatically smoothing down her hair. She drew in a deep breath.

"Thank you for your concern, Mr. Conrad. I have a slight headache and would be grateful if you left now.''

A slight headache, she thought. It was a blinding, pounding headache that was sapping the strength she needed even to stand straight. It was intolerable to have him so close and not collapse into the comfort of his arms, however meaningless the gesture.

"Very well, Clare," Mark said, so gently that Clare had to fight hard not to sway toward him. "You are surrounded by friends. Please believe it."

He turned and left the cottage, closing the door behind him. In those last moments she had grown steadily paler, exerting all her strength to stay on her feet. It was kinder for him to go, leaving her the semblance of dignity. He walked home slowly, trying to puzzle things out. She had expected someone else—perhaps the return of someone, with that remark about taking the damned horse. What had she said the night in the barn—borrowed the horse? Borrowed, meaning taken without permission? And those golden guineas? Had they been borrowed, too? Had both things been taken in an effort to escape some terrifying fate? It seemed logical, but what fate? One whose threat of return could turn a composed girl into a screaming virago? How could he help if she refused to be helped?

Clare lay on her bed in a state of exhaustion. Mark Conrad must think her quite mad, flying at him like some wild creature. Better that than involve him in her affairs. Confessions might be good for the soul, but no one could help her, so why burden others? Lord Rayne had not given up. To describe the horse so minutely, even to the scar behind his foreleg, proved that. He was rich enough to send men to track her down. He would not be content to have his horse and money returned. He would demand some retribution for being made to look foolish in the eyes of his servants.

When Clare woke from a light doze, she felt better, able to think more clearly. She could sell the horse, but wouldn't that look like an admission of guilt to the man who wanted to examine it closely? He knew where she lived now. If only she knew where Lord Rayne lived, she could send him his purse, complete with the guineas. Would that be the end of

it? It was unlikely, with a man of Lord Rayne's stamp. It
would require complete humiliation to satisfy him. How foolish of her to believe that he meant to help her on the night
of her escape from Harcourt House.

She moved slowly around the small cottage, looking at the
home she had made—the only real home she had ever known.
How happy she had been in the cottage and how loath she
would be to leave it. What other course was there? She could
not explain to anyone; she must just disappear. Her gaze fell
on the scarlet silk draped over the dummy. It went against
all her principles to leave things unfinished. Was there time
to complete her commissions—the jet-beaded dress for Mrs.
Foster and the scarlet gown for Eve Patterson? Yes, she must
complete those but accept no new orders. A sick relative, the
offer of a superior job in London—she must concoct some
reason for her departure. Meanwhile, no more visits to Clevedon, and the cottage door would be firmly locked against all
intruders.

For the rest of the day, Clare immersed herself in sewing,
completing orders for muslin dresses, frilled petticoats, and
the wish of two elderly maiden ladies to have simple, high-
necked, long-sleeved nightgowns. These last were the simplest of her tasks and required only plain stitching. Clare
smiled—such wide nightdresses for such diminutive figures.
They always dressed and undressed beneath the folds, they
explained, convinced that exposure of an inch of bare skin
was sinful. Modesty was their watchword. Although not for
a moment endowing the Almighty with human frailties, God
was a man, after all, was he not?

By the time she had parceled up a number of outstanding
orders and laid them all along the length of the sideboard, it
was time to light the oil lamps. She noticed Sara's parcel
then and took it to her sewing table. She stretched, easing
her shoulders and neck, and glanced again at the scarlet silk
on the dummy. Not tonight, Miss Patterson. One needed full
daylight to cut such expensive silk—full daylight and a mind
unclouded by events.

In the kitchen, Clare made tea and sandwiches of the lovely
farmhouse cheese from Mrs. Clark's dairy. The evening was

cooler and she decided to light the fire, draw the curtains, and curl up on the couch with her supper. The door was locked; so were all the windows. Nothing and no one could harm her tonight. She thought of the man who wanted to examine Lord Rayne's horse. He would have no chance tonight, since Sep always locked the farm horses safely into their stables, and the dogs would give voice to any stranger's approach. Until the man had definite proof of the scar on the horse's foreleg, he would not risk wasting Lord Rayne's time, for Lord Rayne must have employed an intermediary. Tomorrow she must warn Sep of rumors about horse thieves in the neighborhood and ask him to keep the horse close. If she could gain a little time, she might escape Lord Rayne altogether. She tried not to think of the scene with Mark Conrad. What point was there in confessing when everything was true? She was a thief, and even he could do nothing to help.

Laying aside her tray, she opened Sara's parcel. It contained dress lengths in pastel shades of yellow and blue, sprigged with flowers. They would be so pretty on a young girl. There was another parcel, separately wrapped and sealed with her name written on the label. It was not Sara's writing—it was too adult for that. Mrs. Winter, the housekeeper, needed something made, perhaps. She unwrapped it carefully, feeling the light silkiness of the fabric. Then she was looking with surprise at turquoise silk in a pattern of brilliant yet delicately woven peacocks, tails fanned out in a display of blues and greens. The eyes in the birds' tail feathers were of emerald green. The silk ran through her fingers. It wasn't a length of silk but a shawl, turquoise-fringed and quite the most beautiful thing she had ever seen.

She stared at it, seeing the background of some exotic, fountained garden. Indian? Persian? Chinese? As she held it up a small white card fell from the folds. The writing was in the same bold hand as on the label. There were only three words on the card— "With grateful thanks." There was no signature or salutation.

Clare dropped the card as if it were hot. Thanks? For what? Since the parcel had been part of the larger one left that morning by Sara Conrad, there was no doubt that it came from Mark Conrad. A shawl so exquisite, and certainly expensive, was a gift more appropriate for a wife or fiancée—or, she thought bleakly, a mistress. But she was not Mark Conrad's mistress, in spite of those two intimate nights. What, then? Was it an apology for not telling her of his engagement to Eve Patterson, a gift to ease his conscience, payment for her silence?

She stood up abruptly and the shawl shimmered to the floor. Damn Mark Conrad! Did he take her for a whore—a girl who required payment for the use of her body? Was that all it had meant to him?

She found her knees trembling and had to sit down again. Anger and humiliation vied with the hurt of this gift. There was no reason for it at all. It must be returned without comment. Such gifts were the prerogative of Eve Patterson, the girl he was to marry. Clare reached down, and without looking at the shawl again, folded it back into its wrappings. Tomorrow she must ask Sep to deliver it to Conrad Place. Let Mark give it to Eve Patterson. She could wear the thing openly and without comment. *How ridiculous*, Clare thought, forcing her mind to replace hurt with scorn, *to suppose that a working dressmaker could wear such a costly article without arousing curiosity.*

Peacocks with glittering emerald eyes walked through her dreams that night—peacocks in exotic, fountained gardens, and striding through them all was a tall, dark figure with eyes of sapphire. There were rubies, too, set in diamonds, but the long, slender hand on which the sapphire-eyed man slipped the brightest stone was not hers. She was not even in that garden, just hovering on the outskirts, unnoticed, part of the background.

Clare opened her eyes to a grey dawn and the pattering of rain on her window. The sun-filled garden faded, and the actors and peacocks strutted off the stage. Reality was back, and with it, all its problems. She must go down to the farm and collect her milk before Milly and Kate had time to bring it up to her. There she could see young Albert and warn him of horse thieves, and beg him to take extra care of the horse. She would need it for her journey to Bristol. The scar behind its foreleg was there; she had verified it after the man had gone. But he must be kept in uncertainty until her plans were complete. She must take the parcel to Sep, first thing, as well.

She rose and went to the kitchen to rake the ashes out of the stove. The scarlet silk would have to be cut today. There was a great deal of work to be done on that gown. Mark Conrad had seen the silk, knew it belonged to Eve Patterson. Would he spare her a thought in the future when his fiancée wore it? Clare shook herself irritably. What languishing nonsense was this? Forget Mark Conrad. He belonged to Eve Patterson. He needed her money and she wanted to be the grand hostess of Conrad Place and belong to a family of good lineage.

At the farm, Mrs. Clark looked at Clare in surprise. "You're up early, my dear. Run out of milk, have you?"

"Not quite, Mrs. Clark. I woke early and decided to save the girls a trip and I'd like a word with Albert. He's still looking after the horses, isn't he?"

"Yes, miss." Mrs. Clark chuckled. "He'd sleep in the stables if I'd let him. Especially if one of the horses wasn't quite up to form."

Clare took the opening. "I'd like to ask his opinion on my horse. He was sweating a bit yesterday when Sep brought him down. Is Sep about, by the way?"

"Probably in the stables with Albert." Mrs. Clark smiled. "You know Sep how loves an audience, and young Albert is swallowing every tale he tells as if it was gospel."

Clare laughed. "You'd think Sep was Admiral Nelson's second in command, from his stories."

"Well, it's all a long time ago, and if Sep embroiders his exploits, he's doing no harm to anyone." Mrs. Clark cast Clare a humorous look. "'Cept maybe to the history books."

Clare found both Albert and Sep in the stables. Albert lifted his freckled face and gave her his urchin grin.

"'Day, miss. Your horse is fine. No need to trouble yourself any."

Clare stood quite still, feeling a chill of unease flit cobweblike through her. She looked into the cheerful young face.

"A bit of wire fence maybe, or a clumsy ostler. Not fresh, anyway." He ran a hand down the horse's foreleg and Clare's gaze followed the movement with hypnotic attention.

"What makes you think I had come about the horse?"

"Didn't you, miss?"

"Well—yes, but how could you know?"

"Easy, miss. That fellow you sent said you'd be down early today." His nose wrinkled in disgust. "What a fusspot he was. Said as how ladies didn't know much about horses —only wanted them fit to ride." He scratched his nose thoughtfully. "I reckon he didn't know much himself. Only seemed interested in the legs, as if that's all there is to a horse."

Clare turned away blindly. She was too late to prevent the man from discovering the scarred foreleg. He must have circled back and watched Sep lead the horse to the farm stables, and waited to speak to Albert after Sep had gone. Albert was young enough to be flattered by questions on horse care from an adult, and eager to show off his acquired knowledge. So now the man knew that the horse he sought was here, and soon that knowledge would be passed to Lord Rayne.

How foolish to think that one could leave the past behind as if it had never existed. Fate had caught up with her, and a price would have to be paid.

◆ *Chapter Twenty* ◆

The sky was brightening as Clare walked back to her cottage. She tried to put herself in Lord Rayne's shoes. It would take time for the information to reach him, particularly if he was in London. Would he act on the man's word alone, or require him to produce the horse? He would take a cautious approach, she judged, for he could not afford to have his actions displayed publicly. She doubted he would invoke the law, for she could claim abduction and the affair would become public, but there were creatures he could employ to do his bidding. All she could do was be alert and watchful. Why should she allow herself to be driven out of this new life she had created?

She lifted her hands and stared at them, frowning. They were empty. She must have left the parcel in the farmhouse and forgotten to collect the milk, after all. One of the girls would bring it, as usual, and since the parcel was clearly directed, it would reach its destination.

She put everything else out of her mind and concentrated on cutting the scarlet silk. If this was the last elaborate gown she would make, she intended it to be a credit to her skill. Her imagination conjured up a picture of Eve Patterson ravishing Mark Conrad's senses in the brilliant, flounced silk, with rubies or diamonds dazzling his eyes. Her lips twisted cynically. Had she the face of a pie dish, Mark Conrad would have taken her, for she had the money he needed.

By evening, the gown was tacked and hung on the dummy figure, a constant reminder to Clare that the owner held Mark Conrad in the palm of her hand.

Friday came and she realized that Mrs. Foster was due for her fitting in the late afternoon. Isobel would, no doubt, come with her. And Mr. Knightly would arrive with the promised jet beads. It couldn't be helped if they met, and Mr. Knightly had not yet been forbidden Isobel's company. Perhaps that would happen when George Palmer came back into Clevedon society. Poor Isobel, if she was forced into marriage with him. Clare toyed with the idea of revealing his perfidy but dismissed the thought instantly. Her own reputation was too fragile to withstand any counterallegation by a vindictive tongue, and Mark Conrad must not be involved. Nor indeed, must the innocent Foster coachman.

Clare checked her appearance in the gilt mirror and smoothed back her hair when the Foster carriage swept up the hill. Joseph was on the box and he gave her a swift grin

as she stood in the doorway before assuming the solemn
expression expected of a coachman. Mrs. Foster descended
as Joseph let down the carriage steps. Isobel followed.

"Good day, Mrs. Foster, Miss Foster. Please step inside.
A fine day, is it not?"

Mrs. Foster inclined her head graciously and Isobel smiled
rather distractedly. Clare closed the door behind them and
motioned Isobel to a chair. Isobel acknowledged the gesture
with a smile but said nothing as her mother began to remove
her gloves and hat. There was an air of strain between the
two. Had Mrs. Foster put down her foot firmly, forbidding
association with Mr. Knightly? Good heavens, Clare thought,
had she not enough problems of her own without concerning
herself with others'?

The black dress was brought and fitted over the tightly
corseted figure of Mrs. Foster. The lady eyed the dress critically in the cheval glass, then pronounced herself satisfied.

"Thank you, Mrs. Foster. All it requires now is the trim-
ming with jet beads. Will you send Joseph to collect it tomorrow? It should be completed by evening."

"Very well, Miss Court. You may enclose your account
in the parcel."

"Of course, Mrs. Foster."

As her mother removed the dress, Isobel spoke.

"May I trouble you for a glass of water, Miss Court?"
Her eyes seemed to hold a message that Clare took as a plea
for a word out of earshot of her mother.

"Certainly, Miss Foster. If you would care to step into the
kitchen, I can offer you some fresh lemonade or water if you
would prefer. It is a rather warm day for driving in an open
carriage. Through here."

Isobel began to speak before Clare had closed the door.

"Mama is determined to forbid Perry the house when she
speaks with Papa tonight. Mr. Palmer has written to say that
he returns tomorrow and we are to dine with him. I just know
that he will offer to marry me, and how can I refuse? Perry
has not offered—how can he, and I have not seen him for
two days—but what can I do? What will he think? I do not,
in the least, want to marry George Palmer."

"Say no," Clare offered mildly.

"Oh, I have tried to, but Mama says it is my duty to obey my parents. I am not as strong-minded as you, Miss Court. Mama goes on so until I feel incapable of resisting anymore. Papa is no help, either. All he thinks about is joining the two companies together. If I could get a message to—"

"Isobel!" Isobel started and turned pale at the sound of the shrill voice.

Clare filled a glass quickly with lemonade. She took Isobel's arm and led her back to the sitting room.

"Do sit and rest for a moment, Miss Foster. The heat has made you quite pale." She guided the girl to a chair by the open window. A quick glance told her that Mrs. Foster was once more dressed in her own clothes. "Rest a moment. I will open the door. Do sit down, Mrs. Foster. Will you take refreshment, yourself? I can guarantee the lemonade."

Mrs. Foster gave Isobel a disapproving look, but seeing the girl's pallor, sat down and allowed that a lemonade would be welcome.

As Clare filled a second glass, she looked hopefully out the kitchen window. There was no sign of Mr. Knightly. What good would it do if he came, anyway? She returned to the sitting room and engaged Mrs. Foster in the conventional trivialities that passed for conversation. Isobel sipped her drink slowly, as if drawing out the moment before being assailed again by her mother's tongue. Clare's own tongue flagged a little as Mrs. Foster's replies became briefer. At last the lady rose.

"Come, Isobel. You look quite recovered, and you know how your papa dislikes being kept waiting for dinner."

As she spoke, Clare heard the sound of someone approaching. Could it be Mr. Knightly? If she could hold Mrs. Foster in conversation over the beads he was bringing, Isobel might yet have the opportunity of a private word with him.

The three women were moving toward the doorway, where a masculine figure had halted, outlined by the sun. It was not Mr. Knightly but Mark Conrad.

"Hello, Clare. May I come in?"

The tone was polite but the glinting challenge in his eyes was unmistakable.

His dress was casual—a checked shirt, open-necked and with sleeves rolled up to the elbows. Tight, dark breeches encased his legs, to meet scuffed, calf-length boots. Black hair, blown wild by the wind, fell over his forehead and on the tanned skin of his face, and his eyes were the deep blue of the sea. He had the appearance of a man just stepped ashore from a tossing boat, supremely unaware of, or unconcerned about, his appearance.

Even as Clare stared her dismay, she felt her bones grow weak. Mrs. Foster was staring, too, her lips tight with disapproval. *Oh, God*, thought Clare wildly, *the woman will be convinced that I have some rough-handed seaman lover and lift her skirts to sweep past him.* How could Mark do this to her?

His hesitation was only fractional, then, as if he divined Clare's skittering thoughts, he said, "Ah, forgive me, Miss Court. I did not know you had company. The coachman must be walking the horses. I did not observe the carriage." He remained in the doorway, showing no sign of moving aside to let the Foster ladies out. Clare felt a reviving flutter of anger and knew she had to speak.

"Good day, sir. I am afraid your daughter's dresses are not yet finished." She was relieved to find her voice sounding normal, if a little cool. At that moment she noticed the small parcel in his hand and her heart gave a sickening swerve. Her own writing was on the label but the name had been scored through. Her own name was uppermost in a hand she instantly recognized as his.

Mark seemed to be waiting. His eyes, under raised brows, were regarding her quizzically. Of course, she realized with shame at her own stupidity—he was waiting to be introduced.

Gritting her teeth, she turned to Mrs. Foster, to whose disapproving look had been added one of puzzlement.

"May I present Mr. Mark Conrad? Mrs. Foster and Miss Foster of Larch House, Clevedon," she finished stonily.

Mark bowed with elegance, so at odds with his appearance, and stepped into the room.

To Clare's surprise, Mrs. Foster's cheeks assumed a pinkish tinge, her tight lips unclosed, and she beamed upon Mark and extended a hand.

"Why, Mr. Conrad, I am delighted to make your acquaintance. I have driven past Conrad Place many a time. Indeed, yes, it is the home of one of our oldest and most honorable families. A military history, I believe?"

Mark was staring at Mrs. Foster intently. "Quite so, ma'am. It is said that one of my ancestors came over from Normandy—with the duke, of course."

"Fancy that," said Mrs. Foster faintly, unable to keep the awe out of her voice. "The one who became king, you mean?"

"Naturally, ma'am. Was there another?"

Clare looked at Mark sharply. Underlying the hauteur of his voice, she detected a hint of mockery in the lazy drawl. She supposed he recognized Mrs. Foster's type and was amusing himself at her expense. Did that indicate a thread of cruelty in his nature? He caught her gaze and smiled most disarmingly.

"Of course, definite proof is quite out of the question after all these years, but Conrads, like many families, have lived here for many generations."

"And all of them claim a similar heritage, I've no doubt," Clare murmured in a voice as silky as his.

Mark eyed her amusedly. "But of course, Miss Court. What cannot be proved cannot be disapproved. A simple philosophy, you will agree. Incidentally," he went on without a change of tone, "I am to return this parcel to you. It appears you left it at the farm."

He laid the parcel on the sideboard and Clare could only utter a muffled word of thanks, but her grey eyes darkened with suppressed anger as they met the smiling blue ones.

They heard another step outside. This time it really was Mr. Knightly. He hesitated, seeing the group just inside the doorway. He also carried a small parcel. Clare stepped forward, glad of the interruption.

"Ah, Mr. Knightly, how kind of you to deliver the beads on the way to your appointment."

"Good Lord," exclaimed Mark Conrad, surveying the
newcomer. "Dashed if it isn't my honorable old friend, Perry.
Haven't seen you since Oxford days."

Mr. Knightly peered forward, then grinned and thrust out
a hand. "Dashed if it isn't that sly bounder who rammed my
shell during eights week. Still ramming boats, Conrad?"

Mark laughed. "Not likely. I sail for Patterson, the shipping magnate. Wouldn't do to hole one of his precious sailing
ships." He turned quickly to the three silent ladies. "Ah,
forgive me, I forget my manners. Miss Court, I see, is acquainted with my old friend, but perhaps you ladies are not."

"No need for introductions, Mr. Conrad." Mrs. Foster's
aspect was frosty. "We have previously made Mr. Knightly's
acquaintance. Come, Isobel."

Mark stared at the disapproving face and noted the pursed
lips. His glance moved to the young girl, whose eyes were
bright with unshed tears. Her lower lip was clamped between
her teeth. She was quite a pretty filly, too, compared to her
dragon mother. He caught Clare's intent gaze—of appeal,
was it?—and noticed Perry's slight withdrawal from the doorway.

"*Mr.* Knightly?" Mark said, emphasizing the first word.
"The *Honorable* Peregrine Knightly, if you please, ma'am."

Mrs. Foster paused, staring at him. She hadn't known
that, then. Mark looked at Perry and laughed. "Hiding your
light again, old son? Always a modest fellow, our Perry.
Thinks being an Honorable comes pretty low in the social
register, but he'll inherit one day. How's the old robber
baron, by the way? Heard he took a toss and rides a wheel-
chair now."

Perry nodded, the flush of embarrassment fading. "Doing
nicely, thanks. Still attends the meets but finds his mount
won't take the jumps." A grin revealed his strong, white
teeth. "Curses like a drunken sailor—if you'll pardon the
expression."

Mark grinned back. "What the deuce are you doing in
Clevedon? Thought you were farming nicely at the castle."

"So I am, but in a smallish way at present. I'm taking
advice about which stock to concentrate on. Which reminds

me, I said I'd drop in on Mr. Clark. He's a fount of knowledge." Perry began to back out of the doorway again.

Clare seized her opportunity.

"How dreadfully crowded we have become, and the day is so sultry. Miss Foster has already been affected by the heat. Do step outside, gentlemen, and escort her into the fresh air. I must ascertain if these jet buttons are to Mrs. Foster's liking. We shall not keep you long."

Her grey eyes held a message as they rested on Mark's face, and the twist of pleasure in his heart surprised him. She needed his help, but for what he could not imagine. Only a few minutes ago her eyes had been dark with anger. He smiled inwardly as he left the cottage. *It must have something to do with the shawl*, he thought. She had recognized the same wrapping, but why the anger? What strange conclusion had she drawn from such a simple gift? He glanced toward Miss Foster and Perry, glimpsed the joined hands, and moved in the other direction. So that was it.

Clare's warm look had not been for him but the way he had responded in her manipulation to allow the two a few moments alone. He stared across the hills and clasped his hands behind his back. Confound the girl. That twist of pleasure he had felt was now a cold spot of desolation. He should never have become involved with her, not a second time. It was not honorable when he was engaged to Eve. Would Eve respond like Clare when they were married? He shook himself. He must not make comparisons—it was unfair, not to mention unfaithful. He was going to marry Eve because he loved her—and because of her father's money, a cynical voice said at the back of his mind. Be damned to you, he returned silently. Patterson must see the future in steam.

Back in the cottage, Mrs. Foster was only half seeing the jet beads. Her nod was automatic as Clare commented on their quality.

"Very nice. Quite suitable. What is a shell and eights week?"

Clare raised her gaze and stopped talking. She thought furiously, remembering her mother's comments. Fragments of memory came back.

"A shell is a light rowing skiff. Since Mr. Conrad and the Honorable Peregrine Knightly were at Oxford together, I believe it concerns rowing competitions held on the Thames River. There are eight oarsmen in each skiff, if I recall my mama's words correctly. It's quite an event in the social calendar, with royalty sometimes in attendance. I have never been there myself. It was rather too far to travel from my home."

Mrs. Foster still wore her bemused expression. "I knew he was a gentleman."

"Who?" Clare probed carefully. "Mr. Conrad?"

Mrs. Foster made a dismissive gesture. "Of course, but I was thinking of the Honorable Peregrine Knightly."

"I think he prefers to be called Mr. Knightly. He's a very modest young man, don't you agree?"

"I understood him, by his own admission, to be poor."

"By merchant standards, I daresay he is," Clare said crisply. Mrs. Foster looked at her sharply, but Clare was tiring rapidly of this line of conversation. "Modesty is the true mark of the aristocrat, Mrs. Foster. He counts his riches in land, not in gold bars or a show of jewelry." She began to put the jet beads back into the packet. "As I said, I will complete your dress tomorrow, Mrs. Foster. Joseph may call in the late afternoon."

Mrs. Foster rose and Clare glanced into her face covertly. She guessed, with a touch of scorn, that the woman was now weighing the possibility of a titled marriage for Isobel against the obvious wealth of George Palmer. She herself had done all she could for the girl, but it had been Mark Conrad who had been the catalyst.

Mrs. Foster took leave of Clare with more graciousness than she had ever shown before. Was this because Mark Conrad had used her christian name, Clare wondered? She stood in the cottage doorway and observed, cynically, the exchange of words between Mrs. Foster and Mr. Knightly. The latter bowed and stood back, his gaze on the now-transformed face of Isobel.

The carriage rolled away. Mr. Knightly lifted a hand to Clare, his smile bright, then he turned toward the farm path.

Mark strolled toward the cottage and Clare braced herself. He stopped before her.

"May I come in now, without risking your anger?"

Clare did not move, although her body willed her to retreat before his. She shook her head mutely.

"Very well," Mark said mildly, smiling down on her. "I only wanted to ask what all the manipulation was for?"

"What do you mean?"

"When anger turns to appeal there has to be a reason. That woman froze solid when she saw Perry. Then, all of a sudden, there was a thaw."

"She didn't know he had a title until you mentioned it. Neither did I, for that matter."

"But you were maneuvering for them to be alone, if I read you correctly."

"Yes, I was. I am fond of Isobel. She is not a bit like her mother, and Mr. Knightly is very attached to her."

"Why the frost from Mrs. Foster? He's a personable fellow. If the girl likes him well enough—?"

"Compared with George Palmer, he's a poor man, and Palmer is favored for Isobel."

"I see. So my revelation brought Perry back into the running."

"I hope so. No girl deserves George Palmer."

"No, indeed. Perry's gone off to the farm, but he is invited to dinner tonight at the Fosters'. We should congratulate ourselves, don't you think?"

The quizzing dark brows over those lazy blue eyes brought Clare sharply to an awareness of her own vulnerability to his charm and the reason he had called on her. She reached out a hand to the sideboard and grasped the parcel. Damn the man and his beguiling ways! He had no right to send her an expensive shawl, except to ease his guilty conscience. And none but a trollop had the right to accept such things from a betrothed man as payment for passion.

Clare held the door in one hand, the parcel in the other. Mark's smile faded as he saw the grey eyes flash with contempt. The change was so sudden, he looked at her in surprise.

Clare thrust the parcel roughly into his hands. "I am not

bought by gifts, Mr. Conrad. Please, in the future, bear that in mind.''

The door shut in his face and he heard a bolt shoot home. For a moment he stared in amazement at the solid oak door, then looked down at the crumpled parcel, his own writing staring up at him.

A smile lifted the corners of his mouth and he pushed his fingers through his thick, dark hair, shaking his head slightly. She had quite misunderstood the reason for the gift and was warning him that she was not for sale. It had been Sara's casual remark that had prompted the offering. He had brought back two shawls from his last trip to India, and had asked Sara's opinion on which he should present to Eve.

Sara had looked at the scarlet one, patterned with exotic flowers, then at the more delicate turquoise with the peacocks displayed.

''Miss Patterson will love the scarlet one, Papa. Fair-haired ladies like bright colors. Have you not noticed?'' Her serious little face had looked up questioningly. ''Miss Patterson is especially fond of colors that match her jewels.''

''So you don't advise me to give them both to Miss Patterson?'' Mark had asked, amused by Sara's perception.

''I think she will wear the red in pref—preference to the other.'' Sara enunciated the long word clearly. ''Miss Patterson has blue eyes, Papa. I think grey eyes, like those of Miss Court, would complement the turquoise better.''

''Miss Court, the dressmaker?''

Sara's lips had pursed as she eyed her father steadily. ''Miss Court is my friend.''

''What about Kate and Milly?''

''They are friends, too, but I play with them. Miss Court is my talking friend. That's different.''

Mark thought of this conversation as he strolled away from Clare's cottage. The child was right—there was a difference. Would Eve take to Sara when she was his wife? Eve liked parties, clothes, and admiration. She used her beauty to command attention, invite complimentary speeches. She would still have these things when they were married, but where would Sara figure in all this? Would Eve insist upon a governess, and could a governess give Sara love and attention? He knew his own inadequacies, since he spent a great deal of time away from home. That night when he had walked in on Sara and Clare, pounding the piano in a laughing duet, passed through his mind. Sara needed someone like Clare, but all association must stop when he married Eve—at least, at Conrad Place.

He shook his head irritably. He had to marry Eve and he had to protect Sara. She had been his responsibility since the day he had brought her back to Conrad Place, barely a year old. She called him Papa and had no memory of her early life. The people of Clevedon and of this small hamlet accepted, without explanation, which he was unlikely to give anyway, that she was his daughter, the product of some secret liaison. It would rest there. Her name was truly Conrad, as had been her mother's, that flighty cousin seduced by a married man. Mark had given her a deathbed promise to care for the child as his own.

◆ *Chapter Twenty-one* ◆

When Eve Patterson came for her fitting, she was accompanied not only by her maid, Marie, but a handsome, fair-haired man. The glossy phaeton that swept up to her door was driven with great skill. Clare watched from the doorway as the man assisted Miss Patterson from her high seat. His dress was immaculate to the point of being dandified. As the sun glinted on his hair, she realized that she had seen him before—on the cliff path and stepping ashore from the *Dolphin*. She also remembered Sep's devastating remarks on his sailing ability, but Sep was naturally prejudiced in favor of Mark Conrad.

Eve Patterson swept toward her, followed by her escort. Neither had looked in the direction of the maid, who was climbing awkwardly out of the small space behind the phaeton's seats. The woman's face was set in an expression of sour acceptance.

"Too fast, as usual, William," Eve Patterson was saying. "No thought for anything but to cut a dashing figure." She turned her head toward the maid. "Do come along, Marie. One would think you were climbing from a stagecoach after spending hours in a sitting position." She turned her head away and only Clare saw Marie's venomous glance.

"Good day, Miss Patterson," Clare said, mentally comparing her own sober outfit against the swirl of green watered silk with matching parasol displayed so elegantly by Eve.

"Good day, Miss Court." Eve's smile was faintly patronizing, as if she, too, were involved in mental comparison. She turned to the man beside her. "This is my cousin, William Oliver, an employee of my father's."

"Captain William Oliver, dear cousin," the man said languidly, but his voice had an edge of unfriendliness in it.

"If you insist, dear cousin," returned Eve, a trace of mockery in her tone. "One is apt to forget, it being such a recent appointment." She smiled at him, but the man was looking at Clare.

There was a flicker of interest in the gaze that rested on her. "So you are Miss Court?"

Clare inclined her head. "Good day, Captain Oliver."

"Haven't we met somewhere before?" he asked. "I seem to recall a meeting."

"I doubt it, Captain, since I do not move in Clevedon society." She turned her gaze to Eve. "Will you step inside, Miss Patterson?"

"With pleasure." Eve shot her cousin a malicious look. "Cousin William believes he must be known to every female in the county, whatever her station."

William ignored Eve and continued to look at Clare, a light furrow between his brows. Clare felt no compunction to help him out. The less she had to do with any member of the

Patterson family, the better. She followed Eve into the cottage and turned to close the door.

"No need for that," Eve Patterson said. "William has seen me in petticoats before, though he would rather someone else filled them." She laughed, delighted at her own wit, and stared a challenge at Captain Oliver, who was now lounging with his back to the door frame. He folded his arms, crossed his ankles, and looked bored.

Eve Patterson tossed aside the green gown and Clare helped her into the scarlet silk. She felt she had cut it well, for the waist fit perfectly and the tacked-on flounces rippled like the petals of a rose as Eve twisted and turned before the cheval glass.

"I do believe I shall look perfectly splendid in this." She tossed her blond head and gave her reflection a provocative, over-the-shoulder look. "What do you think, William?"

He glanced at her, running his gaze over the gown. "I think Miss Court has done a good job."

"I didn't ask what you thought of Miss Court's work," Eve said sharply. "I asked—"

"Oh, I know what you asked," Captain Oliver interrupted. "You wish me to look at you through the eyes of your first mate. I daresay the fellow will be impressed."

Eve stood very still for a moment, staring into the smiling face of her cousin. Her eyes were blue and hard. Clare noted the swift rise and fall of her bosom and feared for the tacking stitches. She knew they were talking about Mark and her heartbeat quickened.

Eve relaxed perceptively and laughed. "I shan't be marrying a first mate, dear William. I shall see that Papa promotes him before the announcement." She put her head on one side and assumed a contemplative air. "Senior flag captain, perhaps, and a seat on the board. Yes, indeed, that would be perfect. I must put it to Papa."

Captain Oliver, in his turn, stiffened. "On the board! Dammit, Eve, I won't have that!"

"Dear William," Eve said with mock sympathy. "I wonder if Papa will agree with you there. You are only his nephew, while I am his daughter, after all. He will want to see me happy."

Clare listened with growing amazement and not a little distaste. She might not have been there for all the notice they took of her. Marie, the maid, was holding the green gown, her eyes downcast in the sallow face. Did they talk this way in front of the household servants? Surely it was better form to keep this kind of verbal sparring confined to the family, out of earshot of the casual listener. Her own mother had once told her that only trivialities should be discussed in front of servants; any serious topic should be kept private. Perhaps times had changed since her mother's society days, but it still seemed wrong to Clare.

Eve had turned to her reflection again, and before either she or her cousin could draw breath, Clare spoke in a calm, matter-of-fact tone.

"Since the fit and length are satisfactory, Miss Patterson, I suggest we concentrate on the neckline. A little higher, wouldn't you say?"

"Higher?" Eve stared intently into the glass that reflected an expanse of ivory skin descending to the swell of her breasts beneath the scarlet silk. "Lower," she said emphatically. "Why, you cannot even see the shadow that catches men's eyes. A little more revealing, if you please, Miss Court." She glanced over her shoulder toward the silent figure by the door and her smile was malicious. "Even William has been known to stare most fondly at a lady's bosom; indeed, long before he notices her face." She smiled brilliantly at Clare and returned to contemplating herself.

The man by the door shifted his position and yawned ostentatiously.

"What a spoiled brat you are, to be sure," he said in bored tones. "Uncle Thomas should have taken you over his knee years ago."

From her position behind Eve, Clare glimpsed Captain Oliver's reflected face. Despite his tone, there was no lazy boredom in his expression. His narrowed eyes were fixed on Eve's back with such a look of hatred that Clare was quite startled. About his tight mouth there was a white line of anger.

No love was lost between these two, Clare decided, but the captain might prove a more dangerous adversary than Eve suspected. No man cared to be mocked in such blatant fashion—even one dependent for his living on his uncle's bounty.

When Captain Oliver spoke again, his tone was as mocking as Eve's had been. "There is still time for correction, although from another quarter, and seaman's hands are invariably rough and heavy."

Eve's eyes glinted angrily as she shot a glance at her cousin. "And what is that supposed to mean?"

The captain's lips twisted sardonically. "You know very well what it means. You've tried the high hand, remember? It doesn't work."

"What rubbish you do talk, William!" Eve tossed her head scornfully. "You're jealous, that's all."

"So are you, I think."

Eve stared at him. "Me? Jealous? There's no one to be jealous of in Clevedon."

"Quite true, but you're forgetting that the child had a mother." He laughed, his temper apparently restored. "You'll be a stepmother. How do you like that thought?"

Eve turned her back on him and regarded the now lowered neckline. "There are such things as boarding schools," she murmured, half to herself.

Clare pressed her lips tightly together to stem the impulse to protest. Shy, sensitive Sara bundled off to a boarding school so that Eve should have no impediment to the gay life she obviously planned at Conrad Place? No need to befriend and entertain a young girl of eight years? Surely Mark would not allow that! But how well did she really know Mark, and how badly did he want to marry Eve Patterson? If he loved her desperately, he might agree to any condition to keep her. She realized that her head was aching and misery for Sara was welling up in her heart.

Dear God, why didn't these two stop baiting each other and go! Why had she ever agreed to make a gown for Eve Patterson? Because she hadn't known of her engagement to Mark Conrad at the time, that was why. Would it have made a difference? She was a dressmaker, and Miss Patterson was a client with influence. How could she have refused without good reason?

When Eve removed the dress at last, pronouncing herself satisfied, Clare gave a silent sigh of relief. The maid dressed her mistress in the green gown and tossed the scarlet silk to Clare, imitating Eve's own carelessness. Her sly smirk brought immediate reproof from Eve, who seemed more concerned with the gesture than the smirk.

"Be careful, Marie. You might pull a thread with your clumsy hands. That silk was most expensive. If you have damaged it in any way, I shall take it out of your wages."

"No harm has come to it," Clare said, sliding the silk over the dummy. "Your maid held it hardly a moment." She smiled at Marie but was rewarded by a sour look.

"All right, Marie. Get into the carriage," Eve ordered, and the woman bobbed and made her way to the door.

Clare could not like the woman, but she felt a spasm of sympathy for her position, at the beck and call of this supremely confident and arrogant girl.

As Eve swept out of the cottage, and Captain Oliver straightened to follow her, he looked at Clare again as the sunlight rested on her.

"I've got it," he said. "I saw you out walking one day on the hillside. Don't you remember? Surely you must, for you waited until I had ridden by."

"Did I?" Clare inquired calmly. "If I did, it would seem preferable to being ridden down, wouldn't you say?"

He gave her a smile of boyish charm—one she calculated he used with great effect on the young ladies of Clevedon.

"It was the dimness in here, you know, for how could I ever forget a pretty face? I remember being intrigued at the time but confess that I could not place you, and you were less than informative." His smile invited her to satisfy his curiosity with, perhaps, a maidenly simper and a flutter of eyelashes.

Instead, she replied evenly, "I am not in the habit of divulging information to passing strangers, Captain. I am merely Miss Court, a dressmaker of this parish."

"But you must have a first name, Miss Court. Will you not do me the honor of divulging that?" His brows were raised quizzically, the winsome smile still on his lips. "I am convinced it will be as charming as your looks."

"You exaggerate both, Captain." Clare smiled faintly and glanced toward the carriage. "I believe Miss Patterson merits your attention at the moment, Captain, far more than I do. It is difficult to climb into a phaeton unassisted. Good day, Captain Oliver."

He shot an irritated glance at Eve, then sighed theatrically, drawing down the corners of his mouth in humorous acceptance.

"We shall meet again, Miss Court. I am determined on it." He bowed and gave her a look that she read very easily, not being one of the bird-brained females reared in the secluded hatcheries of Clevedon society. They might have preened and fluffed out their feathers under the scrutiny of a handsome man, but Clare did not accept that every charming man had a nature to match. Lord Rayne had deceived her and so had Mark Conrad. She had no wish to further her acquaintance with William Oliver. He might know people who knew Lord Rayne. She closed the cottage door.

Was it blind optimism or sheer stupidity that made her decide to stay in the cottage? Why should she allow herself to be driven from her home? Home and friends were to be valued highly. If she disappeared by Lord Rayne's hand, questions would be asked. But who would be concerned with the disappearance of yet another girl in Bristol or London? She imagined the talk in such places, the shrugs and knowing looks.

People would think she had found a rich protector or gone on the streets, maybe. Or run off with a traveling man, or stolen something and thought it best to disappear. Oh, no, the presence of the inquisitive man, his desire to examine her horse, must not drive her into panicked flight. She was far safer here than anywhere she could think of in the whole country.

Putting on the kettle, she began to consider Sara's future when Eve Patterson married Mark Conrad. Although Sara did not remember her mother, she had her father's undivided love. Eve had no intention of adding to that love, but diverting the whole of it to herself by banishing the child to a boarding school.

And what, Clare asked herself, could she do about it? Absolutely nothing. A man might be ruled by his passion for a brief time, but was that not the nature of men? A thinking, ambitious man was not swayed by his body's needs. In marriage to Eve Patterson, all Mark's needs would be satisfied, both mentally and physically. Would he sacrifice Sara on the altar of ambition?

Clare shook herself angrily and carried the tea tray into the sitting room. She was not Solomon, and other people's lives had nothing to do with her. She was a dressmaker, not an arbiter of fate. What will be, will be, she decided, and laid out the cotton prints for Sara's two dresses. The connection between these and the turquoise shawl touched her mind. It had been beautiful. She pictured that silk shawl caressing bare shoulders above a ball gown, gossamer light and vibrant in color and design. Not her shoulders, of course, for she would never go to a ball or possess a ball gown. These things were for people like Isobel Foster and Eve Patterson.

She paused, thinking of the amber silk gown that Lord Rayne had bought. She had it still, tucked away in the back of her wall cupboard. The neckline she had thought so immodest, in her naïveté, was no lower than the neckline Eve had insisted upon. She bent over the cotton print again. That gown would stay exactly where it was, quite unconnected with turquoise silk shawls. She sewed on, determined to finish at least one of Sara's dresses. As the day faded, she lit the lamp and concentrated her mind on seams and the setting of the sleeves.

Clare completed the dresses by early afternoon the next day. She labeled the parcel and laid it on the sideboard, then stretched, easing her shoulders and neck. Glancing into the looking glass, she saw a pale face reflected and smiled ruefully. What a pallid-looking creature, to be sure. Did all dressmakers become colorless and stooped from constantly bending over their sewing? She was not yet nineteen but felt old beyond her years. A walk in the fresh air would do her good. Scanning her order book, she realized that nothing was desperately urgent. Joseph had collected Mrs. Foster's jet-encrusted gown and Miss Patterson's scarlet silk could wait until tomorrow. The sun was shining and the air was cool. It was too tempting to resist.

She would spend an hour being Clare Court again, discarding the sober gown, the chignon, and the restraining hairpins. She changed into a muslin dress of pale yellow and brushed her hair, letting it hang loosely to her shoulders where the breeze could take it. There were coves aplenty to wander in—deserted, rocky places, unlike the busy harbor where she might run across Mark or Septimus, or even Captain Oliver. Today she had no wish for company—not even that of the children. She closed the cottage windows and locked the door, dropped the key into her pocket, and began to walk.

It was a day for new discoveries, so she struck out diagonally across the hilltop, avoiding the farm and the lane up to Conrad Place. A footpath took her over stiles, between blackberry bushes, and around an area of woodland. It turned and weaved through countryside unknown to Clare, descending all the while. She walked slowly, breathing the sweet air and listening to the call of the birds. There were dog roses in the hedges and violet-flowered creepers, and the trees were wreathed by the persistent ivy.

The footpath petered out beyond the trees, running into a wide expanse of common land. Clare found herself looking down an incline to the Bristol Channel. Beyond, to the south, lay the open sea, and she glimpsed the topmasts of merchantmen making for the Atlantic Ocean. She wondered if the *Dolphin* were out there, with Mark Conrad or William Oliver in command.

Directly below her lay a sheltered cove. On the calm surface of the water, a small boat swayed gently against the bank. She judged it to be perhaps thirty feet long, with a mainmast and smaller ones fore and aft. They were all furled, and the deck, boasting a small wheelhouse and cabin, was deserted.

Living in Bradford-on-Avon, Clare had seen few boats, save the occasional canal barge. This one looked cared for —paint and brasswork gleamed in the sunshine. She strolled toward it, wondering if she dare step aboard and discover what fascination held men in thrall to the sea. Even a "beached seagull," as Sep termed himself, could not stay away from the sight and sound of a busy harbor. To men like him a heaving deck, an icy wind that frosted the bristles on his chin and turned his ears dark blue, was a challenge that no true seafarer could resist. It all sounded pretty uncomfortable to Clare, but men still clamored for berths in ships, according to Sep.

Moving soft-footed over the grass, Clare approached the boat. She was moored at prow and stern by ropes attached to convenient trees. The deck was hardly higher than the bank on which she stood, but was protected from having her paintwork disfigured on the shoreline by some kind of inflatable canvas buffer. She looked toward the wheelhouse. There was no sign of life through the small windows. A long step over the buffer and she could be aboard. A quick glance about showed her a deserted common. If anyone hove into sight, as Sep would say, she could hop back onto dry land. The temptation was too strong to resist. She took that long stride. The deck dipped and she staggered slightly. A muffled giggle escaped her. What did she expect a deck to do when somebody landed on it none too gently?

Turning to grasp the burnished brass rail, she was confronted by a small dinghy. A name was painted on its stern. Her hands tightened on the rail and her heart seemed to stop in frozen horror. The name was *Sara*. Dear God, she was aboard Mark Conrad's own boat, the one Sara had proudly said her papa had christened in her honor! She looked about wildly. There was still no one on the common, but suppose he appeared suddenly and demanded to know who had given her permission to board his boat? He could not be pleased after the way she had thrust his gift back at him and dismissed him in such harsh terms.

She stared down at the gap between boat and land. Was

it wider than when she had stepped over it so confidently? It must still be crossed, and the sooner the better.

"Ahoy, there! Is it boarders we're having to deal with now?"

Clare gave a shocked, wailing scream and swung to face the owner of the voice. Sep's head poked out of the wheel-house window, his face split into a broad grin.

Clare slumped against the rail, her legs unsteady. "Sep! What a fright you gave me. I thought there was no one on board. I didn't know whose boat it was until I saw the din-ghy."

"Aye, it's the *Sara*, all right, and you gave me quite a turn yourself. I was just dozing off when I heard someone hit the deck."

"I'm sorry. I must go now."

"Go? You've just stepped aboard. Don't you want to look around?"

"No, no, I've just remembered that Joseph is coming to collect a dress for Mrs. Foster."

"That was yesterday, miss. Saw him myself. You've got your days mixed."

"Well, somebody is coming. I distinctly remember." She glanced quickly at the gap of water. The boat had drifted in the swell to the extent of its lines and the gap was even wider. "Sep, you must help me—get a gangplank or something. If not, I must jump. I have to get ashore."

Sep frowned, looking puzzled at the urgency in her voice. "You can't jump, miss. You're likely to break an ankle. Give her a minute and she'll close with the bank again." He looked at her with concern. "Not feeling queasy below decks, are you? It takes some folks that way—the minute the floor starts moving, you might say."

Clare, about to deny the implication of seasickness, seized on that feeble straw to explain her desire to quit the boat. She smiled an apology.

"A trifle, maybe, which is just deserts for giving in to curiosity."

"No harm in that, miss." He chuckled, low in his throat.

"But you don't have to walk the plank to pay for it. She'll be alongside presently, don't you worry. Why not have a glance about while you're waiting? Staring down into the water ain't good for landlubbers. Makes 'em feel worse."

"I can't," Clare said. "It wouldn't be right."

"Captain won't mind and it's his vessel, after all, but if you're set on asking him first—"

Clare grasped the second straw tossed her way and nodded vehemently. "Yes, yes, that would be far and away the best thing." She noted, with relief, that the gap was narrowing and stared at it, mesmerized. In doing so, she missed Sep's turn of the head, but her own was jerked back sharply at the sound of his voice.

"Ahoy, there, Cap'n. Show a leg, do. There's a fine young lady here, a-wishing to inspect quarters."

The wheelhouse door opened and Mark Conrad stood there, stretching his broad shoulders and running a hand through his tousled hair. He blinked and screwed up his eyes like a man just roused from sleep. Clare felt her heart tilt more than the movement of the boat merited. Her cheeks became hot as she stared wordlessly into the blue eyes.

Mark recovered first. "Why, Miss Court, what an honor you do us. Like to look over the *Sara*, would you? If I'd known you were so interested, I would have piped you aboard in proper style."

"I'm not. I mean, I didn't know she was—or you, in fact. I was passing—"

Mark's brows rose in what she assumed to be derision. "Passing? But you're aboard."

There was no doubt that Mark Conrad was enjoying Clare's confusion. She tightened her lips and faced the bright, mocking gaze, struggling for control.

"Yes, I was passing," she said flatly, "and curiosity overcame me. The deck was deserted and I had no idea who owned the boat, nor did I know her name until I had stepped aboard. Now, if you will excuse me—"

"I fear not, Miss Court. It is customary for refreshments to be offered and accepted by a ship flying the red duster."

"The what?"

Sep grinned at Clare's bewilderment. "The flag of the merchant fleet, miss. 'Tis flown to tell 'em apart from the Royal Navy, which flies the white ensign, save when they run up battle colors or fly the Yellow Jack or the one that means her crew ain't aboard." He turned to Mark. "There's a drop of that Rhenish left, Cap'n. Maybe miss would have a sip of it, just to conform to the law of the sea."

"We're not at sea," Clare pointed out, feeling disadvantaged by this talk on a subject she knew nothing about.

"We're afloat, Miss Court, which is almost the same thing." Mark bowed formally and stood aside from the wheelhouse door. "Please do me the honor of sharing a glass of Rhenish wine. I can guarantee its quality."

Clare hesitated, then moved forward reluctantly. As she passed into the wheelhouse, Mark spoke over her shoulder.

"Let go, Sep." The words were spoken so casually they conveyed nothing to Clare.

"Aye, aye, Cap'n," Sep answered in the same casual tone and turned away, a wide grin on his weatherbeaten features. He would slip the *Sara*'s moorings as softly as he could before Miss Court was aware of it. *Do her good, it will, to get a breath of salt air*, Sep thought. *She looks pale and tense, and no wonder, stitching away in her cottage with barely a moment to be out and about in God's fresh air. Trust Cap'n Mark to notice it, too. He's acquired a deal of common sense about females, having to care for young Sara.*

He glanced at her namesake, now well out from shore, and grinned. Miss Court might be as cross as two sticks when she realized the situation, but no gangplank in the world would reach the shore now. He glanced skyward and nodded to himself. With the wind under his coattails, he might arrive in time for a brew of Mrs. Clark's tea. He set course for the farmhouse.

◆ *Chapter Twenty-two* ◆

If Clare expected Mark to be coolly polite in observing the courtesies he had mentioned, or to jibe at her pretense of just passing the boat, she was mistaken. He seemed genuinely pleased to have her aboard, and led her through the wheelhouse into a small cabin. Two cushioned benches faced each other, obviously bolted to the floor, and between them stood a cabinet displaying many cupboards and a drop-down wooden leaf that might have done service as a bureau or dining table. Whichever it was, it was covered with books and drawings.

Mark swept them aside and produced a bottle and two silver goblets. Clare noted the paneled walls, all bearing prints of ships, from full sail galleons to paddleboats. It was a neat cabin, economically furnished to make the most of its space. Even curtains hung over the two round windows—or were they portholes on a ship? Mark followed her glance and grinned.

"Such refinements are Sara's doing. Heaven be praised she's not the First Sea Lord, or every ship of the line would boast chintz curtains and every sailor's hammock a valance. The enemy would die laughing without a shot being fired."

Clare had to laugh at the vision. "Like a party of dowagers on their way to a picnic."

"Exactly." Mark laughed, too. "I had to draw the line at valances on these bunks." He indicated the one Clare was sitting on. "There's spare canvas and tackle in there when you lift up the lid. Can't afford to fight your way through fripperies in an emergency." He handed Clare a goblet of wine and looked down at her over the rim of his own. "What shall we drink to?"

"Why not the *Sara*?"

"Why not indeed. To the *Sara* and her maiden voyage."

"And when is that to be?"

Mark didn't answer for a moment, but his eyes seemed to glint with hidden amusement.

"Why, right this minute, Miss Court."

Clare stared at him and sudden realization came to her. The deck under her feet was rising and falling with more rhythm than previously. She set down the untouched wine and turned her head. The curtains had been drawn against the sun. She pulled them apart and stared incredulously. The bank was gone, the common land far distant. She turned to Mark, furious.

"We're at sea."

He sipped his wine and smiled. "Not really—only about half a mile into the estuary. We're just drifting."

"You must take me back at once! This is ridiculous, pre-posterous! Why, it's—it's piracy!"

Mark gave a sharp crack of laughter. "Piracy, is it? You have it the wrong way about. It was you who boarded my vessel, unauthorized. I would have invited you aboard had you asked."

"I didn't ask to be taken half a mile from shore," Clare snapped. "Why didn't you tell me you were sailing?"

"Would you have come if I had?"

"Of course not. It is most improper." Her words trailed away as she remembered the two previous occasions when her behavior had not only been improper, but immoral. She stared down at her clasped hands. Who was she to talk about impropriety?

"Will you please turn around and go back?" she asked in a small voice.

"I can't." Mark's voice was soft and sober now. "There's no wind. We're becalmed."

Clare's gaze rose. "You mean, we have to stay here until a wind rises?"

"Yes."

"Did you plan it this way?"

"How the devil could I have planned it when I didn't know you were coming. I was asleep when you boarded."

"Sep must have untied those ropes from the trees."

Mark nodded. "Yes, I told him to let go."

"Why?"

"Because I wanted to talk to you alone, and you would have stormed off if we'd still been tied up."

"Well, I can hardly do that now, and I don't swim that well."

Mark sat down on the opposite bunk. "I'm sorry, Clare. I took a chance on the wind but it hasn't come yet. Do you see now why I am interested in steam power?"

"Very laudable," Clare said crisply. "But your dream of the future does not solve the present problem." She rose quickly and moved to the wheelhouse. "Since your vessel and I are both at the mercy of the wind, I would as soon spend my time in the fresh air and catch this breeze when it comes." She looked through the wheelhouse window at the furled sails, then glanced over her shoulder at Mark with a derisive smile. "This wind you profess to have expected can hardly do its work while your canvas is close-hauled, or whatever the term is. Even a simple landlubber can see that."

She moved to the rail and gripped it tightly, staring shoreward. In the confines of the cabin, Mark was too close. He had only to reach over and she would be in his arms. Could she have resisted, in spite of her hot words at the door of the cottage? She prayed not to be put to the test. A movement behind her told her that Mark was on deck, too, but she did not turn. He moved about, whistling softly to himself. After a few minutes he broke off and spoke to her back.

"Your wish is my command, ma'am. I have laid on aft sail. You'll hear the crack of canvas when the wind comes."

Clare turned her head and saw the spread sail hanging limply. She caught Mark's smiling gaze and scowled.

"Well, at least you're prepared when the wind does rise," was her caustic reply. "How long might we be marooned here?"

"No idea, ma'am. I'd best run out the anchor to hold us steady. No point in drifting out to sea."

"But if the wind comes—"

"Then I shall haul it in again, ma'am."

"Stop calling me *ma'am*. I am not your maiden aunt."

Mark grinned. "Indeed not, although your manner is faintly reminiscent." He disappeared into the cabin and returned with two of the bunk cushions. He made a second trip and returned with the wine.

"Sit down, Clare, and finish your wine. The shore won't come closer because you glare at it."

He sat down himself, his back to the wheelhouse, and stretched out his long legs, crossing his ankles. He looked up encouragingly, his eyes amused. "You're not cast away on a desert island. You'll be ashore in an hour or so and no one the wiser, if it's your reputation you're worried about." There was nothing sly or implied in his tone. They might truly have been mere acquaintants caught in circumstances beyond their control.

She shrugged and let go of the rail. Why make such a drama out of it? The cove was small and secluded. No one had seen the boat leave; why should anyone see it return? She took a step forward and found nothing beneath her foot. Then the deck rose sharply to a sideways swell, jarring her off balance, one-footed. She staggered back, and her heel caught in a ringbolt on the planking. The brass rail struck at waist level. She caught a glimpse of Mark's startled face, saw him start to rise, and then the world tilted into a blur of sky and sea. Her hands clawed the rail but her brain was too shocked to command their strength and the brass rail slid away. A whirling kaleidoscope of color filled her vision, a flash of solid blue and white, then she hit something that parted and closed over her.

The stifled scream was muffled by an inrush of chilling, salty water, filling her eyes and ears. The muslin skirt of her dress entwined itself tightly about her limbs, preventing her from kicking out. She flailed wildly with her arms to halt that downward movement, her brain beginning to work again. Like a stone tossed or an arrow shot into the water, the speed of descent was frightening. How on earth could she have fallen overboard?

The pain in her chest was growing. How far was it to the surface? The descent was slowing. Her hands and arms pushed down in the water. It was imperative that she finish

Miss Patterson's dress. It was for Mark. She couldn't let him down. Her ears were buzzing now and lights exploded behind her eyeballs. She was drowning—knocking on Davy Jones's locker. The surface was too high to reach. She couldn't make it. Her arms were failing and the pain was unbearable. Arms locked about her waist. Was it Davy Jones? Who was he, anyway? She'd never be able to ask Sep now. It didn't matter. She'd find out soon enough.

A wave lapped over her head, then the sea threw her back as if unworthy to be kept. A cold wind struck her in the face and her mouth opened in protest but water streamed out, leaving her retching and gasping. She could breathe again and the sky was benignly blue overhead. Mark's white face, under sodden, streaming hair, was an inch from hers. His eyes were so full of horror that she wanted to comfort him. The pain in her chest was lessening but her breathing was still ragged.

Between gasps she muttered, "What a stupid thing to do. No sea legs—that's the trouble."

The panic was leaving Mark's face. "Hush, my dear," he said huskily. "Let's get back on board and into dry clothes. Thank God I dropped anchor. She could have drifted away from us."

He was kicking out strongly for the *Sara*, holding Clare with almost painful intensity. They reached the side. Mark grasped a trailing rope.

"Can you hold on? Try to climb. I'll push from behind. It's not far."

Clare nodded and fumbled for the rope. Her hands looked like white claws already from being in the cold water, but they obeyed her in part, although Mark's strength forced her up and over the rail, where she collapsed in a drenched heap.

Mark was on his knees beside her, his chest heaving. He raised her head, and through a screen of her own sodden hair, she saw the concern on his face. She lifted a hand to his cheek.

"I'm all right, just wet and—and very cold." As she spoke, a chill shudder racked her body, her lips went out of control, and her teeth chattered. Reaction to near death rushed in and shook her with an intensity there was no way of preventing.

Mark's arms slid under her shoulders and knees. He lifted her and made for the wheelhouse. Through the door and into the cabin beyond, he moved swiftly and laid her on the one still-cushioned bench. He turned and flung open the cupboard doors, and dragged out blankets and towels.

"Clare, darling, you must get out of those wet clothes at once. I'll dry them on deck. Meantime, here's a blanket. Can you manage?" He looked at her, his face full of anxiety.

Clare tried to push herself up into a sitting position, but her strained muscles protested. Mark dropped the blanket and towel and held her steady as she rested on the bunk edge, her legs dangling bonelessly over the side. She looked down at those unruly members and saw with surprise that each ended in a strapped sandal.

"I didn't lose them," she murmured. "Isn't that lucky?"

"What?" Mark frowned, then understood. "Yes, it is, but please, Clare, take off your dress. Neither you nor it will dry until you have done so."

Clare nodded and tried to reach behind her to the buttons of the dress. The fabric was so wet that they clung fast in the buttonholes. Clare's trembling hands dropped.

"I can't. They won't come undone. It must dry on me. There is no other way."

"Yes, there is. I shall unfasten the buttons myself if you'll hold your hair aside. Damned if I know why females put fastenings behind their backs. Seems dashed odd to me."

Clare saw his intent, frowning face over her shoulder as she held her hair aside. A spasm of hysterical laughter added to her shaking body. "We're—we're dashed odd creatures, taken all around. Didn't you know?"

He caught her eye and grinned. "And some are dashed odder than others. There now, stand up and let the thing drop down. It'll soon dry. It's only muslin, isn't it?"

"Yes." Clare stood, Mark's arm supporting her, but the wet muslin refused to drop and clung to her body.

"Oh, confound it," Mark said. "I'll have to peel you like

a banana.'' He suited action to word and the muslin lay in a damp heap at Clare's feet. "Hang on to me and step out of it. Better remove the—er—other things, too. I suppose they lace at the back, too?''

Clare nodded, biting her lip, and turned her back on him. "I'm afraid they do," she said in a muffled voice. She felt Mark's fingers on the strings of her corselet and her body was no longer deadly cold but hot with embarrassment and near hysteria. Dragged from the sea like a gaffed fish, then peeled like a banana. It was too funny for words, and all because of her curiosity. Women were dashed odd creatures, as Mark had said, and he must think her dashed odder than the rest.

The corselet dropped to join the dress and Clare gave a shuddering gasp that was half a laugh. Mark did not recognize the laugh and pulled her about, his arms enveloping her shaking body.

"It's all right, my love. You're quite safe. Forgive me for tricking you aboard. It was an oafish thing to do and I'm sorry. I deserve any abuse you care to hurl at me. What can I do to make amends?''

"You can stop holding me so tightly, for your clothes are wetter than mine.'' Clare smiled shakily. "I can manage perfectly well now, so look to yourself before we both catch a chill.''

"Sensible girl.'' Mark released her and grinned. "I confess, these canvas trousers are damned uncomfortable when they're wet.'' He burrowed in another cupboard and emerged with a dry pair. "No shirt, I'm afraid. Must all be ashore.'' He moved to the wheelhouse door and slipped off his wet clothes, keeping his back to Clare.

She was grateful for his courtesy as she removed her stockings and underwear and began to towel her body. He was not a man to take advantage of her defenseless position, as another might have done. He had tricked her aboard, certainly, but not with seduction in mind. What had he said? He wanted to talk to her? She had been too angry to listen at the time, but now, she reflected ruefully, she had no choice but to stay aboard until her clothes dried and the wind took them back to shore.

She picked up the blanket and draped it about herself. It was thick and heavy. She would be roasted in it if she sat on deck.

Mark spoke without turning. "Are your clothes ready for collection, Clare?"

"Yes."

As he turned, he looked at the swathed figure and followed her own thoughts. "That won't do. You'll be sweltered to death." He looked helplessly around the cabin, then his face cleared. "A sarong would be just the thing."

"A sarong?" Clare had regained sufficient strength to tinge her words with sarcasm. "Don't tell me that you have sailed to the South Sea islands, as Sep claims to have done.".

"No, I haven't," Mark said, smiling. "But one of those curtains Sara insisted upon would serve the same purpose."

He moved to unhook the wire, and pulled one curtain free. "There's yards of it."

"And what am I supposed to do with it?"

"Fold it about your body and knot the ends under your arms. It's long enough to reach your ankles. Your shoulders will be bare, but the sun is warm. Put it on while I take these things to dry on deck."

Clare eyed the flower-patterned cotton material doubtfully. Yes, it would serve and be far cooler than the blanket, and had the advantage of leaving her arms and hands free. Since there was no alternative, she must make the best of it.

With the cotton folded about her body, she knotted the ends securely. Was this one piece of cloth all those South Sea maidens wore? Well, perhaps they added a garland or a large exotic flower behind one ear. She caught sight of Mark's hairbrush and shaving glass on the top of a cupboard. If she did not brush her hair vigorously, it would dry in a tangle of unmanageable curls. At least her hair would reach her shoulders if left loose and make her feel less naked.

Mark had taken her sandals, too, so she must go barefoot. It was just as well, really, since heels that caught in rings and threw one off balance were not advisable on decks that swayed and tilted under one's feet, even on calm days.

She saw Mark before he saw her. He was standing at the rail, wearing only the fine canvas trousers. His back and shoulders were evenly tanned, and her gaze followed the lean lines of his body to the taut waist and narrow hips. The breeze lifted and dried the dark hair, exposing the broad brow and strong profile. Oh, Mark, her heart said silently, if only you saw your fiancée through the eyes of a servant or dressmaker. With you she must be charming and provocative, a beautiful woman of enchanting promise. Ask Marie, or even Captain Oliver, what lies beneath that lovely face, behind those lustrous eyes.

Mark turned suddenly, as if he had sensed her presence. He stared at the grey-eyed girl swathed in flowered cotton, the long, dark hair almost veiling her ivory shoulders. She smiled and Mark felt a strange twist in his heart again. This was not the soberly dressed, disciplined dressmaker with her hair full of hairpins, but an exotic, saronged creature who might have stepped aboard from some tropical island. He found his voice with difficulty.

"Clare." He could think of nothing more to say, and it was Clare who released him from the spell.

She moved to sit on one of the cushions he had previously placed on deck. She looked up at him and spoke politely, as a guest might. "Yes, I believe I will take wine with you, Captain Conrad. Rhenish, wasn't it?"

Mark felt his heart bound with relief. He moved to sit beside her, and his eyes searched her face. "Are you truly recovered? I can't tell you how—"

"Please don't," Clare interrupted. "You have already apologized. It was not your fault that I fell into the sea." She gave a stifled laugh. "They say that curiosity killed the cat. My own almost drowned me. I should learn from experience and leave well enough alone."

Mark handed her a filled goblet and lifted his own. "I drink to you, my dear—a very brave and beautiful girl." He drained the goblet.

"Why, thank you, Captain." Clare tried to keep her tone

light. "Since the recipient of a toast cannot drink to herself, I will repeat the previous one and drink to the *Sara*." Following Mark's example, Clare drained her own goblet. For a second she was breathless. Then she gasped and blinked at Mark.

"That's a powerful wine. Did you say it was Rhenish?"

"No. Sep said that. He must have finished it himself, for I couldn't find any. This is brandy. I thought you would prefer it to rum, which is Sep's sovereign remedy for half-drowned creatures."

Clare smiled and leaned back against the sun-warmed timber of the wheelhouse. "Yes, I well remember the smell of the rum toddy that Sep brewed in my kitchen for you the night the *Venturer* foundered." She raised her face to the sun as the brandy warmed her.

How pleasant it was to lie in the sun with only the softness of cotton molding her body. She had no petticoat or corselet, no stockings or shoes—just the minimum of covering. She closed her eyes, trying not to think of the dresses unfinished—particularly, the red silk gown for Eve Patterson. That thought jerked her into alertness. What on earth would that young lady say if she knew that her dressmaker, clad only in a cotton curtain, was alone with her fiancé on a small boat drifting in the Bristol Channel?

Mark had been watching the serene face, the twin crescents of dark lashes hiding the expressive grey eyes. His glance followed the curve of her cheek, now touched by the sun, and moved on down her slender neck to her graceful shoulders. From there it was no step at all to consider the shape of her body beneath the cotton cloth. It would be taking unfair advantage of her if he began to make love to her, but the temptation was hard to resist.

Clare's eyes opened so suddenly, her gaze intent upon his, that for a wild moment he wondered if he had spoken those words aloud. No, of course he hadn't, but had she sensed what was in his mind? He felt himself grow hot, like some Peeping Tom caught in the act, or some lustful sailor eyeing a voluptuous dockyard harpy.

Her words came as a relief, but a dampening one.

"This really won't do, you know. I was almost enjoying myself until I realized how much sewing I have to do on Miss Patterson's red silk gown." She gave a slight shiver. "I believe the wind is rising."

"Only a little, and not quite in the right direction. If I put on sail now, we'll end up on the Welsh coast. Besides, your clothes are not dry yet. I'll get something to put about your shoulders."

"Thank you." Clare leaned back as Mark rose and made for the cabin. It was a little cooler, but remembering Eve Patterson had chilled her more. If ever this escapade became public, the scandal would ruin her. Why were men admired for scandalous behavior, while women were ostracized? It didn't seem fair that a gentleman known to have mistresses and to indulge in wild excesses was received everywhere as a rakish fellow by his equals. Didn't an air of rakishness attract even the most demure young lady?

But Mark would not betray her. She was comforted by that thought as she heard his footsteps returning. He could have ruined her weeks ago, but he had not done so. She smiled up at him as he slipped something cool and silky about her shoulders.

"Thank you, that's very—" Her voice died, as did her smile. She looked down at the strutting peacocks with their emerald eyes in the turquoise silk shawl. When her gaze rose again, Mark was startled by the angry glitter in her eyes. Two spots of vivid color blazed upon her cheeks and there was a contemptuous twist to her mouth.

"Damn you, Mark Conrad! Don't you ever take no for an answer?" Her fingers gripped the edges of the shawl, but Mark's hands closed over hers, preventing her from throwing the shawl aside.

He knelt before her, their eyes only inches apart. "Tell me," he said, "what this shawl signifies to you?"

Clare glared at him. "Isn't that obvious?"

"The gift is obvious but not necessarily the reason for it. I feel you have misunderstood that."

"Really?" Clare's voice was full of scorn. "Then perhaps you would enlighten me as to why a man would present a gift to a woman who is neither his relative nor his fiancée?''

''You believe it to be for favors received. That is so, is it not?''

''You put it bluntly, Mr. Conrad.'' Clare felt her voice tremble. ''But that is a fair conclusion to draw from so expensive a present. I have not yet sunk so low and I deeply resent the inference.''

''None was intended, Miss Court. Had I realized how you would view the gift, I would not have pursued Sara's reasoning, but left well enough alone.''

Clare's brows drew together. ''Sara? What has she to do with it?''

Mark sank back on his heels. ''Will you promise not to throw the shawl overboard if I release your hands and explain how it came about? It would really be a dreadful waste of something that suits you well.'' He raised his brows in question, but Clare did not respond. He sighed and took his hand away. ''All right. Throw it over the side if you wish. I shall not prevent you or take it back.''

Clare still held the silken edges. It was really a beautiful shawl. She had never owned anything half as fine. To retain it would weaken her position. If he refused to take it back, was she capable of such a grand gesture as tossing it overboard to show her contempt? And what was that about Sara?

She looked steadily into Mark's face. ''Are you asking me to believe this is Sara's gift? No child would hold silent if the recipient made no mention of receipt.''

''That's true. She delivered it, unknowingly, in the parcel containing her own material. I had purchased two shawls in Bombay and asked Sara's advice on which one Miss Patterson might prefer. She was emphatic in choosing a scarlet one, since blondes invariably like brilliant colors. The one you are now wearing was, in Sara's opinion, the ideal color for a grey-eyed, dark-haired lady such as Miss Court, her very best friend.''

''You said she delivered it unknowingly. Why didn't you tell her?''

''As you remarked yourself, a child does not hold silent.

The idea charmed me so much that I could not resist sending it to you, but I now see it was folly.''

"Because your fiancée might come to hear of it?"

"I was not thinking of that—only realizing that you could not wear it openly without inviting comment. I was not the only man to buy shawls in Bombay. I'm sorry, Clare. It was ill judged, but I never thought you would look upon it in that light.''

"It—it seemed the obvious light to me.''

Mark felt a sudden constriction in his throat as he caught the bitter note in her voice.

"It is a gift from a friend, Clare—one who is grateful for your attention to Sara. Please keep the shawl for her sake. Look upon it only in that light. Can't you do that?" His eyes were fixed intently on her face. Clare was very conscious of his nearness—his bare chest with its fine dark hair glinting in the sun and his strong thighs under the taut canvas trousers. He was much too close for her peace of mind. Her body felt weak and she fought the desire that rose swiftly. To succumb to it would make ridiculous nonsense of her anger over the shawl.

A sharp crack jerked her wits out of their lethargy. Mark looked around, then smiled at her.

"That was the aft sail. The wind is rising." He rose to his feet in a lithe movement. "I'll haul up the anchor and put on full sail. You'll be home within the hour."

He moved away and Clare heard the rattle of the chain as the anchor came aboard. She watched Mark loosen sail ropes, then the *Sara* swung, taking the wind in her canvas. The wind was not strong yet, and the sun was still hot, but Clare knew she must look to her clothes. Was she glad or sorry to be reminded of her position by that first crack of canvas? She rose and gathered up her clothes. Perhaps it was for the best. She had been lucky on those two previous nights with Mark. A third time she might not be. He was betrothed to Eve Patterson and his future was circumscribed by that. However much she might desire him and be happy to bear his child, there was only one woman entitled to that privilege, and her name was not Clare Court.

As she dressed, she thought of Sara and the mother the child did not remember. In view of Eve's murmured comments about boarding schools, young Sara was hardly likely to find a substitute mother in Miss Patterson when she became Mrs. Mark Conrad.

◆   *Chapter Twenty-three*   ◆

Clare had dressed and was hanging the slightly crumpled curtain when Mark tapped on the wheelhouse door.

"May I come in, Clare? I must set course for the cove."

"Yes, of course," Clare said without turning from her task. She tried to speak matter-of-factly, hoping he had not sensed how near to surrender she had been. Only that snapping canvas had brought her to full realization. Since her body was not to be relied upon, she must keep her mind doubly on the alert.

"Like a turn at the wheel, Clare?" Mark asked, glancing over his shoulder, his own voice equally matter-of-fact.

Clare joined him and stood for a moment watching the easy way he handled the wheel, glancing down now and then at the compass bearing. He smiled at her.

"No need for the compass really, since I know every inch of this coastline, and every tree and rock is a landmark, but one gets into the habit on the open seas. A slight deviation off course can make a ship miss land by fifty miles. Take the wheel."

Clare took hold of the smooth wooden staves. Mark moved to stand behind her.

"Hold it easy. There's no need to grip the wheel as if you must haul her bodily about." His soft chuckle sounded in her ear and Clare relaxed her fierce grip. The boat answered to the slightest turn and she glanced at Mark in surprise.

"Why, it's easy," she said with pleasure, and Mark laughed.

"On a calm day with only a little wind, and sheltered to landward of the channel, I agree. Try holding a merchantman in hell's weather on the Atlantic."

"You're right, of course. This may be child's play to a real seaman, but it is exciting to a land-bound female."

She watched the prow cut through the water, sending up foam-crested wavelets that slapped the hull of the *Sara* and streamed away, hissing angrily to spread out in her wake. The breeze whipping through the wheelhouse screen brought a flush of color to her cheeks and flung back her hair like a black banner.

Mark stood beside her now, occasionally correcting her course, but mostly watching her enthralled face. After suffering such an experience as falling overboard, here she was as if nothing had happened, completely absorbed in steering the *Sara*. What a figurehead she would have made on some high-sided galleon. Few merchantmen boasted them these days, and certainly not small crafts like the *Sara*.

He looked ahead, thinking of the real Sara. She would be equally entranced at the wheel. And Eve? The thought leaped into his mind and he frowned. Somehow he could not visualize Eve, her blond hair streaming in the wind, too intent on the job at hand to pay heed to the high-flung spray that skimmed and fell like silver droplets on her hair and shoulders. Eve, with her immaculately coiffured hair, straw hats, and parasols to guard her fine white skin from the sun, was as unlikely a seaman as a dead albatross. He smiled wryly to himself. How would she have reacted to falling overboard? Not, he suspected, by admonishing herself for having no sea legs!

He narrowed his eyes as the cove came into sight. He would, of course, invite Eve to the official launching of the *Sara*. Eve would admire the boat and make charming conversation to the guests. If she declined to participate in her maiden voyage, it must not be held against her. Not everyone cared for the sea, especially in a boat the size of this one. Sara wanted a christening party and that she should have, with Sep, the Clark girls, Perry Knightly and his Isobel, if she could be persuaded, Eve and William Oliver, if he wished, and Clare.

He turned to her. "Keep the wheel while I take in sail, will you? We'll coast in on the breeze."

Clare looked at him with shining grey eyes. He thought she had never looked so beautiful. He could not resist the impulse to drop a kiss on her brow. He grinned down at her.

"Don't let go of the wheel to slap me. You've every right, but it might put the *Sara* off course."

Clare grinned back at him. "I wouldn't endanger the *Sara* for the world, but you'd better hurry back and take the wheel in case I drive her ashore."

The boat came gently to rest in the cove and Mark jumped ashore to make her fast, then returned to the deck. Clare looked at him soberly as she pushed her fingers through her tangled hair.

"Such a brief trip can hardly be considered a maiden voyage, so I shall make no mention to Sara, since she is so looking forward to being the first aboard. Do you agree?"

Mark nodded. "Yes, that would be best. I'm sorry, Clare. I didn't mean to take advantage of your curiosity. It was a spur-of-the-moment thing."

Clare smiled. "Very well, I accept that. And you were a gentleman in the cabin." The scene returned so vividly that her voice came out in a stifled gasp of laughter. "You took no liberties, whatsoever."

Mark stared at her, frowning. "And what do you find amusing in that?"

Clare met his gaze, her eyes still full of laughter. "You —you untied my corselet strings in a most gentlemanly manner, for all the world as if you did it daily."

Mark's expression relaxed and he grinned. "Not so, I assure you, but it was the least I could do for a soul overboard—especially one I had tricked aboard and half drowned in the bargain. Mind you—" He regarded her from wickedly glinting eyes. "—had I known how confoundingly fetching you would look in a sarong, I might have dropped my gentlemanly scruples overboard. Ah, well," he shrugged. "Too late for tears." He glanced at Clare's empty hands and the frown was back on his brow. "Are you still going to be stubborn over that damned shawl? If you won't take it, I swear I'll use it to swab the decks!"

"You wouldn't—" began Clare, then caught back the words abruptly as she saw the smile twitch on Mark's lips. "Oh, confound you, Mark Conrad! You knew I should hate the thought of that. You know, equally, that the shawl will never see the light of day if I accept it."

"I know, but I would like you to have it, for I know how beautifully it suits you. Besides—" His lips curved in a grin. "—that paper parcel will not survive another bout of to-ing and fro-ing." He raised a hand as Clare's mouth opened to protest. "I know. Confound me, a plague on my house and all that, but you'll have it in the end, so why not accept the inevitable. Surely it can't be your first gift from a friend?"

He was surprised to see Clare's eyes cloud over and her gaze move past him. What had he said? Something in his words had stirred an unpleasant chord in her memory; that much was obvious. He realized how little he knew of this girl—absolutely nothing of her background, only how self-contained and proud she was.

Clare, for her part, was thinking of the last gift she had accepted from Lord Rayne, innocently unaware of the conditions attached. She was not that unworldly now, yet the threat of Lord Rayne still hung over her. Since that man had been so interested in the horse, she knew that Philip Rayne had not abandoned hope of finding her. What kind of vengeance would satisfy him?

She shook her head, trying to disperse the sudden cloud on her horizon. Mark was looking at her strangely, a question in his eyes.

"What's wrong, Clare?"

"Why, nothing." Clare forced a smile. "A touch of reaction from the ducking, I suppose. I must go now—it's getting late."

"I'll walk with you to your cottage."

"Please don't. We might meet someone, and I am dreadfully untidy. All sorts of conclusions might be drawn that would do neither of us any good."

"Perhaps you're right." Mark smiled as he agreed, but he had the feeling that somehow a disturbing finger had been laid over the day. For the life of him, he could not guess what it was. "I'll get the shawl."

Clare accepted it without further argument and Mark helped her over the side. They stood together for a moment, Mark's hand on Clare's arm. "Thank you for being so—"

"So witless?" suggested Clare, her moment of dark distraction dismissed.

Mark smiled. "Never that, but for being so understanding and forgiving. You looked like a Valkyrie maiden at the wheel, your hair a heavenly banner streaming behind. You'd make an excellent sailor."

"One with a penchant for falling overboard," Clare observed dryly.

Mark laughed. "You'd soon get the hang of it."

"Falling overboard?"

"No, idiot child, the way to roll with the motion of the deck and keep your feet."

"Thank you, but I'll forgo that dubious pleasure."

"You'll come to the launching, won't you? The official christening and maiden voyage, I mean."

"I'm afraid I shall be far too busy."

"I haven't yet told you when it is to be."

"Whenever it is, I shall still be too busy."

"Why? Sara will expect you."

Clare sighed. "Mark Conrad, the sea has addled your brain. Consider your guest list and reason why a nobody dressmaker should be included. Others will wonder—including your fiancée. Please don't be obtuse."

For a moment Mark's eyes held a stormy look, then he smiled ruefully. "I'm sorry. I've no right to use Sara as moral blackmail." He sensed rather than saw the stiffening of Clare's body as he used the term. Had the word *blackmail* touched a chord? His mind flashed back to that first meeting. She had admitted running away from something.

"I must go," Clare said abruptly. "Good-bye, Mark."

Then she was gone, hurrying up the slope. Without a backward glance, she disappeared over the crest of the hill. Mark stood where he was, frowning, trying to decipher the mystery of Clare Court and getting nowhere. He only knew that when she had gone overboard, his heart had frozen in his breast. He could not remember following her—only that the most important thing in his life was to have her back on board. He would have done that much for anyone, of course, since a ship's captain was responsible for the safety of his passengers, but the thought of Clare Court as a limp, drowned body filled him with unbelievable horror. It had been over very quickly and she had taken it well, but would the memory of what might have happened move through her dreams tonight? He went to the cabin to collect his portfolio of sketches, wondering ruefully if he might, himself, be troubled by the same dream.

However, he was due to dine at the Pattersons' tonight. Mr. Patterson had consented to listen to his plans and look over his sketches. With luck and a certain amount of persuasion, the old man might consent to withdraw one of his smaller ships for the conversion suggested. He did not doubt that Eve would support his argument, but William Oliver, since he knew on whom his future depended, would undoubtedly follow his uncle's lead. The simple fact of the old man agreeing to talk after dinner was encouraging, and Mark took leave of the *Sara* in a buoyant mood.

When he presented himself at the Patterson house that evening, he was immaculately turned out. His hair was brushed as flatly as its thickness would allow, his lean brown face shaved closely, and his linen spotless. Clare Court would not have recognized the tall, elegant figure as the same man she had seen only hours earlier in disreputable canvas trousers, barefoot and tangle-haired. But Clare Court was far from Mark Conrad's mind as he was shown into the drawing room.

Thomas Patterson was seated in a deep armchair at one side of the fireplace, William Oliver in a similar chair at the other. Eve Patterson was arranged on the couch, her full silk skirts spread about her. The two men nodded in answer to

Mark's greeting, but only Eve rose gracefully to her feet in a slow whisper of silk and held out both hands. Mark took them as he bowed, and dropped a kiss on each delicate wrist. Eve smiled into his eyes; her own were soft and limpid. Mark surveyed the gleaming blond hair, arranged with precision into a French pleat, allowing a few soft curls to fall over her brow. Her gown was of palest pink, quite unadorned, for she was wearing the red silk shawl he had sent to her.

He remembered Sara's words and smiled. "Yes, that is the better one for you. Do you like it?"

"Dear Mark, it is absolutely beautiful. What good taste you have." She paused. "What do you mean—the better one for me? You make it sound as if you had more than one to choose from, all packed away in Conrad Place." Eve put her head to one side and smiled bewitchingly. "I hope, dear Mark, that I shall not meet a replica of this shawl at some gathering in Clevedon."

Her voice was gently teasing, but Mark knew that her wits were sharp and she had picked up the suggestion of plurality. He must lie by omission.

"Yes, I did say the better one, didn't I? If you had seen the rainbow colors and designs at the silk merchant's in Bombay, you would never have been content with one shawl. Since every conceivable color was displayed, I could only hope that my choice of red would suit you better than any other. If you should come across a similar one in Clevedon, please hold me blameless. I am not the only seafarer to visit Bombay." His tone was mild, his smile affable, and Eve was convinced.

She laughed gaily and patted Mark's cheek. "Oh, my dear, I am not accusing you of playing fast and loose with your fiancée. You are far too honorable for that." Her gaze flickered toward her cousin and the teasing note in her voice took on an edge of mockery. "And too much the gentleman, I vow, to be casting sheep's eyes at a little dab of a dressmaker."

"What?" Mark stared at her, temporarily taken aback. What was she hinting at? What did she know? Then he caught sight of William Oliver's flushed and angry face.

"You really are—" William began hotly "—er, quite wrong," he finished lamely, aware of his uncle's piercing gaze.

"Leave the boy alone, Eve," her father commanded in a no-nonsense voice. "If he wants to sow his wild oats with one of the lower orders, it is not your concern. Help yourself to a drink, Mark, and sit down."

Eve pouted prettily and reseated herself, moving her skirts to allow Mark to share the couch. She smiled at him and continued softly on the same theme.

"It was really quite touching the way William could not take his eyes from the girl."

"What girl?" Mark asked carefully. Eve patronized several dressmakers.

"Miss Court, my new dressmaker. If she pleases me, I am sure that fact will bring her plenty of custom. William escorted me to her cottage for my first fitting. Such a dreadfully out-of-the-way place, and so small, but I daresay it is all she can afford." She glanced over at William and dropped her voice. "Of course, being out of the way has its advantages." She smiled mischievously. "And if William is discreet—"

Mark tried to relax his suddenly tight muscles. He looked at Eve and forced his voice into a lazy drawl.

"And did William's interest evoke a response?"

Eve giggled. "No, I cannot say that it did. Poor William. She's a pretty little thing—far too high in the instep for her position."

"What is that supposed to mean?"

"Why, she had the effrontery to deny me the design of gown I wanted, all because she had made its like for Isobel Foster."

Mark grinned sardonically. "An unusual experience for you, Eve. But nevertheless, she is still making a gown for you, isn't she?" He remembered the red silk draped on the dressmaker's dummy, but more vividly into his mind's eye came the picture of the dark-haired girl in a curtain sarong, the turquoise shawl draping her bare shoulders. He blinked as Eve's voice penetrated that second's oblivion to everything else.

"If the girl does her work well, I will have her make me a simple one for the party at Conrad Place, after the child has launched her little boat. So exciting for the child, I'm sure."

Mark's eyes were a little cool as he looked at Eve. "That child has a name, and if you intend to become her stepmother, it would be well to remember it. You cannot keep calling her *child*."

Eve widened her eyes in pretended bewilderment. "Oh, darling Mark, I meant no disparagement of the—of Sara. How could you think it of me? But you must allow that a girl does not normally envisage matrimony with a ready-made daughter to hand."

She smiled winsomely, relieved to see Mark's eyes soften. She must never forget the strong bond of affection between Mark and the child, and never show her jealousy in any tangible form. There would be time enough when she was Mrs. Conrad to devise a way of weakening that bond. She had no intention of sharing Mark Conrad with anyone—least of all, another woman's child.

With dinner over, Mr. Patterson took Mark into his study. Eve had shown some reluctance to let him go, but her father had patted her cheek with genuine affection.

"If I had allowed your mother to distract me from business, dear child, you would not live in this fine house, with servants and carriages and all the splendid clothes you never tire of buying. Business comes first—you know that."

"Yes, Papa," Eve said with filial sweetness. "You have always been so clever at business, while I have no talent for it at all." She sighed and Mr. Patterson smiled paternally.

"No reason in the world why you should concern yourself with it. Female talents lie in different directions." He ushered Mark through the door and it clicked shut behind them.

Eve glanced at her cousin. William Oliver was regarding her with a cynically amused expression.

"Dear child," he mocked. "Your talents certainly lie in other directions, like flattering the man who pays your bills. You'll not find Conrad so easy to twist around your finger. Besides, he has no money."

"He will have," Eve said airily. "You don't suppose I'm fool enough to marry a poor man."

"Why go to the bother of encouraging him when you could marry a rich man in the first place. There's many a one been angling for your favors, and I've seen you flirting with every one of them. And it's not as if you are mad about the fellow—confess it."

Eve sighed. "You don't understand at all, do you, William? I could marry a merchant's son who is as rich as Papa himself, but how far back can he trace the family tree? Have you noticed ancestral portraits on any wall in a Clevedon house?"

"There must be some."

"Of course, but not in our circle. The really old families keep to themselves and look down on fortunes made from trade, even if they're hard-pressed for money themselves. They judge people by breeding, not money."

"Poor, but well-bred, like Conrad." There was a sneer in William's voice.

"Exactly." Eve ignored the sneer. "I want my portrait to hang at Conrad Place, together with all those earlier Conrad ladies."

"So, to achieve that distinction, you intend to buy Conrad?"

"Don't be vulgar, William. Mark adores me, and he is by far the most attractive man of my acquaintance. Papa will arrange everything to my entire satisfaction; you need have no doubts on that score."

William moved uneasily in his chair and Eve noted the movement with delight.

"Poor William. You don't really like the sea, do you? But Papa will never take you into partnership until you have proved that you are as good as Mark." She paused, eyeing him maliciously. "And a son-in-law is rather closer than a nephew. Who knows, dear William—he may cut you out altogether."

"I'm damned if he will," William muttered through clenched teeth. "I'll see him in hell first."

But Eve was not listening. She picked up a magazine and began to leaf through it, ignoring her cousin's presence.

Mr. Thomas Patterson sat behind his leather-topped desk and adjusted a pair of gold-rimmed spectacles. He looked up at the tall, dark-haired man and nodded.

"Very well, Mark, I have no objection to a lecture on the benefit of steam shipping, but I remain entirely uncommitted. You understand that?"

"Naturally, sir, and I am obliged to you for consenting to this discussion. If you will bear with me for a few minutes, I must explain that this story began in 1806." He smiled as Mr. Patterson raised his brows. "I will state briefly that Lord Dundas commissioned a firm to build an engine into a canal boat. He named the boat after his daughter, Charlotte."

"Obviously a failure," Mr. Patterson commented dryly.

"Since it was a canal boat, the wash from the powered paddles was thought to endanger the canal banks. The idea was abandoned and the *Charlotte Dundas* was left to rot in some inlet."

"So, there was an end to it."

"Not quite, sir. The idea intrigued an American, one Robert Fulton. He visited the site and made careful sketches of the engine. He then commissioned the English firm of Boulton and Watt to copy it. This he took back to America and built his own steam paddleboat, the *Clermont*. This ran successfully up and down the Hudson River."

"A riverboat." Mr. Patterson's tone was scathing. "What good is that to me?"

"Then came the *Comet*, which sailed on the Clyde," Mark went on impassively. He paused, smiling, trying to lighten the atmosphere. "Admittedly, she kept breaking down and the passengers had to take turns at the flywheel, but she did achieve a speed of between three and four miles an hour."

"Three or four—?" Mr. Patterson's face expressed his opinion of so paltry a performance.

"Under steam, sir," Mark interjected hastily. "It was quite an achievement. But one should say that the *Marjorie* in 1817 was the first real steam paddleboat. She steamed from Scotland to London—quite a distance.''

''Where is she now?''

Mark's heart sank. Trust a businessman to find the weak point. ''London to Margate, passenger and freight service.''

Mr. Patterson looked at Mark suspiciously. ''And where is this taradiddle of failures leading us? What the devil do I want with riverboats? My line is oceangoing. You know that very well.''

''Yes, sir.'' Mark felt on surer ground here. ''I was giving background to the theory that steam will come and those fleet owners who recognize the inevitability of it will profit, as it were, from being in on the ground floor. The Atlantic has already been crossed!'' There was a flicker of interest in Mr. Patterson's eyes and Mark went on. ''The *Savannah* came from America to Liverpool in twenty-five days.''

''Under steam?''

''Not all the way, sir, unfortunately. A great deal of fuel is needed to power the boilers. Adequate space for storage is a necessity.''

''Hah!'' Mr. Patterson leaned back in his chair. ''She had sails on her, then.''

Mark nodded, although Mr. Patterson's remark had been more statement than question. He knew exactly what his employer was thinking, and the words came on cue.

''What the devil do I want to be bothering with steam for, when a full head of canvas will take my ships farther and faster?''

''Until the wind runs out and the ships are dead as driftwood.'' Mark must have spoken more sharply than he realized; Mr. Patterson looked up through narrowed eyes.

''You've your heart set on this, haven't you?''

''Yes, sir. I know it means more experiments, better designs below decks for storage of fuel, but the progress from the *Charlotte Dundas* to the *Savannah* has been achieved by men with faith in the future. There's even talk of iron ships, and that suggestion has scoffers aplenty.''

''Since you're favoring me with all this information, I take it you hope to find in me a man of faith in the future, and not one of your scoffers?'' Mr. Patterson smiled thinly.

"Exactly, sir. Allow me to show you the sketches I made myself and the modifications on the original design." Mark swept aside his notes and produced a large-scale drawing. "Here, sir, is a single, horizontal, double-acting cylinder. It has a separate condenser and air pumps, operated from a bell-crank. They're driven from this crosshead, both below decks. Here are the piston rods, in guided slides, and the connecting rod is linked to a crank attached to the paddle wheel shaft at the stern of the ship."

Mr. Patterson frowned. "I don't know what the hell you're talking about."

Mark grinned. "Frankly, sir, neither do I. I'm no engineer, but I'm assured it makes sense to them."

"Engineers, eh? And they'll charge a pretty penny."

Dangerous ground again, thought Mark, but he answered calmly. "A certain outlay, sir, but an oceangoing steamship will not be dependent on wind or tide. The first shipowner to power his ships completely will scoop the market. No port in the world would be out of reach, and—"

"And it will cost a fortune to convert even one ship," Mr. Patterson said. "Have you the figures on that, and the length of time the ship will be out of commission? Every day a ship is laid up, I lose money, yet you ask me to lay up a ship and pay for the privilege of having it tricked out with boilers and pumps and all this newfangled rubbish." He thumped the desk, scattering the sketches that lay there. His face took on a high color as his voice rose.

"The initial outlay will not be cheap, sir, but in the long run—"

"I have twenty oceangoing sailing ships in my fleet, man. If every one costs a fortune to convert, where is my profit? In the long run, you say? Am I to beggar myself for the long run? You have shown me nothing but failures, so far."

"One ship only, sir," Mark said desperately. "A small vessel on which to carry out these trials. I'll engage there'll be no failure with the best engineers I can find."

"You confess to being no engineer yourself. How will you know the best? And who, may I ask, will be footing the bill?"

The two men stared at each other, Mr. Patterson red-faced and scowling, Mark pale and tight-lipped. Both were breathing heavily. There was silence for several moments.

Mr. Patterson broke it. "Come. You look as if you need a brandy. So do I, for that matter." He moved to open the study door.

Mark shuffled his papers into a heap and put them into the portfolio. He felt sick with disappointment. Mr. Patterson left the study, Mark following slowly.

"Come out of the clouds, Mark," his host said, not ungently, as they entered the sitting room. "It's impractical—almost insane. My fleet has sailed under canvas these thirty years and I intend to keep it that way. Steam? Pah!"

◆ *Chapter Twenty-four* ◆

The last words had been heard by both Eve and William. Eve raised her fine brows.

"Steam, Papa? Whatever have you been talking about?"

"Nothing of importance, my dear. At least—" He glanced sideways at Mark's rigid face. "—it appears to be of some importance to your young man. I am sure he has spoken of it to you."

"Why, no, Papa." Eve laughed lightly. "In what connection would we talk of steam? You mean the sort of steam one sees coming out of a kettle?" She looked brightly at Mark.

"The same sort of steam can propel a ship," Mark supplied briefly.

William regarded his uncle keenly. He had heard something of this steam notion. So Conrad was interested, was he, and had thought to interest the old man? From the tightness of his face, he guessed that Uncle Thomas had not received the idea kindly. William smiled to himself. So much for Eve's fine gentleman friend. That should take the fellow down a peg or two. Aloud he said, "Do you set any store by the notion, Uncle?" He had to be sure before adding his own condemnation or praise. Uncle Thomas could be unpredictable when he chose.

"Not in my time, not in my fleet. If men want to try out new ways and ideas, they'll do it at their own expense, not mine."

"Quite so, Uncle. A finer sight than a spread of canvas, I've yet to see. Fast and efficient beyond anything. These steam engines, Conrad—won't they choke the air with smoke and filth?"

Mark looked at him coldly. "Since they need to burn fuel, naturally." He was aware that behind William's bland gaze, the man was enjoying this moment. "But advantages outweigh that consideration."

"Advantages?" William looked puzzled and was rash enough to look appealingly at his uncle. "Do you see any advantages, Uncle?"

Mr. Patterson scowled. "Don't be more of a fool than you can help, boy. Being independent of the wind is a great advantage. Even you should realize that!"

William flushed. "But, you said—"

"I said I would stay with canvas, but that's not to say I don't understand the principles behind the new venture." He glanced at Mark and smiled. "I'm too old a dog to learn new tricks. Have a brandy, Mark."

"No, thank you, sir. If you'll excuse me, I'll take my leave."

"So soon?" Eve complained.

Mark bowed over her hand. "I shall be poor company tonight, my dear. Good night to you." He nodded at William and picked up his portfolio.

William was still smarting from his uncle's words.

"Going to hawk your plans around the shipping fraternity, Conrad?"

Mark stiffened, his eyes glacial. "No, I shall not do that."

"Then you'll have to give up the idea, won't you?" There was the hint of a sneer in William's voice.

"Nor that, either," Mark said, turning toward the door.

"You'll need money," William persisted, not wishing to be denied the chance of scoring over Mark Conrad, who was already opening the door. "That's not so easily come by."

Mark turned in the doorway and favored William with a sardonic smile. "Exactly. But it can be done."

As Mark drove away from the house in his light carriage, he felt the urge to whip up his horse and send the carriage hurtling through the dark night, uncaring of obstacles, just to relieve his intense disappointment. But breaking his neck and injuring an innocent horse in the bargain was no answer. He had been sure, or almost sure, that Thomas Patterson would have backed him in this new venture. One weary old ship laid up was all that he wanted. Well, not quite all, he admitted. There was the question of money for refitting the vessel with machinery. He had failed utterly to rouse any interest in the old man.

That last remark to William had come from hurt pride. It had sounded good, but had been completely meaningless. He grined ruefully in the dark as he guided the horse away from the town. William was right. Money was not easily come by, especially not from the close, hidebound shipowners of Clevedon. Why change their profit-making mode of carrying goods? Only a fool or a philanthropist would dream of something better.

Mark sighed. He did not need either of those, but a rich, young shipping man with a touch of vision. Better still, a group of them. The reins relaxed in his hands as he played with that thought. The horse continued at its own pace, knowing without direction where his stable lay. Mark's mind was engrossed in a world of its own. In the course of his research, he had met many shipping men, some with only a handful of merchantmen but all eager to build up their fleets—elder sons expecting to inherit established lines, but not with any great enthusiasm.

Many of them knew as much as he did about the steam experiments. Cost or parental opposition had always been the stumbling block to any new idea. Glasgow, London, Bristol, Cardiff, and many more ports boasted their merchant fleets. Suppose a company could be formed, each owner contributing to the cost of fitting out just one ship? The more Mark thought about it, the more feasible it became. He would appeal to the younger end of the ship-owning fraternity, naturally, for they would see the future more clearly. Should they build a new ship especially for the job—a fine hundred-tonner, perhaps? Mark leashed back his flying thoughts. One day, maybe, but for now he must be content with a fifty-tonner, perhaps less.

At Conrad Place he unharnessed the horse, strapped the night blanket over him, and provided water and feed. It was all done automatically as his mind made a mental tally of people he could approach. Once in his study, he shrugged out of his evening jacket and began to write letters, both to men he thought might find the idea challenging, and to various engineering firms. A good engineer was a necessity for he had no idea, himself, what the total cost might be. It was no good going off half-cocked, as he had tonight with Mr. Patterson. Businessmen needed facts and figures, not promises of a glorious future.

It was two o'clock when Mark sealed the last envelope. He stacked the letters on his desk and rose. Tomorrow he would drop them in at the post office before taking out the *Firefly*, the second largest of the Patterson ships. William Oliver was captaining the *Dolphin*, heading around the Cornish coast to return with china clay that would then be barged up the Avon River to the potteries. The *Firefly* was making the Cherbourg run to load casks of brandy and French wines.

Mark went to bed. He would have liked to discuss his plans with a sympathetic listener, even if that person knew nothing of steamships. Eve? For her, steam was something that came out of a kettle! He smiled tolerantly. What could you expect from a rich, spoiled beauty? Perry? He was an excellent fellow, but his feet were set firmly on the ground—his own farming ground. And Sep was strictly an old sailing ship man. The name he was trying to keep in the back of his mind floated forward: Clare. Yes, she would listen, ask questions, and try to understand the mechanics of the thing. She might do it, too, for there was intelligence in her—a sharpness of wit and the courage to create her own new world. Yes, she would understand a man's ambitions, for she had them herself.

Had Mark stayed longer at the Patterson house, he would have been gratified by Eve's support for his scheme. His early departure had not pleased her, but she knew better than to rail at him. Mark was his own man and impervious to the tantrums and tears that were usually so effective with other men. She had learned that lesson early in their engagement. He, too, had been dazzled by her beauty and flattered by her attention, and paid court as ardently as any suitor. Not by the remotest chance did he expect to be considered seriously, for all other suitors were wealthy men and Eve was an heiress. But she had shown her preference and had announced to the world, and a bemused Mark, that he was the chosen one. There had been no opposition from Mr. Patterson, much to Mark's surprise. He deduced that Eve had won him around by gentle persuasion, since her happiness was of prime importance to her father.

Eve's partisanship took the form of demanding to know what had happened to send her betrothed into the night so pale and rigid-featured. Mr. Patterson, that hardheaded business man, had told her and been reduced to explaining himself in a splutter of defensive remarks.

William had cast his lightweight support on his uncle's side, but the Pattersons had turned on him as one—Mr. Patterson with relief, and Eve with angry comparisons between himself and Mark. The verbal battle had ended with Mr. Patterson promising his daughter that Mark should immediately be restored to command of the *Dolphin* and the papers drawn up for a share in the Patterson company.

William had listened with horror. ''What—what about me?

You promised me a share, Uncle Thomas. Since you hold most of the shares and Eve the rest—"

"I promised you a share when you had proved yourself, William. Good heavens, boy, you haven't left coastal waters yet! When you've sailed to Africa and India, like Mark Conrad, I'll consider the matter more seriously."

William's stomach muscles tightened and he felt sick. Africa and India? He felt seasick just getting out of the estuary.

"You know, Papa," Eve said, honey-voiced after getting her own way. "I really think William would prefer to work ashore. There must be room for another clerk in your office."

William stared at her in frustrated silence. He would much prefer a land job, but a clerk? A fellow who took home wages at the end of every week, and miserable ones, at that, he didn't doubt. And what chance had a clerk to become a shareholder? He looked at his uncle.

"Very well, sir. I will say no more until I have fulfilled all your requirements." He shrugged. "To the Americas or the Far East, as you wish. I shall not fail you."

Clare locked her door that night and drew the curtains close before spreading the turquoise silk shawl over the back of the couch. She had to admire it just once more before packing it away in tissue paper at the back of a drawer. No one must ever see it and wonder how she came by such an expensive thing. It was still on the couch back when she had washed and prepared herself for bed.

Just once, she thought, she must feel that cool silk about her bare shoulders and see it as Mark had—not over a curtain sarong but a naked body! *Shameless hussy*, she chided herself, but the temptation was too strong to resist. Discarding her nightdress, she stood before the cheval glass and draped the shawl about herself. He was right. The color did suit a dark-haired, grey-eyed girl. The peacocks, undulating to the rise and fall of the breasts they covered, seemed to gaze at her with emerald-eyed cynicism. She smiled. They were right to do so, for had the wind not risen at that precise moment, she might well have cast caution and the sarong aside and been revealed as she was now.

The shawl slid off her shoulders and Clare laid it on the couch again. With the cotton nightdress once more in place, she folded the shawl into tissue paper and carried it into her bedroom.

Isobel Foster called on her the following day, escorted by Perry Knightly. Clare invited them in, expecting to be handed a parcel of material.

"Do we disturb you, Miss Court?" asked Isobel. "This is by way of being a social visit, for I have not brought you anything to sew."

Clare smiled into the glowing faces. "I am honored to be disturbed by such delightful company. You will take coffee, I hope? My cups are not of the best quality, but my coffee is excellent. Will you be seated?"

"In your kitchen, dear Miss Court, if you please. It was in there you gave me good advice, and it's such a cozy room."

"The kitchen?" Clare asked in surprise. "Do I hear aright? You wish me to entertain rich young ladies and honorable gentlemen in my kitchen? Whatever would your mama say to that?"

"Mama is not here," Isobel said with perfect logic. "And anyway, Perry hates to sit on the edge of a chair balancing china cups on his knee, don't you, Perry?"

Mr. Knightly grinned. "Terrifies the life out of me. Especially if I have to balance a tea plate on the other knee. I'm so busy doing a balancing act, I've no idea of the conversation going on."

Clare laughed. "I know just what you mean. The kitchen it is, then. My cups feel more at home there, and I do allow elbows on the table."

As Clare made a jug of coffee, she noted the clasped hands and a thread of envy pulled at her heartstrings. If Mark were free she had nothing to offer him, and he had never said he loved her, anyway. She put the thought aside as she poured coffee into the thick, white cups and brought sugar and milk to the table.

"Do you know, Miss Court, Mama has become quite taken with Perry since our last visit to you. I knew she would be when she really got to know him. Isn't it wonderful?"

"Wonderful," echoed Clare, straight-faced.

"Can't understand it, myself," Perry said. "I never hid the fact that I was only halfway as well off as that fellow, Palmer, but Mrs. Foster said she had to make sure I was not a fortune hunter, so I suppose it stands to reason when you've a beautiful daughter."

Isobel blushed. "What nonsense! You just charmed Mama. It's as plain as a pikestaff to me. What do you think, Miss Court?"

"I think," Clare said slowly, with the air of one who has given the matter deep thought, "our coffee grows cold while you two continue to make each other blush."

Isobel giggled and Perry gave his wide grin. "Drink up your coffee, Isobel," he ordered, "before Miss Court throws us out for ingratitude."

"Yes, Perry," Isobel said meekly, but her eyes were twinkling.

"I hope," said Clare, "that this story will have a happy ending. Has George Palmer been given his congé? I thought your Mama favored him."

Isobel set down her cup, frowning slightly. "She did, and it's rather a puzzle, really. I was sure he intended to propose, as I told you, but I kept Perry beside me, and he sort of loomed over George, which seemed to make him nervous." She giggled again. "He didn't stay long after dinner."

Clare privately wondered if George Palmer believed that Perry might have been his assailant that night in the cottage, and was at pains to avoid a repeat performance with a man of Mr. Knightly's stature.

"Didn't like the cut of the fellow by half," Perry said. "Waistcoat was too loud."

The two girls looked at Perry's disapproving face. There was something so irresistibly comic in the expression that Clare could not help joining in Isobel's laughter.

"Well, there you have the answer to your puzzle, Miss Foster," she said. "What man would not be intimidated by a glowering Mr. Knightly looming over him?"

Perry grinned ruefully. "I was always a big fellow but never went in for fisticuffs—unless it was necessary. My size is handy for things like throwing a cow for branding, though—which reminds me, I want to visit Mr. Clark again.''

Isobel gave a sigh of pure pleasure. ''It's going to be wonderful living in the country and not having to dress up or try to be charming to every young man because Mama is watching.''

''Am I to understand that congratulations are in order?'' asked Clare.

''We have an understanding,'' Isobel said, ''but Papa thinks we should wait a year before announcing anything official.'' She looked broodingly at her beloved. ''So does Perry. It's ridiculous, for I won't change my mind.''

''Neither will I, my love, but you're very young and a year will give me time to get the house in order and the new herd settled. Your papa is right and, after all, you might decide you'd rather have a house in town than one in the country.''

Isobel gave him a long look, then raised her brows at Clare. ''What strange creatures men are. As soon as you have accepted them, they make you wait a year, during which time,'' she looked darkly at Perry, ''they are probably pursuing someone else.''

''Never!'' Perry began indignantly, then saw the smile growing on Isobel's face. He rose to his feet, grinning. ''Come along, minx, and I'll teach you which end of a cow is which. You do ride, of course?''

''Of course, but I prefer to ride horses.''

Perry's lips twitched and he turned to Clare. ''Thank you for your hospitality, Miss Court.'' He took Isobel's fingers firmly in his large hand.

''Thank you, Miss Court,'' Isobel echoed. ''It has been such fun. May we come again?''

''Of course.''

Clare watched them drive down the hill to the farm. She closed her door on the sight of those happy lovers and her cottage became empty again—as empty as it would always be. She shook herself out of her sudden depression. What good was wallowing in self-pity when she had chosen this path for herself?

Shortly after their departure, Clare heard the approach of

a horse. There was no accompanying sound of carriage wheels. Perhaps one of her ladies had sent a groom to collect his mistress's completed garment. Not Miss Patterson's, for she would come herself to try on the gown and ensure its perfect fit. It was for some special occasion, she remembered Eve hinting. Perhaps it was her birthday—an event Eve would view with the greatest importance.

The hoofbeats stopped outside her door and Clare rose, waiting for the knock. It was hardly a knock that came— more a tentative tapping, as if the horseman were unsure of his reception. Clare's heart gave an unexpected jump. It was too fanciful for words, yet her mind sensed nervousness in that tapping and she reacted similarly.

She squared her shoulders, telling herself not to be such a fool. It was broad daylight and the farm was well within screaming distance. She opened the door, her polite, professional smile in place. For a moment she did not recognize the man standing there. He was a few paces away from her door, his head half turned toward the farm. In the brief moment before he faced her directly, her heart jumped again and she knew him.

He was the man who had shown so much interest in Lord Rayne's horse, even going brazenly into the farm stables to establish if the horse had a particular scar behind its foreleg, pretending to young Albert that she had sent him. Clare took a deep breath.

"Well?" she asked harshly.

The man started and slanted a quick look sideways. Clare followed his gaze. Perry was just visible beside Mr. Clark, and even from this distance he looked a formidable opponent, if called upon to enact that role. Clare felt a little easier, understanding now the man's nervousness. He must have been in the vicinity when Isobel and Perry arrived but waited until their departure.

Clare looked more closely at her visitor. He was not a strong-armed bullyboy for Lord Rayne; rather, he was the kind who delved in dark corners, seeking for a fee whatever his employer wanted found. And Lord Rayne wanted Clare Court, formerly Harcourt. Now, he had her.

The man was reaching into an inside pocket of his wide-skirted riding coat. Clare stiffened. Did he have a pistol? She dismissed the thought instantly. It would be too melodramatic and noisy. Lord Rayne's revenge would be more subtle than that.

The hand came out holding a large square of parchment, folded and sealed with a blob of red wax. The wax was indented—with his lordship's seal, she supposed, which would undoubtedly be inscribed on the paneled door of his carriage. It had been dark when they left Harcourt House and her activities the following day had not given her time to study the family arms.

"I don't want no trouble," the stranger said, misinterpreting her look.

Clare was able to regard him calmly. "Then state your business and go about your own."

"I've been ordered to deliver this to you. It's no good asking me any questions. I do as I'm told and don't ask any myself, for it's healthier that way. I don't know what it's about, and I don't want to." The man was breathing hard after his speech and held out the letter to Clare.

She looked at the superscription. Her name was not on it, only the word *dressmaker*. Clare took the letter, her lips curling. A very careful man, Lord Rayne was and she suspected, even without opening the missive, that no names would be mentioned in the script.

As soon as the letter was in her hands, the man climbed into the saddle and was off down the slope and past the farmhouse. Clare went into her cottage and locked the door. She sat down beside her sewing table, broke the seal, and spread out the thick parchment paper. There was no salutation or signature, just a few lines that she doubted Lord Rayne had written himself:

"It is my intention to call on you Wednesday week to proceed with our earlier agreed business. Please prepare for my arrival and believe that my aims are still the same. Should you wish to contact me sooner, you will find I have foreseen this possibility and have set messengers to watch for you in every direction, in order to spare you the need for travel."

◆ *Chapter Twenty-five* ◆

So, Lord Rayne had made his move at last. Clare raised her gaze from the parchment. She felt no fear—only relief that the waiting game was over. Wednesday week he had written, and today was Friday. She thought of the men—messengers, he had called them—patrolling every avenue of escape. How innocuously he had worded his message if she should, by chance, invoke the aid of the law. If she did that, the only outcome would be a forcible return to her father, since she was a minor. No, she would remain exactly where she was and deny Lord Rayne the satisfaction of thwarting her attempts to escape. She would not make his task easier by placing herself in some lonely spot where his carriage could take her up with no one being any the wiser as to her whereabouts.

She folded the letter, took it into her bedroom, and pushed it down into the old straw basket she had brought from Harcourt House. The amber silk gown, fine slippers, and delicate undergarments he had given her were still tucked in the bag. She pushed it to the back, under her hanging dresses. Wednesday week was a generous time limit and one he might judge would reduce her to such a state of nervous dread that future resistance must be mere token. But surely that was ample time to think of something. She was reluctant to involve those she had grown to like in this sordid business—reluctant to have them think badly of her. Whatever she decided, it must be her decision solely. Lord Rayne was rich and titled. No doubt he had friends in high places, as he undoubtedly had in low ones!

On Saturday she worked on Eve Patterson's gown. It was due for collection on Tuesday. During the afternoon, Septimus Thomas rolled up the hill. She heard him long before he came into sight, for he was singing in his gravelly voice. The words were indistinguishable, which was perhaps as well, since sea chanteys were not noted for their refinement. She was standing in the doorway, arms akimbo, when he hove into sight.

He stopped both walking and singing, and looked at her with a sly, ingratiating expression.

"Afternoon, miss. Lovely day, ain't it? Quite a haul up the hill for an old 'un." His intent gaze rested on her un-smiling face.

"Did I invite you to make it?" Clare asked coolly.

Sep scratched his chin, looking away and back again in a slightly perplexed way. "'Tis a fact you didn't, precisely, but I'd a mind to offer my services for—" he paused, reaching for inspiration. "For to spy out that back door bolt, miss. Screeches something 'orrible." He beamed.

"And how would you know, since I don't shoot the bolt until I go to bed?"

"'Twas acting suspicious, like, for I saw rust with my own eyes. Mark my words, I says to myself, miss'll have trouble with that varmint one of these nights, or I'm a Dutchman."

"Septimus Thomas, you've a powerful imagination, but for an excuse to get yourself alongside my teapot, it's the feeblest I ever heard."

Sep looked pained and abashed at the same time. "You don't give a fellow time to take station before you open up on him. As hard a broadside as if I'd scuttled the admiral's barge on account of wanting a bit of whittling wood."

"Septimus Thomas, you're a rogue, a villain, and a be-trayer of females—namely, me."

"Me, miss? I never betrayed a female in my life—least-ways, not a lady female."

"Oh, no? Then who was it who lured me aboard the *Sara*, then cast off as soon as my back was turned? The only thing you didn't do was hit me over the head like a pirate or press-ganger would have done. You cast me adrift without warning, and me not even given time to sign ship's papers." Clare paused for breath, trying to stifle a giggle as Sep began to chuckle.

"Aye, miss, you've a right turn of phrase, there. Captain Mark was aboard and you couldn't have been in safer hands.

Nothing like a sea breeze to put color in your cheeks. Did you enjoy the trip, then?''

Clare decided against telling Sep of her actual trip over the side and said instead, ''Pleasant enough, save when we were becalmed.''

''Aye, miss, that's always been a problem. You can lose a rare lot of time that way. All you can do is sit around gabbing and drinking tea until the wind gets up again.''

''All right, Septimus Thomas, you've made your point. I'll put on the kettle while you deal with that suspicious character.''

''Eh, miss?''

''The bolt, Septimus,'' Clare reminded him, smiling over her shoulder. ''You haven't forgotten already why you came, surely?''

Sep grinned sheepishly and followed her through the cottage into the kitchen.

By Tuesday, Clare was no nearer to finding a way to circumvent Lord Rayne's plot. If his men were watching the byways, others would not neglect the town of Clevedon or the harbor. Every passenger boarding a vessel must be open to scrutiny by men armed with her description. She thought of dressing as a boy and stowing away on a merchantman, but she didn't know how to obtain boys' clothing, or what to respond if she was challenged by a deckhand. She shook her head and prepared for Miss Patterson's arrival.

Once again Eve swept up with her maid, Marie, and her cousin, William, in attendance. The gown had been completed, and once within its folds, Eve posed before the cheval glass, smiling at herself from all angles. Clare had to admit that Eve looked radiant. Miss Patterson beckoned forward her maid, who opened a leather, gilt-edged box to reveal a collection of jewels. Clare stared at the diamond-and-ruby collar. Eve allowed Marie to clip it about her throat.

The maid smiled at Clare, as if her mistress's jewels added luster to her own countenance, but Clare was watching Eve's reflection. How could any man fail to be rendered speechless by this vision?

One, it appeared, could, and the sardonic voice of Captain Oliver made itself heard. "Only you, dear cousin, would travel with a fortune on your lap, just to make sure you had chosen the correct shade of red. Would you have supposed Miss Court could make you another gown before next Saturday, if you had been mistaken?"

Eve replied via her reflection, "I am rarely mistaken, and I matched the silk to my ruby ring."

"Then, why bring the jewel box?"

Eve sighed. "How could I expect you to understand? I might have needed an alteration to the neckline to show off this collar to its best advantage. Everything must be just perfect. After all, a girl is not twenty-one every day of the week."

So that is the special occasion, thought Clare. Aloud she said, "May I offer you my good wishes, Miss Patterson? You will, in truth, have no equal on that night."

"I should hope not," Eve said complacently. "Though all the town will be there."

"Including First Mate Conrad," murmured William.

Eve shot him a vitriolic look over her shoulder. "You are not privy to all my conversations with Papa, William. There will be more than one special announcement on Saturday, apart from the setting of our wedding date."

There was no reply from the doorway and Clare risked a covert glance at Captain Oliver. His face was chalk white, his eyes dark, burning holes in the taut mask of his face. That look should have scorched his cousin, had she not returned her gaze to her own reflection. Marie, at Eve's order, was removing the jeweled collar and placing it reverently into the jewel box.

Clare remembered suddenly, for no reason at all, the sight of the master's wife being rescued from the *Venturer* by the canvas bosun's chair. Women did sail with their husbands and were presumably taken aboard by them personally. Captain Oliver sailed regularly, usually on the *Dolphin*. Could she use him to make her escape? No one would dare interfere with a lady being escorted aboard the flagship of the Patterson line by a relative of the owner, and its captain, no less. Mr. Thomas Patterson was rich and influential, perhaps richer than Lord Rayne. The watchers might inquire about the *Dolphin*'s destination, but dare they make any move to prevent her boarding without further instructions from Lord Rayne?

First things first. She had to make herself agreeable to William Oliver. While Eve was being assisted out of the silk gown, Clare took her opportunity.

"Won't you be seated, Captain Oliver? It will take a little time to parcel Miss Patterson's gown."

He looked at her vaguely for a moment, then seemed to bring his attention back to her words. Clare gave him a gentle, encouraging smile.

"As the captain of the *Dolphin*, I am sure you are well used to pacing your bridge in the course of duty, but even a captain may allow himself a little relaxation. My chairs are very comfortable, I do assure you, but if you doubt me and prefer to stand—" She let the sentence trail and gave him a sad little smile.

Captain Oliver, supposing his gallantry was being questioned, made haste to reassure her that the comfort of her chair was not at all in doubt. He emphasized the fact by accepting her invitation. He bestowed on her his most charming smile.

"As you say, Miss Court, a ship's captain has much on his mind, the least of which is personal comfort. The responsibility, you know," he finished grandly.

Clare clasped her hands together and looked at him admiringly. "Oh, indeed, the burden of command must be so taxing for a man of sensitivity." She glanced toward Eve, now attired in her everyday dress. "Excuse me, Captain Oliver," Clare murmured and moved toward the two women.

"Pack up my jewel box, Marie," Eve ordered as Clare took the new gown from the maid.

The woman went down on her knees while Clare folded the mass of red silk in tissue paper and covered the whole with a cotton cloth. It made a very large parcel and Eve looked at it speculatively.

"Take out my jewel box first, then lay the gown across the rear seat," she said to the maid. "You will have to get the public coach back to Clevedon, Marie."

The woman gave her mistress a sulky look, which seemed to amuse Eve.

"There is not room for you and the gown, and I must have the gown. Do as you are told if you wish to stay in my employ."

The woman left the cottage without another word and Clare kept her eyes bent on her task of folding the unused tissue paper.

"Send your account to Mr. Patterson, Miss Court. I leave all such things to him. Come, William."

She swept out of the cottage and Captain Oliver rose slowly to his feet. Clare smiled at him. Dare she risk a little more flattery?

"I am convinced you would as soon be about your real duty, Captain Oliver, as escorting ladies to dressmakers." She cast down her eyes and said in a voice full of girlish admiration, "I saw you set sail on the *Dolphin* the other day. The sea was quite choppy and I feared mishap, but you took her out so bravely." Her gaze rose, wide and demure. She recalled Sep's gleeful comparison with a sailing haystack and could barely restrain the tremulous quiver of her lips.

Captain Oliver gave her a warm look. If he noted the quivering lip, he must suppose it was on account of the feared mishap and concern for his safety.

"All part of a captain's life, Miss Court," he replied in modest tones, with a dismissive shrug of the shoulder.

They moved to the doorway and into the sunlight. William Oliver's eyes, rested on her face, had become as speculative as Eve Patterson's when they had rested on her new gown, Clare thought a little uneasily. Had she overdone the flattery and led him to believe she would respond to his advances? Was that flattering herself too much?

"Do you often watch the *Dolphin* sail, Miss Court?"

Clare shook her head. "I have little time for that."

"But you watched me take her out."

"I allow myself the occasional privilege," Clare replied primly, her eyes downcast. "She is a fine ship."

"Ah," William Oliver said, and Clare looked up into his smiling face. "And what is your opinion of her captain?"

"An unfair question, sir, since we are so little acquainted."

"Perhaps we may rectify that, Miss Court."

"Perhaps, sir."

"I sail Friday on the early tide."

"A long voyage, Captain?"

"Quite short, but of the greatest importance. I sail only to Bideford Bay in Devon."

"Then, you will be back in time for Miss Patterson's coming-of-age ball?"

"Indeed, yes. It will be quite a splendid occasion, and one I would not miss for the world." He paused, looking down at her. "Perhaps I may see you by the harbor wall on Friday and know that I carry your good wishes with me?"

"Quite possible, sir," Clare said demurely. With Eve out of earshot, this was an opportunity not to be missed. "I am convinced that as a ship's captain, you must enjoy most splendid accommodation aboard."

"Tolerably comfortable."

Clare sighed. "What an exciting life you lead. I have never been on a ship."

"Perhaps we may rectify that, too, Miss Court."

Eve called imperiously from outside. William Oliver grimaced and turned. He smiled at Clare and there was an edge of sardonic humor in the tone of his voice. "Now I expect to be upbraided for keeping my dear cousin waiting. Until Friday, Miss Court." He nodded and strolled away.

Clare was at the harbor wall early on Friday morning. So was Septimus Thomas. He grinned as he saw her.

"Morning, miss. Come to watch the *Dolphin* leave port?" He made a great show of peering around him. "Don't see no press-gang coves about, so you'll be right enough, lest the *Dolphin*'s turned privateer." He looked aloft. "No, she ain't flying skull and crossbones."

He chortled at his own humor and Clare looked at him coldly. "Oh, very funny, Mr. Thomas. About as funny as that bolt on my back door. The knob fell off after you mended it for me."

"Go on, miss, never! I only rattled it about a bit to stop it screeching."

"Which it didn't do before you touched it."

Sep nodded sagely. "Well, there you go, miss. Reckon it was all ready to drop off any night of the week. Just gave it a nudge, like, to prove my point. I'll be over to fix you up right and tight with a new one, so I will. There'll be one hanging about somewhere in the farm junk, though it might take me a while to come across it—hours, maybe."

Clare turned her head to look at him solemnly. "I wouldn't be surprised at all if it took you well into the afternoon. Even teatime, maybe."

"Even that, miss," Sep replied, equally solemn. "There's a mortal lot of bits and pieces all stacked in the barn."

"But you'll do your best, I'm sure."

"I will that, miss. You can count on me."

Clare nodded and turned her gaze toward the *Dolphin*. "Has Captain Oliver gone aboard yet?"

"I've not seen him, miss, but then he usually arrives after all the loading has been done. Come trotting his fine horse down the harbor lane, all smart and gold-trimmed, as if he was the admiral himself, come to lead his men into battle. All show, miss, for he's not a real sailor like Cap'n Mark."

"Well, the *Dolphin* isn't the *Victory*, Sep, and she's not sailing into battle, only running to Bideford Bay."

Sep craned his neck to look at a carriage that had drawn up on the quayside. Captain Oliver stepped from it. For a moment he stood, holding on to the carriage door, then straightened and reached inside. He reappeared, holding a canvas sack. He began to walk slowly toward the gangplank. He looked pale and his gait was unsteady.

Sep sniffed. "Even the sight of the *Dolphin* makes him turn queasy."

Clare watched William Oliver haul himself slowly up the

gangplank. "He doesn't look well, I admit. Maybe that's why he came in a carriage."

"Likely went overboard with the port bottle last night and affrighted he'd fall off his horse." Sep's tone was scathing. "A tipsy hand in my day would be up before the captain and get a dozen lashes to sober him up."

"But Mr. Oliver is the captain," Clare reminded him, "and you're talking of the Royal Navy."

"Aye, well, officers and toffs get away with murder."

They watched in silence as Captain Oliver went below. The coachman was talking to a group of loungers, all intent on watching the *Dolphin* leave her berth. Clare wondered if Captain Oliver would remember her promise to be by the harbor wall.

Some ten minutes later he appeared on deck. *How pale he is*, Clare thought, and in spite of the coolness of the morning, he drew out a handkerchief and wiped his brow.

"In a sweat already," chortled Sep, "and the *Dolphin* is still tied up."

"I think you're wrong, Sep," Clare said slowly. "Captain Oliver is a proud man. He would not allow himself to be the object of ridicule by those he considers to be his inferiors. You said yourself, he is all show. A man of conceit would hide his weaknesses."

Sep narrowed his eyes on the man now gripping the rail. "He's right pale, miss, I'll give you that. What's wrong with the fellow?"

Curious eyes were beginning to focus on the figure of Captain Oliver—crew and watchers alike. The coachman had stopped chatting and was staring up at his master. William Oliver's hand reached for his neck cloth, and dragged it away from his throat as if it were choking him. His gaze seemed to range wildly over the sea of upturned faces. His mouth opened but no sound came out. His hand fell from the neck cloth and his knees buckled. A gasp like the sound of receding ripples over shingle ran through the watchers as Captain Oliver collapsed on the deck of the *Dolphin*.

◆ *Chapter Twenty-six* ◆

The first to move was the coachman. He flung himself forward, clattering up the gangplank. The crew of the *Dolphin* dropped what they were doing and surged toward the recumbent figure. Whatever their personal opinions of Captain Oliver, he was part of the ship's complement, and no seaman ever turned his back on a fellow seaman.

He was lifted gently by large, rough hands and carried down the gangplank. Clare forced her way to the foot of it, in time to see the eyes flicker open in the chalk-white, sweat-drenched face. The coachman was agitated and pale with shock. He stared dazedly at his master.

"Take him home and call a doctor," Clare said crisply in a tone that overrode the babble of sound.

William Oliver seemed to recognize her voice. His heavy-lidded eyes peered up at her. "No, no," he protested weakly. "It's nothing. Must get back on board. Very important." His voice trailed off.

"You're ill," Clare said. "You can't take out the ship."

"Must," he murmured. "Can't let down Uncle—" His eyes closed and he was silent.

The coachman looked at Clare as if awaiting the command of one who had taken charge of the situation.

"Put him in the carriage," she said firmly to the seamen holding William Oliver. "A man doesn't collapse for no reason at all. He must be taken home."

The men obeyed and the carriage door was closed. The coachman climbed onto the box and Clare found Sep at her elbow.

"The *Dolphin* will miss the tide if she's not gone within the hour." He looked curiously after the retreating coach. "Think he's sickening for something, miss?"

"I don't know any more than you do, Sep, but a ship can't

274

sail with a sick captain. Mr. Patterson will just have to send someone else or delay the sailing until the next tide.''

''The *Firefly* came in a couple of hours ago,'' offered one of the seamen to the company at large. ''She's the only one this day. Who's on her bridge?''

''Cap'n Conrad, I reckon,'' a companion supplied.

There was a general lightening of the atmosphere and Sep chuckled. ''I'll lay odds old man Patterson will have Cap'n Mark down here before you can say Jack Robinson. Why, he'll be on the spot making his report right now. The old man won't want the *Dolphin* to stand idle, even 'til the next tide, not if it means paying yon lot to loaf about like gents of leisure.''

Clare left him swapping yarns with the crew of the *Dolphin*. She did not want to see Mark Conrad take over the ship. Instead, she thought of William Oliver. Yesterday, at her cottage, he had been in good health, yet illness could strike suddenly, she supposed. When Eve Patterson learned of it, she would surely be in terror of infection—not on William's account, but lest it ruin her plans for Saturday. The *Dolphin* would be back before then.

Oh, confound them, thought Clare savagely. She must put them all out of her mind and concentrate on her own plans to foil Lord Rayne. Her earlier hope of boarding the *Dolphin* in company with Captain Oliver as escort was unlikely to be fulfilled if the man was seriously ill. She had only a few days left before his lordship tightened the net about her. Should she go with him quietly and hope to escape again? She doubted he would be fooled a second time.

She raised her head as she heard the voices of children. Kate and Milly were waving to her and Milly held a small milk can. Of course, it was the milk they delivered to her as they passed on their way to school. She greeted them and took the can from Milly.

''We've a basket of vegetables set aside for you, miss. The rest are going to market. We'll bring it up after school.''

''Thank you, Milly. I'd forgotten it was market day in Clevedon.''

"Yes, miss. Every Friday. Cattle, as well as turnips and things."

Clare watched them race up the hill. Turnips and things? Did Mr. Clark grow turnips? What was she thinking of? To escape Lord Rayne concealed beneath a load of turnips, like a French milady under the shadow of the guillotine? Ridiculous! Whatever would Farmer Clark think if she put such a proposal to him? He would clap her into the nearest madhouse, most likely, she reflected with a wry smile.

Mark Conrad was on the point of leaving his employer's house when the carriage, bearing the inert body of William Oliver, came to a halt at the front steps.

The coachman jumped down and addressed himself to Mark. "It's Master Oliver, sir. He was taken dreadful ill on the bridge. He fell all of a heap, like he'd been struck down."

The Patterson butler, who had been about to close the door on Mark, came forward quickly. The coachman now had the carriage door open and they all stared in at the figure slumped in the corner of the seat. William's eyes were closed; his skin was still pale and sheened with perspiration.

"Is it safe to move him, sir?" asked the butler in a hushed whisper.

Mark was tired and slightly irritated by the sepulchral tones.

"Well, it'll not improve his health if we leave him where he is. Give me a hand to drag him out."

At the sound of Mark's voice, William's eyelids flickered and a shudder passed through him.

"Let go aft—" he muttered and tried to push himself upright.

"Delirious," the butler said, low-voiced. "A fever, I'll be bound."

Mark spoke impatiently. "You can present your theory to the doctor later, but for now, help me get him into the house."

They managed to bring William to the pavement, where he made a valiant effort to stand but failed and drooped between the supporting arms of Mark and the butler. The front door was still open and William was half carried into the hall. Servants paused to stare and Mark sent them hurrying away to call Mr. William's own valet and acquaint Mr. Patterson of his nephew's unexpected return.

In a moment, Thomas Patterson was on the scene. He frowned.

"What the devil's going on? Hasn't the *Dolphin* left port yet?"

"Apparently not, sir," Mark replied. "Since we hold her captain here."

"What's wrong with the lad?"

"No idea, save the coachman reported his collapse on the bridge."

"Collapse?" Mr. Patterson scowled as if he had received a personal insult.

The valet came clattering down the stairs and Mark gave up his supporting role gladly. The coachman hovered in the doorway. "Shall I go for the doctor, Mr. Patterson, sir?"

William raised his head. "No doctor. I'll be all right soon." His voice sounded weak and very weary. "They shouldn't have brought me home. I must go back—"

Mr. Patterson interrupted, aware of listening ears and the greenness of his nephew's face. "Get him up to his own room. This carpet is too valuable to throw up on," he finished curtly.

"I'm sorry, Uncle. I couldn't—"

"That's enough," snapped Mr. Patterson, glowering at the slow progress of William being helped up the stairs. He waved a dismissive hand at the servants, then came close to Mark.

"You'll have to take her out, Mark. There's nobody else for the Bideford Bay run." He frowned heavily. "You'll go?"

Mark nodded. "I don't seem to have much choice."

Mr. Patterson clapped him on the shoulder. "Good man. I knew I could rely on you. I've got big plans for when you're my son-in-law. You'll be surprised."

"Like investing in steamships?" Mark queried with an ironic lift of one eyebrow.

"Pah! Just forget that nonsense and we'll get along the

better.'' His brows were beginning to converge in a scowl
when he remembered the urgency of the moment and the fact
that Mark Conrad was obliging him by sailing again within
two hours of docking the *Firefly.* ''But we'll talk of it later,
how about that? Take the coach, Mark,'' he continued, the
scowl clearing like magic.

When Mark reached the *Dolphin,* he climbed the companionway to the bridge and gave orders to his crew. Leaning
over the bridge rail, he watched the lines being cast off. He
glanced along the row of faces lining the harbor wall and
spotted Sep waving vigorously, a wide grin on his weathered
face. Mark raised a hand in salute, scanning the female
faces—a few wives and girlfriends of the crew. He thought
of Eve and could not imagine for a moment that she would
ever wave him off in company with these women, hair tossing
and whipping in the early breeze—no, not even if he were
voyaging to China. His lips curved in a sardonic smile as he
recalled Thomas Patterson's flat rebuttal of his remark on
steamships, then the soft turnabout in his eagerness to set
Mark on his way. Both men knew there would be no talk of
it later.

The *Dolphin* heeled as the canvas took the wind and Mark
plotted his course to Bideford Bay. He wondered idly if
William would be recovered in time to celebrate Eve's coming-of-age party tomorrow. Perhaps *celebrate* was hardly the
word, for the two of them were never on the best of terms.

Mark stared ahead as the prow of the *Dolphin* sliced
through the waves, flinging aside white curves of spray that
joined together again in her wake. Neptune's sheep, Sep
would have called them in his fanciful way, to the delight of
his young admirers—Sara, the Clark girls, and now the lad,
young Albert. That line of thought led inevitably to the girl
in the cottage. Mark had not seen Clare since that trip on the
Sara. Was she well? What was it that troubled her? He remembered vividly her attack on him. He should have forced
a confession out of her, but what right had he over her actions?
An intolerable thought struck him, making his heart pound.
What if he should find the cottage empty when he returned
from Bideford Bay?

He banged his clenched fist on the rail and glowered into the water. What the devil was the matter with him? He was engaged to Eve Patterson, yet he didn't want Clare Court to go out of his life. According to Eve, William Oliver was making a play for Clare. Suppose she married William? No, that would be unthinkable! She was his woman. He drew in a deep breath of salt-laden air. No, she was her own woman; and after he and Eve were married, she would be irretrievably lost to him. The thought was like the turning of a blade in his heart, but he was too committed to Eve to draw back now. He went below to his cabin to catch up on a few hours of sleep.

On reaching her cottage, Clare set the kettle on the kitchen range. *A nice hot cup of tea is a panacea for all ills*, she thought moodily. What would she do now? With William ill, she had not the anticipated time to enlist his unknowing support in her bid to escape by sea.

She wandered into her bedroom and, on impulse, pulled out the bag containing Lord Rayne's gown. The amber silk slid lightly through her fingers. It was a revealing gown, more fitted to be worn by a courtesan or fashionable London lady. She carried the gown into the sitting room and slid it over the dressmaker's dummy. Yes, it really was a beautiful gown, but of no earthly use to a provincial dressmaker. She turned her back on it as she drank her tea. If only she could ignore Lord Rayne as easily.

It was still there the next morning when William Oliver called. Clare opened the door and stared into the healthy, handsome face.

"Why, good morning, Captain Oliver. I did not think to find you about so soon. Should you be out of doors?"

"Good morning, Miss Court. It was a passing indisposition, and I am quite recovered. I called on an errand for my cousin and to thank you for your kindness to me yesterday."

"No need for thanks, Captain. Your coachman was quite competent to take you home."

"But the fool would have dithered without a direct order, and the tide would have been lost."

"Do step inside, Captain, and tell me how I may serve

you—or rather, Miss Patterson.'' She gave him what she
hoped was a provocative smile and stepped aside.

William entered the cottage and his eye was immediately
caught by the amber silk gown.

''A superb piece of artistry, Miss Court. Which Clevedon
lady has commissioned such a gown?''

''Why, none, Captain Oliver.'' Clare gave a light laugh
and fluttered a hand toward the gown. ''It is one of my own,
but most unsuitable in my present circumstances. It was a
mere whim in a moment of idleness to look upon it again as
a reminder of more affluent days.'' She widened her eyes as
Captain Oliver regarded her with new interest. ''I was not
always a dressmaker,'' she finished on a gentle, reminiscent
note.

''Quite so, Miss Court.'' He glanced at the gown again.
''I am sure you looked most enchanting in that creation. How
I wish I could have seen you.''

Clare shrugged. ''The turn of fortune's wheel, Captain,''
she said, extravagantly. ''One cannot foresee the future.''

''Very true.'' He continued to stare at her, a half smile on
his lips.

''This errand,'' Clare reminded him gently. ''What does
Miss Patterson require?''

''Ah, yes, the errand. She wonders if you have a little
silver thread left—for her hair, you know.''

Clare moved to her worktable. ''I have a short length. She
plans to wear her new gown tonight, I believe? Her coming-
of-age ball, is it not?''

William nodded. ''It is, indeed.'' He paused, and his lips
twisted with amusement. ''Quite an occasion. I would not
miss it for the world.''

''And when do you sail again, Captain Oliver?'' Clare
asked as she handed him the tiny parcel of silver thread.

William took the parcel, allowing his fingers to linger on
hers for a moment. Clare withdrew her hand slowly, as if
reluctant to break the contact, and smiled.

''I take the *Dolphin* to Cherbourg on Wednesday.''

Clare clasped her hands together and gazed at him admiringly. ''Cherbourg?'' she breathed softly. ''What an adven-

turous life you lead, Captain. I have always wanted to travel on the Continent. Is Cherbourg very gay? How lucky you are.''

"Cherbourg is a port, much like any other, with little to offer," William said, with the air of a man who has traveled extensively. "If it were possible, I would sail to Paris."

"Paris?" Clare gave a light laugh. "Pray do not talk of Paris, Captain, or I might be tempted to stow away on the *Dolphin*."

William laughed, too. "Now, that is a splendid idea. Would you really?" His gaze was speculative, and Clare hesitated before answering. He might, with a little encouragement, smuggle her aboard the *Dolphin*, but the very act of agreeing would brand her as a light skirt, open to seduction. To escape from Lord Rayne was imperative, but to fall into the hands of another like him with no escape once aboard was not her desire. One might disappear in Cherbourg, but one needed to get there first, and she knew from the speculative look that her position would not be that of a regular, fare-paying lady passenger with all attendant courtesies.

Clare decided to play for time before coming to a decision. She smiled coquettishly. "Suppose I said yes. Would it be difficult to arrange?"

William's eyes took on a sparkle. "Not in the least. No one would dare question my actions if I escorted someone aboard. I am the senior captain, after all, and we do occasionally carry passengers."

"It's a tempting offer, Captain, but—I don't know—I must think about it. After all, I don't know you very well."

William put down the parcel and took her hands in his. He bent a sincere blue gaze on her.

"Miss Court, I have admired you from the first moment I saw you. You are beautiful and brave. Fortune's wheel may not have spun fairly for you, but you have proved your ability to make a new life. I would deem it an honor to further our acquaintance."

"By going to Cherbourg?" Clare asked playfully, fluttering her lashes. "I am not a woman of the world, Captain. Would it not raise comment if I were seen to board your ship?"

William paused, looking into the wide, innocent eyes. Behind her mask of innocence, Clare watched with interest the play of emotions on his face. He was easily readable, and she guessed he was suddenly unsure of his direction. Was she a lady fallen on bad times, but still a lady, or open to the blandishments of a handsome man of undoubted wealth and distinction?

He smiled his charming, practiced smile. "Forgive me, Miss Court. I go too fast in my eagerness to know you better. I will not press you on the matter of a trip to Cherbourg, but perhaps we may become better acquainted. Will you drive with me on Monday?"

"I should be delighted, Captain Oliver."

"How formal you are, Miss Court. My name is William."

Clare cast down her eyes. "And I am Clare."

"A beautiful name."

"Thank you—William." Clare raised her eyes.

Captain Oliver smiled, supremely confident now of this girl's eventual submission to his charms. No one had refused his attentions before. Was he not in line to inherit the Patterson empire? He kissed Clare's hand, picked up the parcel of silver braid, and left the cottage with the jaunty air of a man who is completely sure of his irresistible attraction to women, be they lady or wanton.

◆ *Chapter Twenty-seven* ◆

The *Dolphin* dropped anchor in Clevedon on Sunday morning, an hour after dawn. The trip to Bideford Bay had been uneventful, save that the helmsman had reported the rudder a trifle sluggish. Mark promised to have the steering overhauled when they reached Clevedon again. The helmsman looked dubious.

"Not like the old girl to go wandering, sir. Let's hope we've a smooth passage back, for I don't like the feel of her by half."

Mark yawned, feeling sandy-eyed after his few hours of sleep. He stared into the night sky as they cleared the bay.

"Gentle her along as if you were doing the Valeta with your granny," he advised. "She's old but willing and should have us home by morning."

The man grinned. "My old granny never heard of the Valeta, let alone how to do it."

He was glad Captain Conrad was in charge of the *Dolphin*. A man got a bit lonely during the night watch and Captain Oliver would never have lowered himself to crack a joke, however feeble, with a fellow seaman of lower rank. Captain Conrad now, he treated every man as an equal. Funny that, when you came to think of it, for the Conrads were real gentry, yet it was the rich merchants who gave themselves airs. He concentrated on nursing the *Dolphin* along, for she seemed without her usual dash and spirit.

Mark stood on the bridge, his sea cloak wrapped about him, feeling the lethargy of the ship. There was a stiff breeze blowing and the *Dolphin* should have been bowling along, yet she was yawing badly. The steersman was an experienced hand, but Mark was conscious of the persistent corrections of course. He hoped the *Dolphin* would make harbor before any serious situation arose. There was Eve's ball tomorrow —tonight, he corrected himself; it was past midnight. He yawned again. My God, the old man was a stickler for routine. Off the *Firefly* and onto the *Dolphin* with hardly time to breathe—or sleep, for that matter. If Eve expected him to be bright-eyed and full of bounce tonight, she was doomed to disappointment.

A slap of rain took him across the face and he started. Good grief, he was half asleep already! The night had darkened considerably and he had lost sight of the coast altogether.

He pulled the telescope from its housing, extended the tubes, and focused. A pinprick of light caught his eye, not far from the ship. A fishing boat swam into his magnified vision and he saw it was a masthead light. Why wasn't the boat tied up in port like the rest of its fellows, awaiting the early dawn? Was it night fishing or smuggling? Whichever it was, she would veer away at the sight of a well-lit merchantman. He called from the bridge to the watch below.

"Keep an eye to starboard, men. There's a fishing craft ahead."

"Just spotted her, sir. Making heavy weather of it. Give her a blast, sir?"

"Do that. She'll sheer off, for sure."

The single mournful blast of the foghorn brought no response from the small boat. Mark raised the glass again. The vessel was still heading out, and coming closer every second. He ran the telescope lens the length of her decks and saw no movement. Was her crew asleep? Drunk? If she held on course, the *Dolphin* would slice her through.

"Give her another blast," he yelled, the thought striking cold. A collision at sea was a fearful thing, especially at night.

The foghorn blasted its warning and Mark felt sweat on his face, in spite of the cool flurry of wind. Through the telescope, pressed hard to his eye, he thought he saw movement, an upflung hand. Damnation, there were people aboard her! Curse their stupidity in not keeping a proper watch. It was almost too late to avoid running them down, but he had to try.

"Hard aport!" he yelled at the top of his voice.

The *Dolphin* lurched heavily, canting the deck so violently that Mark had to grab the rail to stay on his feet. He dropped the telescope into its housing and jumped the wooden steps to deck level, peering over the rail. His breath came out in a long hiss of relief. The small boat was past and behind them now. Thank God for that.

The *Dolphin* was locked on her port curve and Mark ran to the wheelhouse.

"Put her back on course, Sam." Then he saw the steersman, muscles bulging, fighting the wheel. A crewman was straining beside him.

"She's of a mind to bite her own tail, Cap'n," the steersman gasped. "That hard aport didn't do her a power of good."

The two sweating men managed to bring the wheel over and the *Dolphin* came around reluctantly, but still with a tendency to swing to port.

"'Tis the rudder, for sure," Sam said. "She's not answering proper—she's dancing about all over the place." He grinned at Mark. "She ain't my granny, that's certain."

Mark grinned back and the crewman looked mystified.

"Do your best, Sam. As long as she gets us home, she can do the polka, as well, for my money."

But the *Dolphin* had become a stubborn old lady and refused to dance to any tune. Dawn came, then full daylight, and the *Dolphin* limped along, still many miles from home. The steering barely answered and Sam nursed her gently, fearing that any sharp jerk might sever all connection between wheel and rudder. The wind had dropped to a mild breeze, slowing progress even further, as they crawled up the channel.

The hours passed. Shadows lengthened and Mark leaned on the bridge rail in the twilight. He was unutterably tired and had barely eaten since taking over the *Dolphin*. The ship had not been provisioned for a long run. Tea and hard biscuits did not replace lost energy, and every man aboard had taken turns in holding the wheel on course.

Mark thought of Eve, preparing for her ball. He might manage a late appearance or possibly none at all. That depended on the *Dolphin*. He shrugged philosophically. If William had not collapsed, he would have been the one standing here, not Mark. It was a pity to miss Eve's coming-of-age ball, but there would be others. At the moment, Mark felt more like falling into bed and sleeping around the clock rather than performing either the Valeta or polka.

An hour before dawn on Sunday morning, the *Dolphin* berthed. Every man aboard was exhausted and unshaven. Mark dismissed them to their homes after a few words of praise. He grinned down from the bridge.

"Away with you, you ruffianly horde, and I hope your women recognize you, for you're as much like an unwashed, hairy band of cutthroats as ever I did see. And I'll not dare look in the glass myself until I'm a sight more respectable."

The men grinned back and managed a ragged cheer before filing off the ship, trudging wearily to their homes. Mark went below to fill in the ship's log and gather together the papers needed by Mr. Patterson. It was too early to present himself at his employer's door. He must, in any case, go home to bathe and shave, and to reassure Sara that he had not been lost at sea, merely delayed by a damaged rudder. He gathered his gear together and left the *Dolphin*.

Two hours later, he was backing a horse between the shafts of a small trap. Still gritty-eyed and rather light-headed through lack of sleep, he drove into Clevedon. Eve would accept the reason for his absence at last night's ball. As the daughter of a shipping man, she must know that sailing ships could be delayed for any number of reasons. Outside the door of the large town house in one of the most fashionable streets of Clevedon, he drew rein.

The butler opened the door to him and Mark stepped inside.

"Good morning, Captain Conrad. Glad to see you back, sir. The villagers were getting a mite worried about their menfolk, but if you're back, they are, too."

He beamed and Mark smiled, knowing the elderly man had two sons in the Patterson fleet himself.

"Steering went adrift so we had to gentle her home, slow but sure." He glanced down the hall. "Mr. Patterson about?"

"In his study, sir. I'll announce you."

Mark followed the butler down the hall. "Miss Eve still abed after her ball?"

"Yes, sir." The old man smiled over his shoulder. "But I'll have a message given to Marie when she takes up Miss Eve's chocolate."

Thomas Patterson rose and came around his desk to shake Mark's hand. "Glad to see you back in one piece, Mark. Getting devilish worried about the *Dolphin*. You, too, of course," he added hastily. "What happened?"

Mark smiled. Thomas Patterson was a man to get his priorities right. What was the value of a seaman against the solid worth of a ship?

"I suspect a fault in the rudder cable. It wasn't a complete break, or she wouldn't have answered the wheel at all. It certainly needs looking into before her next trip or she'll only answer to port."

Mr. Patterson nodded. "I'll see to it. Outward bound, was it?"

Mark shook his head, smiling inwardly at the obliquely phrased question. "No, sir. We made the rendezvous. Trouble started on the return leg."

"Well done, my boy. The Patterson line has its reputation to keep up. Promptness and efficiency, eh?"

"Quite so, sir. Sorry to miss Eve's party, but business before pleasure," Mark intoned solemnly.

"Eh? Oh, exactly. My sentiments entirely, but you can hardly expect a female to understand that. Rather put out, she was, but I daresay you'll be able to smooth her down."

Mark gathered from that remark that Eve had been flatteringly upset by his absence. Of course she would understand and commiserate over the bad luck that had kept him from her side.

There was a tap on the door and the butler looked in. "Miss Eve is in the drawing room, Captain. She would like a word before you leave."

Mark looked at Mr. Patterson. "Anything else, sir?"

Mr. Patterson was shuffling papers and did not look up. "No, no. You go along, my boy. I'll get on to those shipwrights about the *Dolphin*."

He frowned down at his papers, and as Mark left, he had the feeling that Mr. Patterson was relieved, and not solely on account of the return of the *Dolphin*. Had Eve wept on his shoulder? Was he now relieved to have the role of comforter taken away? Mark grinned as he headed for the drawing room. Eve was not exactly the weeping sort, but it was flattering to think she might have shed a tear on his account.

As he entered the drawing room, he saw Eve sitting on the couch. She wore a high-necked, flowered dressing gown, girdled tightly at the waist. Her blond hair was loose and hung about her shoulders. He had never seen it other than elegantly arranged. She must have rushed down to greet him without any thought of her appearance.

"Good morning, Eve. How pretty your hair looks when it is loose. You should—"

"Never mind my hair." Eve's pale blue eyes were wide, her voice low. "I hoped you had come here to explain your absence last night."

"Of course I have, and to report to your father, as well." Mark crossed the room and was about to take a seat beside her when she pointed at a facing chair.

"Please sit there, so that I can see your face."

Mark's brows rose in inquiry. "My face? It's not at its best since I have scarcely slept for three nights." He smiled. "You must blame your father for that. Off the *Firefly* and onto the *Dolphin*, with scarce an hour to breathe."

"You only went to Bideford Bay. Does that take two nights?"

"Not normally, but as I told your father, we had rudder trouble. I'm sorry I missed your birthday party, but there was nothing I could do to get back in time."

"You could have come overland and been in plenty of time."

Mark frowned. "Eve, dear, one does not just abandon ship and crew for the sake of attending a party."

"Not even my party? You know how much it meant to me."

"You still had your party, Eve, didn't you?"

"Of course I did, but you should have been there."

"I know and I am sorry. What else can I say?" He was rather puzzled by the edge of curtness in her voice. He had expected the reaction of a relieved woman—a kiss, an embrace—but not this cold quizzing. "Believe me, Eve—"

"Believe you? I wonder if I do. Are you sure you did everything possible?"

Mark stiffened, looking hard into Eve's face. Without her usual paint and powder, she was pale, her eyes hard, her mouth thin. There were angry spots of color on her cheeks.

"What the devil are you implying—that I missed your party deliberately?"

"I planned it so perfectly, and you ruined everything. Have I no right to be upset?"

"You have every right to be upset, but the delay was unavoidable. You must take my word on that." He spoke patiently, trying not to let his irritation show. "Surely the basis for marriage is absolute trust. If you knew a little more about ships and their vagaries, you would understand. Things do not always go according to plan."

"No, they don't, and I had everything planned so beautifully." Eve sounded petulant.

Mark sighed inwardly. "I'm sure your party went beautifully, even without me. We are both tired, Eve, and not at our best. Can we discuss all this later?"

Eve ignored the question and returned to her theme. "Of course it went beautifully. My parties always do, but without you there, how could I make any announcement without looking an absolute fool? I had it all arranged with Papa."

"Arranged? What did you have arranged?" Mark frowned, puzzled. "I don't understand."

"It was to be a wonderful surprise for you." Eve rose and clasped her hands together, her eyes intent on Mark's face. "And so perfect for us both, especially for you."

He rose, too, wondering uneasily what the devil she and her father had planned together with himself the central figure.

"Tell me," he said tersely, watching Eve with tired attention.

"Papa has agreed—when we marry, of course—to make you a junior partner with a seat on the board of the Patterson line. Naturally, you will not sail anymore but spend your time in administration. Is that not a wonderful surprise?"

Mark stared at Eve for a long moment.

"And where does William fit into this scheme of things?" Mark asked quietly.

"William? What about William?"

"Does he not aspire to this exact position himself?"

Eve shrugged. "William will do as he's told. He'll complain, but what of it?"

"You mean he'll dance to your father's tune like a pet dog?"

Eve dismissed William airily. "Of course, if he wants to stay with the company."

"And if I decline to cut him out, what then?"

"What do you mean?" Eve's stare held genuine surprise. "Papa is offering you the chance of a lifetime. Why should you care about William?"

"I don't, but I care about my own integrity." Mark's head was throbbing and his eyes were as dry as dust, but he had to get things into focus. "What you are saying is that you prefer your husband to be a man of position, rather than a common seaman. You will not take me as I am. Is that it?"

"Aren't you being a little dramatic, Mark, dear? You forget who I am. How could Eve Patterson marry a common seaman? I really can't see why you are making a fuss. It's all to your own advantage, isn't it?"

Mark smiled grimly. "I rather think it's to your advantage, Eve. As a condition of marriage, you think I should jump at the chance—and go on jumping, like some pet poodle, at any Patterson command? Would that make me any better than William?"

"Now you're being ridiculous, Mark!" A flush of anger tinged Eve's cheeks and her lips compressed. Without their usual coating of rouge, they formed a thin, straight line. Mark looked dispassionately into the beautiful face. Even a beauty could appear less than beautiful when gripped by strong emotion. Eve's face showed anger, frustration, bewilderment, not to mention complete astonishment at his obtuseness. He suddenly wanted to laugh. Eve had been sure he would come to heel, overwhelmed by the generous offer, which included the gift of herself. It was a good bargain by any standards. Why was he turning it down? It smacked too much of commercialism. He would not be beholden to anyone—not to his employer, or to the girl who sought to arrange his future for her own satisfaction.

He shook his head to clear the fuzziness out of his brain. "Ridiculous? I don't think so. I am my own man and intend to remain so. Don't try to buy me, Eve! I am not for sale."

Eve stared at him fixedly. "Have you no gratitude?" Her voice sounded a little shrill. "You are a poor man. Doesn't money mean anything to you? There would be no lack of it when we married."

Mark pushed back his hair with a weary gesture. "Is money all you Pattersons think about?"

"What else is there?" snapped Eve. "It can buy a lot of happiness."

"Can it buy love? Or is that a lost ingredient in marriage?"

"Love? Really, Mark, you talk like a romantic novel. The most satisfactory marriages are between people of similar background—people who move in the same circles."

"With a little adjustment here and there to make everybody happy."

"What do you mean?" Eve's voice had become sharp. "Must you talk in riddles? I have a headache and planned to spend the morning in bed after so much activity last night. I rose only because Marie told me you were here. Now you are talking nonsense without a thought for my comfort. I really thought better of you. You're not in the least grateful for all my efforts."

Mark felt very calm and very tired. "No, Eve, I am not. I wish you had left well enough alone. No doubt you meant it for the best, but I refuse to spend the rest of my days in debt to my wife."

Eve stared at him, narrow-eyed. The color deepened in her face, making her eyes pale, almost colorless. She opened her lips and her anger seemed to well up and explode in a fury. Gone was the caressing, teasing, provocative contralto of former days. The harsh voice issued from the mouth of a raging virago, unused to rebuttal.

"How dare you throw my generosity back in my face? I would have made you one of the richest and most respected men in town. Our house would have been the center of social life, our parties famous. You turn all this down because of some silly scruples." She was twisting the ruby-and-diamond ring about her finger in her agitation. The glint of it caught her eye and she pulled it off with a savage movement. "Do you expect me to stay engaged to a pauper?"

The sneer in her voice ignited Mark's own anger. He looked at her coldly and spoke in a deliberately provoking slow drawl.

"Miss Eve Patterson to fall so low and forget her position? Never, my dear—it would be too dreadful to contemplate. A pauper and a common seaman! Good heavens, what a comedown—"

"Be quiet, damn you!" Eve screamed. "You're—you're despicable. I never want to see you again. Take your ring and get out of this house! You'll pay for this insult, I swear it!"

"Don't swear, my dear. It's not at all ladylike."

The slam of the drawing room door seemed to shake the house, and Mark found himself alone, the ring in his hand. He stared at it idly, as if he had never seen it before, then dropped it into his pocket. The noise of the door slamming still reverberated through his head and he moved like a sleepwalker into the hall and out the front door. On the front step he stood for a moment breathing deeply, his eyes on the sky. Dear God, how tired he was. The trap was at the foot of the steps. He climbed into the seat with an effort and took up the reins.

◆ *Chapter Twenty-eight* ◆

The ground began to rise under the trap and Mark realized they were now ascending the hill to the farm. The horse knew its way home without direction from him. The pace slowed as the farmhouse came into view. The Clarks would be about their duties, the children at Sunday school. Sara, too, would be absent from Conrad Place. Only Mrs. Winter would be about.

Out of the corner of his eye he glimpsed the short, sturdy figure of Septimus Thomas as he drew level with the farm stables. Sep was scuttling furtively toward his own tiny cottage, attached to the stables. Whatever he was up to was his own affair. Mark decided to drive on. Not even Sep could cheer him up today. But Sep had heard the trap. He peered around, half in and half out of his cottage. A broad grin of relief spread over his face and he stepped out into full view.

"Belay there, Cap'n," he called, and began to amble toward the trap.

Mark sighed and drew rein. He didn't want to talk, but he could not ignore the old seaman. Sep was a friend, a commodity he might soon find in short supply! He forced a smile as Sep came puffing up.

"Morning, Sep. What are you up to?"

"Up to, Cap'n?" Sep looked innocent. "Nothing at all."

"Is that right? Do you normally scuttle about like a mouse when the ship's cat is on its trail?"

Sep gave a sheepish grin. "Well, seeing it's you, Cap'n, I'll tell you. I thought it was the missus on my track and she's a rare one with the tongue-lashing when she thinks it ain't right."

"What ain't right? What have you gone and done now, you old ruffian?" Mark smiled in spite of himself. "Mrs. Clark is a kind, honest, and sober lady. There's none more generous."

"I know." Sep drew a circle in the dust with the toe of a very disreputable boot. "It's the sober bit that goes against my nature, you might say." He raised his gaze. "The wagoner brought me a bottle on the quiet and hid it in the stable. I was just going to put it somewhere safe, so that young Albert wouldn't fall over it and hurt himself—a sort of charitable act." He squinted up at Mark.

"A full bottle?"

"Aye, Cap'n. A real good drop of Nelson's blood. I just thought I'd give it a taste, like."

Mark swung down from the seat of the trap. "A damn good idea, Sep. Invite me to join you, will you?"

"Of course, Cap'n. Not too early in the day for you?" He grinned slyly. "You always said—"

"Be damned to what I always said!" The voice was so harsh that Sep's grin died and he stared closely into Mark's face.

"You look as if you could do with a tot, Cap'n. Come on in, do." He glanced sideways at the tall man and observed the shadowed eyes and grim set of the mouth.

"A bad trip, Cap'n?" Sep asked as they sat at his table, the rum bottle between them.

"Bad?" Mark laughed without humor. "You could say that."

Sep held his tongue and watched Mark drain the glass of rum in one swallow.

"I'm not overfond of this stuff, Sep, but I'll trouble you for another. Get the wagoner to bring you a barrel next time and send the bill up to me."

Sep refilled Mark's glass, smiling a little uneasily. There was something wrong here. Captain Conrad was not a man for the strong drink, and he had never downed two such measures of rum in so short a time in all the years that Sep had known him. A bad trip, he had said, but the run to Bideford Bay on a calm night should not have had Captain Conrad looking like a man who had battled through the Atlantic in the teeth of a storm.

When the captain thrust forward his glass again, Sep's uneasiness gave way to alarm. He hesitated, the bottle in his hand, and squinted across the table. "Something's shot you amidships, Cap'n, but this stuff don't shore up timbers. It only gives a fellow a powerful urge to lay down and die, somewhere quietlike."

Mark peered into the hazy face across the table. Strong drink on an empty stomach made Sep's head sway like an anchored balloon in a breeze. He bared his teeth in a ferocious grin.

"I'll be doing that soon enough, God knows! Now, be a good fellow and stop your gabbing." He paused, eyeing Sep through narrowed eyes. "Is it an empty bottle you're worried about?'' He tried to stand up, determined to stalk out with majestic dignity, but found his legs too weak to carry the weight of his enlarged head. Dear God! What a weight! He slumped down, glowering. ''I know what it is, you miserable old sea gull. You think I won't pay my reckoning, damn your eyes.'' He delved into his jacket pocket, his fingers closing about the ruby-and-diamond ring. His head was now swimming so much that he had difficulty in finding Sep again, once he had removed his gaze from the man.

''Where are you?'' he roared, but the words came out husky and slurred.

Sep had moved, but only as far as his doorway. He needed help with this situation. Short of dragging the captain to Conrad Place, which he knew was physically impossible, he was quite at a loss. He had never seen Cap'n Mark like this before, but it would not do to let him be seen by any Sunday guest on her way by carriage to Miss Court's cottage. He peered about, seeking guidance. A farm cart, perhaps? Mrs. Winter, up at Conrad Place, would never consent to his taking the carriage. Besides, a carriage needed those four-legged fiends to pull it, and he was no coachman.

His breath came out in a sharp sigh of relief as he caught sight of Miss Court herself, coming up from the farm. A good lass, that, and one who could hold her tongue. Hadn't she taken in the captain the night the *Venturer* was wrecked?

Clare saw Sep and raised a hand in greeting. Sep beckoned, his face urgent and distressed. She walked toward his cottage.

''What's wrong, Sep? You look as worried as—'' Her voice trailed away as Sep stood aside and she saw the face of the man slumped over the table. Her heart jerked violently and she took in the haggard face and unfocused eyes.

''Oh, my God, Sep, what has happened? Is he sick?''

Sep shook his head. ''Not yet, miss, but I'll bet a year's pay to a rusty anchor that he'll be off-loading before long. He's—well, miss, he's just plain got a load of rum aboard, you might say.''

''Drunk?'' Clare stared. ''Is that usual with Captain Conrad? I have never seen him so myself, but—''

"Nor me, miss. It's not like him at all. I reckon some-thing's hit him mighty hard, but I've no notion of what it is."

"What do you want me to do?"

Sep scratched his chin. "Don't know, miss. Get him home, I suppose."

"No, you can't do that. Sara might be at home. There's Mrs. Winter, too. They'd be shocked, and you know how gossip gets about."

Clare approached the table with some trepidation. Mark saw the blurred outline of an oval face, tendrils of dark hair falling over brow and cheek as the face leaned forward. A memory unrolled in the back of his mind, confused and dis-jointed. He knew this face.

"Want to see the color of my money, is that it? A fine tavern wench you are, arguing the toss with a well-heeled customer as you did with that lost little maid. Roll out a barrel, confound you. I can pay the reckoning." He drew himself up, fixing his gaze unsteadily on Clare's face. "As a token of my good faith," he began grandly, "of my munissi—munifi—" He gave up and raised a hand slowly and dramatically aloft. The fingers loosened. Something dropped and bounced on the table, then rolled to the floor. Mark slumped forward and laid his head on the table.

Clare watched the object come to rest. Light glinted on the ruby-and-diamond ring—the ring she had last seen adorning the finger of Eve Patterson. Clare felt her throat tighten. She tried to swallow, but the thick, bitter taste of dismay made the act impossible. For a man to get so deathly drunk as this, he must have loved Eve Patterson with an intensity that could only be borne by resorting to the bottle.

Sep looked at Clare blankly. "What's it mean, miss—the ring and all?"

Clare swallowed hard and turned to Sep, trying to keep her voice steady. "It gives reason for this strange behavior. This is the ring he gave to Miss Patterson on their engage-ment."

"Gawd," Sep breathed. "So that's what hit him so hard. Returned his ring, did she?"

"I suppose so," Clare said dully. "He would not be in this state if it had been by mutual agreement."

"What are we going to do, miss?"

Clare lifted an eyebrow. "We?"

Sep looked at her appealingly. "You said yourself we couldn't take him home, what with Sara and Mrs. Winter there. What about the farm?"

Clare bit her lip. "No. There are too many eyes there. It would get about and he wouldn't like that, although it would serve him right for getting into this state. How stupid men can be!"

"Aye, miss, that's true, but we rely on a good woman to steer us back on course."

Clare gave him a sardonic look. "Bilge water, Septimus Thomas. You rely on us only when you're in trouble."

"Yes, miss," Sep answered meekly.

Clare took in a deep breath and hardened her heart. "He'll have to sleep it off, that's all there is to it. And mind you put a bucket beside him for the—the off-loading, as you call it."

Sep glanced over at the semiconscious man. "Here, miss?"

"Where else? It was your rum," she finished brutally.

Sep regarded her reproachfully but said nothing.

"Damnation, Septimus Thomas," Clare exploded. "You're not suggesting I have him in my cottage?"

Sep put his head on one side and scratched his chin thoughtfully. "Well, the lasses are in and out of here, not to mention young Albert."

Clare stared aghast. "I don't believe I'm hearing aright! Do you expect me to give up my bedroom to this—"

"Just an idea, miss."

"Well, think of another one," Clare snapped. "If any of my ladies called—" She paused as a thought struck her. "Don't drunken men burst into song if the fancy takes them?"

Sep allowed the possibility and Clare tried to banish the vision of Mrs. Foster's face if the sound of a masculine voice raised in bawdy song should issue from her bedroom. Clare gave a muffled gasp that was half laughter.

"Absolutely not, Septimus Thomas! I refuse to have any

part of this. Lock your door. Tell the children you've caught
a fever. Run up one of your famous flags—the Yellow Jack,
for instance. Good heavens, the man can't stay drunk indef-
initely! He'll get over it. Hide your rum and make him drink
black coffee when he's capable. And put that ring back in
his pocket. He'll probably make it up with her.''

She walked out of Sep's cottage and made her way up the
hill. She was half amused, half indignant that Sep should
expect her help with Mark Conrad for a second time. Was
she some kind of seaman's mission, where nearly drowned
or fully drunk sailors could recover? Confound Septimus
Thomas and damn Mark Conrad! What concern was he to
her? Had she not enough troubles on her own without giving
comfort to a man who had been rejected by another girl?

Damn, damn, damn, she thought savagely, fitting the key
into the lock of her cottage door. Of course she would have
comforted him, but she had no claim, and he had no right to
expect it. Not that he had asked, but his troubles were his
own.

◆ *Chapter Twenty-nine* ◆

When William Oliver called for Clare on Monday afternoon,
she had taken great pains with her appearance. Her curls were
loose under a small straw bonnet and she wore a wide-skirted
muslin dress. A matching parasol hung elegantly by its ribbon
from her wrist. William jumped down from his glossy-
paneled phaeton and helped her into the high seat. She smiled
her thanks and prepared to enjoy the unaccustomed pleasure
of a drive in the afternoon sunshine. Her mind was easy;
there was nothing to be dreaded today.

''We'll go over the hills and to a delightful little place I know," commented William. "They serve a delicious cream tea, if that is to your taste."

"It sounds splendid," Clare said demurely, meeting William's eye. "Is tea to your liking, also?"

"Rarely," he said, smiling. "But I will make the sacrifice for your sake."

The smile died from his face as they came abreast Conrad Place, to be replaced by a sneer.

"You'd think that fellow would be skulking indoors, licking his wounds, wouldn't you? But there he stands, brassfaced as you like."

Clare looked at him in surprise. "How indignant you sound, William. What has the man done? Is he not betrothed to your cousin?" she asked innocently.

"Not anymore. She threw his ring back at him, and not before time."

"I'm so sorry. Is she very unhappy?"

William gave a short laugh. "More furious than unhappy."

"I don't understand."

"Of course not, but it serves her right for aiming to be the lady of the manor. I knew he was not suitable all along, but she wouldn't listen to me. Oh, no, he must have a seat on the board when he married into the Patterson family. But that's all over now. Ignore him, my dear, when we pass."

Clare glanced out of the corner of her eye at the tall figure of Mark Conrad, lounging by his front door. His gaze was upon them as they approached, and she saw that William was staring straight ahead. Her own feelings were mixed until she remembered the disgusting sight of the drunken man in Sep's cottage. She raised her chin and stared ahead, but not before she had noted the sardonic smile on Mark's face. Her heart beat a little quicker but she stared resolutely before her. She sensed that William was not displeased by the turn of events.

There was no acknowledgment on either side as the phaeton swept past Conrad Place. Clare obeyed William's injunction to ignore Mark, for he was her only line of escape. As they reached the hilltop where the track curved onto the main highway, Clare looked at William.

"I had the impression that you and your cousin were not

on the best of terms. Perhaps I was wrong and family feeling is stronger than personal differences, especially as you say the engagement was broken by Miss Patterson, herself?''

William's eyes narrowed slightly in a look of suspicion. "You seem mightily concerned, my dear. Do you, by any chance, have some compassion for the man? Are you acquainted with him?''

Clare relaxed her expression and smiled back. "I have seen him about, naturally, but I am better acquainted with his daughter, Sara. She is a sweet child.'' It would do her own cause no good if she showed further interest in Mark Conrad.

William seemed satisfied and pointed ahead. "There it is, my dear, just by the wayside, under that enormous thatch. Why, you can scarcely see the teahouse door for that trailing clematis. You will like this place. I have patronized it often, though not in the tearoom before.''

He drew the phaeton to a halt and Clare noted the quick flicker of his eyes over her head. There were small, latticed windows tucked under the eaves—some upstairs accommodation, certainly, for discreet, out of the way renting by Clevedon's young bucks.

"The taproom serves excellent ale,'' William went on as if unaware of his upward glance. "But one does not entertain young ladies there.''

"Of course not,'' Clare responded, giving a delicate shudder. She was about to say that she had never entered a taproom in her life when the memory of her first encounter with Mark came to her. Her cheeks turned pink but William smiled, attributing her sudden flush to maidenly modesty. He looked pleased and led her masterfully into the small, oak-beamed tearoom.

The hot scones with cream and strawberry jam were excellent. William was treated with what Clare considered a slightly familiar respect by the ample-bosomed landlady. William seemed either unaware of or unconcerned by the easy manner of the bold-eyed woman. Clare caught the speculative gaze upon herself as the woman served them and wondered uneasily if the soberly dressed landlady threw off her respectability after dark and became a renter of rooms to the young blades of Clevedon, no questions asked! Was she viewing William's companion along those lines? Clare lifted her chin and returned the woman's look with a touch of hauteur in her stare, remembering William's quick glance at the upstairs window.

It was pleasant to sit in idleness, eating scones and sipping tea. The conversation was rather one-sided, but Clare was content to listen to William's talk of people and parties. It was certainly a world unknown to her. She smiled and nodded, certain that his discourse was meant to impress her. She was, indeed, impressed as he spoke of the expense incurred by Mr. Patterson to celebrate Eve Patterson's coming of age,

"You never saw so many jewels all in one room," he said. "But Eve made sure that no one outshone her." His smile held scornful amusement. "She had every fellow drooling at the mouth to dance with her."

"Except one," Clare reminded him.

William waved a dismissive hand. "Good riddance, I say."

He spoke no more of Mark Conrad, but turned the conversation to his forthcoming trip to France and sought to enthrall her with its delights.

They drove back to her cottage, meeting no one on the way. William was in a cheerful, carefree mood.

At the door of the cottage, Clare thanked him prettily for the outing and William preened visibly, convinced of his conquest.

"I will call tomorrow, my dear, for your decision." He lowered his voice, although there was no one about. "Our little trip to Cherbourg, eh? Be sure to pack your amber silk." His eyes twinkled boyishly and Clare gave him a flutter of eyelashes and a maidenly simper.

Once inside her cottage, Clare slid the bolt on the front door and leaned wearily against it as she took off her hat. She eyed the amber silk dress on the dummy with loathing. Was she to step out of Lord Rayne's reach, only to fall into the clutches of William Oliver? His intentions were quite clear. She was not of Clevedon society and was therefore fair game—especially after he had glimpsed that dress! The silk seemed to mock her for a naive fool, and on a sudden savage impulse, she strode forward and hooked her fingers into the neckline. She would tear it into shreds and blame the farm cats! Her fingers tightened and a low, amused voice spoke, making her jump visibly.

"My dear girl, if you need to vent your spite on something, let it be on your dowdiest gown, not on that scrap of exquisite silk. Which brazen hussy commissioned that whore's gown? Certainly not my late, unlamented fiancée. It's too small by half."

With her fingers still frozen on the gown's neckline, Clare turned her head slowly and saw the figure of Mark Conrad lounging on her couch. She stared coldly but her heart pounded with shock.

"What are you doing here? How the devil did you get in?"

"You left your back door open. I came in that way."

"Then you may take yourself out the same way," she snapped, recovering.

Mark did not move. "Do you treat all your visitors like this?"

"Uninvited ones, yes."

Mark rose slowly to his feet and Clare had time to notice the tired lines on his face. She felt a stab of sympathy but suppressed it fiercely, keeping her expression stony.

"I'm sorry for intruding," Mark said. "It was stupid of me to come."

"Very stupid," Clare agreed, and her anger rose, burning its way jealously into a spate of hot words. "If you seek comfort to soften your rejection by Eve Patterson, you have come to the wrong place. I am sure you will find a willing girl and you may both get blind drunk with my blessing."

Mark stared at her. "What the devil are you saying?"

"Isn't it obvious? You have tried the bottle and all you got was a sore head—at least, I hope you did—so now get out of here and leave me in peace." Her voice broke. She swung angrily away and stormed into the kitchen. She opened the door wide and stood watching Mark pointedly.

He had followed her into the kitchen and they faced each other. Mark's lips began to twitch, then he chuckled.

"Little spitfire," he said, his tone admiring.

"Drunken lecher," she retorted, then gasped at her own language.

Mark laughed delightedly. "You don't mince words, do you? I admit to being drunk in Sep's cottage, but I don't admit to being a lecher—not in the presence of a girl I care for greatly."

Clare stiffened. "Pretty words won't get you sympathy."

"I know, but they might get me a hearing."

Clare frowned. "Why not take them to Miss Patterson? She rejected you, not I. What has your broken engagement to do with me?"

"Forget Miss Patterson, Clare. It is to you I make an apology."

"For what?"

"For yesterday morning at Sep's cottage."

"There is no need—" Clare began stiffly, but Mark interrupted.

"Indeed there is every need, and dammit, Clare, won't you let me sit down before I fall down? I didn't get much sleep last night and that makes four nights in a row. For pity's sake, let me talk to you. That's all I want."

Clare hesitated, then nodded. "All right. Will you take tea? I'm afraid I have nothing stronger," she added caustically.

Mark sank gratefully onto a kitchen chair and shuddered visibly. "Thank God for that! Two glasses of Sep's rum would strip the paint off a battleship. No wonder I felt keelhauled when I woke up."

"It was your own choice," Clare said primly as she spooned tea into the pot.

"I know, but it was a damn fool thing to do on an empty stomach and an even emptier head. I'm sorry you were there."

Clare shrugged. "What does it matter? You had your reasons."

They were both silent until Clare had placed two steaming mugs on the table. She sat down across the table from Mark.

"You said you wanted to talk. What do we have to talk about?"

"You were out with William today. Did he seemed pleased by Eve's rejection of me?"

"Immensely."

Mark frowned into his mug. "As pleased as if he had arranged it himself?"

Clare looked keenly into Mark's face. "For what purpose?"

"To keep me from attending Eve's party. She meant to make various announcements, or so she told me yesterday."

"Like a seat on the board?"

Mark looked startled. "How did you know that?"

"People like Miss Patterson forget that their inferiors have ears. During her fittings, she infuriated her cousin by hinting at her future plans for you."

"Plans that might not be to his advantage?"

"Yes."

"Then he had good reason to tamper with the steering gear. The shipwright swears it was tampered with when he examined it today." Mark frowned thoughtfully. "We had to crawl back under half sail. Even William would know that."

"Would it have taken long to damage the steering?"

"Not if you knew where to find the connections to the wheel."

"William was below for quite a while. I was at the harbor with Sep. I thought William looked ill when he arrived and then, of course, he collapsed on deck."

"Leaving me the only available captain to take out the *Dolphin.*"

"He seemed really ill."

"But he refused a doctor! I heard him."

"I was surprised to see him looking so well on Saturday when he called on me."

"A convenient illness, wouldn't you say?" Mark asked dryly.

"A passing indisposition, William called it."

"A very quick passing, which allowed him to attend the party."

"You can't really prove it, can you?"

"No. And it doesn't matter now."

"But it must have upset Miss Patterson."

Mark grinned. "Oh, indeed it did. I was really hauled over the coals, and do you know something, Clare?"

She shook her head.

"They didn't burn one little bit."

"But you got drunk," Clare accused.

"Reaction and meeting a friendly face. I know it was stupid. I should have gone home to bed. I'll steer clear of Sep's rum bottle in the future, if I have a future!" Mark stood up. "Thank you for listening to me, Clare."

Clare regarded him curiously. He looked so much younger than the man who had entered her cottage—almost cheerful and confident.

"What will you do now?" she queried. "If you make it up with Eve, your future is assured."

Mark shook his head. "What happened was no fault of mine, and a man is only accountable to his employer. Good night, Clare."

Long after Mark had gone, Clare sat on in the kitchen, the tea growing cold. He must make his peace with Eve. What other way was there to rescue his future? Eve would get over her disappointment and regret the outburst of temper against her errant lover. She should have known better than to rail at a tired man, especially after her own exertions the night before. Neither of them could have been in the best of moods.

Clare rose at last and carried the used crockery to the sink. The day after tomorrow, she would board the *Dolphin*. There was a future somewhere else for her, and the inhabitants of Clevedon were well able to sort out their affairs without any help from Clare Court. Her last act that evening was to remove the amber silk dress from the model and stuff it back into the straw bag.

Sara called early the next morning on her way to school. She was growing taller and prettier as the weeks passed and

Clare acknowledged that her own affection for the child had grown, too. What would Sara and the Clarks think when she suddenly disappeared without explanation? The Clark girls might accept it philosophically, but Sara was so sensitive, she was bound to be hurt.

"Will you come to tea again, Clare?" Sara's grey-green eyes were so eager and trusting that Clare felt a sharp pain in her heart. As she hesitated, Sara rushed on. "Do come, Clare. It was so much fun last time, and Papa says he will be busy in his study and not mind in the least how much noise we make playing the piano. Of course," she added hastily, "it is not noise when you play, but only when I hit the wrong notes. You will come, won't you?"

"Thank you, Sara. I shall be delighted, if you are sure it will not disturb your papa's work."

"Oh, no, Clare, not at all. In fact, he agreed immediately when I asked permission. He was in very high spirits this morning and said it was a splendid idea."

When Clare arrived at Conrad Place, there was no sign of Mark. Sara welcomed her with enthusiasm and Mrs. Winter greeted her politely. Clare left her gloves and bonnet in the hall and followed Sara into the same sitting room as before. Clare looked about her. She would remember this beautiful room and think of Mark, long legs outstretched, reclining in one of the comfortable easy chairs by the fireplace, and Sara, too, perhaps sitting on the rug while the glow of a winter's coal fire touched her hair with reddish-golden glints. Would Eve Patterson sit across the hearth from Mark in the other easy chair? Such reflections held no comfort so she turned her attention to Sara, who was now presiding over the tea tray.

Sara Conrad was an intelligent, sensitive child. With loving encouragement, she would become a clever, well-read young lady. Would Eve give her that impetus? With her talk of boarding schools, it was unlikely that Eve would have the slightest interest in the girl, even if Mark refused the suggestion of sending Sara away to school.

Sara was eager to show Clare her new batch of sheet music, which was a step up from the simpler pieces of before.

The music stool was wide enough for the playing of duets and Clare took the end close to the window in front of the bass notes. She sat back while Sara showed off her new pieces.

"How much more accomplished you have become since we last sat here," Clare said, and Sara glowed under her praise. "Indeed, it will be I who hits the wrong keys, for I have no piano to practice on. What a lovely tone this instrument has. It deserves the most delicate touch and loving handling. Your fingering is excellent, Sara. What a good teacher you have in the vicar's wife."

The ring of the front doorbell coincided with the opening chord of the duet Sara placed on the music stand. Neither of them heard it and were well into the music when the sitting room door opened. Still they played until a voice, high with irritation, spoke.

"Good heavens, Mark! Am I supposed to compete with that noise?"

Sara looked up first and gasped. Her hands faltered on the keys and hit a very unmelodic note. Clare's hands slid off the keys and dropped into her lap. Glancing across the room, she saw Eve Patterson framed in the doorway, beautifully dressed and immaculately coiffured. Behind her stood Mark, frowning slightly, with the bemused air of a man newly roused from sleep or deep thought.

Only Clare and Sara saw the hard blue light in Eve's eyes as they rested on the child. Sara's left hand moved in a convulsive gesture of distress. Clare grasped the trembling fingers and pressed them between her own two hands, trying to instill some of her own strength into their limpness.

◆ *Chapter Thirty* ◆

Eve turned a smile onto Mark, her blue eyes now soft. "We really must talk, Mark darling. I was upset on Sunday morning—too distraught by worry to treat you fairly. Do send the child from the room, darling. Then we will talk, just the two of us."

Mark regarded Eve steadily for a long moment, then said softly, "The child has a name, Eve."

"Of course, darling. A most pretty name. Sara, isn't it?"

Mark spoke in the same soft voice. "My daughter, Sara, is presently entertaining a guest. It is for us to leave the room."

"A guest?" Eve's head jerked around sharply.

Clare realized that, although Sara was quite visible with the sunlight behind her, her own figure was shadowed by the velvet curtain. Coming in out of the bright sunlight, Eve had been unaware of the second person on the piano stool.

Clare rose. "Good afternoon, Miss Patterson."

Eve's eyes widened. She swung again to Mark. "A guest, you said."

Mark inclined his head. "Indeed, I did."

"A guest? That—that tradesperson! How dare you invite her to your house?"

Clare pressed Sara's hand tighter as the child seemed to shrink at the tone of outrage in Eve's voice.

Mark's tone was even softer and the words came in a laconic drawl. "I dare anything, my dear, and your displeasure moves me not at all. Why should it?"

"I am your fiancée."

Mark smiled. "Since you were the one to break the engagement, I find that a strange claim."

Eve reached out a hand and laid soft white fingers on his coat sleeve. She smiled enchantingly.

308

"Dear Mark, I have had time to reflect and reconsider. That's what I came to tell you."

Mark looked down at the elegant hand. "I have had time to reflect, too, Eve. Our engagement remains broken."

"What?" Eve stared, then drew back her hand quickly. Her gaze flashed over the room and rested on Clare. Her eyes narrowed in suspicion. "That woman—is she your mistress? If so, I will hound her out of town and make sure that no respectable lady patronizes her squalid establishment—"

Her words were cut off sharply as Mark spun her about and showed her to the door.

In the doorway she shook off Mark's hand and stood completely motionless. Her expression was unbelieving. For Eve Patterson to be dismissed by a man was beyond all comprehension.

Mark seemed to divine her confused line of thought. "If someone had taken a stand against you a dozen years ago, it would have improved your character immensely. I fear this comeuppance has arrived too late."

Eve recovered her wits and glared at him. "Much too late for you, Mark Conrad! I was a fool to take up with you, but I'll make you pay for this insult. Uncle Thomas will dismiss you from his service when I tell him of your callous behavior. I'll tell everyone how you ill-treated me."

To Clare's astonishment, Mark began to laugh. "Bravo, Eve. Tell the world of my insolence and mark yourself as a fool for taking up with me. They will all commiserate but laugh behind their hands at your folly." He paused, sobering. "May I show you to your carriage?" he continued with the air of a polite host.

Eve tossed her head angrily. "I can find my own way out." She pushed past Mark and paused in the doorway to deliver a parting invective. "I hope you'll remember that you brought it on yourself when you and your brat end up in the workhouse. As for that creature—"

Something in Mark's expression must have hinted at danger, for she closed her lips tightly and swept out of sight. The front door slammed. When Mark returned to the room, he found Clare embracing Sara, who was sobbing almost noiselessly on her friend's shoulder. Clare looked at Mark over Sara's head.

"I'm sorry. I shouldn't have come here. My presence was an irritant to Miss Patterson. You could have become reconciled, but my being here just made things worse."

Mark smiled. "Nonsense, my dear. It all went splendidly. I have long wanted to answer to that young lady's arrogance. Her abuse gave me the perfect opportunity. Here, let me take Sara. Come, my darling, and sit on Papa's knee."

He lifted Sara, who threw her arms about his neck, and they sank together into a deep easy chair. Clare watched him stroke the child's hair and wipe away the tears. She envied the bond of love between father and daughter. It was something she had never known in her own early life.

Mark glanced up, his expression still gentle. "Play something for us, Clare. Something gay, for we need to mark this occasion."

Clare gave him a bemused look but lifted her hands to the keys in obedience to the strange request. She chose Chopin's "Minute Waltz," which took her all of two minutes to complete. When she glanced over at Mark and Sara, they were both smiling, Sara's tears forgotten.

Clare gave a wry smile. "My apologies to Mr. Chopin. One needs to be very experienced to complete the piece on time. If Sara goes on the way she is doing, why, she'll have the piece finished in half a minute—or less."

Sara giggled and Mark laughed.

"Mr. Chopin might not like that at all. Thank you, Clare. That was most enjoyable. Sara, my love, go and ask Mrs. Winter to make fresh tea, will you?"

"I really should be going," Clare said, rising from the piano stool.

"Not before I tell you my news, surely? I did say this was an occasion."

"You did," Clare admitted. "But to me it seemed more of a catastrophe. You have lost your fiancée and possibly your employment, yet you seem bent on celebration. I don't understand."

"You will when you see the letters I have received. I am

not alone in visualizing steam power for ships. I have a dozen or more supporters, all willing to invest in a new company to further the idea. We plan to meet in Bristol next week to launch our new project and have everything placed on a legal basis by a company lawyer after discussions with engineers and shipbuilders.''

"What about the Pattersons?"

"Who?" Mark laughed. "That's the past, my dear. I look to the future now.''

"Without regret?"

"Completely. Eve showed her true colors today and on Sunday morning. I have William to thank for my release and I truly feel like a reprieved man.''

After more tea, Clare rose to leave. "I wish you every success, Mark." She looked at Sara and touched her gently on the cheek. "Good-bye, my dear. Keep practicing, won't you?''

Mark escorted her to the front door. He was frowning. "You said good-bye as if you meant it.''

Clare was annoyed at herself. He had too much perception. "Did I?" she asked lightly.

"Are you afraid that Eve will ruin your professional reputation?''

Clare shrugged. "Clevedon is a small place. A hint of impropriety dropped here and there will not add to my standing in the community.''

"No need to leave town," Mark said slowly. "You could stay here and marry me.''

"What?" Clare's heart gave a violent lurch. She stared at Mark incredulously. "Marry you?" she asked faintly, feeling the ground move beneath her feet.

Mark's lips twisted into a self-deprecating grimace. "I'm not much of a catch, I admit. A man without a job and only a long-term chance of prosperity is a poor prospect.''

Clare gathered her wits together. "And a man on the rebound is an even poorer prospect." She looked at him steadily. "Your suggestion does not honor but insult me." She gave a short, hard laugh. "Do you suppose I have so little pride as to take a rejected suitor of a mere two days' standing?''

"But you don't understand, Clare. I love you. I was a fool not to see it before, and—"

Clare cut in sharply, her hurt and anger building. "Then you'd best be a fool again, Mark Conrad, and find yourself another heiress. How would marrying another pauper help in your fine schemes? It's a quixotic gesture, I grant you, but one you'll have regretted before dawn, by which time I'll be—" She bit back the words that had been tumbling off her incautious tongue. Why should she explain anything to him?

Mark grasped her arm. "You'll be what? Tell me. I have a right to know."

"A right? You have no rights over me whatsoever. What a curious idea. I go where I wish. Let go of my arm, if you please."

Mark's hand dropped. He looked angry and frustrated. In her present mood, Clare gloried in his bafflement. He didn't love her and she resented his proposal, convinced that for him it was a face-saving, second-best, spur-of-the-moment thing.

Mark stood aside, saying nothing as she walked swiftly out of Conrad Place. He had not put forward any argument or detained her further. She was right, and he knew it, but that did not help the hollow desolation that crept over her as she entered her own cottage.

William called an hour later. Clare greeted him calmly, although her smile was a little hard to keep in place.

William glanced at the dummy, now denuded of the amber silk dress. He smiled. "You have packed your beautiful gown. That pleases me enormously." He gave her a quizzical look. "Are you sure you will wake in time to catch the tide? It's very early for a lady to be about, if she has no one to wake her."

His smile was suggestive, but Clare chose to ignore his meaning. If she had to give in to William Oliver, it would not be before she was safely aboard the *Dolphin* and en route for Cherbourg.

Was it really true, as Sep had implied, that William suffered from seasickness? How convenient that would be! She would pray to heaven for a rough crossing.

She smiled archly at William. "I think I may prove a poor sailor, sir."

William's smile was almost smug. "Since you told me yourself that you had never been on a ship, your fear may prove groundless. I shall be beside you, never fear, and will devote myself entirely to your comfort. The outlook is good. We shall have a smooth crossing."

That night, Clare found sleep difficult. Her mind would not rest. At last she rose and began to pack the old straw basket she had brought from Harcourt House. She discarded Lord Rayne's gifts and filled the basket's capacious depths with her own purchases. For the last time she sat at her walnut bureau, composing a letter to the Clarks. They had been so kind, she could not leave without a word of explanation— not the true one, of course, but the vague suggestion of investigating new premises in Bristol. She tried not to think of Mark and his offer of marriage. It would have been simple to accept, for she loved him, but could she have lived under the shadow of Eve Patterson and the possible regret he might have felt in the future? Then there was the complication of Lord Rayne.

Her gaze rose and she stared blindly out the window into the darkness of night. She knew she would have been a loving wife to Mark and a devoted mother to Sara, but not this way—not picking up the pieces of a broken romance and expecting a wholehearted man. She would leave a note for Sara, perhaps with a hint of being called away on unexpected family business and a hope of meeting again in the future.

She left the note for the Clarks in a prominent place. Milly or Kate would see it and take it to their mother. She slipped Sara's letter into the pocket of her cloak. If Sep was at the harbor, he would deliver it after the *Dolphin* sailed.

As the faintest glimmering of dawn warmed the sky, Clare left her cottage, front and back doors closed but unlocked. It was far too early to go straight to the harbor. Over the fields, the long way around, would be best, and not even the earliest cowman would be abroad.

The dew in the long grass wet her shoes, but it didn't matter. Nothing mattered now save to escape from the one man she loved and the other she hated. A very young voice lifted high with frustrated imprecations assailed her ears, startling her into sudden stillness.

"Come here, you wicked, thieving, ornery, four-legged son of Satan! I'll have you flogged on the gratings and hung from the yardarm—you see if I don't, you pesky, bony bag of horse meat. Come here, do, you useless critter."

Clare let out her breath, recognizing the voice of young Albert. His wiry young body flung itself across her path and skidded to a halt as he saw her.

"Morning, miss. 'Tis rare early for a body to be about."

"Just what I was thinking, Albert. I—er—gather you're in search of something four-legged?"

He grinned sheepishly as the dawn light touched his face. "Aye, miss, reckon you could say that. There's always one, isn't there? This critter must have known it's his turn to pull the milk churns. He took off afore I could even get a rope on him. He's as sharp as a bosun's rope end." He peered up the hill. "There he is, just looking at us, calm as you like." He paused. "No, that ain't him. 'Tis a cove on horseback. What's he staring at?"

Clare followed his gaze. She just had time to glimpse the man's face before he wheeled his horse and galloped away. It was the man who had delivered Lord Rayne's letter and previously been so interested in Clare's horse—or rather, Lord Rayne's. She was conscious of the large basket on her arm. He must have seen it, too, and at such an early hour, guessed it was her last-ditch attempt to escape. Now he would be on his way to pass the news to Lord Rayne.

"I'd best be off, miss. If I don't catch that critter soon, there's folks who'll find their milk cans empty come eight o'clock."

"Milk cans?"

"Aye, miss. Folk hereabouts rely on Farmer Clark delivering their milk."

"Yes, of course." Clare remembered the Clark girls bringing up her own milk. She looked at Albert speculatively. "Do you deliver to Conrad Place?"

"Every day, miss. Eight o'clock sharp."

Clare reached into her pocket and drew out the letter to Sara. With that man now on his way to Lord Rayne, she could not wait for Sep to appear at the harbor. It was better that she should go aboard and be hidden from view long before the local people gathered to wave off the ship. She held out the letter.

"Albert, will you give this note to Miss Sara when you deliver the milk, please? I haven't time, myself, and eight o'clock or later will be fine."

"Of course, miss." Albert tucked the letter into his pocket and grinned. "Got to find that danged horse first."

Clare watched him race up the hillside like a young gazelle and head toward the woods. The *Dolphin* would be well gone by the time Albert delivered the note. She turned away and began her descent to the harbor.

◆ *Chapter Thirty-one* ◆

Mark Conrad had also passed a troubled night. He cursed himself fluently for mishandling the situation with Clare Court. After closing the door on an ex-fiancée, only a crass fool would propose to a girl who had witnessed the whole scene. She was right, of course. Clevedon would say she caught him on the rebound after Eve's rejection. They wouldn't know that Eve had figured less and less in his thoughts and Clare Court more and more. What a sane man would have done was to allow this business to fade into the background before paying his addresses to Clare. He knew now that he loved her—in fact, he had loved her without really knowing since that night in the barn. Clare was beautiful, serene, without artifice or coquetry—but with a secret she would not share. What had she been running from? He didn't care what it was, if only she would let him help her solve it.

He climbed out of bed, strode to the window, and opened it wide. Dawn was here already and the hills were rimmed with gold. He breathed deeply, leaning his elbows on the sill. A small, dark shape caught his eye—a slow-moving figure, half crouched, silent. Mark frowned, peering from his window. What the devil was going on? The figure made a quick, mad dash, than a crow of delight exploded into the still air.

"Got you, you blamed critter! Thought you'd hide here, did you? Now, you come along with me, for it's your turn on the milk cart and no mistake."

Mark leaned out the window, grinning as he recognized the voice. It was the lad off the *Venturer* who had been taken on by Farmer Clark.

"What's going on down there, lad? Such a bawling is enough to wake the dead, let alone law-abiding folk who expect to sleep the night through."

Albert's voice came breathlessly. "Sorry, sir, but this old brute has been giving me the slip half the night and I've got to get him down the hill and in the shafts of the milk cart. They'll be milking 'fore too long." There was the sound of a snuffle and Albert's voice became shrill. "Bite me, would you, you evil heathen. Sir, would you be having a bit of rope, like, for there's the devil in this fellow. He'll not walk nice and easy—give over, do."

"Hang on, lad. I'll be with you in a minute."

Mark pulled on his trousers and boots and went to help the struggling boy. They got the horse haltered between them and Albert looped the leading rope about his wrist. He was red-faced and fulminating. He glowered at the horse.

"Can't think why I bother with 'em. They're mean, bad-tempered, ungrateful brutes." There was something in his voice that belied the harsh words and the horse, now passive as a lamb, thrust forward his head and nuzzled the boy's neck.

Mark grinned. "Now, you'd not get the bosun to kiss your cheek after keeping you on the trot all night."

Albert chuckled. "You're right there, sir. 'Tis proper

soppy, this one, trying to make up now he's ketched. Well, I'll be off, sir, or the missus will be for chasing me out if the milk delivery's late, which it will be and t'ain't no fault of mine. Morning, Cap'n.'' He began to lead the horse down the slope, then stopped, fumbling in his pocket. "Oh, sir, I've just recollected, talking of milk and such. I've a letter for Miss Sara. Told to bring it on the milk round, but seeing as it'll be late and I'm here now—''

Mark took the letter, now creased and grubby. He stared for a long moment at the writing he had seen before on the label of the parcel containing the turquoise shawl. Why was Clare writing to Sara?

Albert was moving away again and Mark called after him. "When did Miss Court give you this letter, Albert?''

The boy looked over his shoulder. "Maybe an hour since, Cap'n. I was still chasing—''

Mark interrupted. "An hour since? It was dark then. What was she doing at that hour? Was she alone?''

Albert stared blankly, taken aback by the sharp, questioning voice. "Aye, sir. Miss was alone. In a hurry, she said, and eight o'clock would be fine.'' He paused, wrinkling his brow. "Stands to reason she'd be in a hurry.''

"Why?''

"She was carryin' a bag and all. It's a tidy stride to the crossroads.''

"Thanks, Albert.'' Mark tossed the words over his shoulder and made for the house. In the hall, he paused by a lamp and turned up the wick as he tore open Sara's letter. If there was a clue in it, he had to know long before Sara rose. He stared, baffled at the wording. There was nothing but an expression of affection and hope of a meeting in the future. He laid down the note and ran upstairs to dress.

Half an hour later he was at the crossroads, staring up at the signpost. Which coach route would she take—Bristol or London? A thought cheered him. Both coaches must take the same way from Clevedon, diverging here for their ultimate destinations. All travelers would assemble a mile down the road unless they boarded in Clevedon itself. She must be at the King's Head, unless Albert's estimation of time had been incorrect and she had caught an earlier coach. That good-bye had been real then, and his own stupidity in proposing had driven her into instant flight. She would not come back, he was sure of it. Therefore, she must not be allowed to leave until he had convinced her that he loved her beyond measure.

The lighted windows of the King's Head came into sight. The forecourt was empty save for a few lounging ostlers. One straightened and approached as Mark reined in.

"What time is the coach due?" he asked.

"Bristol coach anytime, sir, but if it's the London you want, that'll be along in half an hour." He peered up at Mark. "Every seat is booked inside, and a mill of folk are here already for the outside places."

Mark dismounted. "I'm not traveling. I'm here to see someone who is, that's all. Take my horse while I go inside."

He strode into the crowded inn, looking about him. He didn't see Clare so he pushed his way through groups of people, scanning every face. The breakfast room, parlor, and taproom opened before him but no Clare Court came into view. Could she have gone into Clevedon? It didn't matter, for the same coach had to stop here to pick up passengers. When it arrived he would be outside and in position to see all inside travelers.

He stood aside to allow a man to enter the taproom. A wave of perfume enveloped him and Mark glanced at him without real curiosity. He was a Londoner, perhaps, considering his elegant style of dress. It was rather excessive for the country, and he wore rather too much jewelry—several rings, a jeweled brooch in his neckcloth, and an ornate gold watch chain across a brocaded waistcoat. Shorter than himself and running slightly to plumpness, the man had corn-colored hair and the face of a fallen angel.

Mark, while listening for the coach, leaned against the wall and watched the man idly. Surely such a prettily dressed gentleman in his pale buff attire was not going to scramble aboard the public stagecoach and risk the stain of travel, either to Bristol or London? One would suppose him well able to travel by post chaise, at least.

A red-faced, sweating man detached himself from a mug

of ale at the bar, and hurried toward the fine gentleman, who stared at him coldly.

"Well?"

The red-faced man wiped a sleeve across his forehead. "It was just as you said, my lord. She cut and run in the dark at the last minute. She was heading this way, too."

Mark looked again more intently at the well-dressed figure—a lordship, no less, and hardly likely to be taking the stagecoach. Like himself, he was expecting someone.

"Get me a brandy."

"Yes, my lord, right away." The man scuttled off and his lordship sank onto a cushioned bench, staring about him with undisguised disdain. He caught Mark's eye, ran his gaze up and down the tall figure, and decided, Mark thought with amusement, that this obviously local person might be worthy of a civil remark.

"I suppose we can hear the coach arrive from this room?" His faint smile was condescending.

Mark crossed his arms. "Yes."

His lordship looked at his minion. "Go outside and wait. You know who to look for. I'm damned if I'm going to hang about in a cold yard."

"Yes, my lord." The man hurried away.

Few people were left in the taproom and his lordship eyed Mark again. "You're local, I suppose?"

"Yes."

"Know everybody hereabouts?"

"Yes."

His lordship sighed. "You don't say much, do you?"

"No."

"Close-mouthed, you country folk, but there'll be a guinea in it if you tell me something. This fool of mine might have made a mistake, but since you're local—" He spread his hands.

Mark said nothing.

His lordship drained his glass and called for another brandy. He looked at Mark. "Does the name Harcourt mean anything to you?"

"No." As Mark made the denial, he felt a sense of unease

creep up his spine. Harcourt? It was not far off from Court. He made his voice deliberately casual, injecting a trace of the Somerset dialect in his words. Since he had dressed hurriedly and not spared a moment to shave and brush his hair into order, snatching up the old tweed jacket that was nearest to hand, he must look like the bumpkin this man supposed he was. A straw between his teeth would have completed the picture.

He looked reflectively at the seated figure and spoke. "Your man called you a lord. Don't get many lordships around here." His gaze took in the furnishings of the small country inn, then came to rest on the slightly florid face. "Not around here, we don't," he finished pointedly, a smile lifting his lips.

The seated man bridled at the disbelieving tone and stared haughtily. Mark held the gaze impassively, aware that he was expected to break the contact.

"Damn you for an impudent rogue! I am Lord Philip Rayne and your hearing was not at fault."

Mark shrugged and stared at the smoke-blackened ceiling beams. His attitude of indifference provoked Lord Rayne into further angry speech.

"I wouldn't be in this wretched hovel if it wasn't for that ungrateful ward of mine. She shall pay for this indignity when she arrives."

"Coming on the coach, is she?" Mark probed.

"Of course she is. Why else would I be here? But I'll have her off it and into my own coach before she knows what's happening." Lord Rayne drained his third glass of brandy. "Defiance won't pay. I've the law on my side and she knows it." He stared at Mark from bloodshot eyes. "She'll not dare run away again, won't Miss Clare high-and-mighty Harcourt."

♦ Chapter Thirty-two ♦

Mark still leaned against the wall, his eyes on Lord Rayne's face, but he was not seeing the man. His mind was occupied with fitting the pieces of Clare Court's life together. Was this man, already showing signs of debauched living—the sagging facial muscles and thickening body—really her legal guardian? Was she bound by law to remain under his protection until she had reached the age of twenty-one, unless she married before then?

He remembered the guineas she had left in the barn, and her misdirected fury over the horse. She was a runaway, stealing money and horse to make her escape—but escape from what? Or from whom might be nearer the truth? This man who purported to be her legal guardian had searched her out and set a man to watch her movements. He now proposed to drag her off a stagecoach, fling her with indecent haste into his own carriage, and make off with her. Legal or not, it was decidedly underhanded, more the action of an unprincipled man than of a responsible guardian. Now, there was a thought.

He said on a guess, "I expect your lady wife is distraught with worry over this headstrong girl."

Lord Rayne looked startled, then reddened, his eyes flickering away briefly. "Yes, of course. Quite out of her mind with worry as to what may have happened to the unfortunate creature."

Mark knew he was lying, and that his reason for kidnapping his so-called ward was of a personal and very basic nature. Why the devil hadn't Clare confided in him and sought his help? Why the devil should she? he acknowledged bitterly. He had been betrothed to Eve, talked only of his ambitions, and taken advantage of her loving nature. My God, what a crass fool he had been.

The rumble of coach wheels brought Lord Rayne to his

feet. Mark read the excitement in his expression—he ran his tongue over his lips, his eyes eager, like those of a dog preparing to sink its teeth into a tempting delicacy. Lord Rayne was out of the taproom, Mark close behind him into the hallway, both men shouldering aside the outgoing travelers.

Few people descended from the coach. Lord Rayne's man was peering intently into the compartment. He turned a strained face as his lordship came up to him, and shook his head.

"What?" Lord Rayne almost screamed the word. "Look properly, man!"

The man obeyed but no passenger bearing the slightest likeness to Clare Court looked back. Lord Rayne's face turned red with frustrated anger. He rounded on his man and dealt him a stinging blow across the side of his head.

"Stupid, useless imbecile!" he snarled. "You swore the wench would be aboard."

The man shook his head dazedly. "I saw her, my lord. How else could she leave? All the roads are watched, day and night."

Mark backed slowly out of the thronging passengers. He knew there was one other way and cursed himself for not thinking of it before. Lord Rayne would not be far behind in his own thinking. Clare knew she was being watched. She would not have been fool enough to try and escape by public coach. It had to be on the *Dolphin*, and William was taking her out this morning. He ran to the stables and led out his horse. The thought of William and Clare together was like a knife wound. He could not let Clare go out of his life aboard the *Dolphin*. Her farewell of last night and the letter to Sara had been her way of saying good-bye forever. Another thought struck him like a blow. Was William a means to escape Lord Rayne, or did she really love the fellow? He kneed the horse into a mad gallop. Maybe the *Dolphin* had already cast off and she was gone.

Despite the chill air, Mark felt the heat course through his body. He glanced at the sky, willing the dawn to halt and the tide to be less than at the full. If the *Dolphin* had shipped her anchor and cast off, Clare could arrive in Cherbourg and lose herself in France before he had a hope of another ship. He was moving fast, but a glance over his shoulder showed a distant carriage on course behind—Lord Rayne, with two magnificent and fresh Thoroughbreds between the shafts. The early sun flashed on their burnished bridle chains as their heads tossed in unison.

Through the outskirts of Clevedon, Mark held the horse in a thundering gallop, ignoring the startled looks from wagon and farm cart drivers proceeding sedately into town. With luck, Lord Rayne's carriage would be forced into a slower pace. As he neared the harbor, his heart gave a lurch. The topmasts of the *Dolphin* were visible. Even as he thundered down the stretch, the aft sail unfurled, then the small forward sail. Only a few minutes were left before she cast off, turning into the wind with the mainsail down. For the moment he had lost Lord Rayne, but the chase was on.

With his eyes on the ship, Mark was unaware of the heads twisting to discover the source of the pounding hooves, the reason for Captain Conrad's headlong dash to the harbor. There was a hum of speculation as the disheveled rider threw himself off the sweating horse. Men stood ready at the bollards, awaiting orders to cast off. Mark's heart pounded with elation. The *Dolphin* had not yet sailed, although the dripping anchor was shipped.

From the bridge, William saw Mark, tousle-haired and breathing hard. He could not have come from Uncle Thomas since, at Eve's insistence, Mark Conrad was no longer employed by the Patterson line. He could not know that Clare Court was aboard—how could he? She had arrived cloaked and veiled and was now hidden away in the captain's cabin. Anyway, the damned fellow was not coming on board. He had forfeited all rights by his rejection of Eve's attempted reconciliation. William raised a hand peremptorily.

"Cast off both," he shouted, putting all the authority he could manage into his voice. The men bent to the bollards, watching Mark out of the corners of their eyes. What was Captain Conrad doing here—and come in a devilish rush, it seemed. Their overflowing curiosity slowed their hands on the ropes.

"Belay that order!" roared Mark in a voice so full of savage authority that the men froze.

"Let go, damn you!" William's voice rose. "At once, I say, or I'll have you flogged for disobeying your captain."

The men straightened and looked from William to Mark in puzzlement. Captain Oliver was captain of the ship, all right, and they should obey his command, but Captain Conrad must have some reason for belaying the order, and they'd like to know what it was before letting go.

An indignant voice crackled behind Mark's shoulder. "Now there's a right liberty, so it is. Flogged, indeed!" The words issued from the truculent face of Septimus Thomas. "'Tis only the Royal Navy that has the right to flog a fellow. 'Tisn't proper in the merchant fleet."

There was so much outrage in Sep's voice that Mark grinned, despite his anxiety. The old seaman's chin was out-thrust, every bristle aquiver, as if the privilege of being flogged belonged exclusively to the man who sailed in the service of the sovereign.

The *Dolphin* was tugging gently on her lines, as if eager to be off down the Bristol Channel. The rattle of coach wheels had every head turning toward the flying coach, the sun picking out the gold-outlined crest on its door panels.

"Hold fast," Mark shouted to the men at the bollards as he leapt for the ship's rail.

He swung himself over and was halfway to the companionway before Lord Rayne's coach halted. William hurled himself down the bridge ladder.

"Get off my ship—" he began, but Mark was not listening.

He took the companionway in great downward leaps and threw himself toward the captain's cabin. The door crashed back on its hinges and Mark paused, his gaze flying around the dim interior. Clare sat stiffly on the edge of the bunk, her cloak tight about her, the bag at her feet.

Clare stared into the unshaven face under the wild tangle of hair. The blue eyes were hard, the lips compressed, as if holding back a flood of furious words.

"What—what do you want?" she asked faintly.

An expression of exasperation crossed Mark's face. "You

lead me the devil of a chase and now you have the nerve to ask that! I want you, of course. You'll take no sea voyage this day.''

Clare looked at him coldly. ''Since you are no longer in the employ of Mr. Patterson, you have no right to be aboard this ship. Who are you to tell me what I must or must not do?''

''No right at all, but I will take you off this ship, with or without your consent.''

''You will do no such thing,'' Clare snapped. ''I happen to be a passenger and a guest of Captain Oliver.''

Mark eyed her in silence for a moment. ''Since the policy of the Patterson line is to carry fare-paying passengers only, I assume you have come to terms privately with William?'' He raised his brows in sardonic question. ''Have you paid your fare already or is that a pleasure in store for Captain Oliver?''

Clare paled at the insulting note in his voice. ''How dare you speak to me like that? You are no gentleman, Mr. Conrad.'' She turned her head so that he should not see the hurt in her eyes.

''And you, Miss Court, are no lady if you consider William Oliver a fair exchange in your bid to escape.''

''Escape?'' Clare turned to look at him. ''Escape from what?''

''Your past and me.''

''I don't know what you are talking about and I would be obliged if you would leave.''

Boots clattered on the companionway and Mark smiled sardonically. ''Your lover is galloping to your rescue, my dear.''

''He is not my lover,'' Clare said hotly, caught off balance. ''Why, I don't even—'' She stopped abruptly, biting her lip.

''Like him?'' Mark asked silkily, a new light in his eyes.

''Oh, confound you, Mark Conrad! Why can't you leave me alone?''

''No chance of that, my love, for your past sits outside in his carriage.''

''What?'' Clare's eyes widened. ''What do you mean?''

"Your legal guardian, he claims."

"My father?" Clare's face went chalk white. "I will never return to him."

Mark frowned. "You have a father? Then who the devil is this Lord Rayne who claims to be your legal guardian?"

"Oh, my God, not him." She sank back against the cushion, looking very small and lost.

William came hurrying into the cabin, followed by Lord Rayne. Both glared at Mark, then looked at Clare.

"There you are, my dearest," said Lord Rayne heartily. "Come along, and we will say no more about it."

William took the hand Lord Rayne extended. "You are very civil, my lord. Had I known the young lady was your ward, I would never have acceded to her request for a passage. I cannot be involved in criminal proceedings. The honor of the Patterson line is paramount to me." He gave Clare an accusing glance.

"Of course, my boy, I understand." Lord Rayne beamed. He waved a delicate hand in Clare's direction. "Such a headstrong child. My patience amazes me, but I know my duty just as you do, my dear captain. I wonder I took on the guardianship at all. Such a whimsical child."

Mark had been staring at Lord Rayne with rising dislike. "Then why did you take it on, Lord Rayne?"

Lord Rayne seemed to see him clearly for the first time. "Good God! You were that uncouth fellow at the inn. What are you doing here?"

"I might tell you if you answer my question first. Why did you appoint yourself legal guardian to this lady?"

"Because she was given into my care."

"By whom?"

Lord Rayne stared into the hard face and lost a little of his confidence.

"The lady has a father," Mark persisted. "Is he not her legal guardian?"

Lord Rayne lifted his chin and tried to look down his nose at Mark. Since Mark had the advantage of several inches, the exercise failed.

"There were circumstances," his lordship said with dignity. "A matter between gentlemen. You would not under-stand."

Mark looked at Clare, silent and pale. He crossed the cabin floor, went down on one knee before her, and reached for her limp hands.

"Clare, do you wish to go with this man? If you do, then I will not prevent you. William has disowned you so you must now leave the *Dolphin*, anyway."

Clare looked up and Mark was shocked at the dark despair in her eyes. His hands tightened on hers. She shook her head.

He rose, pulling her to her feet. He picked up her bag and faced Lord Rayne. "Since the *Dolphin* must sail, I suggest we leave the ship and discuss this matter somewhere else."

"There is nothing to discuss," Lord Rayne said. "My carriage is outside. My ward and I will be gone directly."

Mark walked past his lordship, holding Clare's hand in a warm clasp. Lord Rayne was forced to follow and they left the ship in silence.

On the harbor side, Mark turned a derisive grin on William, who had regained his position on the bridge.

"Carry on, William. You're captain again." He grinned at the men by the bollards. "Thanks, lads. Cast her off now."

"Aye, aye, Cap'n." They grinned and bent to the lines.

As they drew level with the carriage, the *Dolphin* had already put several feet between herself and the harbor. Lord Rayne paused by the carriage door, held open by a wooden-faced coachman.

"Here we are, my dear. In you go."

Clare made no move to obey. Lord Rayne's geniality was wearing a little thin. It was so damned early for a gentleman to be about.

"Will you do as you are told? These common people have had enough entertainment for one day."

"I am not going with you," Clare said, low-voiced.

"Yes, you are, my girl! You have given me enough trouble already, and I don't intend to let you out of my sight again. It is your duty to obey me."

Mark felt Clare's hand tighten in his. "What duty would that be, Lord Rayne?" he inquired.

His lordship looked Mark over with an air of disdain and dismissed him as another common person.

"It is no concern of yours. Be a good fellow and take yourself off." He turned toward Clare and held out a beckoning hand, unaware that Mark's eyes had darkened with barely controlled anger at being so summarily dismissed. His voice, when it came, was mild, but held an edge his own crew would have recognized. Lord Rayne did not.

"The lady is reluctant to enter your carriage. How do you explain that?"

Lord Rayne turned in simulated surprise. "You still here? I thought I told you to be off. What makes you think I need to explain anything to you?"

Through clenched teeth, Mark said, "Perhaps you would rather make explanation to the local magistrate. He resides close by."

Lord Rayne looked at him closely. This disheveled young man might cause trouble if not dealt with quickly. He turned to his wooden-faced coachman.

"See the fellow off, Jenkins. If a gentleman can't travel about without being accosted by the riffraff of the docks, it's beyond anything."

Jenkins, a short, stocky man with a thick neck and paunch to match, lost his wooden expression and advanced upon Mark with pugnacious intent. His sneer was a replica of his master's.

"Push off, you scum. Didn't you hear what his lordship said?"

He paused fractionally as he caught the sudden blaze in Mark's eyes. The hesitation was brief, but in that second Mark had closed, delivering a fierce right to the jaw. Jenkins fell back, measuring his length on the wet cobbles.

The horses threw up their heads and sidestepped nervously. After one horrified glance at his prone coachman, Lord Rayne stared with alarm into the dark face.

"If it's money you want—" he stuttered, delving into his waistcoat pocket. "I've a couple of spare guineas. Here, take them."

Two gold pieces lay on his trembling palm. Mark struck

the hand aside and Lord Rayne shrank back against his carriage door.

"Don't you dare lay your hands on me. I'll have the law on you."

Mark dropped his hands, restraining the urge to plaster his lordship over the cobbles alongside his coachman.

A cheer from the onlookers brought Mark's head around. He had forgotten how public the harbor was. In the forefront was Septimus Thomas, a wide grin splitting his face. He was almost dancing with delight as the coachman scrambled to his feet.

"A mill, lads. My bet's on Cap'n Mark. Give him another, Cap'n. Go on, do—he's a high-nosed coachy if ever I saw one."

"Shut up, Sep. There'll be no mill. Go away and make yourself useful. Finish off the *Sara*, there's a good fellow."

"She's as spick-and-span as an admiral's lady already. There's naught else to do aboard her."

Mark sought for inspiration. Without Sep as ringleader, the spectators would lose interest.

"Well, go and sandpaper the bloody anchor!" he roared.

Sep almost choked with laughter at this suggestion. It was an old joke in the Royal Navy—a pointless task you pretended to be about when caught in a moment of idleness by a new, raw young officer who didn't know any better. Well, here was Cap'n Mark telling him to clear the decks while he had his argy-bargy with the toff. His eyes fell on the two gold coins lying on the cobbles. He bent furtively to pick them up. Jerking his head to the onlookers, he shambled off in the direction of the harbor pothouse. He could watch events just as easily from the window, and it didn't do to argue with Cap'n Mark when he had that look in his eye.

Lord Rayne had regained a little control but he sweated still. He needed a brandy badly. His first instincts were to have the fellow taken in charge, but common sense told him it would be unwise. The last thing he wanted was an encounter with the local magistrate, but how the devil was he to rid himself of this headstrong yokel, this self-appointed protector of his property?

Jenkins was swaying unsteadily on his feet, his eyes wary as he looked at Mark. Lord Rayne looked at the girl he considered his property. She was pale but, by God, how he desired her! She was even more beautiful than when he had last seen her in that ridiculously old-fashioned bonnet, and later in the amber silk dress. There was something different about her—more maturity, perhaps. She must have learned a thing or two about the elegance of dress from her clients. A dressmaker, indeed! What stupidity compared with what he could offer.

Lord Rayne fingered his cravat, trying to decide his next move. Force and bribery had failed. Only sweet reason and rightful proof were left. He glanced into the hard face of his adversary and smiled his most sincere smile.

"Since we appear to have reached an impasse, I suggest we adjourn to the privacy of a room in the tavern yonder. It would be a decent sight more comfortable to talk over a glass of brandy than argue the toss in front of these loiterers. What do you say?" He eyed Mark warily and was relieved to be answered by a brief nod. "Walk the horses, Jenkins. I will call you when I need you."

"Very good, my lord." Jenkins was wooden-faced again but his mind seethed with resentment. Not for him a brandy, even though he'd been the one clobbered by that young jackanapes.

They entered the tavern, bespoke a private room, and Lord Rayne ordered brandy. He looked inquiringly at Mark, who shook his head.

"Too early in the day for me. Order coffee for the lady."

Lord Rayne's mouth opened in protest at the curt order but he restrained himself—no sense getting the fellow's back up again.

"Of course, of course. Coffee it shall be for you, my dear."

Clare made no reply, but stared into the fire in brooding silence. How could things have gone so awry? If Mark had not arrived when he had, the *Dolphin* would have been in open waters by now, all danger gone. But she was not beaten yet. She had to think of some way of evading the two of them.

The coffee came and Mark filled two cups in silence, then pushed one toward her across the small table. It was hot and strong. Lord Rayne drank his brandy quickly and called for another.

"Drink your coffee, Clare," Mark said, and Lord Rayne stared at him.

"Clare? That sounds mighty familiar. You told me you knew no one called Harcourt."

"Nor do I," Mark replied evenly.

Clare looked at Mark, a frown between her brows. "You have met before?"

Mark nodded. "At the King's Head coaching inn. It seems we were both waiting for the Clevedon to Bristol coach."

"Why?"

"We assumed you would be on it."

"Why should I be on it?"

Mark grinned faintly. "You fooled us both by taking a sea passage. It was very clever, but you would have paid for it. Why in God's name do that, Clare? Why didn't you tell me the truth? You knew I would help you."

"I didn't want to involve you in my sordid past. I also have pride." She tried to speak lightly but her voice betrayed her by trembling on the last word. Her head bent over the coffee cup.

Lord Rayne's voice cut in harshly. "A sordid past, indeed, from which I saved the lady. Tell him, Clare."

Mark looked at him sharply. "Tell me what?"

Lord Rayne had drunk enough brandy to renew his confidence. "Tell him, Clare, how your father sold you to the highest bidder in order to marry his doxy and secure a snug income."

"Good God!" Mark said, appalled. "Is this true, Clare?"

She nodded without raising her eyes. "Lord Rayne slipped away and came to warn me in the middle of the night. He persuaded me to leave immediately. He promised me his protection."

"Protection?" Mark looked puzzled.

Lord Rayne sighed inwardly, his irritation rising against

this obtuse young man. He took a gulp of brandy to steady himself.

"I intended to take her to London and place her in the care of my lady wife."

Clare's head came up and her face flushed with color. She was over her shock now and prepared to fight.

"A wife you did not have when you proposed to me. I only learned of her existence when I heard your coachmen talking."

"So that's why you stole my horse and ran. You misunderstood my intentions, my dear. What a silly child you were, to be sure. How could I propose marriage to you when I already have a wife?" He smiled genially at Mark. "There, the matter is all cleared up. I am obliged to you, my boy. We'll not detain you any longer. My ward and I will be off to London directly."

"I am not your ward," Clare said flatly. "Why do you persist in calling me so?"

"But you are, my dear. Your father agreed to it." Lord Rayne had drunk just enough to become overconfident of his victory. "He had to agree since I hold your—shall we say, bill of sale—over his head."

"My what?" asked Clare faintly.

Lord Rayne laughed, his eyes brandy-bright. His triumph was as intoxicating as the brandy. "Haven't you understood, my dear? Would I risk my reputation by taking you from Harcourt House without first purloining the incriminating bill of sale? It guarantees your father's silence, don't you see? His signature is upon it, together with that of the gentleman who bought you. Neither dare risk the bill coming to the attention of the authorities."

"This is quite barbarous," Clare said fiercely. "It is your duty to expose them."

"No, no, my dear, the scandal would ruin them both. I have a generous heart and prefer only to hold them under obligation to me. The matter will never be made public." He smiled kindly at Clare. "You would not wish your name to be dragged through the mud, would you? Best leave things as they are."

"But the other man, who is he?" Clare persisted.

Lord Rayne shook his head in a sad gesture. "A man of excellent character, save for this one lapse from grace. Better that you do not know, my dear. I hold the proof quite safe. Be glad that I saved you from such a fate." He gave the untidy young man a beaming look. "My ward is obliged to you, sir, but no longer requires your protection. We shall leave right away."

Mark rose, his expression impassive. Clare felt the panic run through her. He was leaving her with Lord Rayne, accepting his dismissal. She choked back the words that rushed to her lips. It was so sordid a story, she could not blame him for wanting to walk away. She stared fixedly at her empty coffee cup, despising herself for the prickling of tears behind her eyelids.

Mark spoke. "This document, Lord Rayne. You have talked of its existence but shown no proof of it. Why should the lady believe you?"

Lord Rayne's geniality deserted him. This insolent young scoundrel was questioning his word. It was an outrage, coming from such a common person. Unconsciously, his fingers moved to the breast pocket of his jacket.

"I have been patient, God knows," he snarled, the broken veins on his cheeks standing out like faint red cobwebs. "But I will not be cross-examined in this manner by a country lout playing Sir Galahad! Be off with you before I call the constable. How dare you doubt the word of a gentleman?"

"Methinks this one doth protest too much," Mark misquoted softly.

Lord Rayne paused, his eyes narrowing on the hard face. "Well, well! So we think to try a little Shakespeare, do we?" His voice held a sneer. "I didn't think the village school went in for the classics."

Mark shrugged. "I wouldn't know. I didn't go to the village school."

Lord Rayne almost laughed aloud. No schooling? This oaf was, without doubt, illiterate. He pulled the paper from his pocket and waved it under Mark's nose. "Is this proof enough? I'm sure you can recognize writing, despite your lack of education.''

Mark smiled and laid a hand on the paper. ''You misunderstood me, Lord Rayne. I didn't go to the village school, but I don't lack education. I was at Winchester and Oxford.''

Lord Rayne stared, his face going slack. ''You—you don't look like—'' he began.

''Seamen seldom do. They grab the first thing to hand when they're in a hurry.''

His lordship seemed unaware that Mark now had full possession of the paper. ''What's your name? You never told me.''

''You didn't ask. It's Conrad—Mark Conrad.''

Mark was scanning the paper swiftly and Lord Rayne recollected himself with a start. He made a grab for it, the blood pounding in his head as he realized the enormity of his mistake.

Mark's face darkened as he read.

''Give it back,'' Lord Rayne almost screamed. ''You have no right to read my private paper—'' He was silenced by the look of sheer savagery on the young man's face.

''You damned, unscrupulous, conniving bastard!'' Mark threw the words at him so fiercely that Lord Rayne backed away.

Clare stared up at Mark. The fury in him was almost tangible. Her heart thumped as she rose, steadying herself on the table edge. ''Mark, tell me.''

Mark was looking at Lord Rayne with utter contempt. ''You disgust me, you lecherous devil. Your purchaser, Clare, was this odious object here.'' Mark tore the paper in half and tossed it into the fire, dusting his hands as if they had touched filth.

Lord Rayne watched the flames take his precious letter and turned furiously on Mark, all caution forgotten as he saw his hold over Clare Harcourt go up in smoke.

''How dare you—'' he spluttered.

For the second time that day, Mark Conrad knocked a man down.

♦ *Chapter Thirty-three* ♦

Lord Rayne lay slumped against the paneled wall of the small, private room. His eyes were open. Mark's blow had not rendered him senseless, although he might have preferred unconsciousness to the sight of this young giant towering over him with fists clenched and the utmost savagery on his face. Lord Rayne lay where he had fallen. If he rose, this angry fellow might knock him down again. The prospect did not appeal.

Mark's fingers uncurled as Lord Rayne made no move to rise. "Gutless," he said, and the single word, uttered with such contempt, was like a slap to his lordship.

He reddened, his eyes hostile, then his gaze flickered away. *Good God, the brute might kick me like a dog if I show too much hostility*! he thought. He looked away.

Mark gave a harsh bark of laughter and stepped back, the anger draining out of him.

"On your feet, you gutless coward. Get out of here and take your bully boy with you."

Lord Rayne was only too eager to be out of range of those fists. He scrambled up, gathering the shreds of his dignity together. At the door he paused, confident of his escape route, but determined to have the last word.

"You've not heard the last of this," he snarled. "I'll have you before the county judge for assault."

Mark grinned unexpectedly, making Lord Rayne blink. "Judge Conrad? I haven't seen Uncle Henry in years. He'd be very interested in your story." He turned his back on Lord Rayne.

Clare had slid down into her seat again and the hand she had clapped over her mouth to stifle her gasp as Mark hit Lord Rayne was still there. It was all so unreal, she thought, like a theater drama without an audience. No one had come

in to see what was amiss. Had it all gone without notice from
landlord and customers alike? She was light-headed from lack
of sleep and food. Yes, that was it, but why was she afraid
to remove her hand from her mouth? She had to hold back
the hysterical laughter that was already threatening to break
through her tightly compressed lips. That, indeed, would
bring the landlord running. Only she and Mark were in the
room and he was gazing at her with a puzzled but tender
look. That look almost broke her tight control. A gasp—half
laughter, half scream—wrenched at her throat, then Mark
was beside her, enveloping her in his arms.

With her face buried in his shirtfront, Clare shook with
laughter and the tears coursed down her cheeks.

"Hush, my darling," he whispered. "Everything is all
right now."

He might have been comforting Sara, she thought wildly,
but it was a comfort she badly needed and she gave herself
up to it.

At last she drew away from him and accepted his proffered
handkerchief. She wiped her face and smiled.

"What a patient, kindhearted man you are, Mark. No wonder Sara thinks you the best father in the world."

Mark smiled. "My patience earns me a lot of wet shirts."

Clare gave a giggling hiccup. "I'm sorry. I promise to
wash it for you."

"I would rather you promised to marry me."

Clare looked away. "How can you say that after hearing
of my sordid past?"

Mark took her chin in his hand and turned her face toward
him. "Your past did not soil you. Who better to know that
than I?" He smiled. "I think it your duty to make an honest
man of me." He paused. "Besides, you don't hold the mo-
nopoly of family skeletons in the cupboards of Harcourt
House."

"You mean you have some, too?"

Mark grinned at her look of surprise. "Don't all the best
families? I will tell you all about them one day, including
the truth about Sara's mother."

"Your—your wife?"

Mark shook his head. "I was never married and I had no part in Sara's conception."

"But you are her father?" Clare said, bewildered.

Mark shook his head again. "No, my love. To the world in general and to Sara in particular, I have taken on that role. Her father was a wastrel who seduced a cousin of mine, then took himself off. My cousin never recovered from Sara's birth and wrote to me in desperation before she died. I brought the baby to Conrad Place and vowed I would treat her as my own. There was curiosity, naturally, but it was never satisfied by me, and I have come to love Sara as if she were really my own."

"And now you are entrusting this secret to me. Why?"

Mark leaned forward and kissed her gently on the cheek. "I don't believe in secrets between husband and wife."

"I don't recall your proposal of marriage," Clare said, rallying her wilting forces. "Why do you assume I shall marry you?"

"Because you love me. Don't you?"

Clare frowned. "Yes, confound it, but a girl likes a proper proposal."

Mark laughed. "All right, my love. Will you marry me, darling? I love you, too, confound it, whoever you are—Clare Court or Miss Harcourt. I'll take either or both of you."

Clare bit her lip on a stifled giggle. Was there ever such a ridiculous proposal? Her head felt as light as her heart. "We both accept your kind proposal, Mr. Conrad, but don't get ideas about starting a harem. We shall be united in opposition."

"I promise to be true to you both," Mark said solemnly.

There was a moment of silence as Clare found herself kissed soundly, then she took Mark's right hand in hers and peered at the skinned knuckles.

"You'll have to give this up, you know," she said, raising solemn eyes to Mark.

He looked at his knuckles reflectively. "A fellow can get a taste for fisticuffs. I've a mind to punch the landlord on the way out."

"You'll do no such thing—" Clare began, then saw Mark's grin.

"You sound like a wife already. Is there time to withdraw my proposal?"

Clare shook her head. "No, there is not, and since I have no engagement ring, you will not have it thrown back at you, so resign yourself to your fate."

"Yes, ma'am." He pulled her to her feet and they clung together, still laughing. "Let's go and find Sara. She'll be overjoyed to have you permanently at Conrad Place. She'll be a great help with the children, too."

"I—I think we should get married first," Clare gasped as Mark hurried her out of the tavern.

Mark threw her a glance of amusement over his shoulder. "Of course, my love. We must take things in their proper order, just like respectable people. Saturday, by special license—will that do?"

They had reached Mark's horse. He hung Clare's basket on the pommel and lifted her up to sit before him in the saddle. His left arm held her close as the horse began to trot up the hill.

The weather could not have been better for the launching of the sailing ship, *Sara*. The invited guests began to assemble in the cove under a cloudless blue sky at two o'clock in the afternoon. A long trestle table had been set up on the flattest ground. A white damask cloth covered the table, and that in turn had been covered by an array of dishes and plates containing the buffet luncheon.

The children came first—Kate and Milly Clark, scrubbed and almost polished, wearing spotless cotton print dresses—followed by Mr. and Mrs. Clark. Despite the request for informality, Farmer Clark seemed to have been thrust into his Sunday, churchgoing attire by his bonneted wife. Mark, in open-necked shirt and twill breeches, pointed out that seawater was the ruination of good clothes and suggested that they abandon both bonnet and jacket for the maiden voyage. The Clarks accepted the suggestion with obvious relief.

Isobel Foster and the Honorable Peregrine Knightly ar-

rived, having left their phaeton on the lane above the bay.
They came hand in hand, aglow with their own happiness.
Clare smiled at them. She had once envied their happiness,
but not anymore.

Behind the trestle table stood Mrs. Winter, with Septimus
Thomas co-opted as helper. She would rather have had one
of the Conrad Place housemaids, but the master had been
adamant that this old seaman, with his badly shaved chin,
was entitled to be present, since he had helped rig the *Sara*
for sea. She kept an eye on him just the same.

Sara stood between Mark and Clare as they greeted the
guests. Her smile was brilliant and her air of suppressed
excitement—almost smugness—seemed extravagant for the
occasion.

"I shall burst soon," she whispered to Clare, "if Papa
does not make the announcement."

"Patience, darling," Clare whispered back. "Papa is waiting for Cupid. Ah, here he comes."

Sara glanced over at the small, racing figure and frowned.
"That's Albert. He doesn't look a bit like Cupid."

"Not many people do," Clare answered, smiling. "He
appears in many guises."

Sara look mystified but Albert was already among them
and Papa was already rapping the table for silence. Sara and
Mrs. Winter changed secret smiles. They knew what was to
come. They had been there, hadn't they?

Champagne glasses were filled and handed around. Young
Albert, a startled expression on his face, found himself holding a delicately stemmed champagne glass. He looked around
and caught Clare's eye. She smiled and nodded. He would
never know how his early delivery of Sara's letter had
changed her life. Mark had told her of it on Wednesday night
in the privacy of her cottage. That letter and the one she had
left for the Clarks had disintegrated in the flames, just as
surely as the one Lord Rayne had flourished in Mark's face.

Their own flame of passion that night in the cottage had
not died but intensified, bringing them both to exhausted
satisfaction. Freed from Lord Rayne's pursuit and the prospect of Mark's marriage to Eve Patterson, they had spent the

night in love and laughter, giving themselves utterly to each other. And tonight, Clare thought, they would share their passion in the marital bed at Conrad Place.

Mark glanced at Clare and, as if drawn by an invisible silken thread, she moved slowly to his side, holding Sara by the hand.

Mark looked about him. "We are here, my friends, for a double celebration. Miss Court and I were married this morning. Will you raise your glasses to toast my bride, Clare Conrad? After which, we shall launch—" He got no further, for the guests were surrounding them in delighted congratulations.

Perry's voice rose as he grinned at Mark and pumped his hand. "Curse you, Conrad. You've done it again. Stolen my thunder, as always."

Isobel kissed Clare warmly on the cheek. "Miss Court— I mean, Mrs. Conrad—"

"Make it Clare," said the bride.

Isobel giggled. "And I was going to tell you this very afternoon, dear Clare, that Mama has given in, and Perry and I are to marry next week. Oh, I am so happy for us both. Isn't it wonderful?"

Clare felt Mark's arm tighten about her shoulders. "Truly wonderful," he began and was once more silenced, this time by Sep's rasping voice for three cheers for Cap'n Mark and his lady.

When a modicum of order had been restored, Mark handed a champagne bottle to Sara.

"Your turn now, my pet. We must launch your namesake in style."

"A terrible waste of good liquor," Sep muttered, and earned himself a sharp glance from Mrs. Winter, who had retreated to the far end of the trestle table when Sep's cheer had shivered the air. He grinned at her placatingly. "Still, 'tis all in a good cause, ain't that so, missus? Go on, Miss Sara, give the old girl a right good thwack. 'Tis no matter if she wants a lick of paint afterward. Old Sep will do it, just like he sandpapered—"

"Hold your tongue, Sep," Mark interrupted, grinning, "or

you'll find that article sandpapered, too." He glanced down at Sara. "Ready?"

Sara hesitated. "Can I ask Clare something first?"

"Of course, darling." Clare went down on one knee before the child. "What is it?"

"Can—can I stop calling you Clare? Now that you are married to Papa, may I call you Mama?" The intent, grey-green eyes looked appealingly into the grey ones. "I would so like to have a mama, like everyone else."

Clare felt her throat constrict and she put her arms about Sara, meeting Mark's eyes over the child's head. He was smiling, but there was a tenderness mixed with amusement in his voice.

"You've joined the wet front brigade."

"What?" Clare looked down.

The champagne bottle, bedewed from the ice bucket and still clutched by Sara, had left its mark on both dress bodices. Clare glanced expressively at Sara, who giggled.

Clare straightened. "All in a good cause, as Mr. Thomas says." She smiled at Sara. "Come along, daughter mine. Let's get on with the launching."

"Yes, Mama." Sara's face glowed and they moved to the water's edge.

Later that night, in the marital bed at Conrad Place, Clare lay sleepily in Mark's arms. What a wonderful day it had been, every precious moment of it. Mark's fingers caressed her body, halting on her stomach.

"That reminds me," he said. "I have something to give you."

"You have already given me everything," Clare murmured. "What is it?"

"The thing that brought us together. I have held it as a keepsake since that night in the barn."

He unclenched his fingers and laid the gold coin on her stomach. Clare peered down at it, then raised her eyes to Mark.

"Are you trying to buy me, sir?" she asked on a choke of laughter.

"You bought me with that selfsame guinea." He touched the coin reflectively. "I believe I will have it mounted and attached to my watch chain. What do you think?"

"A good idea, for it will not lie flat on my stomach for long."

Mark gave her a startled look. "You don't mean—"

Clare reached up for him, her eyes mischievous. "No, my darling, not yet, but if you put your mind to it—"

Mark grinned, flipping the guinea aside. "Your obedient servant, ma'am."

GET LOVESTRUCK!

AND GET STRIKING ROMANCES FROM POPULAR LIBRARY'S BELOVED AUTHORS

Watch for these exciting romances in the months to come:

January 1990
TO LOVE A STRANGER by Marjorie Shoebridge
DREAM SONG by Sandra Lee Smith

February 1990
THE HEART'S DISGUISE by Lisa Ann Verge

March 1990
EXPOSURES by Marie Joyce

April 1990
WILD GLORY by Andrea Parnell

May 1990
STOLEN MOMENTS by Sherryl Woods

POPULAR LIBRARY